DARK DECEPTION

Dr Gary Lapham

Dr Gary Lapham MRCP

About the Author

Gary Lapham is a UK Medically trained Physician with extensive experience in Hospital Medicine and General Practice.

He has worked in the Pharmaceutical Industry in both drug development and Product launch.

Gary has Published Medical and Scientific clinical trial data, Personal Perspectives and Articles on issues including Ethics and the European Law.

"Dark Deception" is the Author's inaugural fictional Publication from a trilogy to be Published Worldwide from 2020 to 2022.

The Second book in the series entitled "The Visionary" will be published on-line in 2021.

Contact the Author:

email: garylapham.author@gmail.com

Part 1

Chapter 1

Dark Velvet

Wednesday 25th January 2017

Surrey, United Kingdom

Shards of amber light cascaded across the immaculately white tiled bathroom as Dr Christophe Schultz stood naked and opened the pristine white venetian blinds to his en-suite. Dawn had always encapsulated a magical quality for him: *sleep is for the dead* me mused.

Christophe held a stainless steel scalpel in his left hand: the razor sharp edge glinting in the exquisite hue of the rising sun.

Knife to skin felt good. A single horizontal incision. As Christophe's blood oozed from the delicate white unblemished skin of his right forearm he gently sighed; embracing the warm release he felt. He closed his eyelids lightly together and relaxed his breathing, gently and rhythmically inhaling and exhaling; welcoming the temporary escape from reality.

He showered vigorously in the second of his daily rituals; a waterproof plaster covering his newly incised forearm.

Toccata and Fugue in D minor played soothingly in the background as Christophe repeatedly re-tied his purple woven wool tie until he achieved a flawless symmetrical Windsor knot; before donning his favourite dark blue silk jacket and trousers.

He stood transfixed in critical self-appraisal as he viewed his suit in the full length mirror to ensure his appearance was immaculate.

Today would mark the zenith of seven years of passion, persistence and disingenuous politics in his role as UK Medical Director with Utopia Pharmaceutical Company.

Christophe exited his apartment building and operated the electrically powered rollover garage door with a single nudge of the power fob on his key-ring. The rear-end of his beloved offspring from *Zuffenhausen*; steadily emerged before his eyes.

Not for him a modern replica of German engineering, with parts sourced from other Companies or even Countries; he remained true to the design specifications of his aged Porsche. It mattered little to him that nay-slayers derided his vehicle as a *"hair-dressers car"*, whilst they drove their loathsome monstrosities.

With a flick of his right wrist, the low rumble of the engine stirred into life and he pulled down the hood lock and depressed the toggle switch; then waited the twelve seconds until the power-hood had retracted completely and the red warning light on the dashboard had turned off.

The cold January air immediately heightened his senses as he reversed into the communal turning area in front of the apartment block, before exiting the drive onto the deserted road towards West London.

The early morning grit scattered wildly as Christophe gathered speed passing through sleepy local villages and the throaty roar of the engine grew more intense as he approached Sunny Oak Village level crossing and slowed in readiness for the clearly marked speed camera; the yellow casing already visible in his left peripheral vision.

The road ahead was narrowed due to road works and seeing the temporary lights at red he slowed and waited; suddenly acutely aware of the cold morning air gently burning the soft pharyngeal mucosa at the back of his throat. A lone worker in a fluorescent canary yellow coloured jacket stepped forward towards the right side of the car and gestured to speak.

"Need to close the road temporarily mate; can you detour via Archway Road?"

With only a cursory nod, Christophe made a swift tyre scrunching U-turn and took an immediate ninety degree right turn before picking up speed and following the curve of the bend. With traction control set to off, he felt the rear wheels slip momentarily on a small patch of ice; as he took the second right turn towards the arch of the bridge over the road.

Unexpectedly a low-loader sat ahead of him, straddling both lanes of his exit; hazard lights flashing like hypnotic strobes in the early morning light. Without hesitation Christophe depressed the heavy clutch pedal and selected reverse gear, only to find another vehicle behind him; lights on full beam. Dazzled and momentarily irritated, Christophe leaned down and forward to disengage reverse gear and switch on his hazard lights. As he did so he felt a sudden intense pressure and searing pain in the right side of his neck. He lifted his right forearm in protest, opened his mouth wide but only a silent scream passed his lips.

A strong hand covered his mouth; the distinct smell of leather and the metallic tangy taste of blood. His vision dimmed and the dashboard became a swirling frenetic firework display of multi-coloured neon lights. Deafening drums began to hammer in his ears; as he heard distant voices and then, there was only darkness.

Minutes later Christophe's car was fastened securely onto the low-loader and driven away.

Chapter 2

Six months earlier….

Monday 8th August 2016

Heavy steel security gates mounted on powerful industrial rollers cranked steadily apart as Christophe swiped his identity card and slowly approached the main entrance to *Utopia Pharmaceuticals Ltd* [UPL]. The early morning sun reflected on the metallic facade of the building and illuminated the multicoloured rows of Rhododendron and assorted rose bushes; all of which served to architecturally soften the edge of the concrete pavement which skirted the modern seven-floor building.

By passing the largely empty rows of parking slots at ground level, Christophe headed down the sharply winding spiral slip way to the underground bay where he selected his usual parking space; sandwiched between two uniformly white-washed concrete pillars at the far end of the car park.

With a second swipe of his identity card, Christophe entered the central glass encased lift shaft and was whisked swiftly to the Sixth Floor of UPL. A burly clean-shaven security guard with a number one haircut and rugged facial features, was sat behind the desk as Christophe entered the Reception area. He stood up and greeted Christophe with a cheery smile.

Rob Masters was dressed in a black two piece suit and sported a contrasting starched white shirt with an immaculately ironed collar and cuffs: a throw-back to his Military days. His silver coloured tie caught Christophe's attention as he approached the long oak wooden desk.

"*Good Morning Dr Schultz – how are you today*?"

"Good Morning Rob - I'm good, thank you. *Great tie.*"

"Glad you approve Doc'; the wife bought it for me for our Wedding Anniversary."

Rob nodded his appreciation for the complement and watched as Christophe headed off down the corridor towards his office; automatic energy-saving lights triggered by each strident step. His shoes as always were immaculately polished black Brogues; he might easily have been mistaken for an ex-military man mused Rob.

But there, the similarities between them ended. Not for the first time, Rob wondered what kind of life the Doctor enjoyed outside of UPL; given the long hours he worked and his habitual arrival by six-thirty a.m. five or six days a week.

As a former Platoon Sergeant with an Infantry Battalion; Rob had worked for four years as a Security Officer with UPL: married for twenty-five years he had three teenage boys. The lads shared a passion for football and basketball; each already blessed with a stance well over Rob's 1.89 metres. Rob competed with fearless composure: wearing the number eight shirt for the combined Tri-Services Forces' rugby team.

Entering his four digit Pass-Code Christophe opened the door to his office and glanced at the electronic clock which displayed 6:20 a.m. precisely. He placed his right hand on the security pad which automatically activated his customised sleek black computer stack. It came to life with a gentle electronic purr and he entered a further alpha-numeric password via his keyboard to enable entry to his Personal files.

Scanning his unread emails he clicked on a *"Certification request"* red-flagged as *urgent* and clicked his knuckles as he sat down; by hyper-extending his interlaced fingers.

Christophe sat back in his black leather swivel chair and made a conscious effort to relax his shoulders as he read the final revision of a proposed Company Statement; which was tagged to remind him that it was scheduled for release in the next twenty-four hours.

The eyes of the Company' Shareholders and investment Brokers, to say nothing of Competitors and Journalists World-Wide; would scrutinise every detail. It had to be accurate and unambiguous in content; reflecting the contemporaneous views of quoted Contributors. The

Company Lawyers had already made amendments to the Disclaimers during the review of previous versions. The final document would be approved by Christophe's electronic signature and the countersignature of the CEO [Chief Executive Officer] of Utopia.

Christophe's life had been dominated by the *anti-viral product U0008* for the last six years and the run up to launch was gathering increasing momentum. Every piece of Promotional Material related to the Launch of the Product to Market, crossed his table and passed through his electronic inbox. Some days the burden hung like a heavy mantle on Christophe's shoulders. Today felt like one of those days for no good reason, other than he had a long to-do list and the Press Release was a pivotal part of a complex jigsaw of Company Strategy and vital to the Company's projected success in the fiscal cycle.

He stood up and systemically stretched his neck, arms, shoulders and back; flexing to touch his toes before settling back in front of the computer screen. He logged into the electronic Promotional Copy Approval Platform and painstakingly scrutinised the Statement; word by word, reflecting on each claim; then read the document backward to ensure there were no spelling mistakes.

Press Release [*Final Version For Approval*]

STRICTLY CONFIDENTIAL

Utopia Pharmaceuticals Ltd [UK] has been granted a license for *hepcretrovir* [formerly known by the acronym *UP0008*]: for the treatment of Pan-Genotypic Chronic Hepatitis C infection [HCV]. The single tablet, once daily formulation has been evaluated in a World-Wide cohort of patients including those with severe chronic renal impairment and a surgical population Pre- and Post- liver transplantation. It is estimated that *185 million patients* World-Wide are infected with HCV.[1]

Utopia Pharmaceuticals Inc. [USA] announced the final Phase IIIb clinical trial results for *hepcretrovir* on May 10th 2015. In clinical trials conducted on a total of 22,125 subjects infected with Chronic Hepatitis C infection, consistent SVR rates of 99-100% were attained at 12 and 24 weeks after treatment exposure ranging from 4 to 12 weeks. Patients included those with cirrhosis, high viral loads and hitherto treatment resistant genotypes.[2]

Mr George Latimer CEO of UPL [UK] said: "The Chairman and Board of Directors would like to acknowledge the dedication of Principal Investigator Professor Karl Linz and the Global Team of Clinicians who implemented the Clinical Trial Programme for UP0008. Professor Linz will continue to oversee the Safety of the Product in Post Authorisation Efficacy and Safety Studies as mandated by Competent Authorities".[3]

On June 14th 2015, The Pan European Transatlantic Drug Evaluation Unit [ETDEU] granted the drug "Unified Fast Track Status", thereby deploying the Global Regulatory Resources of the United States of America and the 28 European Member States in the simultaneous Assessment of the Quality, Efficacy, Safety and Health Economic Impact of *hepcretrovir* [U0008].

Professor Edwina Justin MBE, the Chairperson of the National Institute of Chemotherapy and Oncology [NICO] said: "The Cooperation between the National Institute [NICO] and the Pan European Transatlantic Drug Evaluation Unit [ETDEU] marks a paradigm shift in the future of the Research, Development, Approval and Distribution of Medicinal Products across the Global Market Place. The impetus created by the adoption of the Unified Fast Track Status for those drugs such as hepcretrovir which provide a significant advance in the treatment of hitherto unmet clinical need; will impact those who have most to lose by their illness: *patients, their families and caregivers*".[4]

Further information: The National Institute of Cancer and Oncology [NICO] is a wholly Independent Registered Charity with a Board of Trustees, Chaired by Professor Edwina Justin MBE. NICO was established in April 2016 and is based in London, United Kingdom.

Press Release ends

Christophe reviewed the further information, superscripted references and notes and Legal Disclaimers listed as Appendices on Page Two of the Release; cross-checking the library copies and ensuring that his previous comments and amendments had all been incorporated. He electronically countersigned his intention to sign-off the final hard copy version of the Press Release, by inserting the approved electronic watermark.

He sat and reflected on the document before pressing the send button which electronically conveyed the document to the Originator's inbox. With a flick of his index finger, the document was sent and he sat back with his fingers interlaced and tented, deep in thought: trying to anticipate what hurdles lay ahead.

"The unforeseen quagmire of trips and falls; waiting for the unwary."

That's what his first mentor in the Industry had warned him about ten years previously when he had joined a small Biotech Company working on an innovative manufacturing process designed for enzyme replacement therapy; ultimately destined for an inherited metabolic disease.

"Always expect the unexpected." This had always been Dennis Cooper's advice to him.

At 8:15 a.m., an electronic ping from his computer diary broke his chain of thought and reminded Christophe that he had fifteen minutes until his first scheduled meeting of the day. He stretched, logged off from his computer and headed out into the corridor.

The carpet clad corridor was unusually quiet for the time of day. Most of the Company managers and Directors would normally be in their offices by eight o'clock. It felt like the calm before the storm.

"'Morning Christophe!" called out *Peter Adams* from behind his desk, as Christophe passed through the large suite of offices into the open work area marking the perimeter of the Marketing Department.

He retraced his steps over the dark blue carpeted floor towards Peter's enclave.

"*Good morning Peter.* I've approved the Press Release and sent it back to you as job bag Owner."

"Good Man. I want to be sure I have George's paw print on that by the end of the day."

"Then *Monica* in Corporate Relations can set the ball rolling and get it out to the distribution list before it goes live on the Company Intranet in 24 hours time."

"Remembering of course - George and I have to sign-off on the Paper Copy; *before* distribution." reiterated Christophe.

"Yeah sure, I have read the *revised* Standard Operating Procedures [SOPs]. *When have I ever let you down Christophe?*"

Christophe raised his eyebrows and gave him a playful knowing glance.

One of the more onerous tasks which fell to Christophe was the oversight and revision of Protocols, covering a wide variety of Company procedures: anything related to the Advertisement, Safety, Efficacy, Registration or Distribution or Withdrawal of a drug from market: being of paramount importance.

"Okay, point taken, *but that was just the one occasion*; are you 'heading off for a coffee before we kick off?"

Christophe nodded affirmatively and they marched off to the kitchen for a black coffee before mounting the single flight of stairs to the Boardroom.

Chapter 3

"*Gentlemen*, let me remind you, we are *Lawyers*: he gestured to the two men sat on his left hand side as he spoke. If we decide that the liver is made of *chocolate* we need only persuade the Tribunal of Fact, based *on the Balance of Probabilities*; and our case is made out".

"The disclaimers will undoubtedly address the points you raise Dr Schultz."

His determination was clear: his decision was final.

Christophe once again, felt the need to suppress his distaste for Clive McGregor; as Senior Counsel for UPL he was feared and respected in equal measure by any candid enough to voice an opinion. Rumour had it that McGregor's father had always hoped that his son would follow him to the lofty heights amidst the High Court Judiciary, but he never made the grade; leaving him with a large chip on his broad Etonian shoulders.

His mocking reference to liver structure and reiteration of the power of reasoned argument; was as always, the Trojan horse for his closing argument and suppression of dissent.

McGregor however, gave Counsel to and deputised for; none other than *George Latimer*. He was *God's right hand man* you might say; but few did: whilst everyone acknowledged his lofty status.

McGregor looked younger than his fifty-two years; immaculately dressed in a high end suit, from *Bond Street, London*: Christophe surmised. He always wore a gold tie pin having long since cast off the eccentricities of a bow tie or brightly coloured socks. Clive McGregor clearly had a vast array of cuff links to match endless supply of silk shirts, that part of his persona at least; gained Christophe's approval.

McGregor continued to hold the teams' attention, even when he was silent. He sat squarely in his chair at the head of the table, his perfectly manicured broad fingers crossed and laid on the oak table in front of him. The thick band of gold on his left hand glinting in the early morning sunshine added further credence to the God-fatherly demeanour he cultivated.

He slowly but deliberately scanned attendees faces one by one, fixing his gaze for a few moments on Christophe; before continuing.

"So if there are no further pressing comments or requests for clarification, he paused for a final glance at Christophe; *Iris* will distribute minutes this evening and send electronic invitations for a follow up meeting at eleven o'clock tomorrow morning. By that time, we will have the Board's recommendations in place."

Without further comment he rose from the table and strode purposefully toward the door; his highly polished brown Brogue shoes audibly striking the wood block floor as he left.

Christophe watched him leave and was suddenly aware of a low grade occipital headache; no doubt from the tension in his neck muscles he concluded. He mentally self-prescribed more neck stretching exercises for the day ahead.

As the room cleared of meeting participants he felt a quick tap on his right shoulder. *Steve Goodge, National Sales Manager*, smiled down at Christophe and with a Geordie chuckle added:

"'Chocolate *liver*?"

What next kidney truffles; coconut *sweetbreads* – good enough to nibble?"

Not sure he quite got the joke, Christophe laughed anyway.

Peter smirked, rolled his eyes and shook his head as he left them to it.

"A few of us are heading for a glass of Chardonnay or two and a bite to eat at the *Anchor* tonight; you up for it?"

"No thanks Steve, 'appreciate the offer, but big day tomorrow, early night for me." replied Christophe with a sigh; gently massaging the nape of his neck with his thumbs.

"Lightweight, that's what you are." retorted Steve with a playful snort.

"I've got a mounting pile of data, slides and *Peter's* Promotional Material Approvals to get through."

"No rest for the wicked!" he called after Steve who was heading for the door.

"You know you love it!"

 "If you change your mind *Seven o'clock*…I'm off to meet the Key Account Managers in Ascot for lunch; I'll send your regards shall I..?"

His voice trailed off as he entered the corridor and hurriedly caught up with Peter.

Chapter 4

Christophe lowered himself into the soft cool leather seat of his car. He sighed with relief as he exited the Company gates and began weaving his way through the congested early evening traffic which was snarled up due to a traffic light failure adjoining the A4 main arterial route out of London. He began humming along to a classical rock selection to ease his anxiety. He could already feel his excitement rising in his trousers as he felt the throaty engine vibrations gently permeate through his genitals.

He checked the glove-box whilst sat in stationary traffic. A pack of latex surgical gloves, size eight, lay sealed and sterile. He gently stroked his groin, fuelling the tension behind his zip as he hit sixty miles per hour passing the Wentworth Estate, burning off an Audi boy racer on the inside lane. He cranked up the volume and submerged himself in the lyrics.

"Eat my dust."

He muttered to himself with a huge smile forming across his face as he accelerated up the incline towards the next Village; whilst the Audi merged into the background traffic left trailing in his wake.

An hour later with garlic, ginger and spring onions sliced on the wooden chopping board, Christophe selected a generous handful of prawns from the freezer and defrosted them in the microwave oven; as the glorious smell of fried charlottes gently wafted through the kitchen in his Apartment.

The extractor switched onto maximum was no competition for the cacophony of rich odours which regularly filled his kitchen and suffused his sinuses. His mother had taught him to cook as a child; his father unflinchingly insistent on fresh food, especially fish and vegetables.

The buzzer on the cooker signalled the passage of nine minutes since his white rice had come to the boil and he plated his meal adding a side helping of spinach, before pouring himself a generous glass of Chardonnay. *Steve would doubtless be on his third glass by now,* mused Christophe, flicking a look at the clock. In the lounge he heard his phone buzz with a new message, which he happily ignored as he chomped into his third garlic flavoured prawn. His favourite collection of *Mozart* filled the kitchen with majestic strings of violin admixed with exquisite harpsichord.

Firing up his laptop, Christophe opened his presentation entitled: *Board v4*.

Two hours later he had finished his final amendments to the slide presentation he would deliver in the Boardroom in nine hours time. Checking the distribution list again, he sent the amended slide-set but not before double-checking he had copied in George's secretary, *Annalisa*; to ensure she was updated on any last minute changes George might request.

Time to chill he decided. Christophe turned down the lights and selected a CD from his catalogued collection and inserted it into the player. He retrieved his latex surgical gloves, still double wrapped and laid them on the glass table next to the sofa before heading to his en-suite shower room.

The vanity cabinet in his bathroom contained three neat rows of toothpaste, shower gel and shampoo; immaculately arranged like sentries on duty at *Buckingham Palace*. Christophe selected a new container of gel and shampoo and set about his ritual: cleaning his body scrupulously from top to toe. Twenty minutes later he emerged in his robe; his cheeks glowing from the comforting warmth of the shower.

As he sat on the sofa, Christophe remotely started his CD player. Then slowly and methodically he opened the outer layer of the surgical gloves and discarding the wrapper in the stainless steel bin to his left; he carefully flicked back the sterile inner layer covering the gloves and placed the forefingers of his left hand inside one glove, followed by the right into the other; before gently easing the flexible latex up over his hands.

He stretched out on the sofa and closed his eyes, taking six long slow deep breaths, each followed by a longer exhalation. He tensed all the muscles in his body, then relaxed them and luxuriated in the feeling of controlled relaxation and mounting anticipation.

He visualised the long white curvaceous sandy beach ahead of him, as the pale blue waves lapped gently over the soft comforting sand, swirling around his feet; the water cleansing as it massaged his toes. He felt his skin rejuvenate as the deeper layers progressively soaked up the sun's rays like a camel taking on water in an arid desert.

His muscles felt strong and his body was once again invigorated and he began to jog along the beach; the serenity interrupted only by the sound of thunderous waves crashing against the distant craggy headland. The sand massaged the balls of his feet as he moved rhythmically and effortlessly down the beach. The sun beat down on his back and neck and he breathed in revitalising warm air, tinged with the scent of lemon grass.

He could already see her reclining resplendently naked and feral against the rocks in the distance, her lower body moving with the swell of the sea as the waves pounded her shoulders and firm dark breasts. He ran with renewed vigour and sprinted around the arc in the coastline towards the jagged rocks.

As he moved closer to her the roar of the waves grew more intense and he could feel the swell of the waves against his own body pushing him back and suddenly they were united, their tangled naked bodies writhing together in the powerful waves. He could feel her heart pounding like a drum against his naked chest as his breathing deepened. Her deep brown eyes were closed as they embraced and their tongues entwined and he tasted her sweet puckered lips. Their breathing grew deep as the water swelled around them and they were engulfed: her hands around his manhood which grew as hard as the rocks that savagely cradled them as her hands explored his shaft.

She arched her slender back, forcing her mound towards him, gently rubbing his tip as she swayed and he sank down, bending his knees, then thrust up deep inside her body until he could hear her cry out; her scream muffled only by the waves crashing around their ears. The rise and swell of the waves was matched by that of his lower body as it engorged and they rhythmically pounded together against the headland: *their lips united in rapture.*

Christophe's gown fell open and he placed his hands firmly around his throbbing shaft. The deep heavy beats from the sound system pounded around the room and he began to match their rhythm, slowly at first and then with increasing vigour until with a final exaltation the crest of the wave erupted over him and he lie panting and satiated. His eyelids remained closed as his eyes met hers, locked in the exaltation they'd shared; uniting their souls.

Chapter 5

9th August 2016

Annalisa Devlin did not acknowledge Christophe as he quietly entered the Boardroom. Dressed in a dark grey two-piece suit and pale pink blouse she stood preparing the video conferencing facility. Annalisa wore 6-inch black stilettos which honed her legs exquisitely.

She made sure that the remote tracking cameras responded to her movements as she repeatedly tested voice responsiveness.

"One, two, three." Annalisa repeated with a soft Western Irish lilt; as she moved deftly around the table perimeter.

She sat momentarily at the head of the table to examine the video imaging quality before systematically checking place markers against the spread sheet on her black clip board.

Annalisa repositioned several small plates of Belgian chocolates which had already been arranged strategically around the table. Finally she made sure everyone would be in reach of an array of spring water, soft drinks and freshly delivered fruit smoothes; the latter one of George's favourite breakfast tipples.

As Christophe organised the area around his seat at the far end of the table, closest to the projection screen, Annalisa finally spoke.

"Good morning Dr Schultz."

"Thanks a million for incorporating the last minute changes to your presentation which George had recommended: I distributed the final slide-set to the Board an hour ago."

"Thank you Annalisa." replied Christophe with a warm smile. He had fired up his computer at 5 a.m. unusually early, even by his standards.

Christophe knew how much pride and effort Annalisa put into her work: tirelessly working later than most of the team in the evenings; and arriving promptly at six-thirty in the morning.

"I am sure your efforts will be most appreciated by the *Senior Leadership Team*: the table looks sumptuous!"

"Thanks a million Christophe!" Annalisa smiled warmly and wished him *"Good Luck,"* crossing her fingers in front of her, before heading off in the direction of George's office.

Christophe checked his watch for the third time in fifteen minutes.

He clearly had time for a quick run through his presentation before the heads of department arrived.

Moments later his solitude was interrupted as *Therese LaMere* popped her head around the door.

"Good morning Christophe: are you all set?"

Christophe instinctively locked his keyboard, smiled and walked across the boardroom to greet Therese and she reciprocated by meeting him half way; delivering a swift kiss on his left cheek as she gently held his forearms.

She smelled divine, thought Christophe but could not place her scent; it reminded him of lemon grass. An evocative vivid memory stirred momentarily and he re-focused his attention on Therese immediately.

Her long slender brown fingers finished with red varnished nails were adorned with a variety of slim fashion rings and she sported a sleek grey silk dress which hugged her figure and finished modestly above her knees. As they parted from their embrace their eyes locked for a moment and he felt himself blush, hoping she hadn't noticed; she had.

"I'm good and you look your usual chic self Terry!"

"*Flattery will get you everywhere* Dr Schultz." she teased, raising her eyebrows and widening her eyelids further revealing her huge brown eyes; a testimony to her Anglo-French Algerian ancestry.

"I just popped in to make sure you have everything you need?"

"*Everything except* you!" replied Christophe, matching her playfulness.

"*By the way, how is your swimming tuition coming along*?" he added as a self-indulgent vision crossed his subconscious and he inhaled the Ocean admixed with the temptation of lemon grass once again.

"*Now now, what are you two medics cooking up*?" boomed Steve as he entered the room.

"Keeping Sales and Marketing out of the loop *again*?" he teased without conviction.

"*You know us*." replied Therese, half turning and flashing him a smile.

"We're always conjuring up new ways to keep you guys on the straight and narrow."

"Okay children, time for the big boys to come out to play!"

"Mmmh *allegedly* Steve: time I wasn't here."

"*Have fun boys*." She teased and pivoting neatly on her left foot she breezed from the room.

"*What I wouldn't give*." said Steve wistfully as she left the room.

"*Out of your league my friend*" replied Christophe, giving Steve a friendly slap on the back.

Steve shook his head, patting his beer belly absent-mindedly and headed off to his assigned seat diametrically opposite Christophe at the Board table. He promptly fired up his laptop and sourced the all-important Sales Projections ready to present; his slot scheduled for 9 a.m.

Five minutes later the room began to fill and as Christophe quietly scanned his opening presentation slides he glanced up as he heard *Clive McGregor* arrive with *Josh Edwards*, Head of Communications for the Corporation; both looking conspiratorial but sounding in high spirits.

Josh made a bee line for Christophe and thanked him for turning around the Press Release in good time. Both final signatories having approved the piece, it was good to go once the fine detail of the data had been discussed at the forthcoming Board Meeting; he advised Christophe in hushed tones, as if the news was likely to come as a complete surprise to him or anyone else in the Boardroom.

A quiet buzz of anticipation spread around the room and as Christophe's computer marked eight o'clock *George Latimer entered the room.*

"Good Morning Team!" bellowed George effortlessly, as he headed to his seat, pausing momentarily to shake the hand of Josh to his left and Clive to his right: *the right hand of God*, thought Christophe.

The unified and enthusiastic response of the room to George's salutation was a measure of the respect which George had earned during his fifteen years with the Company. He was a Visionary and had charisma by the bucket load; to say nothing of the rise in Share Price since he took over the reins as Chairman of the Board of Directors for UK, Europe, Asia-Pacific and Latin America.

The rest of the Board would join the meeting remotely at eight-fifteen, GMT. George wanted to rally the UK audience before Colleagues from the USA and Asia-Pacific, both parties assembled in Hong Kong, and teams from wider Europe; dialled in.

George rose to his feet and the team fell silent.

"Right" said George with a definitive tone. *"Let's crack on!"*

"Today is a momentous day for Utopia Pharmaceuticals and I am absolutely delighted to welcome everyone around the table this morning."

Twenty-two individuals around the table gently rapped the table with their outstretched hands to create a virtual drum roll. A UPL tradition since George had joined the Company.

George Latimer beamed with delight and nodded as he looked appreciatively at each and every smiling face around the room.

His eyes met those of Christophe and he nodded with unspoken gratitude. That was one of George's natural gifts: he made everyone feel valued.

"*Now Ladies and Gentlemen*, before we are joined by our overseas colleagues I want to outline this morning's agenda."

And so it began. The day that would change one Doctor's life: *forever*.

Chapter 6

"Well that went remarkably well, *if I say so myself.*"

"Your modesty does you credit Steve."

"*Thanks Christophe*, appreciate the vote of confidence."

"What do you think Peter. *Did we nail it or did we hammer the shit out of it*?"

"George looked like a Cheshire cat by the end of the call; so yep': I'd say you guys nailed it firmly to the Board..... '*no pun intended.*"

Do you think the detail was about right for our colleagues in the Far East?" asked Christophe; ever modestly self-critical and analytical in equal measure.

"You worry too much mate. It was on the button. They're very clued up on the Genotype stuff and you remember they meet frequently with that retired Professor of Virology; what's his name Peter?"

"*Professor Wang*. He presented to our Key Account Managers last year at the update meeting in Sheffield if you remember Steve?"

"Yep, that's him. He's a great guy. We sat and chatted over a Chinese afterwards."

"Trust you to bring it all back to food Steve." Christophe joked.

"So what is it Steve, are you already losing your short term memory or is last night's Chardonnay dulling your senses?"

Steve gave Peter a quick dig in the ribs for his jibe.

"Fighting again *boys*?"

Therese was stood in the doorway, running the fingers of her right hand through her long dark hair as she spoke. Her large brown eyes highlighted by her renewed eyeliner.

"You know us Therese; anything to draw *your* attention." Steve responded in an instant.

"*Always so impetuous, Steve.*" retorted Therese.

"Careful Therese, you know how it turns me on when you talk dirty with those big words!" Steve sniggered as he spoke.

"Spontaneous is fine Steve, but you must to learn to focus your energy."

"Let me know when you want me to focus it on you!"

Therese laughed showing her gleaming white teeth. She wagged her finger at Steve before disappearing back into the corridor. The three of them stared at the figure-hugging grey dress she wore: like boys wistfully surveying a candy store; without pocket money to spend.

"You don't suppose Therese would like to come and work for me in Sales; rather than report to you Christophe?"

"*Don't even go there.*" responded Christophe as he retreated to gather up his computer.

"She'd eat you alive."

"*That's what I was hoping.*" Steve stood laughing like a naughty schoolboy, voraciously licking his lips.

"You set them up and I'll knock them down Christophe."

"Clearly the alcohol is still impacting your judgement Steve." Peter said dryly.

"Cheer up Pete; it might never happen!"

"Not if I have *anything* to do with it." Christophe said with feeling.

"Now I am off to get my head in gear."

"Ahh' so your mind is back to cars already then?" Steve counter-attacked.

"Touché." responded Christophe, a hand across his chest feigning injury.

"Sorry to break up the fight. But I need to speak to Christophe."

Therese was back at the door; minus her playful banter and broad smile.

"He's all yours." Steve retrieved his computer as he spoke.

"Be gentle with him." Steve turned over his left shoulder and winked at Christophe as he followed Peter out of the door and put a fatherly arm around his friend's shoulder.

Chapter 7

"Let's chat in Elizabeth Tully's meeting room, please Christophe. She is already waiting for us."

Therese's tone of voice imparted a sense of unexpected urgency foreign to his ears. *"Terry"* ordinarily took everything in her stride: she was smart, resourceful and dependable. At times she seemed to positively effervesce with the Joy of living. Christophe put it down to *Karma*. She felt like the *Ying to his Yang*: the antidote to his stress; she was someone Christophe could trust and believe in and at times; *she felt like so much more...*

The two walked the short distance in silence. Christophe could sense his day was about to take an unexpected turn.

He felt a sinking feeling in the pit of his stomach and his mouth felt suddenly dry.

"Good morning Christophe. Thank you for coming immediately. *I'm sorry if it sounded as though I had summoned you to this meeting.* I can imagine you've already had a stressful morning, what with the Board meeting and so on."

Elizabeth waited for Christophe to adjust the height of his seat as he sat opposite her in the small square room which contained only a simple wood laminated table, four chairs and a telephone. It was linked to Elizabeth Tully's room by a connecting door. She orchestrated so many meetings these days that she had disciplined herself to separate meetings with Colleagues *spatially and mentally* from her daily activities.

From the sanctuary of her larger adjoining personal office space, she could work without interruption on busy days: which outnumbered quiet days by an unenviable margin.

Therese sat on Christophe's right and Elizabeth's new deputy for Pharmacovigilance *Helen Vance*; sat to his left. Elizabeth gestured to Helen as she spoke.

"Helen has been collating the latest *Serious Adverse Events* for our latest hepatitis C antiviral; candidate U0008." Elizabeth spoke always with reference to the Company allotted nomenclature before moving forward to the assigned generic name, it was an old habit from her previous Biotech role where everything ended in [-*imab*] *or* [-*onovir*];.....she liked belt and braces:

"Consistency of process encourages connected thinking and minimises the chances for error."

This was Elizabeth's mantra for her new staff.

"We are very concerned by what may be a *significant safety signal* for "*hepcretrovir*" and I wanted you to be fully aware of the facts - *immediately."*

Elizabeth emphasised the words "significant safety signal" as a prelude to her reveal: already managing Christophe's expectation and reinforcing the sinking feeling in his stomach.

"That sounds worrying Liz'". He spoke with clear concern audible in his voice.

"Well, in a word yes; Christophe."

"You've seen the latest figures for bone marrow suppression from the amalgamated safety reports from the data base?" (A rhetorical question: *consistency of process.....*)

"Yes. The External Safety Monitoring Board, *the ESMB*: appeared satisfied that the number of cases were a reflection of co-existent disease processes in patients with Chronic HCV infection."

"Yes so I understand. But they met again three days ago and the *cumulative* results for bone marrow damage are alarming. There may be

an indication that the drug is suppressing the production of both red and white blood cells as well as platelets."

"So the picture is one of *pancytopenia*?" Therese interjected for clarification.

She thought for a moment then decided it would be to Helen's benefit to hear an explanation of the impact of the diagnosis on the patient. Therese had worked as a General Practitioner for five years before joining the Company a year previously and was always enthusiastic to share knowledge.

"The risk to the patient may translate into severe anaemia causing extreme lethargy and shortness of breath. A lower white cell count implies a susceptibility to bacterial infection, which may cause overwhelming infections called septicaemia."

"Last but not least, suppression of platelets interferes with blood clotting; so the patient may bleed excessively from minor injury or bruise spontaneously. As you know many drugs can suppress individual blood cells lines, but *a reduction of all three cell lines is very serious and potentially fatal*."

Elizabeth smiled and nodded her appreciation to Therese. Elizabeth always encouraged impromptu training of her team and Therese always intuitively went the extra mile; without being asked.

"*Thank you Therese*. The ESMB team were not surprised to see reductions in cell counts but unfortunately the number of cases of overwhelming infection, of *sepsis*; may well be mirroring the bone marrow cell counts."

Elizabeth looked unusually concerned as she spoke; the crows feet around her eyes now matched by the wrinkling of her brow and glabella: the skin covered area between her eyes.

Christophe had known Elizabeth for over eight years. Furthermore he had been instrumental in her appointment to UPL after settling into the nuanced Company politics and leveraging his influence. During that time she had been steadily promoted through the ranks of the Pharmacovigilance department: steadily increasing her influence [through *consistency of process*], on the safety of drug development and adverse event reporting.

Elizabeth had an impeccable approach to her work and always aligned herself with Patients' best interests: with safety at the forefront of her mind. Christophe regarded her as punctilious in all aspects of her work and voiced his opinion at every available opportunity with Senior Management.

She took a sip of water and waited for Christophe's response. Elizabeth realised that with an imminent Press Release the news could not have come at a worse juncture and conceivably he might be placed in an invidious position within the Company. The future of the drug as a treatment option; could well be compromised by significant safety concerns and it was Christophe's responsibility to assess the evidence and advise the Company accordingly.

"Can I see a copy of the latest figures please Elizabeth?"

Thinking aloud Christophe said: "So these figures were evident and discussed on Saturday, that's the 6th of August..." He always spoke dates aloud it was a sure-fire way of him memorising them quickly.

Elizabeth turned her computer screen round for him to see and Therese moved closer to him, their knees touching, as they looked at the rows of neatly presented data; reflecting the impact of *hepcretrovir* on different cell lines within the blood results.

In her usual pragmatic style Therese thought out loud as she digested the impact of the recent data on the proportion of patients who had developed bone marrow impairment. Christophe wondered whether she had consciously decided to mimic his traits as a form of convergence...

"So the historic trend is around *one in four thousand patients* go on to develop *pancytopenia*; whilst on long term treatment of up to 24 weeks?"

They collectively sat quietly looking at the data and waiting for Christophe's opinion.

Finally Christophe spoke, rather more slowly and deliberately than was normal for him.

"The six previous cases of sepsis were compatible with the patient's *past or existing history of deficient bone marrow function*, whilst on historical anti-viral treatment; or as a consequence of co-morbidities.

But these ten new cases have been labelled *Serious Unexpected, Serious Adverse Reactions* [SUSARs], by the ESMB."

"I have already reported the list of cases to the Competent Authorities of course." confirmed Elizabeth. She looked down at her keyboard as she spoke and typed commands.

"Thank you. Is there anything else I should know?"

"Not at this stage Christophe."

"Okay Elizabeth. Could you send me a copy of the case narratives if available, and the updated figures for me to study please?"

Elizabeth's fingers were already typing as Christophe articulated his request.

"Consider it done." Elizabeth made eye contact again as she pressed the send key.

Christophe stood up sensing a heavier weight now pressing down on his shoulders.

"Thank you Elizabeth. *I guess you're working late*?"

She nodded.

"Catch you later then." he added as he smiled at Helen and closed the door behind Therese.

Christophe walked silently alongside Therese for the second time that morning as they headed towards his office.

Chapter 8

"Well that's a blow." Therese stated the obvious as they slumped down on adjacent seats in the corner of Christophe's office.

"Sorry to have collared you the minute the Board Meeting was over."

"You did the right thing; the three of us were just shooting the breeze anyway." Christophe stood up as he spoke.

He walked to his desk and illuminated the *"Do Not Disturb"* sign with his remote control then poured them each a glass of mineral water. He drained his glass before he spoke. Therese sat with her notepad and pencil poised to write as he sat back down.

"Let's prioritise." Christophe focused on the clock as he spoke; already anticipating his 11 a.m. meeting with his least favourite lawyer.

"I will forward the case narratives and data to you as soon as we finish our meeting."

"As you know, the narratives will give an overview of the patient's history, ongoing treatment and response to *hepcretrovir* with appropriate blood test results."

"Review everything and assume nothing."

Louise nodded affirming her response to his ritual mandate.

"First, take a good look at treatment exposure periods in the narratives and details of concomitant diseases and drug therapy. Ensure you fully appraise the data and *details for all sixteen cases of pancytopenia in the database for this particular study.*"

"Second, prepare a simple slide overview of the bone marrow suppression data."

"Finally, prepare a detailed slide listing timelines and eventual *patient-specific outcomes: all of which will need careful follow up documentation.*"

"Let's be sure we can define the size of the problem and the impact on patient well-being."

"Needless to say Therese, we need all of this done by Close of Business today."

Therese smiled and knew she need say only one thing in response.

"*I'm on the case.*"

She stood up, readjusted her dress momentarily and headed for the door.

She hesitated for a moment, turned and remarked.

"*By the way; I like your shirt and tie combo'.*"

Christophe looked across at her and gave her a broad smile in return.

"*That's more like it*!" she said.

"*See you later Boss.*"

Chapter 9

"Hi Annalisa. Is George available?"

"I'm afraid not Christophe. He's already on the plane bound for Chicago and I don't expect to see him before next week. He will be calling me from time to time of course."

"Is it urgent? Shall I ask him to call you when I speak?"

"No don't worry. I will email him, thanks."

Christophe licked his lips and frowned as he stroked his chin. Unusually be shuffled his feet as he spoke. Annalisa sensed his anxiety as he half turned to leave. *Keen to support him, she carried on talking*:

"I gather the meeting went well? George was *very pleased* with your presentation."

"He mentioned it?"

"No I heard him on the phone to Asia. They were very complimentary about all your hard work and the quality of your slide presentation. I am sure he'll be in touch soon."

"Thanks I appreciate that. See you later."

Annalisa felt uncomfortable to see him leave without further explanation. She quickly typed an email to her boss as a heads' up on recent warehouse data and included a line concerning Christophe's enquiry. If a member of the Senior Leadership Team was worried: George expected to be updated.

He sat on the Company' private jet and read her email twenty minutes after she'd sent it; as the jet reached cruising speed.

Chapter 10

Christophe sat in his office analysing his options. The recent email from Elizabeth was open on the screen and he looked at the Serious Adverse Event data relating to bone marrow function and haematology.

He checked his watch again: 10:25 a.m. Less than three hours before the Press Release embargo would be lifted at 2 p.m. C.E.T. Timed to ensure the U.S. markets got an early heads' up for the start of Wall Street trading.

His mobile phone buzzed in his pocket. *A private number he noted*; but instinctively answered anyway.

"Good morning Christophe."

His pulse rate instantly rose as a surge of adrenaline coursed through his veins. He responded unusually slowly.

"Professor Justin? *Edwina...... how are you?*"

"Are you alone Christophe?"

"Yes Edwina. I'm very surprised to hear your voice; *but very pleasantly surprised.*"

He had recovered his composure by the time he replied on this occasion. He could feel his face was flushed none the less.

"Let's hope you feel that way when we have finished our conversation." She responded curtly.

"Christophe I'm *very* concerned."

Christophe shifted uneasily in his seat. He loosened his shirt collar and swallowed hard; sensing more troubled waters ahead.

"Professor Jenkins from the External Safety Monitoring Board rang me this morning."

"He rang *you* Edwina?"

"Why would he?"

"He expressed....concerns about your Company data."

"You're referring to UP0008?"

"*Yes. What else*?" Her manner was unusually brusque; bordering on sarcasm.

Did he mean so little to her now?

Christophe felt more than a little hurt by her approach.

"*You're fully updated on the latest bone marrow and sepsis data?*" She persisted in the same tone, with no sense of empathy towards him.

Edwina paused, clearly waiting for an unwavering reply.

"*Yes of course.*"

Christophe could feel a further wave of anxiety rising in the pit of his stomach. He waited for Edwina to continue. This was clearly no time for personal sentiment.

"*There's no easy way to say this Christophe, so I will get straight to the point.*"

"We've become aware that one of the Contract Research Organisations [C.R.O.] used by Utopia; has been *manipulating data.*"

Her words were incisive and cut through him like a surgical laser.

Christophe audibly caught his breath. The silence on the phone was deafening. He stood, bent forward and re-illuminated his "*Do Not Disturb*" sign and then sank back into his chair. His pulse was pounding and he felt light headed. He took a sip of water from his glass: his mouth felt desert dry all of a sudden.

"*Let me elaborate Christophe.* As you are well aware I chair NICO. For reasons I cannot go into over the phone, we commissioned duplicate *independent* laboratory analysis on a consecutive series of blood tests for patients in a study which *we as an organisation: funded, designed and implemented."*

She paused; realising what she was revealing could be catastrophic for Christophe, the Product and the Company.

"I'm listening carefully Edwina." His auditory cortex was already firing at a frenetic rate; he heard a tap on his door and jumped like a frightened hare caught in the headlights of a speeding car. He focused only on Edwina's voice: *right now, nothing else mattered.*

"We instigated an immediate audit of the Company Procedures at the site; as a consequence of the discrepancies we uncovered: we have reported our findings to the European Competent Authorities and National Regulators for the region."

"How does this directly affect Utopia?"

"At this stage I cannot give you a firm answer to that question. What I can say is that your haematology results *may vastly underestimate* the scale of Serious Adverse Events for your study population."

"Are you implying that the external Company concerned *intentionally falsified results?"*

"That's a matter for the Authorities and not for me to judge. But if you ask for my personal opinion: then the answer has to be a resounding YES!"

Her voice was calm and pragmatic.

 "The source data verification process looks clear enough."

"From your perspective; you will need to CANCEL the Press Release Christophe."

The words hit him with the force of an express train and he felt physically propelled back into his chair.

He drew breath slowly and deliberately, as his heart rate aligned with the notional express train, travelling at 124 miles per hour. His heart was thumping inside his chest as more adrenaline was squirted into his circulation by his *adrenal medulla.*

"A reanalysis of data sets originating from that particular C.R.O. will be essential to ensure the validity of your combined study results on Safety. I understand from my conversations with *Professor Jenkins* that your analyses were undertaken by two different Companies in different geographic regions. So your database arising from Latin-American countries *may not be impacted*."

"Christ; I can't believe what I'm hearing. "

Christophe sat with a stunned expression. He started to perspire and small beads of sweat broke out on his brow.

The pain in his neck returned with a vengeance. He absent-mindedly took off his tie.

"So what you're saying Edwina, is that the blood results for thousands of patients, coming from one of the major analysis laboratories, *from Mumbai specifically*, are suspect; and in the worst case scenario, may have been *falsified*. Furthermore, this may have been intentional: *a Criminal Act*?"

"At the very least, you must assume that the laboratory results may not be a true reflection of the accurate values."

"Your product launch will need to be delayed pending a re-evaluation of your entire Clinical Trial Results."

Christophe looked at his watch again; he felt sick and retched involuntarily.

He caught his breath and took a drink of water to wash down the acrid taste of bile in his mouth.

"I need time to take this in Edwina."

"I understand Christophe. I will text you my mobile number in case you want to talk about next steps."

"In the meantime, *I need your undertaking that the Press Release will NOT be issued.*"

"Neither the Data Summary, nor my Endorsement, is appropriate under the circumstances."

"*I understand; but…*"

"*Thank you. Take care.*"

The line abruptly went dead.

Moments later, Edwina's mobile number appeared with a ping on Christophe's mobile. He saved her number to memory immediately, then tightly closed his eyes and tried to focus his thoughts.

His heart was racing and he could feel the carotid pulse in his neck keeping time with the thumping in his chest. The pulses in his fingers joined the orchestra; triggered by sequential surges of adrenaline: transmitted throughout his arteries.

Sweat dripped from his brow and he felt his back sweating against the leather of his chair.

With his fingers trembling on the keys, he sent an immediate cancellation notice for his 11 a.m. meeting with legal, sales and marketing. He sent an urgent meeting request scheduled for 11:30 a.m. with *Josh and Clive* in his follow-on email; marked CONFIDENTIAL and red flagged. He elected to use one of the small meetings rooms in the Legal Department as he selected a venue for the meeting.

Christophe felt drained. He closed the electronic blinds to his office and closed his eyes; composing his thoughts in preparation for what lay ahead.

Chapter 11

"Have you any idea of the *SHIT STORM* you are about to detonate Christophe?"

"How can you be sure the Data are corrupt?"

"It may well be that *our* Clinical Trial Data is clean!"

Josh Edwards sat forward on his seat waiting for a reply as he fired questions at Christophe. When he realised he was not going to provoke a response he carried on his rant regardless; gesticulating wildly with his arms.

The veins on the side of his forehead assumed abnormal prominence as he continued raising objections. His eyes bulged as he retracted his eyelids, further exaggerating his prominent globes; arising from his historically overactive thyroid gland.

He hesitated momentarily and looked at his watch.

"We have less than an hour before the press release is due to be released and you want me to withdraw it? *Are you fucking serious?"*

He shook his head disbelievingly.

"We have had Board Approval and George was *unequivocal* with his instructions on timing."

"Do you have any idea of the damage to our reputation, any idea of the number of Press Agencies who will draw their own conclusions if we withdraw the announcement?"

".....To say nothing of the bloody share price?" He could envision his Mercedes 2017 upgrade disappearing before his eyes as he spoke.

He nervously licked his lips for the third time in ten minutes and rubbed his forehead, exasperated. His voice had risen an octave and his throat felt strained.

"Professor Justin was clear: *we must not* issue *the Press Release*."

Christophe stated in a factual, down to earth manner; sounding pragmatic but feeling nauseated with a tinge of panic now setting in. His tongue stuck to the roof of his mouth as he spoke and felt tongue tied.

They both glared at him across the table.

"So you answer to *her* now? Since when did she sign your merit awards?" Josh spat out the words sarcastically.

"It's not a case of *answering to her* Josh; *SHE CHAIRS NICO!*

"She is hugely influential and that's the very reason you were adamant that she is cited on our Press Release."

"So we remove her Endorsement and go ahead with the planned press release."

Josh tented his fingers as he spoke, trying to regain his composure as much as trying to portray the impression that he was in control of the situation. He spoke at a steady pace and lowered his voice but his eyes were darting back and forth as he spoke belying his feelings.

"*Are you serious*?"

Christophe looked incredulous and shook his head as he shifted uncomfortably in his chair. He continued, struggling to take back control of the conversation: feeling as though he was clinging to the edge of a precipice.

"You would be willing to go ahead despite such doubt hanging over the *validity of the SAFETY data*?"

"And when we have a spate of cases of sepsis and an unprecedented number of deaths...."

Clive McGregor finally spoke; laying his hand on Josh' right forearm as he did so.

"As I understand, it the Efficacy data are *not* in doubt. We have established that *hepcretrovir* works for patients with Chronic Hepatitis C."

"*The central laboratory* in Virginia which analysed the viral loads was used to quantify *the entire sample range*. There is no doubt that hepcretrovir suppresses the virus and contributes to a potential lifelong cure."

Josh nodded in agreement appearing buoyed by Clive's composed reasoning: sensing light at the end of the tunnel where ten minutes ago there had been only darkness.

"*That may be so; as far as we know.*" Christophe responded cautiously.

"But Efficacy and Safety go hand in hand; we cannot claim one without the other. *The balance of benefit and risk MUST be appropriately apportioned for us to Market the Drug.*"

"So now *you* of all people, doubt our efficacy data?" Clive looked indignant; his tone almost sarcastic as he glared at Christophe and leaned across the desk towards him.

"But the laboratory in question analysed a large portion of the routine haematology and biochemistry data. There has to be doubt raised about the veracity of the database."

"*But surely the individual clinicians involved in the trial would have raised concerns about patient welfare if patients had deteriorated under their care?*" Clive insisted.

"Not all changes in blood results will impact patients' well-being *immediately*. The blood test changes may take a while before they manifest. That's why long term data are vital."

"*And that's precisely why we have Post Authorisation Safety and Efficacy studies in place: correct?*"

Clive and Josh exchanged glances. Josh began to sweat visibly. Clive glanced at his watch.

"So let me summarise, you don't have *any* firm evidence to confirm that the data were falsified or to suggest that the safety data for *hepcretrovir* are inaccurate." This was a statement and not a question.

Clive McGregor's face turned stony hard the instant he had finished the statement.

Christophe looked at Clive McGregor, opened his mouth to speak and hesitated.

"I suggest you speak to Professor Justin and tell her to contact *YOU...*"

"*IF and only IF:* her suspicions mature into concrete evidence of wrong doing."

He pointed his left forefinger at Christophe as he personalised the directive.

"The Competent Authorities have already been informed." protested Christophe.

Clive's eye's widened and his pupils dilated.

"*Why would Utopia have been included in that discussion*?

Clive McGregor demeanour switched to furious as he fixed his icy stare on Christophe, tracking his eye movements; but outwardly keeping his composure.

"*You clearly told us* that *the Study in question was an oncology study independently funded and instigated by NICO*?"

He enunciated each word slowly and deliberately.

 A statement not a question.

"It was Professor Justin's responsibility to raise concerns about the study or studies within her remit. As I understand, she has had no involvement in our Study Cohorts whatsoever."

An unequivocal statement.

Christophe gritted his teeth, realising he had to concede that point.

"Whilst that may be so, her call has given us significant doubt concerning..."

Clive had heard enough.

"Her call *specifically* to you; and *you alone*: has raised *your* doubts."

"You have nothing but hearsay to report."

"And... what of Professor Jenkins' concerns?"

"DEAL WITH IT!"

DO YOUR FUCKING job."

"Do whatever you need to do."

"*The Press Release goes out*."

Having delivered his ultimatum, he glared at Christophe: stood up and closely followed by Josh; left the room: firmly closing the door behind him.

Chapter 12

14:35: Christophe Schultz' Office

"What were you thinking Christophe?" Edwina sounded angry now. He could sense her usual calm demeanour beginning to fracture as her voice intensified.

"How could you of *all people* countenance their decision?"

She sounded almost spiteful thought Christophe as he listened to the edge in her voice.

"I didn't."

He uttered defensively. He crossed his arms as he spoke and his lower lip trembled as he retorted.

"So they published the Press Release *without your Authority*?"

"How could you be so foolhardy as to let this happen?"

"I didn't just let it happen."

His protests fell upon deaf ears.

"Well you didn't stop them Christophe."

"By failing to act you are complicit in their deception."

"YOU are the MEDICAL DIRECTOR!" What could you have been thinking?"

Christophe felt on the edge of panic. He was tired and his head was spinning.

He consciously tried to control his breathing to abate the pins and needles around his lips and permeating his finger-tips: clear signs of hyperventilation.

"Well I tried to persuade them and in the end; there was nothing I could do."

"I hoped *you* of all people Christophe would have shown more metal; more stele."

"*You leave me with little choice I'm afraid.*"

"What do you mean Edwina?"

"I will need to speak to the Authorities; to the relevant Regulatory Agencies impacted by your decision: *or lack of it.*"

"Edwina, at least give me some time, to speak to George and the team; they're all travelling to the USA at present."

"Time is precisely what we don't have Christophe."

"Think about the PATIENTS: think about their SAFETY!"

"*I am; that's all that drives me in my work.*"

"That's not how it looks to me. I gave you fair warning."

"*Goodbye Christophe.*"

The phone went dead for the second time that day.

There was a finality in her tone as she hung up.

Christophe sat; momentarily paralysed by fear and indecision.

He closed his eyes and took several long slow deep breaths and felt his mind clearing.

Christophe dialled Edwina's number; her phone went straight to voicemail.

He had only one course of action open to him.

The tenor of his message was clear.

"Please do nothing until we have discussed the matter in London: we have to meet face to face, this evening."

Part Two

Chapter 1

08:30 a.m. Friday 12th August 2016

Ordinarily, *Molly Hull* abhorred indecisiveness.

But today, just like yesterday, was turning into anything but an ordinary day.

In fact, it very much looked as though she was destined to spend the whole day cancelling meetings and reiterating trite apologies.

In truth, Molly didn't like apologising, particularly when the short comings were not of her own making.

Everything in Molly's life was ordered and tidy; it had been ever since childhood. From the age of three, a single speck of dirt or spilt food on her outfit merited a change of clothing. That trait had followed her throughout her life; one that *Harold*, her late besotted husband, willingly endured; during their twenty-seven years of happy, albeit childless, marriage.

Molly's orderliness was one thing *Professor Edwina Justin* valued above all else; that and her undivided loyalty. Professor Justin had used almost those precise words, during Molly's tenth annual appraisal in January 2016; several months before their combined workload escalated after Edwina's new high profile appointment to Chairman of NICO: the *National Institute of Cancer and Oncology*. Over the last few days it seemed that the whole Institute needed an appointment with Professor Justin and all were predestined for disappointment.

The telephone rang for the eighth time that morning and it was still only 8:30 a.m.

On the second ring Molly lifted the receiver to her right ear: instant recognition as she heard the caller's cultured, slightly dismissive tone as he enquired regarding "*Edwina's*" availability.

Molly disliked the disrespectful approach inherent in failure to refer to *Professor Justin* by her title.

"I'm sorry *Professor Stanley*; I haven't had a reply from Professor Justin, as yet. I have left a number of voicemail messages precisely as you requested and forwarded your email and the relevant attachments."

"Yes I can confirm that the email was sent to her private email account."

She listened, shifting the receiver to her left ear; an outward sign of her growing irritation.

"It is unusual, I agree and ordinarily Professor Justin does keep me updated with any unintended or unexpected last minute changes to her itinerary and meeting schedules."

As she listened to *Morton Stanley* bleating on, she could imagine him stood in his herringbone tweed jacket with blue shirt and matching dark silk tie; toying with his latest golf trophy or planning his next trans-Atlantic flight in search of further self aggrandisement.

("Never one to hide his light, under a bushel:" her beloved Harold would have said: if he'd known Morton Stanley, *which thankfully he did not.*)

June Brett provided a welcome distraction as she popped her head around the office door and gave Molly a brief wave. Molly gestured five minutes with her outstretched fingers whilst she silently mouthed the confirmation. June nodded and closed the door quietly behind her.

"You have my word Professor Stanley. The moment I hear from her I will ask her to call you."

"*Goodbye*" Molly had gratefully seized the opportunity to terminate the call.

She breathed a sigh of relief; yesterday it had taken her a solid ten minutes to extricate herself from his phone call; same agenda, same promise, remaining unfulfilled. She tugged at the waist of her woollen skirt and straightened her blouse.

Molly studied one of her many spreadsheets, this one populated with a growing number of outstanding fields which remained pending; a series of traffic-light priority flags attached, with an ever increasing number of amber transitioning to red flags.

"My God Molly" June Brett, her close friend and confidant would say: *"Do you have a spread-sheet for everything?"* She did. It was the secret of her success in many ways: order was her best attribute in times of trouble.

Molly opened another tab on her Dell® computer screen and surveyed the back-to-back appointments in Professor Justin's diary and felt that sinking feeling again. On a more typical day, Professor Justin would be at her desk working, armed with her second or third black Espresso of the day; by the time Molly arrived at 7:30 a.m.

Friday morning: it was now day three and she'd heard nothing from Edwina since she'd left the office on Tuesday evening around 6:30 p.m. Molly recalled Edwina had looked flustered as she'd bid Molly a brief goodbye, mobile in hand; exiting the office without their habitual daily de-brief.

Molly stood up and took let out a deep sigh. She adjusted the collar of her white silk blouse and lifted her grey jacket carefully from the top hook of the ornate iron coat-stand which stood in the corner of the room behind the office door. She straightened her pencil grey skirt and adjusted her belt ensuring her blouse hung neatly over the waist-band, which was finished off with a thin black soft Saint Laurent leather belt from Selfridges Department Store in Oxford Street, Central London.

With a cursory look in the mirror to the left of her desk she straightened her pearl necklace and took a longer look at the photograph hanging alongside. She stared upon her beloved Harold, immortalised on the 8x10 inch photograph hanging in its golden frame; taken by a hospital photographer at a Gala Dinner charity event 5 years previously. Happier days she sighed; a tear appeared briefly in the corner of her left eye and she brushed it away.

She headed for the door but the phone halted her progress.

She grabbed the headset on the third ring.

"Good Morning: Professor Justin's office."

Dr Constance Blake MD had been working for four weeks on her latest research proposal; consuming all her spare time between clinical commitments, endless meetings and political wrangling with clinical colleagues at the Institute. Everything from on-call duties to Outpatient commitments seemed to be ripe for change or up for grabs; depending on your political or financial viewpoint.

"*Molly this really is terribly frustrating.*" Constance Blake continued, as Molly stood and soaked up the diatribe in her right ear.

"I can only sympathise." Molly responded genuinely. "For what it's worth, I have had to cancel or reschedule dozens of meetings in the last few days and..."

Constance Blake cut her off mid-sentence.

"I don't want *sympathy*." she snapped back. "I want confirmation of the meeting."

"And as I have explained Dr Blake, I cannot confirm the meeting until I speak to Professor Justin."

Constance Blake could feel a migraine coming on. She had a dull occipital headache and her vision was blurred around the edges as she looked at her computer screen and her scheduled commitments for the following week; wondering when she was ever going to schedule a week off.

"Look Molly, I'll pitch up at 1:30pm today as planned and would be grateful if you could ensure that Professor Justin is available; as previously agreed."

She now felt nauseated and her vision started to tunnel.

She replaced the receiver before Molly could reply.

"God what an infuriating women" thought Molly; *"and rude to boot."* What had Edwina called her in an uncharacteristically unguarded moment? Ah yes, *narcissistic*. Molly sat down in front of her computer and checked her own schedule.

The time for indecisiveness was over: time for her to act!

Molly gathered up a file of paperwork requiring Edwina's signature from the middle tray of her filing stack. Having set the call forwarding function of her office telephone, she amended her personal email out-of-office for mid-day; before locking and detaching her laptop computer from its docking station. With paperwork and laptop safely secured in her large purpose made Italian leather shoulder bag; she checked she had the keys to Edwina's London Mews and rang *Frank* on speed dial using her mobile.

"Good Morning Molly; to what do I owe the pleasure?" Frank's broad Cornish accent cut through his welcome like a hot knife through Devon clotted cream.

"Oh Frank you are such a charmer." replied Molly, a smile breaking the harsh frown she'd been wearing all morning.

"Ah: but only for the *right* Lady." Frank replied chirpily.

"I rather think you mean ladies *plural*?"

"Oh dear, I think I may have been rumbled." Molly could hear Frank beginning to belly laugh at the end of the phone situated on the ground floor; in the concierge department. She pictured his ruddy complexion gradually deepening.

"Professor Justin is always remarking about how you could charm the birds from the trees."

"Maybe it's got something to do with your hobby?" she continued.

"And no doubt my *bird fanciers' lung*?" Frank raised his bushy, overgrown eyebrows.

"I think you mean *pigeon* fanciers' lung Frank?"

"*Do I*? You do seem remarkably well informed about *my health*. I do know *you always manage to make me breathless Molly!*"

Molly could feel herself start to blush and could hear Frank doing his best to suppress a cough as he audibly wheezed into the telephone receiver.

"Well now I'm definitely out of my depth." laughed Molly, feeling somewhat embarrassed; yet suddenly acutely aware that it was the first time in several years that anyone had paid her such a blatant compliment. In fact: the first time since Harold's death.

Frank held the receiver of the telephone away from his mouth, then placed it on the table, and started to cough repeatedly. He braced himself with outstretched arms and took a couple of deep breaths before instinctively breathing out through pursed lips.

Molly waited, knowing that Frank would want to recover his composure before continuing. Her thoughts regressed three years in time; recounting the painful months when Harold was in the final stages of his illness. The daily ignominy of breathless conversation with cherished family and friends and the long lonely nights he had spent pacing slowly up and down the living room; insomnia his veritable enemy; *his nemesis*. Despite her reassurance and encouragement, he had resolutely refused to wake her in his hour of need. Even then, dying inch by inch, racked with metastatic lung cancer, he didn't want to burden her with his distress, his loneliness and enforced isolation. He refused to wake her: precious realising that she lay awake just one storey above him, lonesome in their marital bed, acutely aware and tortured by his suffering a floor below.

Then witnessing the deep sadness in his once joyful brown eyes as the days became shorter, his time confined to chair, then bed: tears welled up in her eyes as she glanced at his photograph on the wall.

Pulling herself together she none the less stood wondering how on earth a rough diamond like Frank could have such a positive impact on her. A smile, even a blush.....did she simply feel sorry for him with his personal daily battle with shortness of breath?

Empathy or sympathy, she couldn't decide but either way, he managed to touch her emotionally and it gave her a warm feeling inside.

Frank composed himself and took a large swig of water from the litre bottle on his desk.

"Sorry Molly: *you rang me for more than my silly banter. How can I help?"

His tone had switched abruptly to professional mode.

Molly wondered whether someone had come into earshot or whether he was simply deeply embarrassed by his coughing fit.

"Frank I need a driver in the next twenty minutes or so. I am visiting Professor Justin's apartment in Mayfair."

"Give me ten minutes to bring the car around and I will take you myself Molly."

"Well if you're sure? Thank you. I'll meet you in the car park."

"Right you are: *Parker at your service M'lady."*

Molly ended the call on her mobile. She would miss Frank when he retired next year. Who on earth ever made *Thunderbirds' jokes* these days?

Chapter 2

June Brett had her blue-tooth audio earphones inserted deeply inside her ears and was staring intently at her computer screen, scrutinising the integral medical dictionary, when Molly entered the small office; three doors down from her own.

June glanced up, smiled and popped one earphone out which immediately halted the *Mozart Piano Concerto No. 21*, playing on her *mobile*; as background music whilst she worked.

"Hi Molly: *Happy Friday*!"

"You too: June!"

(*Fred Patterson* in procurement had started the trend towards the "Happy Friday" salutation when he joined the Institute three years previously; just after Harold's death. At the time the weekly greeting seemed hollow and over familiar to Molly and she guessed he must have thought her stilted and unfriendly. Now with the growth in headcount over the last year, she had to admit she found it a comforting when colleagues she barely knew, greeted her on dreary mornings with a smile and friendly wave. Even Edwina had recently proactively adopted the practice of greeting visitors with a "Happy Friday.")

(Times move on and so must I: she had counselled herself. That was what Harold would have wanted.)

(She'd always had a knack for second-guessing Harold; at heart they were both true romantics and enjoyed nothing better than curling up together on their comfy sofa at home with a classic black and white movie: preferably featuring *Dirk Bogarde* and *Katharine Hepburn*: she'd lost count how many times they'd watched *The African Queen* together.)

"How's the Institute Research Composite Dossier coming along?"

"*Steady progress Molly*. Professor Justin made a fair number of technical Medical amendments but I'm determined to have it completed by the end of the day; before heading off for the weekend. You'll recall I've booked Monday and Tuesday off to give me time with *Ted*."

Molly nodded; she'd not forgotten and knew that if June had set herself a deadline: she'd meet it.

(June and Ted met on an internet dating site in 2014: three years after June's late husband died of a sudden heart attack [myocardial infarction]. That was one of the reasons Molly and June had grown close; sharing grief, sharing fond memories and expressing their individual hopes and aspirations for the future. Molly doubted she would ever re-marry but admired June's fortitude and spirit for adventure: re-marrying at the age of fifty-three. To June, so set in her ways, and eight years June's senior; she could only envisage a quiet retirement and time to immerse herself in books and gardening: her two passions in life). Being fifty-three felt a lifetime ago and now she counted her blessings with the birth of each new day.)

June lowered her voice, as if the walls had ears. "Talking of Edwina, *any news yet*?"

"No not a word. That's why I'm heading off to her Apartment now."

"I haven't been able to reach her by 'phone; her mobile is going straight to voicemail and I want to be sure everything is okay at her Apartment; water the plants and take in her mail *etcetera*. As you know, I tend to pop over regularly when she's away or out of town for a few days."

"So do you think she's taken an impromptu holiday, *in Italy perhaps*?"

June gave Molly a playful wink as she spoke.

"*I do hope you have not been listening to tittle-tattle or gossiping with Constance Blake*?" barked Molly, maybe a tad too loudly in the confined office.

June looked a little sheepish and gazed down at her keyboard: looking every inch like a scalded child, taken to task by her headmistress for talking out of turn in class.

June regarded Molly as a good friend but also respected her as a no-nonsense line manager. Ordinarily there was no conflict of interest, but she recognised Molly's fierce loyalty to Professor Justin; especially since Harold's demise.

"Sorry Molly, I didn't mean to..."

In a more level tone, Molly responded with her eyes fixed on June's forehead.

"Between you and me, I hear Constance Blake has been spreading rumours and all because she'd seen Professor Justin having coffee in Venice with one of her Italian delegates from Milan University at the recent oncology conference in March."

Molly bristled at the thought of Constance Blake holding counsel with the other Consultants; always looking to undermine Edwina's position: gaining political points to use in the Boardroom.

(*"There's bad blood there and 'no mistake"*. Harold would have remarked in his broad Yorkshire accent.)

"That said..." Molly went on to admit, lowering her own voice: "I did have a similar thought and rang her apartment in Milan, but no luck. Phone just kept ringing."

She sighed and in a more decisive tone continued.

"So I have put my call forward to your extension June for the next couple of hours and expect to be back by mid-day."

Molly glanced at her watch. "I'd better be going; I need to stop off at the Secretariat on route."

"Of course, anything I can do to minimise your work-load Molly; just ask: you know that." June looked contrite and looked Molly squarely in the eye as she spoke.

"Thank you June." she headed for the door but stopped momentarily; looking over her right shoulder before turning the brass handle.

"Oh and I'm sorry June, I didn't mean to bite your head off just now. *It's just so unlike her.*"

"Try not to worry Molly; I'm sure everything's okay."

But Molly did worry and had a feeling that everything would not be okay. She was wrestling with a nagging feeling in the pit of her stomach; which despite her best efforts, wouldn't go away.

Ten minutes later Molly exited the lift on the lower ground floor and headed for the car park.

Molly smiled inwardly to herself. '*Good old June*, always the optimist and always ready to roll her sleeves up when the job demands". She made a mental note to make a recommendation to Edwina during the next round of pay reviews.

Frank stood waiting by the black Institute courtesy vehicle: a Mercedes C Class, which he had taken through the car wash before she'd arrived. He gave her a smile as broad as his shoulders as he held the rear passenger door open for her.

"You're carriage awaits ma'am!"

Molly flashed him a smile though couldn't bring herself to meet his gaze. *Had he noticed her blush*?

He had and that had made his day, did she but know it.

Chapter 3

10:15 a.m. Friday 12th August 2016

Six white marble steps rose up to the imposing entrance of *Melway Mews*; in the heart of Mayfair: Central London, UK.

The entrance to the Georgian property was flanked by two large black marble pillars; weathered by years of rain and traffic fumes, as were the approaching steps.

Molly stood in front of the highly polished solid black veneered front door with bright brass fittings. The entrance towered above her fragile frame as she reached inside the integral zipped pocket of her laptop bag, for the keys to the Apartment block.

She lifted the brass metallic flap and entered the *six digit numerical password* into the entry key pad before unlocking the heavy front door: the communal entry to the 14 luxury apartments within. The most prestigious apartments occupied the third and fourth floors: mostly second or third homes for the well healed or famous occupants who valued their privacy and opulent accommodation in equal measure.

As she stepped onto the diamond pattern black and white Marble floor of the entrance hall, Molly felt a flush of pride. She stopped for a moment to admire the imposing ornate crystal chandelier suspended over the vaulted stairwell. The early morning sun danced around the atrium walls, adding to the glamour of the facade. She imagined the aristocratic families who had once owned the entirety of the building, hosting extravagant parties: the likes of *Katherine Hepburn* escorted down the stairs, her beauty matched only by a stunning diamond-studded necklace creation; worn as if created bespoke for her elegant neckline.

Molly recalled the first time she had been invited the Mews, two years previously. She remembered the occasion as if it had been yesterday; her feelings of awe and humility: gaining an insight into the personal world of Professor Edwina Justin. Molly knew she was one of the very few from the Institute trusted enough to enter the *"inner sanctum"* of *Edwina's private life*; a public figure who treasured an intensely personal life.

But a decade spent as Edwina's P.A. [Personal Assistant] had been so much more than a typical employer/employee relationship; especially since the death of Harold. Edwina had been there for her, every step of the painful journey during the last months of his illness. *Empathy, compassion, generosity and warmth*; all words which were totally inadequate to convey the strength of support she had received from Edwina.

When Molly's friends and family were lost for words or incapable of finding the right ways to support her during Harold's illness; Edwina had always been there. A gentle reassuring squeeze of Molly's hand or a warm embrace; she always seemed to have the measure of compassion.

Molly unlocked the rectangular post box: simply labelled *Apartment 14 Edwina Justin.*

Her eyes skimmed along the row of boxes to other names, now familiar to her; some in the public eye: a Conservative Politician and famous writer, alongside an actress known for her proclivity for cocaine; a fading Hollywood star.

This building their London retreat from the blinding spotlight of celebrity status.

The small bundle of letters and single package fitted neatly alongside the laptop computer in her shoulder bag as she secured the postal box with the small silver coloured key.

The clear glass lift glided effortlessly to the fourth floor and Molly glanced up at the sunken CCTV camera in the transparent roof; wondering whether anyone was watching her at that very moment. The days of a concierge standing behind a small desk in the lobby of even the most exclusive apartment complex were becoming a distant memory; *more cost-cutting reflected Molly*. She tucked back her short grey hair behind her ears and absent-mindedly straightened her pearls again as she left the lift; turning right towards apartment 14 down the short connecting corridor.

The plush beige carpet silenced her footsteps. The corridor was empty and quiet. She glanced at her watch: *10:20 a.m.*

Molly rang the doorbell and the familiar simple church chime provoked no response from within. She waited a few moments then opened the deadlock. No chain in place: Edwina was certainly not at home.

She stepped inside the hallway and called out Professor Justin's name for good measure. Immediately, Molly's throat and nose were accosted by a pungent, yet vaguely familiar smell. She placed her laptop bag down alongside the ornate Chinese telephone table, noting the flashing digital light: signalling messages waiting. As she'd surmised: no one at home.

So she had been right to tend Edwina's Apartment.

She lingered for a moment wondering where the smell coming from? She felt slightly nauseous as the atmosphere seemed to claw at the back of her throat. The thermostat on the wall in the hallway was set at 21 degrees Celsius.

Nothing seemed out of place.

The lounge was picture perfect; as if staged for a home-buyers' photo-shot in a high end Estate Agent's window in Mayfair or Knightsbridge.

Molly retraced her steps and opened the front door to help dissipate the odour, then headed for the kitchen; by now strongly suspecting the freezer had defrosted.

"*Oh God*" she blasphemed under her breath and instinctively touched her breastbone, feeling for her crucifix with her right hand. At times she still forgot that she'd removed her 22-carat gold crucifix, given to her by her mother; when Harold had died. Molly had buried Harold with her most valued keepsake.

As she opened the kitchen door she peered around the corner, looking for the tale-tale puddle of stained water. She thought of the time she'd returned from a Caribbean holiday many years before, when a power surge had blown the fuse to the freezer. She had sudden olfactory flashbacks to a similar nauseating kitchen odour which she had not managed to clear for a week after cleaning up the mess: hands and knees, two bottles of bleach and still the smell had lingered. She shuddered at the memory.

The floor was clean and the fridge light illuminated. The freezer LED registered minus 18 degrees Centigrade.

Molly immediately opened the door to the fridge and above it the freezer; everything normal. Cheese, yoghurt, unopened, semi-skimmed milk within date; and fresh vegetables. Nothing out of place; nothing perished.

Molly opened the small kitchen windows and checked sinks; the draining rack was clear.

Next step the toilet thought Molly: she silently prayed there would not be some kind of blockage; Harold always dealt with that kind of problem: a plumber's privilege. She was sure he'd spared her some of the more sordid details from derelict or neglected households he had visited during his thirty-five year professional life.

"*Overcrowded squats and temporary shelters for the homeless*" he'd say: "*all deserved better.*" He always bought a copy of the *Big Issue*: his social responsibility from his selfless viewpoint.

"*Five selfless acts a day Molly; that's all it takes: good Karma for us all.*"

Crossing the living room Molly side-stepped the delicate Persian run and rounded on the bathroom to the left of Edwina's bedroom. The smell seemed stronger as she approached the bathroom door, which was ajar. The white toilet suite, tiled wet room and triangular bath unit were all spotlessly clean; with none of the familiar odours Molly recalled from having visited the nursing home when her late mother had become first bed-bound, then *doubly incontinent*. She recoiled and shivered momentarily at the memory.

Somewhat mystified, Molly re-entered the lounge and turned left; hesitating for a moment and knocking on Edwina's bedroom door before entering.

Chapter 4

Molly took the full force of the brutal assault on her senses as she opened the bedroom door.

A billion neurones fired with terrifying intensity in her occipital and olfactory cortices and she could no longer visualise the image which would forever be indelibly engrained in her Psyche.

Her entire body and life force felt crushed, her senses overwhelmed by the smell which deprived her of breath and splinted her breathing; she gasped for air and began to retch and swallowed back vomit.

Her head began to swim and she steadied herself against the door frame; willing her body to move: to carry her away from the bedroom. But her legs began to buckle and shake and she reeled stumbling backwards onto the floor as the vile contents of the room swirled around inside her skull like an unrelenting hurricane of horror.

Molly was overwhelmed, panicked by what she seen; her mind was racing uncontrollably, but time seemed to stand still.

She rolled over onto her hands and knees and crawled to the bathroom, willing her body around the doorway and heaving herself up against the doorframe. She reached the toilet bowl and retched and repeatedly vomited, then heaved a lung full of air before retching and vomiting again. Her legs gave way again and she kneeled over the toilet; gasping for breath as her abdominal muscles contracted involuntarily.

Tears flooded Molly's eyes and she sobbed incessantly as she tried to push herself up using the toilet bowl for support. She slipped on her own vomit. Her legs would not move and she lay down on her side, bringing her knees up to her chest. The tiled floor felt cold, but safe.

She willed herself to visualise Harold's face but she could only see gruesome flashbacks from the bedroom. She lay slowly mustering her strength; knowing she must make the call, knowing her life was irrevocably changed, touched by something evil and degrading.

Molly wiped her hands down her skirt and pushed forward onto her hands and knees again. Her heart was pounding in her chest and a heaviness pushed down on her breastbone, as she edged forward knowing she had to pass in front of the bedroom, past....she couldn't say it....she could barely think it; images uncontrollably flooded her mind. She turned her head away from the bedroom as she crawled slowly across the carpet and turned onto the short corridor in the direction of the door to the apartment.

Molly lay next to the Chinese table her mind racing; yet she couldn't organise her thoughts. She felt cold and she shivered involuntarily and uncontrollably. Finally after what seemed a lifetime she lifted her left hand, feeling for the telephone keypad. She pulled the handset to her left ear, suddenly aware of sweat dripping down her face.

Holding the handset in front of her she tried desperately to focus on the keyboard; wiping away her tears. Slowly she pressed the keys...9...9...9...

Her heart pounded in her ear over and over like a bass drum. She cried out for Harold but the voice at the end of the phone was barely audible, unfamiliar and cold. Pain radiated up her neck into the base over her skull.

Chapter 5

Detective Chief Inspector [D.C.I.] *Sally Benson* stepped out of the passenger door of the black Five Series BMW and stood on the pavement for a moment to admire the magnificent façade at the entrance to Melway Mews.

As *Detective Sergeant* [D.S.] *Brian Mann* joined her she furnished her warrant card for Woman Police Constable [W.P.C.] *Paula Jones* who stood at the entrance to the foot of the steps. Paula Jones duly recorded both detectives' names on her clipboard and they passed under the blue Police Incident Tape which was secured at each end to the pillars at the entrance to the Mews.

"'Originally owned by *Lord Anthony Reginald Melway*, Boss: a shipping magnet."

Sally raised her eyebrows; ill-prepared for a history lesson after a night where sleep had evaded her and a pile of paperwork had been her only distraction as the minutes ticked by endlessly.

"Have uniform secured the rear entrance Brian?"

"Already done Boss - two 'up: checking all residents in and out: no visitors permitted access until we give the order. Dave is overseeing process."

Sally nodded.

"Get the CCTV footage from that camera ASAP."

Sally pointed up to the strategically mounted camera, secured high up in the left hand corner of the building, positioned on a hinged metal arm, with an apparently uninterrupted view of the steps leading up to the communal entrance to the Mews.

They paused for a moment to look at the lobby.

"Geez' how the other half live, 'eh Boss?"

Sally quickly scanned the two rows of letter boxes inside the building. A forensic scientist was already dusting for prints as they scanned the scene.

"Get a list of the residents Brian. Let's see who lives here as well as who comes and goes."

They both donned a pair of white plastic gloves taken from a box on a forensics' portable stand positioned near the mail boxes.

Brian was already taking notes as they entered the lift and Sally depressed the button to the 4th floor.

"*I'll do likewise with the CCTV from this one.*" Brian gesticulated to the roof of the lift with his biro.

They stood momentarily in front of the scene of crime tape; erected at the entrance to the short corridor leading to Apartment 14. They each donned a plastic forensic zip up suit, shoe covers and fresh latex gloves; overseen by a wiry young constable who meanwhile scrutinised their warrant cards and recorded their names.

Sally noted his fresh face and rather grey demeanour.

"If you are going to *throw up*, do it in a bag and bin it. Understand?"

"*Yes Ma'am.*" He nodded apprehensively and shuffled his feet awkwardly feeling deflated and more than a tad nauseated; wishing he had not had toasted sausage sandwiches for breakfast earlier that morning. A sickly odour emanated from the apartment directly behind him and he'd been one of the first on the scene after the Emergency 999 call from Molly. He'd been patrolling in the Area Car with W.P.C. Jones and he had no doubt he'd drawn the short straw by remaining inside the Mews: checking in forensics' and detectives.

Brian felt his stomach rumble. Sally heard it too.

"'*Christ* what is it with you men and your stomachs." derided Sally shaking her head.

By contrast, she'd not yet eaten and was beginning to feel grouchy.

"*These fucking patches...*" Sally spoke under her breath and absent-mindedly rubbed at her left upper arm walking toward the entrance to the Apartment.

She'd been using nicotine replacement patches for four weeks and the cravings felt as bad as ever; particularly in the morning, at night, after a curry, with a coffee or a beer; in fact, pretty much all the bloody time! Her abstinence was beginning to wind her up.

"*They irritate and they're useless.*"

"*Sorry Boss*?" Brian looked quizzical as he spoke over her shoulder.

"Forget it Brian. I just need a cigarette at a time like this."

"*Not in here you don't!*" He regretted the witticism the second he'd cracked it: it was greeted by a stern look from Sally.

She stopped at the Chinese table just inside the front door and noted the flashing message monitor.

She gesticulated with her silver metallic pen: "let's get forensics onto this as soon as we've seen what we've got inside."

They walked silently across the living room, past the white leather sofa set against the wall and headed directly towards the bedroom.

Sally and Brian stood shoulder to shoulder watching the three ghostly figures, clothed in white coveralls from head to toe, going methodically about their task: akin to *actors* in a slow motion horror movie with carefully scripted movements.

The team in forensic overalls were *Dr Caroline Crunch* and *Mike Simmonds*: both stooping over the victim. *Tony Bailey* stood taking digital images: working the victim's bedroom from the left side of the bed and following Caroline's systematic instructions. The three of them had been working crimes scenes together for just short of two years and each knew the pattern Dr Crunch would follow in the event of a crime scene involving an unexpected death.

The victim's body was obscured from their line of sight as Sally and Brian stood like two perverted voyeurs; huddled in the doorway craning their necks to view the body of the deceased.

Caroline turned to greet Sally; and moved to the right, Mike following her initiative moving left: giving Sally and Brian their first uninterrupted view of the late *Professor Edwina Justin*.

Sally exhaled and grimaced momentarily and quietly took in the scene: scanning left and right and back to the victim.

A minimalist design was evident throughout the bedroom canvas. Sally observed the plush fabrics with matching floral curtain materials and duvet cover; the latter lay discarded on the floor to the left of the bed: just as the team had found it.

Ornate Chinese black lacquered furniture and a pair of matching pale blue bedroom side lamps adorned the hand-made tables. In the centre of the room a large queen sized bed dominated the scene.

The room appeared normal: but for the highly sculpted body of the deceased on the bed and the pink, yellow and brown stains visible on the otherwise vibrant white bottom sheet of the bed. Sally thought it likely that the stains were due to early decomposition of the body which lay ahead of them.No blood spatters or signs of a struggle were evident on cursory examination.

The body was naked, Caucasian, but positioned in anything but, a typical prone position.

Sally had taken a step back and had her head cocked to the right side: her *thinking pose*; as her late parents had coined it some two decades previously.

"No signs of a struggle?" Sally spoke almost rhetorically and Caroline waited before replying. She stood watching Sally intently: conscious of her huge experience of graphic crime scenes and her ability to read a scene swiftly.

"No signs of a struggle or violence in the bedroom and from our initial appraisal, it looks as though she was very carefully posed: *peri- or post-mortem.*" Caroline spoke pragmatically.

 "It certainly looks intricately staged... almost..... analogous to the Japanese furniture which has been so meticulously arranged around the room ..." Sally agreed.

"Are you thinking what I'm thinking Caroline?" Sally asked without expecting a reply.

She had worked many frenzied crime scenes and by contrast very few scenes as immaculately presented as this example. No blood, or signs that the victim had urinated or heavily defecated during or after death; bar the small multi-coloured fluid pattern she'd observed.

"'*Bit like the camera view on a B movie.*" pronounced Brian; stood to Sally's right hand side in the doorway.

"*We'll take your word for that D.S. Mann.*" Sally shot him a side-wards glance as Caroline responded: her comment accompanied by raised eyebrows. She added: "'*Morning Brian: very little good about it though.*"

Caroline proceeded to give an overview of the crime-scene.

"This is the late and eminent Professor Edwina Justin: a highly respected Immunologist from the *National Institute of Caner and Oncology* [N.I.C.O. for short]: just thirty minutes drive from here."

She was highly influential and was discovered by her P.A. around 10:30 a.m. this morning. She dialled 999 and we've been here around half an hour so far."

"The duvet was on the floor as you observe, when we arrived."

 "You'll notice how anyone entering the room gets a direct view of her vulva."

"There's a pillow positioned under her perineum and her hips have been thrust backwards and upwards."

"Her right leg is flexed under the torso and left leg extended."

"With her head turned to the right and her right arm up underneath her chin it looks almost like the.."

Sally interrupted: "*the recovery position*? Like the paramedics use to protect the airway of an unconscious patient."

"*Oddly, that was my first impression too, Sally*." Caroline gave a fleeting nod.

"Cause of death?"

"Too early to be sure; and apart from gentle rotation of her neck, we haven't moved her yet and we're about to start sampling."

"I can see what look like finger marks on the exposed part of the right laryngeal portion of her neck, similarly on the left side and they're virtually symmetrical in location: so my money's on manual strangulation. No ligature marks as far as I can see; either on her neck or wrists or ankles.

"Any idea on how long she's been dead?" Sally asked.

"Given the thermostat reading 21 degrees celsius, ambient humidity and her rectal temperature, with early tissue degradation: somewhere between three and four days. We'll know more later on today once we've looked at tissue degradation in detail. I'll call you personally Sally as soon as I can narrow the window."

"Thanks Caroline: it would also be helpful to have a transcript of the messages from the home phone as soon as you can." Sally added.

"No worries. Tony can you take care of that as a priority please?" Caroline asked.

Tony looked across and nodded to Sally. "Will do."

Sally reciprocated with a nod and remained silent. The sooner Caroline and the team completed their initial survey; the sooner they'd be able to perform a full post-mortem.

"*Mike* if you could label the tubes please?"

Caroline spoke slowly and deliberately as she proceeded to take a series of samples; each carefully inserted into a labelled tube held by Mike.

"*Anus, rectum*; notice the possible bruising around the anal verge: *Tony* can we get some close-ups here as I work please? No signs of tears, haemorrhoids or prolapsed rectum."

"Okay Mike: *I'm taking a vulval swab and vaginal to follow*."

Sally and Brian had seen enough. They began their initial survey of the lounge and kitchen; nothing appeared disturbed, no sign of a struggle. No broken ornaments and a noticeable absence of photo- graph frames.

"*Always ask yourself what's missing*." This was one of Sally's mantras which had always added greatly to her personal appraisal of crime scenes.

There was a single photograph placed centre-stage on the white and black flecked marble mantel-piece over the faux fireplace which housed a modern wood burner.

A stylish glass "Outstanding Achievement in Oncology Research Award" inscribed with Professor Justin's name and title; adorned the ornate Chinese lacquered side-board. Notably absent were family portraits or graduation photographs; none of the usual crop of telephoto lens shots of small children with loving parents, or doting grandparents.

Brian was busily sifting through paperwork in the bottom drawer of a small bureau next to the dark wood desk in the far right hand corner of the room; adjacent to the only window offering daylight within the lounge. He picked out a large black leather wallet: clearly designed for travel, from the bottom unlocked drawer.

"*Here we go Boss*: passport, assorted credit cards and what looks like her personal mobile phone."

"*Edwina Florence Justin*: date of birth: *25th December 1963*."

With his latex gloves on the mobile was less responsive to his touch as he navigated the screen; noting 15% charge remaining. The mobile had been left on: maybe since here demise?

"*Unbelievable*: no password lock on her mobile."

"*It doesn't look like she had kids, so probably no need.*" Sally responded dryly.

Sally picked up a silver photo-frame from the mantle piece and found herself looking at the late Professor Justin in happier times: stood next to a middle-aged oriental lady of similar height; each posing hand on alternate hips in front of the Great Wall of China. Wearing a broad smile, Edwina Justin was dressed in a pristine white blouse and colour matched full length trousers. She had a light tan which complemented her short brown hair. Sally noticed her high cheekbones and slightly pinched expression making her look older than her fifty-two years. But she was an attractive lady without a doubt.

"*Let's get Louise working on next-of-kin [N.O.K.] ASAP*; before the press get hold of this."

Brian was distracted and didn't respond.

Replacing the photo-frame she walked across and looked over Brian's right shoulder as he interrogated the mobile; giving a running commentary as he did so.

"So what have we got: high end mobile spec'; certainly doesn't have the hallmarks of a work 'phone, least ways, none that I have ever seen."

Brian was working down the list of calls received and dialled. He exited and went straight to SMS messages.

"*The last message was on Tuesday evening: 9th August 2016, received at 20:15.*"

"The message reads: "*expect to be with you at 9 p.m. or shortly afterwards. Christophe S.*"

"An earlier message from the same mobile says: "*must speak to you, please call me back soonest. Regards, C.S.*" That message was received at 17:55.

Brian scrolled down the list of calls again.

Footsteps padding across the corridor carpet alerted Sally who looked left to see who else was entering the crime scene. Fewer visitors meant less chance of crime scene contamination.

"Good morning Boss, Good morning Brian."

Detective Constable [D.C.] Louise Shepherd stood at the entrance to the lounge.

"*Okay to come join you*?" She was already wearing her over-shoes, a forensic suit and gloves.

Sally nodded: Brian carried on interrogating the mobile phone as they spoke.

"I've just taken a brief statement from *Mrs Molly Hull* who found the body. She's been Professor Justin's P.A. for ten years. She was very distressed and she's being checked out at the hospital. The paramedics ran an ECG on her in the ambulance given her history of high blood pressure and the shock of finding her boss dead. She'd had chest tightness and discomfort in her neck, so the doctors want to exclude a heart attack."

"Apparently they were very close: Molly Hull and the late Professor Justin."

"I'd avoid the bathroom Boss; it was clean when Molly arrived but she repeatedly vomited before emergency services arrived. Probably the shock, but the paramedics wanted to be sure she didn't suffer a heart attack or stroke at the scene. She seemed very weak, and in light of her discomfort....."

Nodding her approval Sally cut Louise short: "*Why was Molly here in the first place*?"

"She last saw Professor Justin at around 18:30 on Tuesday, three days ago; and had not seen or heard from her since. Molly looked after the Apartment when her Boss was away.

"*Any update on next of kin*?"

"As far as Molly is aware, no one close. Both parents are already dead; she was an only child and may have distant relatives in the Far East."

That fits with the photograph: thought Sally. And as usual, Louise was already on her toes, anticipating the need to track down N.O.K. ASAP.

"If it is okay with you and Brian, Boss; I'd like to get back to the Hospital to be with Molly as soon as she's well enough to give a full statement?"

"Sure, thanks for coming back Louise."

"No problem: I wanted to give you these too."

"It's the mail which Molly had collected from the mailbox this morning."

Sally took the items which were already in a Police evidence bag which Louise had marked up.

Louise turned and headed off with a quick nod and smile towards Brian who was studying the mobile.

"*She'll go far that one*." Sally remarked as she rejoined Brian.

"So here we go: Professor Justin made three consecutive calls to the same mobile number at: *10:15 and 14:35 and 18:25* respectively on Tuesday 9th August. The mobile is listed in the people category as C.S."

"So it's not too much of a stretch that's the same Christophe S as sent the SMS."

"Exactly Boss."

Brian had already started taking notes as he began to scroll down the list of phone calls.

"Since that time the call-log records....a total of fifteen *unanswered* calls from 21:30 onwards on Tuesday 9th August; eleven of which are calls from "*Molly*"."

"That would be Molly Hull, her PA; she last saw her on Tuesday evening around 18:30. That's plenty of time to get back to her Apartment and meet Christophe S."

"So we have a possible murder timeline: three days ago." Sally concluded.

She went to the entrance of the bedroom, where Caroline and Mike were taking *buccal swabs*; directly from the deceased' oral cavity.

"It looks like we *may* have a time-line for you Caroline."

"What already?" Caroline looked up; surprise audible in her response.

"Last SMS made from her private mobile at 18:25 on Tuesday evening, and she last received SMS at 20:15 on Tuesday evening with a visitor by the name of *Christophe S. scheduled to arrive at 9 p.m*: *less than 3 days ago*."

"We already knew the deceased was alive at around 18:30 on Tuesday when she left the 'Institute. So with say an hour max to get home she may have been the one to receive the text at 20:15....as it was already opened. That said, her phone was not password protected."

"All subsequent calls from 21:30 onwards on Tuesday evening; remain unanswered."

"So we could be looking at time of death somewhere between 20:15 and 21:30 on Tuesday 9th August." Sally surmised.

"Right, thanks for the heads up' Sally; speak later." Caroline didn't look up as she worked.

"Okay Mike let's take nail scrapings; right hand. No rings of any kind."

Tony instinctively took further digital images as the painstaking work continued.

Caroline would leave no detail undocumented; she knew just how damaging a shrewd Defence lawyer's cross examination of forensic evidence could be: potentially damaging to her Department's reputation, and more importantly they had a moral and ethical obligation to ensure Justice for the deceased'. Caroline had little doubt that a second Post-Mortem examination would be requested by the Defence team as soon as a suspect was charged.

Sally popped her head around the door peering into the vomit ridden bathroom. She gulped and left swiftly closing the door firmly behind her.

She felt relieved that forensics would take care of any possible evidence from the shower room given the contamination left by Molly. Louise' advice to avoid the bathroom had been fully justified.

Sally headed into the kitchen, conscious that the windows had been open when they'd arrived. She felt relieved to clear her lungs and airways of the odour of vomit and took a few deep breaths as she inhaled the cool fresh air: meanwhile surveying pristine clean work tops and immaculately kept white goods. She inspected the fridge and freezer compartments and glanced inside cupboards. Everything was minimalistic and signposted a person living alone: meagre cupboard supplies of essentials and very few tins or packaged supplies. She recognised her own traits reflected in the kitchen.

Moving into the hallway Sally inspected the answering machine; modern with multiple key options. The message indicator was flashing but the messages would be extracted by Tony Bailey. It was all too easy to lose or damage valuable finger print evidence with a gloved finger or even a detective's pen; used in haste and causing irretrievable damage to a crime scene.

Sally was inspecting the front door, safety chain and area immediately outside the apartment when Brian had finished bagging the mobile phone, travel bag and a few letters and documents from Professor Justin's bureau.

"A high quality dead-lock and no signs of a forced entry. Looks like our victim invited the killer in. Either knew him or trusted him."

"Or.....them?"

"Perish the thought." Sally responded; recognising how common group sex, supposedly consensual porn' and gang rape, had become. At first blush: this didn't have the appearance of either.

She entered the short corridor leading back to the central lift area.

"Right I need a few lungfuls of good old fresh air and a cigarette, in that order."

They ducked under the Police tape and removed their plastic overalls as they spoke; retaining their gloves.

"That's one request I can deliver on immediately." Brian headed for the lift in his enthusiasm to finally distance himself from the crime scene which always left a bitter taste in his mouth.

"No: we'll take the stairs down and take a look at the rest of the building on route."

"I want the lift sealed and checked for prints Brian: arrange that before we leave. It's a long shot, but let's be sure we don't lose valuable finger print evidence."

"Ask Dave to check out the CCTV and garage facilities for Professor Justin's car and footage from any nearby outbuildings. He'll need to determine who manages the building and security. *Karl* can start the interviews with the other residents, starting on this floor and working down."

The stairwell was wide and carpeted in beige for the entire length. The central lift well occupied what would historically have been a view from top to bottom of the grand house before it was segmented into apartments by the developer.

Windows illuminated each floor to the front and rear of the property; but what were once sash windows and wooden frames had been replaced with modern sealed unit plastic UPVC frames: heat efficient and tastefully styled in gun-metal grey in keeping with the properties' facade.

They reached the entrance hall without meeting any residents on route.

An SMS pinged on Sally's mobile. The Chief Superintendent wanting an update.

They entered the Mews' underground garage via the rear entrance to the Foyer and walked the perimeter before pressing the exit button which raised the roller driven exit door. Two uniformed Policeman stood at the entrance to the garage and P.C. Coombes greeted her as "Ma'am" when they stepped outside to examine the garage entrance control pad.

"PIN pad entry system." Brian remarked.

"So one external camera on the adjacent building Brian:" Sally pointed up to her left as she spoke and "one internally we passed as we entered the garage; near the entrance to the Mews."

"We'll need CCTV footage from them all ASAP please Brian."

They circumnavigated the Mews taking in the nose to tail parking and grandeur of adjacent local dwellings on Atlantic Street as they returned to the Front Entrance steps to the Mews where Brian Brian issued instructions for the lift to be sealed until forensics' review had been completed.

The forensics team member who had finished dusting the mail boxes, responded immediately and took a reel of blue and white scene of crime tape and sealed off the lift before taking the stairs to the fourth floor to repeat the procedure.

Brian could see Sally back inside the BMW so he climbed swiftly into the driver's seat.

"Right Brian change of plan. We head back to the 'Station: no smoke break."

"Make sure Louise gets hold of Professor Justin's laptop and other computer equipment from her office at *NICO* as soon as she's spoken to Molly; who can hopefully give her a heads' up on the Office politics at the Institute.

Chapter 6

13:05 Friday 12th August 2016

"Okay you lot; heads up." Brian called above the office buzz of activity.

Briefing with the D.C.I. and Chief Superintendent: at 1:30 p.m. *pronto*.

Sally and *D.C. Mark Fletcher* walked in moments later. She caught Brian's eye and the three of them headed off to Sally's office and Brian closed the door.

"Okay, Mark's secured a list of the Mew's residents; it's a bit of a *"who's who"* with some high profile names including a Conservative Member of the European Parliament [MEP]."

"So the 'Chief Super will be all over this like a rash." muttered Brian.

"So what this means is we can't afford any careless whispers: we need to keep the team tight on this one Brian. Mark I'd like you to work with Karl and dovetail with Brian on the interviewees: doubtless you'll need to go through the letting agency to make contact with some of the residents. Rather like the *deceased*, you'll need to run the gauntlet of P.A.' and a few agents...for the Actors. Make a start now please Mark."

"Will do Boss." Mark left Brian and Sally together.

"'Christ Boss, this one could be a hornet's nest with the press crawling all over us in no time."

"Yep, the A.C.C. [Assistant Chief Constable] has just collared me in *Ballard's* office. That's why I want you to check over Mark's shoulder and make sure the troops don't step out of line. I want everything by the book; and no cock-ups. Karl can take the lead on interviews; I want him to step up his game.

Brian nodded, conscious of how much of her energy Sally spent encouraging her team and supporting their development.

"'Find anything else of interest on Professor Justin's mobile yet?"

"*Nothing yet Boss*. The majority of contacts look like clinical colleagues. Similarly, the majority of messages relate to meetings; mostly as a result of the late Prof's absence from work.

"Absolutely no personal messages or anything from family members."

"*So we don't have a next-of-kin*?"

"No, and no one cited in her passport. Louise has made no headway either."

"So there's a risk that family will get to hear via the media at this rate."

Brian nodded, looking pensive."

"*Shit*. Okay Brian. Let's make sure Louise stays on top of her debrief with Molly; she's doubtless our best hope at this stage."

"How is the background search on '*Christophe S.* going?"

"I will update you shortly Boss, just as soon as I double check with the Network Provider.

Sally swivelled back in front of her computer and Brian took that as his cue to exit.

"Okay, Boss: see you shortly."

Sally nodded; already searching *Wikipedia*® for Professor Justin's Webpage.

Chapter 7

Murder Investigation Central Office

The team were assembled in a semi-circular arrangement which Sally felt strongly encouraged sharing of information and discouraged hierarchal behaviour. She'd attended a number of team building exercises which were typically externally moderated and she implemented her learning points at every opportunity. Aware 'Ballard would be showing his face it was a show of team integrity by equal measure.

"Right here's what we know so far."

The team fell silent as Sally spoke.

"The body of Professor Edwina Justin, aged 52 years was found at her Mayfair Mews this morning by her P.A of ten years standing: *Molly Hull* at 10:30 a.m."

"Professor Justin had been recently appointed to Chair the National Institute of Cancer and Oncology: known by the acronym *NICO: the appointment was made in April 2016."*

"She was Academically a high flyer at the top of her game: by all accounts managed patients with complex liver disease and advised *Competent Authorities; Governments and Statutory Bodies:* on the suitability of new drugs for licensing."

"As yet; next of kin have NOT been informed; *and are unknown.*

"Louise is at the Hospital as we speak, with Molly Hull: it's possible her nearest relatives may live in the Far East, possibly *China."*

"Molly was understandably very distressed, after seeing the deceased and is being assessed by the doctors to make sure she's not had a heart attack or stroke. She's a spritely sixty-one year old."

"Professor Justin was an only child; both her parents are dead."

Heads turned in synchrony as the door to the briefing room banged open and *Chief Superintendent (C.S.) Edward Ballard* entered the room.

"*Don't get up*." Edward Ballard gestured with his hand, and smiled at Sally.

 "*Carry on please D.C.I. Benson*."

"Thank you Sir."

"So as I was saying, no NOK yet identified."

"Molly Hull, Professor Justin's P,A., discovered the deceased body at 10:30 a.m. this morning.

"Molly said "Goodbye" to her Boss on Tuesday evening, the 9th August [2016] around 18:30: since which time they'd had no further contact."

"Briefly, her mobile phone logged three calls to *Christophe S;* with whom she had spoken earlier in the day and *she may or may not have picked up his message received at 20:15 indicating his anticipated arrival at 21:00.*"

"*Brian will take you through the detailed timings.*"

"Professor Justin has not been at work for the remainder of the week and most of the telephone calls on her landline at her apartment, related to missed appointments and *NICO* clinical workload."

"So Molly was probably the last person to see the Prof alive Boss?"

"That's our working assumption *Karl; other than her killer of course.*"

"As you'll be interviewing residents with Brian, we may strike lucky but at first glance of the resident list for the other thirteen Apartments, there's a fair smattering of fading film stars and VIPs so the chances of a fortuitous citing look a little remote to me."

Karl nodded.

"*Dr Caroline Crunch* and her team are working the Crime Scene. In short, no signs of forced entry, nothing out of please except for the deceased body found in her bedroom. She *may* have died by *manual strangulation*: but this is a preliminary comment as bruising was noted by 'forensics on initial examination of the body. We'll know more later; there may have been a sexual element to the murder."

"Here are the preliminary crime scene photos." Sally pinged up the photos on the electronic white board, via her laptop, as she spoke.

"Certainly looks sexual from the apparent posing of the deceased."

"So we're thinking strangled from behind Boss, during the act?" ventured *Dave*.

"It certainly looks the most likely scenario at this early stage. No ligature marks visible but as I alluded to likely finger marks on the victim's neck either side of the trachea; which would certainly be consistent with her having been strangled from behind, possibly during sex."

"We expect a forensics update later this afternoon and we'll have the usual sample and finger print data 'soonest.'"

"What about the.... *posture*....I know that's not the right word but... the deceased body Boss...we don't see many in such a *ritual position*?"

"*You're right Karl*, but let's be very careful of our choice of words at this stage: the last thing we need in Press are comments pertaining to a *"ritual killing!"*

"'Got it Boss." Karl nodded affirmatively.

"At this stage we rule nothing in or out of the investigation but let's wait until we have 'forensics."

"Brian: would you review the detail of the mobile phone evidence please."

Brian detailed the timelines and SMS and call details relating to *Christophe S* and the remaining list of contacts.

"So the last known contact was with Christophe S." Concluded Sally.

"We've requested phone records and his mobile number will reveal his full identity."

"So we may already have a suspect?" Chief Superintendent Edward Ballard spoke.

"It's possible Sir. As soon as we can identify him, Brian and I will pay him a visit."

"Anything else I need to know Sally?"

"Not at this stage, Sir."

"The details of this case remain <u>absolutely confidential</u>: no leaks, no un-guarded comments over coffee in the canteen. *Is everyone crystal clear on this point?"*

C.S. Ballard surveyed faces one by one as he walked forward and stood alongside Sally to deliver his instruction.

A ripple of *"Yes Sir"* and his message had been duly delivered.

He nodded, smiled fleetingly at Sally and left.

Chapter 8

18:45 Monday 15th August 2016

Christophe had just stepped out of the shower when the intercom buzzed. He grabbed his white fleecy bathrobe and went to the entry control panel next to the front door to his Apartment and depressed the intercom button.

"Hello?"

"Dr Christophe Schultz?"

"Yes, who is it?"

"I am Detective Chief Inspector Benson and have with me Detective Sergeant Mann. *We'd like to speak to you please.*"

A long pause ensued.

"Give me a moment and I'll buzz you in. I'm on the second floor, apartment 12A."

Brian looked around the parking bays outside of the apartment block and a sleek metallic black *Porsche Boxster 3.2s convertible* caught his eye in the fading light. He wandered around the car, taking in the sleek lines, unmarked alloys and distinctive red brake callipers.

"Forget it on your wages." Sally said dryly looking across at the car. She regarded cars as necessities, rather than an essential extension of a man's vanity or virility.

"I can dream can't I?" Brian retorted playfully.

"Maybe when I'm on a D.I.'s wage Boss?"

Before she could reply, the electronic door release buzzed loudly and Sally held the door as Brian caught up with her.

Christophe stood in the doorway of his Apartment as Sally and Brian approached with their warrant cards open.

"*After you Dr Schultz.*" gestured Brian as Christophe led the way into the small lounge.

Sally sat on the green leather sofa with her back to the window and Brian took a matching arm chair to her right. Christophe sat directly opposite Sally in the black leather recliner with headrest.

"*Superstitious* are you Dr Schultz?"

"Sorry?" replied Christophe, bemused by Brian's opening gambit.

"I notice your apartment is numbered 12A not 13?"

"A decision made before my time."

"How long have you lived here?" Brian continued.

"Three years, give or take."

"Schultz, is that a German name or Swiss?"

"Yes German. My family are from Stuttgart. Do you know it Detective Sergeant?"

Brian shook his head.

"So what's this all about….D.C.I…?" Christophe looked directly at Sally as he posed the question.

"*Benson, Sally Benson.* We're from the Murder Investigation Unit."

"Ah, I see."

"*Do you*?" replied Sally, disingenuous surprise registering in her voice.

"*Well…it's been all over the news…Professor Justin's death.*"

Sally held his gaze for a moment before he looked away. She sensed he'd made an effort to look her in the eye, but he looked uncomfortable. She watched his larynx move as he swallowed involuntarily several times. He wore a white cotton shirt with a small crest replacing a pocket; open at the neckline with sleeves rolled up to the elbows. Designer clothes head to toe, thought Sally as she looked at his denim jeans and laced up white Branded pumps.

"So how well did you know Professor Justin?" Brian asked, note book on his right knee and black Biro poised in his left hand as he posed the question.

Sally watched Christophe intently; studying his body language.

He uncrossed his arms and leaned on the arm rests of the chair as he shuffled back on the black leather recliner; he then adjusted the backrest electronically, using the control panel under his right hand; before he answered.

Gathering his thoughts Sally surmised, ready to choose his words carefully, his postural adjustments an outward sign of his inner struggle to deal with the information and anticipated questions.

"I knew her through my work."

"Ah I see." Sally subconsciously mirrored his language as well as his body posture; arms now unfolded; relaxed shoulders.

"You're a Medical Director I understand?" she clarified; noting his measured responses. No added detail.

"That's correct." He regained eye contact.

"And what does that involve *exactly*?" God it's like pulling teeth thought Sally.

"I lead a small team at *Utopia Pharmaceutical Company:* we're based in Hayes, Middlesex."

"I am responsible for the oversight of new drug evaluation: making judgements on the efficacy, that's the effectiveness of the new treatment; and the safety of the compound: the benefit/risk ratio."

"*How well it works and if it has any side effects*?" prompted Brian.

(What is it with *bloody doctors*, thought Brian, always overcomplicating it when a few well chosen words would suffice?)

"Essentially, that's it: yes."

(*Essentially – in other words: Yes! See how hard was that*? He shoots, he scores. Brian smiled inwardly.)

"And that's how you met Professor Justin?" Sally interjected.

"Yes, I first met her at a Safety Review Meeting."

"In what capacity was she present?" Sally gave her quizzical look again as she posed the question.

"She chairs".....Christophe cleared his throat...."*chaired*..NICO..the National Institute of Cancer and Oncology."

"Where and when was that meeting held?"

Christophe paused: visibly controlling his emotions. He took a number of deep breaths.

Christophe looked distant as he contemplated the question; then closed his eyes. Sally and Brian exchanged glances.

"It would have been Quarter 4, 2015. It was around the time of an International Hepatology Symposium in London: from memory the first or second week of November. "

"*Hepatology – that's the liver right?*" Brian asked.

"Yes."

"And did you meet *publicly*?" Brian put heavy intonation on the word publicly.

"*What do you mean?*"

"It's a simple question Doctor – did you meet in a large gathering of doctors or..."

"It was a round table meeting. We...I had organised a meeting of around 12 to 15 Specialists in that field."

"Specialists in Hepatology: the study of liver function and liver diseases." prompted Sally pedagogically; once again grateful for her background research with Wikipedia before their meeting.

"Yes. I presented the data on *U0008*: a novel drug treatment for patients with Hepatitis C.

"And that was Professor Justin's area of expertise?"

(Christophe couldn't help but be impressed by D.C.I. Benson and her cool manner: she had obviously prepared carefully for the Interview. He was aware he was starting to perspire under his arms and could feel sweat drip down his back. *He was sure they'd noticed his emotional response to the question of his last meeting with Edwina Justin* and this only exacerbated his feelings of anxiety which were increasing incrementally; question by question.)

"Yes, amongst others.. Edwina"...he quickly corrected himself: "*Professor Justin* had a wealth of expertise in a variety of disease areas, including Oncology, the study and treatment of Cancer; and the immune basis of disease."

More bloody big words to impress us: thought Brian.

"I'm sorry I haven't offered you both any refreshments. Can I offer you tea or coffee or...?"

"*We're fine*. Don't let us stop you though Dr Schultz. I know this can't be easy for you."

Sally smiled at Christophe as he stood up and walked across the lounge into the small open planned kitchen which was fully visible from the lounge where they had gathered. The smell of Chinese cooking lingered in the air: chicken stir fry if Sally wasn't mistaken.

(It was a favourite from her own cooking repertoire when she took time out to cook: which seemed to be less and less these days as murder investigations became ever more complex and time consuming.)

She watched as he opened the fridge door and poured a large glass of sparkling water. He drained the glass and refilled it before returning to his seat; placing the glass in front of him on the frosted-glass table.

"Can I ask?"

Sally nodded assent.

"Do you know why Professor Justin was murdered?"

"What makes you think she was *murdered*?" Brian asked, looking up from his notebook and resting his arms on the leather chair.

"Well, you said you were both from the Murder Unit, so I assumed..."

"That she was killed deliberately?" Brian didn't take his eyes off Christophe as he posed the response.

"We are treating the death as suspicious, yes." Sally's face was stern.

 "Can you think of anyone who would have wanted to harm Professor Justin?"

"No....Edwina was....I mean...no... I didn't really know her that well...."

"So how many times did you meet her Dr Schultz?"

(Brian had not broken his stare since the last question; Christophe could feel his eyes boring into him like a hot poker, even as he answered Sally's questions. It was beginning to feel like a Punch and Judy show. He could feel cold sweat on his back. Not for the first time, he wished he'd not had a hot shower immediately before they'd arrived; *unannounced.*)

"A few times...." Christophe looked distant again as he replied; staring towards the window.

"How many times *exactly* Doctor?" Brian was unrelenting.

Sally could see the tension in Christophe's face; he was beginning to frown and he licked his lips repeatedly.

"November as I've said... and again in late December: the week before the Christmas recess."

(Another clever word, thought Brian; why couldn't he say *holiday* like the rest of us. *Who on God's Earth says recess*?)

"Another....let me see" Brian appeared to hesitate and referred to his notes: *"round table meeting* with other specialists?" Brian held his pen poised as he spoke.

"No, it was just the two of us."

"Oh and was that in a public place?" Brian's voice was tinged with more than a hint of sarcasm.

"Yes of course, in a coffee shop."

"Where was that *exactly*?" Strong intonation again was evident in Brian's tenor.

"A large bookshop actually; *"Garroways"*: we met by chance on the Tottenham Court Road."

"Yes I know it...." Brian wanted him on the back foot again. "I buy my history books there; great range."

"Small world: Doctor." Brian laughed at his own trifling humour.

"Is that a question?" Christophe bristled.

(He was fast losing his patience, his brain was telling him he needed to regain control; that this banter was all part of their routine: but he felt irritated none the less. He didn't like unannounced visitors at the best of times, especially when all he wanted was to chill down after a long hot shower.)

"Just the two of you meeting like that, of all the places in London. How far would that be from..." he feigned hesitation again..."The *National Institute of Cancer and Oncology*......?"

"*Well how should I know;* you're the one who patrols the streets!"

(Christophe' cheeks were now the colour of a bright red *Sir John Betjeman English shrub rose*: blood red. Meanwhile, Brian kept up his unrelenting gaze.)

Sally sensed the need to interject.

"What did you discuss Doctor?"

"Oh just mundane stuff.... *day-to-day Doctors' Politics*.... the recent *new NHS Contract for Consultants* and potential strike action: that sort of thing."

(*In other words, things that don't concern you mere Police Officers*; was how Brian interpreted that comment: condescending to say the least...evasive at best.)

He took up the line of questioning again.

"Which coffee shop did you meet in?" He followed up quickly before Christophe could reply.

"Remind me Doc' which floors are the coffee shops on?"

"The fourth floor: there is only one."

"*So there is, so there is.*" Brian changed pace again.

"How long did your meeting last?"

"Maybe... *half an hour*?" His answer sounded unconvincing; even to him as he gave it: phrased more like a question than an answer.

"Well you would know Doc' was it half an hour: could it have been an hour? *You sound unsure*?"

"*Did you talk about U008?*"

"That's U-0-0-0-8!"

Christophe responded uncompromisingly: enunciating each letter and syllable.

"My humble apologies..." responded Brian: looking anything other than humble as he replied stagily.....bowing his head.

"No, the meeting was by chance *as I've stated*; we didn't have an Agenda to discuss the Product. In the Industry we adhere to Codes Of Practice and don't simply engage in idle discussion of Company Products or data."

Christophe Schultz sensed he had the whip hand now and sat forward as he spoke engaging eye contact with Brian.

"So what did you talk about for half an hour?" Brian persisted.

Christophe looked hesitant for a moment.

Brian seized his chance to interject again and keep him on the back foot.

"Do you have family in England Doctor?"

"No." He stated flatly.

"Do you and the late Professor Justin have *friends in common*?"

"No....maybe work colleagues from the Institute...but..."

"That would be the NICO Institute?"

"Yes of course."

"Well we must be certain Doctor, not to make mistakes...an extra *zero* or the wrong address...makes all the difference, wouldn't you agree Doctor?"

Christophe said nothing.

(The Detective's sarcasm was laid on thick as he delivered his line theatrically. As far as Christophe was concerned that was a rhetorical question and he was in no mood for this guy's games.)

Sally was sensing how far out of his comfort zone the young Doctor was; already clearly rattled.

Sally sat forward on her chair as Brian continued to push and she summarised:

"So let me get this clear in my mind...you had met previously at a meeting with colleagues....you met...*by chance in London*...talked for thirty minutes; *without discussing the new drug* 0008;...so my question is..*what did you talk about*?"

Sally was clearly on Brian's wavelength. They could both see Christophe was flustered and his answers were at best, unconvincing.

Christophe stared out of the window again. The light was fading fast and the setting sun cast dark shadows around the room. Christophe felt his world was closing in on him. He had to stay focused.

"Can I use your bathroom please doctor?" Brian stood as he asked the question; putting his notepad and Biro inside the pocket of his blue cotton jacket.

"Yes it's just down the corridor on the right."

That was Sally's cue.

"Dr Schultz, we know this must be hard for you." her voice was softer, reassuring in tone.

"Do you really?" Christophe looked offended and hurt in equal measure. "Do you know what it's like to lose a respected colleague in this way?"

"What way Dr Schultz?"

"So suddenly, so..."

Sally sat forward, now on the edge of her seat; empathy emanating from her honey coloured eyes. Christophe caught her eye briefly and looked away again.

"You must meet lots of Specialists and Consultants in your line of work Doctor, and you must have seen plenty of death, personally witnessed death, before you took up your current duties?"

('Another rhetorical question was his interpretation and he could feel an emotional "lump" arising in his throat.)

"But Professor Justin had clearly made quite an impact on you."

"*If you mean, am I upset by her death: yes of course I am.*" He chewed his bottom lip absent-mindedly again and shifted his gaze back to Sally.

Sally could see his eyes were moistened and she could detect a fine tremor in his facial muscles. He was clearly suppressing emotion.

Sally sat back in her seat and remained silent until she heard the lavatory flush and Brian returned. She was sure Christophe was holding back tears. She looked around the Apartment: nothing out of place. The kitchen appliances and breakfast bar looked spotlessly clean.

(A good external cleaner or a Perfectionist Personality: maybe? She plumped for the latter. He struck her as a very private person and she was sure that they were seriously invading his private place by their presence.)

"*Did you meet Professor Justin again, after that?*" Brian already had his pen out of his pocket again and posed the question before he took his seat.

"Yes one further, final time. *9th April 2016*. That was just after Professor Justin's appointment as Chair of NICO. That date, I am sure of."

"*What did we talk about?*" Christophe pre-empted Brian's next question and shot him a candid look as he spoke.

Brian now registered annoyance in the bright blue piercing eyes that met his own. Sally noticed it too. His body posture became more rigid and he sat forward and emptied the glass of water.

He's taking back control thought Brian; knows he's appearing more aggressive; almost defensive.

They sat in silence. A timer device switched on a lamp in the corner and the room grew brighter as the element warmed up.

"To be clear: *the meeting was pre-arranged* and was to agree the final wording of a statement which Professor Justin would make; endorsing the Efficacy and Safety Profile of U0008."

"The statement would ultimately be incorporated in the Press Release; to be posted at a later, mutually agreed time-point."

"And such an endorsement would carry considerable gravitas in the Scientific Community? No doubt that would provide a good platform for your drug launch?"

Sally's comment was not so much a question but a clear indication of her political insight; thought Christophe.

"*Sure.*" He shrugged his shoulders: looking nonchalant with his reply.

Back to brevity, thought Brian. He's asserting his control again.

"Tell me more about the...*what did you call it...the benefit/risk ratio doctor*?" Brian cocked his head to one side: (a habit he had clearly acquired from Sally.)

This time he didn't refer to his notepad as he posed the question.

"Well it's an evolving review of all the efficacy and safety data; a way of ensuring that the benefit to patients of prescribing the drug outweighs any serious or significant side effects or health risks."

"*Evolving*...what does that mean...*in this context*?"

"Well, as more information about the drug becomes available, the benefit may be undermined by the risks if they become.....*significant*."

"Like thalidomide you mean?"

The speed of Brian's response took Christophe by surprise. His eyes visibly widened.

Brian clocked his reaction immediately. Sally naturally was watching every nuance of Christophe's behaviour.

"*Well yes*; although that's an extreme example arising in the offspring of pregnant women who took the drug for the nausea of pregnancy, *but you're right*."

"So did Professor Justin's opinion of the risk/benefit ratio *evolve or change in any way*?" Brian had manipulated the ratio intentionally.

Christophe caught his breath momentarily as if he'd been stabbed with a sharp object. Sally noticed his mouth open transiently and then close again whilst he reconsidered his response.

He's keen to tow the Company line, she thought; a prepared statement for such a question, whatever the source.

"Not to my knowledge."

"And *you* of all people would know if it did." Brian's question was incisive.

"Yes, that's my responsibility ultimately."

"*So you mean other people are involved in the assessment*?"

"Yes of course, can I ask where all of this is leading?"

"We're just trying to understand the nature of your relationship with Professor Justin." Sally sat forward again in her chair as she spoke.

"There was no *relationship* as you persist in describing it Detective Chief Inspector!"

Sally sat back; surprised by the ferocity of his response. Christophe sat forward in his chair, his blue eyes flashing with indignation. His face flushed for the second time. She could see beads of sweat breaking out on his forehead.

"None the less it must have been quite a shock when you heard about her death." Came her riposte.

"Yes of course."

"*And how did you hear about it*?"

"I'm not sure, radio, TV...yes the radio I think.."

"*You're not sure*?" There was more than a hint of incredulity in Sally's voice as she stared at him with her eyelids widened.

"Well there was quite a lot of discussion at work and..."

"Brian where were you when heard about *Michael Jackson's death*?" Sally turned her legs and upper body towards Brian as she spoke, away from Christophe. She felt his eyes on her body as she posed the question.

"*I was at the Feathers in Newcastle*."

"And where were you?"

"*I was taking tea with my mother in Preston*." Sally promptly responded.

"What about when *John Lennon died*?" she asked; ignoring Christophe and keeping her eyes on Brian.

"Gosh now you are going back in time Boss: 1980.

" *I was at infants' school*. The headmaster announced it in assembly and we held a two minute silence in 'Lennon's name. Such a sad day, he touched so many lives and we can all relate to his lyrics. The man was a genius, *nothing short of a musical genius*."

She turned back to Christophe; moving her whole body and crossing her legs at the ankles. Her skirt rose a few inches up her thigh as she did so. She watched Christophe's eyes dart momentarily down and back up to her own gaze. He blushed visibly.

"You see my problem Dr Schultz. Brian can remember exactly where he was at the time of two completely unrelated deaths, both well known Public figures; *neither known to him personally.* In the case of John Lennon: a sad death occurring nearly four decades ago. But you don't remember where you were when you heard about Edwina Justin's death just a couple of *days* ago?"

(Sally had made the question even more personal by dropping the late Professor's title…)

"I simply said I wasn't sure that's all." He added swiftly: "It would have been the radio."

"I'm sorry, it's late and you have so many questions…"

"So since you last met in April, have you seen or spoken to Professor Justin?" Brian's tone was flat, non-confrontational; pragmatic."

"Doctor Schultz?"

Christophe studied his nails and chewed his bottom lip again.

"No." He replied quietly.

"Not for any reason?" Brian repeated the question and wrote down the answer. He paused.

"Do you have a telephone number for Professor Justin?"

"Yes, I believe I have her office number."

"Would that be a mobile number or land-line Doctor?"

"Maybe….I'm not sure." Christophe was staring down at the floor now; looking down-hearted and exhausted.

Sally noticed faint scars on his right forearm as he adjusted his shirt sleeves.

Christophe started to roll his sleeves down.

So he'd noticed her looking at his arms? Maybe he wasn't as tired as he was claiming.

"Good with your hands Doctor?" Brian had a smile as he spoke.

"Sorry, what do you mean; *as in artistic?"*

"Well it's just having trained as a doctor, I kind of assumed you have to be good with your hands: and yes maybe *creative?"*

"Not especially." Christophe shrugged. "As a General Physician, yes I do have a degree of competence in procedures such as...intubation or venous and arterial cannulation."

"What about resuscitation?"

"Yes that too, in my Clinical days."

"Before going into Pharmaceuticals you mean?"

"Yes"

"And why did you?"

"I don't see what that question has to do with your inquiries Detective."

"Like D.C.I. Benson said; we're just building up a picture at this stage, of everyone who knew the late Professor."

"Well I think that's enough for today Dr Schultz. Thank you for your time. Let me give you my card."

Sally handed Christophe her contact details as she interjected and stood up.

"If you do think of anything else that might be helpful to our inquiry, please call me on the office or mobile number on the card: *day or night.*"

Christophe nodded. Sally stood and looked at him for a moment. He didn't engage.

"Just one last thing doctor, is that by any chance your personal Porsche Boxster outside?" Brian asked.

"Yes it is." Christophe forced a smile; it was evident to them both as he did so.

"Absolute beauty it is too!"

"*Well thanks doctor; enjoy your evening.*" Brian offered his hand to Christophe and received a firm albeit clammy handshake as they left.

Outside the apartment block with only the external security lights for illumination, Brian took a final look around the Porsche; long enough to ensure he had Christophe's attention. He glanced up and waved as he saw him silhouetted at the window to his second floor apartment. He saw the figure move swiftly away from the windows and the curtains drawn as they turned their backs and headed for their BMW.

"*Well that was interesting.*" He took his place in the driver's seat and started the engine as Sally took a long deep inhalation from her cigarette and blew the smoke out of the passengers' window.

"I thought you'd quit?"

"I had until earlier today. I couldn't use one more of those bloody patches Brian. If it kills me so be it."

She added as an afterthought: "A better way to go than most of our victims."

"So what did you think of 'Schultz?"

"There's clearly much more to the good Dr Schultz than meets the eye." Replied Sally cryptically.

"Put your foot down Brian; I need a G&T."

As Brian took a sharp right turn out of the drive a white van man accelerated up behind them and came perilously close to his rear bumper before turning right.

"You bloody arsehole." Brian muttered quietly as he watched the tail lights disappear.

Sally was already making notes in her black leather-clad notebook; deep in thought: it had taken barely twenty seconds for the nicotine to reach her frontal lobes and calm her racing thoughts.

Chapter 9

The pub was only half full; mostly regulars sat around talking as the two of them walked up to the bar together.

"I'll get these in."

Brian gestured to a table in the far corner, away from the TV which was showing Germany versus France; a so-called friendly. A battle too far for Sally tonight: Brian was mindful she wanted to de-brief.

He ordered a double G&T for Sally and a large diet Coke for himself: plenty of ice.

"Cheers Brian. What's with the fizzy?"

"I've got to shift this lot somehow." Brian grabbed a roll of abdominal fat and wobbled it up and down." G.P. says I'm two stone overweight. I'll end up with diabetes, like my old dad."

"Girls like a man with a bit of padding."

"And which girls are those exactly Boss?"

"What's wrong Brian, are you missing Annie?"

"Don't even go there." He said shaking his head.

"Trust me: Since the day I signed the divorce papers a couple of years ago, there's not a day goes by I don't *"Praise the Lord."*

He placed his hands in the prayer position and looked skyward as he uttered the words with feeling.

"What about your ex: do you miss him?"

"Not since he told me I had a simple choice: *him or the job.* Only one of those two options pays the Mortgage; and he certainly never did that. Glad to see the back of him."

"Kindred spirits 'eh Boss?"

"Or sad bastards married to the Job: take your pick!"

They laughed heartily until Sally's smokers' cough kicked in.

"Okay let's crack on with business. What did you make of the good Doctor?" Sally took a gulp of her drink; then squeezed the lemon slice before allowing it to drop into the glass as she posed the question.

She had her back to the wall and had a full view of the pub. No one within spitting distance: but none the less she was guarded when talking in Public, especially with high profile cases. Never knew when a journalist would spot her. Like the Police, they were never Off Duty. She was sure they'd not been followed from London; but was a strong believer in serendipity.

"He's coiled tight; very tight." *Brian clenched his fists as he spoke* using hyperbole to good effect.

"I think you got under his skin and no mistake." Sally let out another chuckle as her Gin and Tonic started to kick in and relax her.

He nodded with a smile, knowing it was a complement; part of his job to unsettle his witness.

"For an experienced Doctor he seemed remarkably cut up about the death of a Colleague. He was very defensive at times, not atypical for someone grieving; a loved one or close friend. But someone he had only met on a professional basis, just three times?"

Brian was clearly not convinced.

"I agree and I was very sceptical about his chance meeting in London; thirty minutes of discussion, but couldn't remember anything concrete. Hard to believe they didn't discuss either the Product or Results of Drug Trials for U0008."

Sally took another sip of G&T, savouring her first, but maybe not her last 'mixer of the evening.

"So even if his longer term memory is not up to scratch, he seemed rather conveniently to have developed a short-term memory loss as well. *No mention of the telephone conversations just six days ago.*"

"I figure that we have enough to pull him in formally for questioning but guessed you would want to speak to the 'Chief Super and arrange a Warrant before we go steaming in?"

"So you think he's our man Brian?"

"Certainly a worthy contender Boss. Struck me as very....what's the word...*Conformist*... but he's clearly a guy who needs to be in control. His bathroom cupboard was stacked with fresh tubes of toothpaste, toothbrushes and floss; neatly arranged in rows, bit like that film with you know who....beautiful girl from the Perfume advert....."

"Julia Roberts in *Sleeping with the Enemy.*"

"Yes exactly: how the hell on Earth do you do that?"

Sally parried the complement with a wave of her hand and a knowing look..and continued:

"Exactly; a bit of a Perfectionist I think. So IF he's our man, why with his training and background would he *potentially leave clues on the deceased' phone at the scene of the crime and leave behind DNA evidence and finger prints?*. That makes no sense at all; he must have known it would take only a day or two for that kind of evidence to be leveraged." That's always assuming the samples are a match with his DNA of course.

Did you notice his right forearm by the way?"

"Yeah the horizontal scar lines you mean. *He's been a self-harmer*, if I'm not mistaken."

Sally nodded in agreement. "I've seen it many times when working with Vice."

"When I shook his hands as we left, they were very clammy. He was clearly nervous." Brian observed.

"So what about flight risk?"

"Any chance he'll do a runner do you think Boss?"

"Let's not take any chances. Alert the Ports and Airports. I'll give *DCI Hugh Mortimer* from Surrey CID a call back as we're on his patch; and update him superficially on progress. Enough that he knows we will probably be back."

"*Good shout Boss*. Don't want any local politics clouding the issue when we move in."

"Right, let's run some additional background checks on him. What's the update on the mobile phone Company; are they going to give us the transcripts or do we need a Court Order?"

"They're dragging their feet a bit. The guy I spoke to kept talking about needing Authority: Company phone and the usual red tape heightened by Prof's high standing and access to all kinds of Medically and Government sensitive information."

"Okay. Speak to our German colleagues as agreed and see if they have anything on file in addition to our own databases Brian. We need his landline phone records too; we can request those as soon as we've secured a Warrant for his apartment."

Sally emptied her glass. "Right you finish up, I'm heading outside for a cigarette."

"*Another*?"

"*What are you, my mother all of a sudden*? 'Back off, Soldier!" She shot him a devilish smile.

"See you in five." Sally headed outside.

Brian swivelled round and watched a couple of minutes of the football. Even the regulars looked bored. He swallowed the remainder of the drink and headed for the car. It began to rain as he started the engine.

"Indian or Chinese takeaway back at the Nick; my shout?" announced Sally sounding up-beat.

"In that case, a Chicken Madras and Peshawar Nan sound perfect. I might even stretch to a beer."

"Done; I'll leave the choice from the High Street to you."

Chapter 10

Tuesday 16th August

Brian checked the wall-clock: 07:15.

"Right listen up: team briefing fifteen minutes."

Brian knew it had been short notice for some of the team who'd worked into the small hours of the morning. *Louise Shepherd* came through the door as he spoke. She shot him a smile and took off her black raincoat.

The rain had gotten a lot heavier since Brian had arrived at 6:30 a.m. He watched Louise as she shook off the worst of the downpour from the sodden coat before hanging it on the communal coat rack. She was wearing a long black woollen dress which hugged her slender figure and finished just below the knee.

He knew she'd been back to see *Molly* late last night; keeping her abreast of developments, constantly information gathering; "family" liaison *Detective style: at its best.* During the weekend they'd worked together, interviewed Professor Justin's Colleagues from *NICO*; discovering that all Institutes and Professions were plagued by Politics: but otherwise gained little of use as regards the Investigation; no-one with a grudge or axe to grind.

The NICO Institute was clearly in mourning for the loss of one its true visionaries and someone with the credentials and visibility to attract considerable charitable funding and prestige.

As the troops gathered for the briefing *there was a palpable air of expectation.* The Chief Superintendent, Edward Ballard was standing at the back talking to Sally Benson as the team filed through the single door and took up the semi-circle of seats in front of crime scene photographs; displayed over three large pin up boards.

"Right then team: let's start with forensics."

The room fell silent as Sally walked briskly to the front of the room and began the progress update.

"As preliminary examination at the crime scene had suggested, the cause of death is consistent with *manual strangulation*."

"Having worked through the weekend: this news is familiar to most of you: but let's complete the scenario for Jock's sake."

"Post-mortem examination revealed skin and soft tissue bruising bilaterally; and a *fractured hyoid bone* to complete the picture of death my manual strangulation."

She pointed to the relevant photographs as she spoke: each enlarged to show fine detail of three bruises bilaterally caused by finger imprints on the skin adjacent to the trachea.

"No evidence that the attacker wore a ring of any kind."

"So the perpetrator strangled her from behind: using both hands evidenced by lighter bruising on the back of her neck over her occipital musculature created by pressure from his thumbs used to pivot his hands on her neck."

"Nothing to indicate a ligature was used and no marks on Professor Justin's wrists or ankles."

"So nothing to suggest she'd been tied up or physically restrained boss at any time Boss?"

"That's correct Louise." Sally nodded affirmatively.

"Defence wounds?" asked *Dave*.

"Nothing Dave and scrapings from under her finger nails were negative."

"So if she did put up a struggle it was short lived, or she was overpowered quickly."

"*Or she was sedated*?" suggested Louise.

"There's nothing on the usual toxicology report to suggest that. Certainly no benzodiazepines: specifically, there were no traces of *Rohypnol®* or GHB [Gamma-Hydroxybutyric Acid] in her bloodstream."

Louise had studied Forensic Psychology for her Masters' degree; a great asset to the team and the key reason for her selection to join the close-knit team.

"*Dr Crunch* found light bruising on the skin covering the back of Professor Justin's gastrocnemius muscles.... the back of the lower legs to the non sportsmen and women amongst us: that's consistent with her assailant having sat astride her as he strangled her."

Sally pointed directly at the photographs as the bruising was subtle and difficult to identify.

Louise stood up and looked closely at the two pictures and raised a further query: "*Boss what did the victim weigh?*"

"*Good question*" responded Sally. "*A mere 49 kg post mortem.*"

Expanding on her answer for the sake of completeness; Sally added:

 "So not hard to pin down: with a suitable weight advantage: or with the element of surprise."

"Do you think she knew her attacker Boss?"

"Let's stick to forensics first Dave; but it's looking that way."

"There we no signs of forced entry at the Apartment as you're aware."

"Okay, moving on. *Semen samples* have been isolated from *rectal and oral swabs*. So as of this morning: we have his DNA."

A ripple of applause spontaneously erupted around the room.

"The samples were small, especially in the case of the oral [marked buccal, samples C19875/6 respectively], and the lab used the latest PCR: that's Polymerase Chain Reaction technique: to expedite the replication of the original DNA segments isolated from the deceased: to enable the DNA to be fully characterised.

"We have partial finger prints from the blue bedside table lamp to the left of the bed and bed frame itself."

Without prompting, Brian pointed out the locations on photographs from Professor Justin's bedroom.

"No finger prints were found after a detailed review of the victim's neck or laryngeal region." Sally continued.

"So the perp' may well have used gloves. No tell-tale signs of talcum [silica] powder that we used to find in the old days when gloves contained such additives for ease of use." Brian added.

Chief Superintendent Edward Ballard's phone rang twice before he answered the call.

"*Yes, as we speak Sir.*" The call ended abruptly.

Without waiting, he interrupted.

"*Any promising updates on other lines of inquiry D.C.I. Benson?*"

Sensing he needed to be somewhere else and the team needed to debrief; Sally was diplomatic.

"*Can I update you later in the day Sir?*"

"Fine make it before 3pm Sally: my office."

Sally nodded as he left.

Brian glanced across at Sally knowingly. The A.C.C. wanted an update.

"Right let's get some updates from you lot."

"Brian?"

"Thanks Boss."

"*Karl*: where are we with Mews' resident interviews and door to door interviews?"

Detective Constable Karl Madding had been just twelve months with the team. He stood with a slight stoop as he spoke; conscious of his six foot five inch stature Sally surmised. After three years spent patrolling the streets of London, he'd expressed an interest in working with the Murder Unit and had already earned his place. He had an eye for detail and put in the hours: always volunteered for stag duty. His father had risen swiftly to the ranks of D.C.I. thirty years before his son's entry to the Force.

"*No leads so far Boss*. Most of the residents keep themselves to themselves and only the Conservative MEP: *Michael Hampshire*; knew the victim well. He had invited her to provide expert testimony at a number of Standing Committee meetings in Parliament *prior to his EU appointment*: largely to discuss updates in Cancer management and the likely impact on Government ring-fenced spending."

"He works long hours and travels extensively. Last saw Professor Justin about four weeks ago. As far as he is concerned, she was revered as an expert in her field and drew admiration from all who knew her."

"His wife had met her twice socially at cocktails parties, Fundraisers and the like; but nothing more. They both seemed genuinely shocked by her death. They live at Apartment number 7."

"We've spoken by telephone to a further four of the six residents from numbers 1,3,4, 5, 8 and 9: for whom the apartments are second homes."

"I have put their details on the website. We hope to have face to face interviews with all six of them by the end of the week as they're all out outside of London."

"We have not managed to speak or directly contact three residents: *Charlie Roth* from Apartment 11, who's filming in L.A. and has been there for the last two months according to his PA; and *Christina Hall*, the model from Apartment 6 - who has been travelling on a variety of high-end magazine fashion shoots for the last six weeks or so, mostly in the Far East and Hong Kong dominantly. I've checked with Immigration officials and their passport information tallies."

"*Okay for some*." Brian scoffed. "*Charlie Roth* – I can't believe he's still going strong. I grew up watching his detective series, based in New York and the Bronx."

"*Ahh, so he was your inspiration Brian: your role model*?" Louise was beaming at him showing her playful side; duly noted again by Sally who could see her body language plain as day.

"Yeah thanks for that Louise; he must have been fifty in those days..."

"*And not another word: Detective Constable*!" Brian raised his hand; anticipating her replay. But his smile belied his good humoured response.

"Thanks Karl. You mentioned a *third person*?"

"Yes. Apartment 10, on the third floor, is owned by a Russian Diplomat: *Anton Yurichev*."

(*Oh God, not another one with Diplomatic Immunity pondered Sally.*)

"He's lived in the Mews for two years. Currently in Russia on State Business; where he's been for the last two weeks. His Secretary was very helpful. She offered to provide a breakdown of this travel plans. She doesn't expect him to be back in the country for at least two weeks."

"*So his Apartment is empty*?" challenged Brian.

Karl nodded affirmatively.

"Wife lives in Russia with their two daughters."

"*Anything further to add, Karl*?"

Dave spoke to the elderly actor, turned writer from number 13: Mr Leonard Elkin and that leaves Mrs Elstree from Apartment 12, an elderly lady who spends an increasing amount of time with her family in Maidenhead: they are currently in Spain on holiday.

Apartment number 2 is currently vacant. The agent inspected number two with us present: completely empty Boss.

"Anything further to add, Karl?"

Karl shook his head. "That's it for now boss Boss."

"OK let's get hold of the keys to Apartment 10 and check it out. We'll need Mr Yurichev's permission of course and a Home Office Search Warrant if he resists; given his Diplomatic status: let's just make sure no one unauthorised has been inside given the proximity of the apartment to Professor Justin's former residence."

"Will do Boss."

"Dave: bring us all up to date on the CCTV footage from outside the Apartment block at the Mews; *Camera A*: Brian pointed to the camera placement on the scaled drawing of the Mews.

Dave checked his notes and moved forward to the board to the far left, showing the building layout.

"The CCTV footage is from Camera A; situated at roof level on the left hand side of the building. There's an uninterrupted view of the flight of six stairs that lead up to the entrance but the view of the front door is partially obstructed by the vertical column to the left of the entrance."

I've reviewed fifteen days of footage so far, working back from the 12th August when the body was discovered by *Molly Hull*. Nothing unusual, but very hard to discern identities of visitors, so I've concentrated on *Camera B*: the lift camera.

"Apart from residents: *nine visitors* prior to the day of discovery of the victim's body, six of whom have been identified and been accounted for by residents. I've filed a list on the team website along with stills taken from the CCTV."

"No unusual behaviour. Only two visitors to the fourth floor; both destined for *Mr Leonard Elkin* the semi-retired method actor who works three days a week as a novelist; during which time he lives in Apartment 13. The two women were his publisher and PA respectively. "

"*Just one young male unaccounted for so far.*"

"The images are exhibit 1262D, 1263D and 1284D Boss."

Brian pinged the images up onto the white board above the hard copies of Crime Scene evidence.

"Distinctive red cap and sporting a black back-pack . We don't get a view of his face. We don't know which Apartment he visited and he was only observed travelling up in the lift to the second floor and he was not observed leaving the building."

"So we've assumed he used the Fire Exit rather than the main door to the block when leaving."

"Okay, keep working on that individual. Let's get some enhancements of his back pack. 'Seems to be some sort of insignia on the flap." Directed Sally peering closely at the image as she spoke.

Dave got up and stood alongside Sally with his glasses on as her examined the enlargement closely.

He retreated to his seat.

"Will do Boss. I've had a word with Forensics and they have very few distinct finger prints from the lift buttons or interior of the lift thus far. This guy pressed the lift button on entry to the lift, so Forensics have been back to the lift for a second run on finger prints to ensure they have a clean sweep."

"The lift has been cordoned off since the murder and power cut off at source so we should have avoided further contamination."

"Which just leaves *Camera C* from the underground car park?" Brian asked.

"Exactly Guv', bad news at this point: unfortunately no CCTV available footage for the last camera."

"The ceiling mounted camera is fully intact, no signs of vandalism or disablement. However, there was a technical problem with the remote recording equipment. It was reported to the maintenance arm of the Security Company; but *not acted upon*."

"Bloody typical, how often....." Brian shook his head trailing off as he spoke.

"The wall mounted camera the Boss and I spotted when we looked at the rear entrance to the garage from the opposite side of the street; has not worked for years as you all know." Brian reminded the team.

"Okay so to summarise: nothing to go on from CCTV?" Sally interjected.

"One outstanding visitor: identity and purpose of visit unknown." Dave summarised and added:

"I have put all the images from CCTV on the team site alongside all the interview transcripts and resident details." He nodded at Karl as he spoke.

"OK keep us updated on the unknown male."

"Right Boss."

Sally thought for a moment, then moved on.

Brian had clocked her moment of hesitation and made a note to follow up with Sally when they had protected time.

 "So any thoughts around the room speak up: *Louise* what are you thinking?"

Sally knew Louise would have a profile in her mind and wanted the team to hear her thoughts: strength and trust grows with sharing. As a team they were well aware of the short-comings of *Profiling* but none the less, this topic had been the focus of Louise' MSc at University which gave her credibility.

"Thanks Boss."

"The Crime Scene, Post-Mortem results and posed position of the body suggest two things.

"Firstly: *the manner of the sexual assault, subsequent murder and the posing of the body of Professor Justin post-mortem, held some form of "symbolic" significance for the attacker, it's unlikely to have been a random attack..."*

"........and secondly *the victim may well have known her attacker."*

She paused; the team tuned in to her dialogue and all heads turned to her as she sat bolt upright in her chair at the far end of the semi-circle.

"To deal with the second aspect first:"

"No sign of forced entry: Professor Justin let him into her Apartment and thereafter into her bedroom. So unless he brandished a gun or weapon which put her in imminent fear for her life: *she knew him.*"

"There were absolutely no signs of a struggle."

"In addition, the victim had semen traces in her oral cavity, without signs of bruising or abrasions around her lips or mouth. There were no oral traces of mucosal tissue damage or bleeding from her gums to suggest she'd bitten or resisted his penis; so it may have been consensual oral sexual activity." Louise paused.

"Semen was recovered from Professor Justin's rectum, but not her vagina. She had peri-anal bruising so that element of the sexual activity may have been rough or non-consensual; we know she was strangled from behind; so there may have been a withdrawal of Professor Justin's presumptive initial consent."

Louise paused and Sally interjected: changing track for a moment: holding her hands in a prayer like position as she spoke:

"Remember that the communal front door to the Mews is accessed via a six-digit code and key. The garage roll-over door likewise requires the identical six-digit code and the limited number of bays are ordinarily occupied by resident's cars; especially when they're overseas."

"*Karl – whilst I think of it*: check out the valet provisions for the residents' cars whilst they're away. The Management Company should be able to advise us. Who keeps the car batteries charged up and who valets the cars?

Let's be sure we don't miss an opportunist; despite the profile.

"*Carry on Louise*." Sally encouraged with a smile and a nod.

Louise stood up and walked over to the photographs showing the position of the body.

"To point one: the *personal element of the murder:*"

"The way in which the body was posed Post-Mortem suggests the killer took his time. He had no concerns about leaving his DNA; didn't use a condom. That suggests we won't find him on our databases, he knows he's not on the radar. He's not known to us in any other capacity: no known history of burglary or serious sexual assaults...."

"*Or he's a bloody careless Bastard*." piped up *Jock McKenzie*; who'd been uncharacteristically silent until that moment.

Jock was nursing a hang-over from his previous night out with his brother: before he had taken the red-eye down that morning. He had cut short his fly-fishing holiday when he heard about the murder. His presence was one of the reasons Sally was rehashing information with which most of the team were already familiar.

"*Profiling would suggest otherwise*." Louise responded thoughtfully...

"...But on the other side of the coin, he wore gloves which for the strangulation, which would have appeared odd if the sex had been consensual up and until the moment he took up position behind her in preparation for anal sex: you'd expect Professor Justin of all people, would have been suspicious; unless that was part of her routine sex play."

"Never know with these kinky Medical types eh Boss?"

Sally acknowledged Jock's input with a repetitive nod of her head: despite the apparent jokiness of his comment, she knew he had a rich vein of experience to tap into.

Brian made an entry in his note book as if to underline Jock's contribution and piped up:

"Fair point Jock: Karl check the inventory from Professor Justin's apartment: make sure there are no unusual medical items to suggest any unusual sexual proclivities on the late Professor's part."

Louise let the scenario play out then continued:

"Perp's likely to be a confident, white well-educated man in his 30's to 50's. He'll be physically strong, or athletic and likely to be a narcissist."

"So that would fit with the need to control the scene, sculpt the body position post-mortem: in short demonstrate his omnipotence."

Sally commented.

"It might suggest a need to be in control: perhaps that's an element missing in his daily life.. or perhaps that's how his life is lived: in a constant struggle to assume control."

Brian was immediately reminded of their initial discussion with Christophe Schultz as Sally spoke.

"Would you think cohabiting, in a relationship or single?"

Brian asked Louise.

"I don't think the nature of the crime carries any persuasive view one way or another Brian. History bears witness to multiple examples of killers who have been in stable relationships and are married with kids in some cases."

"Entirely agree." responded Brian; nodding thoughtfully.

"He left fingerprints on the light and bed-stand as well; what do you make of that Louise?" Jock asked.

"It fits with his concept of his own invincibility. He's confident he'll not be caught."

Sally interjected again:

"No recent murders in the last three years with a similar M.O. that we're aware of."

Sally had painstakingly searched the Police Database personally at the weekend, not wanting to miss a killer escalating in his behaviour with a similar M.O. [*modus operandi*].

Louise waited patiently before pressing on:

"We're talking Mayfair, so unless he visited Professor Justin's apartment very late at night; we wouldn't expect him to look out of place in that location."

"The SMS messages and mobile phone data might suggest a time-frame between 20:15 and 21:30: the former being the last message opened on Professor Justin's personal mobile and the latter representing the first missed call of the evening; Molly Hull, her P.A.; having made the call - Jock."

"Aye, thanks Louise." Came Jock's reply.

With that, Louise gave a cursory nod to Sally and sat down.

"*Excellent: thank you Louise.*" Sally beamed.

"*Better watch out Brian, she'll be after your Job soon!*"

"Cheers Boss, great to feel wanted."

"Well that leads us nicely to our interview with *Dr Christophe Schultz.*"

"Brian here's your chance to shine again!

Sally shot him a warm smile.

"Right Dr Christophe Schultz hails from Stuttgart."

Brian jumped to his feet enthusiastically and summarised the interview from the previous night.

An hour later Sally concluded....

"So he's a forty-two year old single white male. He knew the victim and his medical knowledge would be a passport to ingratiating himself with her. His behaviour was defensive and his answers inadequate: we came away feeling he'd been economical with the truth."

"So he was *visibly* upset by the death of the 'Prof, and *must have known we'd link him to her by virtue of his work and the Drug Company!"*

"I hear what you say Jock: he's by nature controlling and the scene is consistent with having taken time, to contrive and stage the body and yet he may well have left behind DNA evidence that would convict him!"

"A lover's tiff: turning pleasure into murder?" Brian challenged.

"Or autoerotic asphyxiation: gone too far?" Sally responded.

"Geez, far enough to fracture her hyoid bone: and leave her with deep tissue bruising?" Jock looked unimpressed. He'd seen his fair share of murder victims in Glasgow. *"And no signs they were stoned at the time?"*

"No signs that she was." Sally corrected him.

"Aye: fair point Boss."

"Schultz didn't strike me as your typical addict; *what-ever that is.* We've all seen what some of the coked up' City Boys are capable of. But again, that's at odds with the sense of control from the scene and the lack of controlled drugs anywhere at the Crime Scene."

"But Schultz' did have what looked knife marks on his forearm. So self-harming opens up all kinds of possibilities..."

"Brian: anything on *'Schultz* on our databases?"

"Not so much as a ticket for speeding Boss."

"I am waiting for our German colleagues to return my call. For good measure I ran it past a colleague from Interpol; likewise awaiting the outcome."

"*Jock, work with Louise*, let's trawl the database to see if there have been any similar cases in the last ten to fifteen years, lacking or including forensics but with a similar M.O. Maybe our boy is starting to toy with us if he's a repeat offender."

"I started the process at the weekend and drew a blank. Review all crimes which involve *any forming of staging of the body*, the use of sex toys or medical paraphernalia."

"Start with London and trawl nationwide."

"You thinking: "copy-cat" Boss?" Brian clarified.

"Let's not rule anything in or out at this stage. Christophe Schultz said he'd been living in his apartment for three years. Dig a little, previous address, employers, background. To Jock's point, we know how over-represented the Medical Profession and Nurses are in the ranks of Serial Killers."

Jock beamed and nodded as she gave him a mention. Sally knew how long he'd waited for his fishing holiday and his dedication to duty and loyalty to the team was outstanding.

"Louise – when have you planned to speak to *Molly Hull* again?"

"Later today Boss: around 2pm. The doctors should have finished their rounds by then and further investigations by then. Unfortunately she suffered a small *sub-endocardial infarct: a heart attack which damaged the inner liner of the heart muscle.*"

"The Doctors reckon it was the shock of finding Edwina Justin: they'd known each other ten years and Molly considered her akin to family. Incidentally, she's unaware that Edwina Justin had any family."

"Take her back to the Crime Scene when she's ready Louise. Be guided by the Doctors, *Duty of Care and all that.*" Sally responded and continued:

"Although she goes in regularly I doubt she snoops around, but get her to focus on the contents of the rooms. Is there anything missing or out of place?"

"Are you thinking trophy collection?"

"Exactly: if we execute any Search Warrants in the near future, it would be good to know if we should be looking for any specific added extras".

"Doubt we'll find any heads in freezers this far South of the Border."

Jock's gallows humour caused Louise to wince.

"Molly provided you with a full list of Colleagues with whom Professor Justin had recently connected. Did you unearth anyone or anything of interest Brian?"

"*Yes, with full being the operative word Boss*. More a case of who she hadn't been in contact with. Everybody wanted a piece of her since her appointment to NICO. A whole load of Politics going on, but everyone seemed genuinely shocked and upset by the news of Professor Justin's death."

"What about the Italian apartment she owned; any update *Gloria*?"

Gloria was the only Civilian Member of the team. She turned her hand to whatever Sally or the team needed and was a veritable whizz' with technology having come from the telecoms industry two years before joining Sally's team.

"The Manager of the Complex had not seen her since her last trip to Milan prior to attending a Cancer Conference; held in Venice, in March this year."

"The Milan apartment is cleaned weekly and only the Management and Professor Justin would have held a key."

"Did we find that key Brian, is it on the inventory?"

Brian flicked on his laptop and opened the file of items bagged by forensics.

"No boss.....nothing..."

"Follow up on that please Gloria: double check with the Forensics log thru' Chris'."

"One more thing Boss:" Gloria continued: " The small package in the post - it was a miniature theatrical mask sent from Italy: the type you see in Venice. I've posted it on the website. No notes or other clues as to the sender's identity."

"Okay thank you Gloria."

"A secret admirer...?" Brian suggested.

"Louise 'speak to Molly: she if anyone might know."

"Louise nodded her assent."

"Did you find anything noteworthy from Professor Justin's mobile phone?"

"Not so far. I've not yet had any follow-up from Brian's request for transcripts but I'll get back onto that shortly." Gloria stated.

Sally's phone pinged.

"Okay thanks. That's it for now. Get to it. Brian let's catch up in my office after I have spoken to the A.C.C."

Chapter 11

2:45p.m. Tuesday 16th August 2016

"Right Brian, Christophe Schultz: *let's bring him in*."

"*You think he's our man*?" Brian registered no surprise in his voice as he asked the question.

"*He troubles me Brian*. On one hand his profile fits: middle-aged Caucasian, smart, knew the victim, a degree of emotional instability *maybe*: clearly he's calculating and obsessive. "

"By contrast and by the same token, *his labile mood is an issue*; particularly when we interviewed him. If he did murder Edwina Justin in the way the evidence suggests, that would make him nothing short of a *cold-hearted bastard*. Calculating and callous….."

……So way the emotion when he talks about her?"

"A lovers' tiff: a game which went too far?"

"Then why not 'fess up because he must know that if he has left his semen and finger prints they will incriminate him?"

"I certainly didn't get the impression that any of his reaction to our interview was game playing; despite the way you two fought for the upper hand at times!"

"But something doesn't fit. No previous…"

"*That we know of*." Brian interjected.

Sally nodded, preoccupied; then she continued thinking aloud.

"There's his *aggressive side*. We both saw that; he was rattled by your questioning and the mere hint of any intimate relationship seemed to put him on the defensive big time. The self-harming, that signals his vulnerability or maybe a Psychiatric history."

"Do you think we have enough to track down and speak to his G.P; always assuming he's Registered in the U.K.?"

"*Not yet;* I don't want him getting any kind of a nod or a wink from a fellow Doctor."

Sally hesitated.

"……We both know they can be *thick as thieves and stick together.*"

"Changing tack Brian: when do you expect to hear back from Germany and your mate in Interpol?"

"I'll get straight onto it as soon as we're done."

"I've been thinking about the SMS messages too on Edwina Justin's mobile: have we checked deleted text and chat?"

"Okay Brian…" Sally cut short their conversation.

"Get both of those items sorted. I'm going up to see the 'Chief Super."

Jocelyn Wilson was touch typing with unrelenting speed as Sally exited the lift and headed for Edward Ballard's office. With windows floor to ceiling on three sides she could see him pacing up and down talking on his mobile phone; as she approached. He beckoned her into his office as soon as he saw her. She instantly smelled a mixture of stale tobacco and aftershave.

"*She's just joining me now Sir. I'll put you on speaker-phone if that's okay?*"

He placed his mobile on the desk, speaker-phone activated.

"I've got the A.C.C. on the line Sally."

"*Good Afternoon Sir.*" Sally readied herself for *Henry Curzon's agenda*.

"*Right as I've just advised Chief Superintendent Ballard, we need to expedite the Edwina Justin case.*"

"The Home Secretary has taken a particular interest and I shall be updating him this afternoon."

"*What progress have you made D.C.I. Benson?*"

"The cause of death was manual strangulation and we have both the murderer's semen and finger prints from the Scene Sir."

"*That's always assuming he who made the deposit, committed the deed.*"

"Well, yes Sir. But in the absence of any contradictory evidence to date...."

"*Okay yes, I get the picture.*"

(*'God why does he always have to be so obnoxious thought Sally*. Not for the first time she wondered how he'd risen to such a lofty height without the good grace to reciprocate when greeted or even acknowledge progress.)

"*And do we have any suspects on our database with matching DNA or prints?*"

"Not so far Sir."

"*We interviewed a forty-two year old Stuttgart born doctor from Surrey yesterday evening*. He knew the deceased as a consequence of his work in the Pharmaceutical Industry. He met her three times by his own account, last occasion four months ago. However, he may have been one of the last people to have talked to her before she died; at least according to her mobile phone entries."

"What do the mobile phone transcripts show?"

"We haven't been able to access those as yet; working on that now Sir."

"So that's what I have to tell the Home Secretary later today: *nothing new to report*?" His tone was contemptuous.

"With respect Sir, it's been barely four days and..."

Sally looked pensive. She sensed a shit storm brewing and she'd be the one left without an umbrella if there were any cock-ups.

"Okay Sally: let me be crystal clear." He spoke slowly and deliberately as a Head Master might lecture his kids in assembly after a breach of school protocol:

 "Professor Justin was *hugely respected* and was a key scientific player in our research work and collaboration with the EU and the U.S."

"'Since the *bloody "Brexit" vote* we have lost both clarity and momentum in our negotiations on both sides of the Atlantic'. As you might imagine, the P.M.'s team have lost a strong ally on the research vanguard. *He is not impressed.*"

"Now do I need to spell it out or do you have a clear vision?"

"That's perfectly clear Sir."

"Okay, Edward, we're done here."

The line went dead.

"Sally, is there anything you need, resource wise?"

"No Sir not right now. I am arranging a Search Warrant for Dr Schultz' Apartment, his mobile and land-line records. We'll bring him in for questioning as soon as that's issued I expect that to be later this evening."

Edward Ballard gave his customary fleeting smile as Sally left.

Once again, Jocelyn Wilson didn't look up from her computer screen as Sally exited Ballard's office. *Rather you than me*, thought Sally. *Give me villains over Politicians any day of the week.*

'God she needed another cigarette.

Four floors below in the car park she found Brian under the smokers' shelter taking a quiet moment to top up his nicotine levels.

"Great minds think alike." he smiled as he blew a smoke ring towards Sally, seeing the look on her face he added:

"I sense the A.C.C. was in good form?"

"What are you bloody psychic or something Brian?"

"My mother used to say so. Her aunt was a medium you know."

"What Ouija boards and all that paraphernalia?"

"Yep: made a good living by all accounts."

"Gives me the creeps all the same, all that voodoo stuff."

Sally felt a cold chill run through her.

"More the living I fear; the dead don't carry knives and guns..or Rohypnol."

"Talking of which: Christophe's training. He would know all about toxicology and drugs."

"Pacifying his victims you mean....knowing what would turn up on a routine toxicology screen...."

"I had the same thought as Louise was talking Brian."

"You want me to talk to Biscuit Boss?"

Sally started to laugh and then coughed on her cigarette smoke.

"For God's sake don't let her hear you calling her that. It must have been bad enough going through school with a name like *Caroline Crumb*. I cannot begin to imagine how she'd have been teased at Medical School. You know the kind of reputation doctors have for their sense of humour."

"Yeah, or lack of it; in the case of 'Schultz."

Brian was still smiling as Edward Ballard walked into the car park and looked at his watch. Moments later his driver pulled up alongside him and opened the rear door for him. Executing a swift U turn they left the car park.

"*How was happy Teddy today?*"

"He kept his toys in his pram and even asked me if I needed extra resources!"

"'Feeling the heat from the A.C.C.: Edwina Justin was clearly well connected in the corridors of power."

Sally put a finger over her lips.

"That's all we need. We're always in the shit; it's only the depth that varies."

Brian recited one of his favourite lines for the third time in Sally's recent memory.

His mobile rang.

Seeing the numerals his spirits lifted.

"*Ahh Germany calling...*" He stepped out of the shelter to ensure a good connection.

"*Frank Guten Tag [Good Day]: what news?*"

Brian listened intently, stubbing out his cigarette in the deep metallic container embedded on the frame of the shelter.

Sally finished her cigarette and then rubbed her shoulders to keep warm as she waited for Brian to complete his call. She was wearing a thin black blazer and was beginning to wish she'd put on her denim or warmer jacket. The rain was now a drizzle and rather reflected her mood.

"*So you've already spoken to Lars?*"

Brian's voice began to rise half an octave with each statement at the other end of the phone.

"*Frank I owe you big time*. Sally Benson is with me now."

'Yeah she's still my D.C.I. *Danke Gott*. [Thank God!].

Speak soon *tschuss*!"[Good Bye!]

Brian stood processing the information.

"Dr Christophe Schultz: arrested in Sweden for driving under the influence; he was nineteen years old at the time."

"So they'll have his dabs on record. You've requested them?"

Sally needn't have asked.

"Right let's pay our Doctor a home visit."

"'*How about the Search Warrant*?"

"I'll get right onto it. 'Get the dabs' update sent through on route."

"Right Brian '*bring Jock along for the ride*; especially since he flew down mid-holiday. Get Gloria to ring ahead of us and check whether 'Schultz is at work or at home."

"Going back to the issue of drugs used to pacify victims...ask Caroline Crumb to widen her search of the post-mortem blood samples procured from Edwina Justin: looking for *anything unusual......*"

Chapter 12

19:30 Tuesday 16th August 19:30

'Schultz checked in sick and has been working from home all day."

"Are we sure of that?"

"Dialled in remotely apparently; Gloria spoke to the IT guys at his Internet Service Provider: called in a favour from one of the contractors who she knows from her penultimate role in the telecoms Industry."

"Small world." Sally smiled.

Brian beamed back as he hit the gas and steered a wide birth around a group of Journalists at the front entrance of the Police Headquarters.

Sally sat deep in thought as they drove. Jock started to snore within ten-minutes and Brian shot him a look in his rear-view mirror.

The rain started coming down harder as they drove; Brian had already put his flashing blue lights on the unmarked BMW M5 he was driving in the heavy evening traffic. A moment later as they hit the M3 Westbound he activated the siren and Jock woke with a visible jolt.

"Geez, took me back to Glasgow for a moment. Where are we Boss?"

"We're on the M3: enjoy your rest?"

"'Aye Boss grand. *The red eye was crammed with Business types.* You know what the Monday morning commuters are like on domestic flights?"

"Thankfully that's something I've managed to avoid."

"Okay; we won't delay with 'Schultz. I want him on record; so assuming he's at home we'll Arrest him Under Caution and get him back to the Nick soonest."

Sally's mobile rang.

"*That's great Gloria*. We can send the team in later. Give Dave the warrant and tell him to take Karl with him……on second thoughts, I will call him myself."

"Get hold of the phone records *pronto* please Gloria. Good work, see you later."

Sally speed dialled Dave. He answered on the second ring.

"Dave, the Search Warrant is issued for Christophe Schultz' Apartment. Take Karl with you. Thereafter, given your science background, research Utopia' and see what you can dig up on U0008. I'm conscious you've done all the background checks on line, but let's flesh that out by going direct to the Company tomorrow morning....."

"Find out who apart from Schultz' is responsible for safety and these Benefit/Risk ratios we've heard about and go push their buttons...."

"Speak soon." Sally sat back with a broad smile on her face.

"Okay Warrant issued. Jock I want you to stay once we've cautioned 'Schultz and await Dave and Karl who will follow us up as soon as they've got the document in their hands."

Sally rang Edward Ballard and updated him on progress.

"Okay Sally. Let me know when you're back." The phone abruptly went dead.

She sensed wherever he was; now was not the time for conversation.

Chapter 13

"The time is 07:30 a.m. and the date is Wednesday the Seventeenth of August 2016."

"Those present Detective Chief Inspector Sally Benson, Detective Sergeant Brian Mann; and the defendant: please introduce yourself Dr Schultz:"

"Dr Christophe Schultz." He spoke in a monotone.

"May I remind you Dr Schultz that you remain under Police Caution and your are being detained in connection with the Murder of Professor Edwina Justin."

"You have been detained since 22:30 last night: Tuesday Sixteenth August and have declined legal representation."

"Is that still the case?"

No response.

"Do you wish to reconsider that decision having had a night's sleep?"

"Yes" came the muted reply.

"Yes you decline legal representation; or yes you'd like to reconsider that decision?"

"I don't need a lawyer: I've done nothing wrong." His voice was barely audible as he talked down towards his feet; head hung low.

"Louder please Doctor; for the benefit of the tape."

"I do not require a lawyer." Christophe took a deep breath after replying.

Sally sat directly opposite Christophe.

He was wearing a light blue designer denim shirt and matching denim jeans. Sally noted the faint whiff of aftershave which she couldn't pinpoint and the dark circles under his eyes. He sat composed as he spoke; albeit staring at the ground.

"As yet you have not been formally charged as you have agreed to help us with our enquires, but there are a number of inconsistencies between the evidence you provided during your first interview on Monday 15th August and evidence which has come to light."

"I would like to clarify several points arising from your statement which you made to D.S. Mann and myself when we interviewed you on Monday evening Dr Schultz."

"*I will do anything I can to help you find Professor Justin's killer.*" replied Christophe; lifting his head and looking Sally directly in the eyes as he made his commitment.

"*Let's start with the last time you met with Professor Justin.*"

"*The 8th of April 2016.* We met for lunch in Professor Justin's office."

(Sally noted the date discrepancy from his previous statement, but elected not to interrupt the flow...)

"What was the agenda for your meeting?"

"We met to agree the precise wording for a forthcoming Press Release: for U0008."

"Who prepared the wording?"

"We had an exchange of emails and thereafter I wrote the text which was agreed by our Company Lawyers. The final draft needed Professor Justin's approval before we could hold it on file ready to incorporate into our Press Release."

"How long did your meeting last?"

"About an hour; we had our discussion then ate a sandwich lunch and coffee which was delivered by her P.A."

"Do you remember her name?"

Christophe hesitated for a moment; *"Yes, it was Molly."*

"When your meeting was over did Professor Justin agree to any further meetings?"

"No there was no need. We agreed to correspond by email if there were any major amendments to the Press Release."

"And did that need arise, were there any amendments?"

"No."

"So the last time you spoke to Professor Justin was on the *8th April 2016.*"

"Correct."

"Have you had any conversations since that time?"

A moment of hesitation, then: "No."

"And you are completely sure?"

"I've said so."

"Okay Dr Schultz. Do you have the late Professor Justin's telephone number listed in your mobile phone?"

"I believe so."

"And is that number a landline or mobile number?"

"Both. I checked Monday evening after you took my Statement."

"And when did you last dial that number, *for whatever reason*?"

Christophe looked uneasy for the first time during the interview.

"I suppose it was in April, before our meeting."

"You spoke to Professor Justin on your mobile phone to arrange the meeting?"

"I believe so."

"You didn't make those arrangements via her P.A., via Molly? Why was that Doctor?"

"Well, we'd met before and I guess she agreed that approach..." His voice drifted off.

"Okay."

"Let me turn to the nature of your relationship with Professor Justin."

"It was *purely* professional."

"So you stated previously; in your first Statement."

"Let's return to the first two meetings with Professor Justin, the first in early November 2015 and thereafter in December 2015. Tell me about the nature of those meetings."

"The first in the second week of November was a round-table meeting of Liver Specialists. I arranged the meeting and sent out the invitations personally. Most invitations were sent out about four to six months in advance to ensure that the Invitees were available and able to save the date in their schedules."

"Go on." Sally nodded as she spoke.

"The meeting was an opportunity to share the efficacy and safety data for U0008; a new drug to treat patients with chronic hepatitis C."

"And you presented the data?"

"That's correct. I also Chaired the meeting."

"Did any of your colleagues from the Company attend: from Utopia Pharmaceuticals?"

"No, just me."

"Did Professor Justin play a key role in the meeting?"

"No more so than anyone else; but her opinion is...was.... very well respected."

"Ordinarily....She does little in the way of collaboration with the Pharmaceutical Industry."

"So she was seen as someone who was not....." Sally continued choosing her words carefully:

"In the pockets of the Industry..?"

"Exactly so..."

Christophe once again realised the D.C.I. had a good grip of Politics.

"'Although that's a very jaundiced way.... of viewing the relationship between Big Pharma' and Health Care Professionals: we are guided by stringent rules and Operating Practices are pretty clear on what's acceptable and what's not."

Without acknowledging his point Sally continued:

"This Meeting pre-dated Professor Justin's appointment to NICO: The National Institute of Cancer and Oncology?"

"Correct. That appointment was made *4th April 2016*; shortly before we met: which was on the 8th April. I believe on Monday night I may have stated that our meeting was on the 9th April."

(Error noted: thought Sally and watched Brian out of the corner of her right eye.)

Brian noted the change in his notebook in which he was making aide memoirs from the interview.

"So your first meeting was with Scientific Colleagues; a round table meeting in London."

"Yes, we met at the Royal Hotel in Canary Wharf: the venue was very close to an International Hepatology meeting; to which most if not all of our round-table delegates would have been attendees."

"And did you have time to talk privately with Professor Justin at that time?"

"No, she was presenting at the Symposium so joined us for the two hours of our round-table meeting; then left promptly. I don't recall her staying for refreshments."

"Tell us about the second time you met: in *December 2015*."

"It was about a week before Christmas.."

"Can you be more precise? Surely you would have the details in your mobile phone?"

"Yes I can check for you."

"*Later Dr Schultz*": directed Sally.

"*Please continue.*"

"I was shopping in London on the Tottenham Court Road. We met in *Garroways Bookshop* and had coffee together; around mid-morning."

"Where precisely did you meet?"

"We were both in the travel section of the bookshop. I was looking at tourist guides to the Far East. Edwina tapped me on the shoulder."

"*Just like that: out of the blue*?" Brian interrupted.

Christophe looked at Brian briefly, then back at Sally.

"*Yes just as I've described.*"

"Who suggested coffee?"

"*I did: or is that a Crime now*?" his response to Brian was snappy, indignant even.

"I suppose that would depend on your Code of Ethics, Doctor Schultz."

Christophe gave Brian a puzzled look.

"Meaning what precisely?"

"You told us that there were Rules." He referred to his handwritten notes from the previous interview; then he continued.

"We adhere to *Codes of Practice* and don't simply engage in discussion of Company Products or data."

"Can you confirm those were the words you used when we took your statement?"

"That sounds about right; yes."

"Okay, so you were not there to discuss the Company' product: U0008?"

"No. It was a chance meeting as I've stated. No agenda."

"*What did you discuss*?"

Christophe took a deep sigh.

"The Doctors' *amended NHS Contract*, changes to the NHS etcetera: nothing specific."

"*For half an hour*?" Brian interjected.

"Surely Professor Justin must have had many commitments that day, her being so eminent and all that?"

Before Christophe could reply:

"And did you make any follow-up arrangements at that point?"

"No."

"What did you both *eat* doctor, with your coffee?"

"*What did I eat*?"

"Yes it's a simple question." Brian looked stoney faced.

Well..I think Ed...Professor Justin had a piece of carrot cake."

"And who paid?"

"Well I did of course."

"*And is that allowed*?"

"What?"

"Under your Rules: your Codes of Practice and Ethical Behaviour?"

"Doesn't that constitute entertainment? A gift...so to speak."

"As a Policeman I am duty bound to declare any such *inducements..*"

Sally was impressed; she had a shrewd idea Brian had checked on the Code he was referring to.

"Well..that would depend...and it was not an inducement of any kind..I resent...."

Brian cut through Christophe's statement with his own sword...

"*Depend on whether you were discussing Business or just meeting up as friends..*"

"*Well yes..where is all this leading Sergeant?*"

"*That's Detective Sergeant Mann.*" Brian corrected acerbically.

(*"Quid pro quo"* smiled Sally inwardly: true to form, Brian wouldn't let the U0008 correction from Monday night's interview go without a swift riposte at some point. *Game on...*)

"Did you make any plans to meet up *socially, at Christmas for example*?"

Christophe took a sharp intake of breath and swallowed hard. Clearly wrong footed by the question.

He shifted in his chair and pulled his legs back under him.

Brian persisted:

"*With mutual friends: or family?*"

"No on both counts; I don't think Edwina had any family."

"*How would you know that?*" interjected Sally.

Christophe hesitated. "Edwina must have mentioned it."

"*So you did talk about private matters with Professor Justin?*"

"Well, I suppose we must have."

"When?"

Christophe looked bemused.

"Doctor?"

"I don't know..."

"*So what did she tell you about her family?*" Sally leaned in towards Christophe as she posed the question.

"As I've said...I don't think she had any family...at least in the UK."

"*So she had family elsewhere?*" Brian sat forward too.

"Well..."

"Yes or no Doctor..."

"I really don't know..."

"So to summarise:" Sally began.."You talked about Professor Justin's *personal life*..but you can't remember when?"

'Schultz fell silent and looked at the floor.

"Is that a fair summary doctor?"

"Yes."

"For the benefit of the tape please Doctor.."

"YES!"

"So what did she know about your Personal life?"

"Like what?"

"Did she know you live alone Doctor?" Probed Brian

"I really don't see…"

"Let's move on Dr Schultz." Sally interjected.

"When did you learn of Professor Justin's death?"

"I think it was on Saturday 13th August."

"Two days ago you were unsure?"

"Is that a question or a statement Detective?"

His blue eyes burned with irritation.

"How did you hear about it?"

"It was on the radio."

"Where were you when you heard the News?"

"Whilst driving to work'. I was on the way to Hayes in Middlesex."

"On a Saturday morning…?" Brian asked and continued:

*"Is that normal for you…*to work at weekends?"

"Sometimes.."

"And you're sure that's when you learned of Professor Justin's murder?"

"Yes."

"Two nights ago you seemed much less certain."

Christophe sat impassively.

"How did you *react;* when you learned about her death?"

"*I was shocked. I......*"

"You what: Dr Schultz?"

Sally sat forward again in her chair.

"I heard colleagues talking about it as soon as I arrived at work."

"How well did your Colleagues know Professor Justin?"

"*By Reputation: of course*. She was a leading figure in a therapy area where we have several treatments available."

"Were you upset?"

"Yes of course, she was.....*special*." he lowered his tone as he pronounced the word *special*.

"Do you mean special to you: *personally*?"

Christophe bit his bottom lip.

"Could I have a glass of water please?"

Brian passed him a plastic bottle of water, having broken the seal.

He drank hurriedly from the bottle and wiped his mouth.

"Thank you."

"*I'd like to reconsider; I would like a Lawyer present before we continue.*"

"Okay. Do you have someone in mind? If not we can..."

"A Duty Solicitor will be fine."

"*Interview suspended at 8:05 am.*"

Chapter 14

Sally depressed the record button and waited a few moments.

"The time is 10:15 a.m Wednesday 17th August 2016."

"Those present D.C.I. Sally Benson, D.S Brian Mathews…..

After Christophe Schultz and his lawyer Ms. Georgina Townsend, had both introduced themselves, Sally continued:

"May I remind you Dr Schultz that you are still under Police Caution?"

Georgina was wearing her signature white silk blouse and plain grey suit. Her blonde hair was tied tightly back and her flat black shoes were highly polished.

(Her father had risen from Accounts assistant to Branch, and thereafter Area Manager for a High Street Insurance Company; and was always client-focused and immaculately dressed. He did his best to pass on his wisdom to his only daughter before his death.)

(*"If you're going to Practice Law Georgina, always dress formally and be under no illusion: first impressions always count."*)

Sally noticed the decorative ring on the middle finger of Georgina's right hand; it looked antique: a family heirloom she guessed. Georgina looked young for the role of Duty Solicitor; but they all did these days.

(Maybe she was getting older and that was the pertinent issue.)

Christophe Schultz looked more composed as he sat opposite Sally; his lawyer to his left opposite Brian.

Georgina smiled at Brian as he sat down; his face remained impassive.

"So let's begin where we left off…." Sally spoke first.

Georgina interrupted her.

"*Before we continue D.C.I. Benson, my client would like to make a statement.*"

(Bloody hell thought Brian, only been here two minutes and she's calling the shots!)

"*Go ahead Dr Schultz.*" Sally sat impassively watching Christophe as he composed himself.

"*I wish to amend my Statement.*"

He paused and looked at the table for a moment."

"*Take your time.*" Sally encouraged him.

"When I met Professor Justin on the second occasion, in London, we had coffee precisely as I described; on the Tottenham Court Road. It was a week before Christmas and neither of us had plans for *Boxing Day* so we agreed to meet up; at Professor Justin's Apartment in Mayfair: at *Melway Mews.*"

Christophe looked side-ways at Georgina. She simply nodded.

"*I drove to her Apartment and arrived around 1pm on Boxing Day: 26th December 2015. I parked as instructed in the Underground Car Park at the Mews. We had lunch and relaxed; listening to music for several hours. Later that afternoon we had sex. I left her Apartment around 8pm and that was the first and last time I visited her Apartment.*"

"Thank you. Is there anything further you wish to add?"

"No." Christophe looked relieved and looked Sally directly in the eye as he responded.

"So when you met in *December*, at *Garroways bookshop*; who suggested you meet up on Boxing Day?"

"*It was Edwina's suggestion.*"

"How did she phrase the invitation?"

Christophe looked blank for a moment.

"……..She asked me about my plans for Christmas. I explained that as I don't have family I was meeting with friends for lunch on Christmas Day and had no plans for the 26th."

"Let me be clear. *The invitation was for lunch*?"

"Yes."

"Did Professor Justin ask about your Private life?"

"Yes. She asked me if I was single and whether I'd had any recent girlfriends."

"I hadn't and I was honest about that with her."

"How long had it been since you had last had sex, before you spent the afternoon and early evening with Professor Justin?"

Georgina interrupted: "*I don't see what relevance..*"

Sally raised her right hand. "*I'm coming to that shortly.*" She maintained eye contact with Christophe as she spoke.

"*Please answer the question.*"

"I don't know; maybe two years."

"And was that part of a relationship or a one-off; *a one night stand*?"

Georgina opened her mouth to speak: but Sally had the upper hand and Christophe nodded at Georgina as if to signify that he was comfortable as he answered.

"*As you say, a one-off; it was a work Colleague.*"

"Have you had *any* lasting relationships Dr Schultz?"

Georgina interrupted and this time stood her ground.

"Please get to the point 'Chief Inspector: this is beginning to feel like a fishing trip."

"It's okay. I'll answer the question. I haven't had a lot of time for relationships; my work has been my focus: *always*."

"Returning to Boxing Day: 26th December 2015: what kind of sex did you have with Professor Justin?"

Christophe looked hesitant.

"It was consensual."

Sally nodded and waited.

"We began touching on the sofa and she took me to the bedroom. We had sex in bed and I used a condom."

"Who made the first move to the bedroom?"

"She stood up...reached for my hand..and led me slowly to the bedroom and closed the door."

Christophe cleared his throat and took a sip of water from his bottle before replacing the screw top lid.

"Who supplied the condom?"

"I did."

"Did you have full intercourse?"

"Yes."

"With full Vaginal penetration?"

"Yes."

"What about anal penetration?"

"No." Christophe scowled. *"I don't do that."*

Sally thought about the position of Edwina's body post mortem.

"When you had intercourse, what position did you use?"

Georgina raised her hand but Sally pressed on.

"Were you on top of Professor Justin in the Missionary position?"

"We had sex in the Missionary position. Now can we move away from this detail please; I am uncomfortable."

"Did *she* straddle *you* at any point?"

Silence.

"I am sorry if this makes you uncomfortable Doctor Schultz, but this detail is very important. Please answer the question."

"Okay, okay."

"Edwina did straddle me: just before she had an orgasm."

"And what about you; did you climax?"

"No."

"Did you penetrate her from behind: the common term is the colloquial, *doggy position?*"

"No."

"How did you feel about not having an orgasm?"

"It was fine."

"You weren't angry or frustrated?"

"No......well.....maybe a little... ....*frustrated*. But it was not unusual for me."

"Did you have sex in any other position?"

"No as I told you..the Missionary and then briefly as Edwina straddled me. She looked directly into my eyes.....as she climaxed. Then......rolled over and fell asleep briefly."

"For how long?" asked Sally

"Maybe ten minutes: just a nap."

"I had the feeling......" He spoke quietly...his voice trailed off and looked away from them.

"Yes Doctor?"

"*Nothing.*"

"Christophe...." Sally probed gently; her voice maternal rather than threatening.

"*You had something more to say*?"

"Do you suffer from any sexual problems?"

"No: *none.*" Christophe stated categorically with an instant retort.

Then more slowly he added:

"I was going to say....I think Edwina needed the sex more than *me*: I think she was lonely."

"I think...I....I..."

He paused and took a deep breath and opened his bottle for another sip of water.

"I think she chose me...*for sex I mean*.... simply because I was alone, like her; *uncomplicated and available.*"

"Thank you Christophe. I know that can't have been easy for you to discuss."

"Did you have any other forms of sex whilst you were with Professor Justin?" Brian interjected.

"No, I already told you." He stared at Brian...more irritation than anger.

"Fellatio?" Brian now led the questions in rapid succession.

"No: it was the first time we'd met. I think that would have been too personal for her."

"Did she say so?"

"No."

"Did you ask her to perform any other sexual acts with you?"

"No."

"Did you want any other forms of sex with her?"

"NO!"

"What did you do after you'd had sex Christophe?" Sally asked in a gentle tone.

"We took separate showers. Relaxed with some music and then I drove home."

"Did you arrange to meet again?"

"No."

"Speak by phone or message?"

"No; not until I contacted her about the press release."

"In April 2016?"

"Yes."

There was a loud knock at the door.

Sally looked around; paused momentarily and then spoke again:

"For the benefit of the tape, interview suspended at 10:40 a.m."

"*I suggest you have a cup of tea with your lawyer Dr Schultz. We will resume again shortly.*"

Brian held the door open for Sally as *W.P.C. Rita Datta* brought in two plastic cups of tea and placed them in front of Christophe and Georgina.

"Sorry about the interruption to bring you out of the interview room Boss; but I have an important update for you. We have full transcripts of the telephone conversations between Professor Justin and Dr Schultz and a forensics update."

Louise looked liked the cat who'd got the cream.

Chapter 15

"Dr Crunch has checked Christophe Schultz' dabs against the partial prints found at the Crime Scene Boss."

"The bedside lamp and bed stand?"

That's right." replied Louise. *"They're a perfect match."*

"His well-timed statement pre-empts us from using that to implicate him. He'd have known his dabs were in the bedroom so he's covering his tracks."

Brian replied with a note of irritation.

"It might be a bit harder for him to explain why his semen is in the deceased body." Louise responded.

"Assuming that's a match: that would be the icing on the cake…." Sally responded, then winced at her unguarded analogy.

"Particularly given his supposed distaste for anal sex." replied Brian.

"How long did the lab say it would take to compare the DNA from his buccal sample and the semen sample found at the crime scene?"

"They're working flat out boss. ASAP was all she would say. She promised to text you as soon as the result is available as well as ringing me."

"Okay."

"What about the Prints from Interpol?"

"All three are a match Boss."

Sally put both thumbs up and looked resolute.

Sally read the transcripts and passed them onto Brian.

"Right well that explains a lot! Concluded Sally.

Sally, Brian and Louise headed back towards the interview room, where Christophe was sat drinking fresh tea alongside Georgina. His demeanour was relaxed.

Sally and Brian stood and watched the two of them through the two way mirror.

"What are they talking about Louise?"

"Stuttgart; where he grew up. Travel around Europe."

"They're well aware of the two way mirror and she's a smart one Boss. She'll not let him make any unguarded comments."

Sally was in reflective mode.

"I'm sure you're right about him covering his tracks, Brian."

"Do you think the statement was her idea?"

"*Reckon so*. Be interesting to see how they react to the forensics. Do you plan to wait for the DNA from the semen analysis or shall we have another crack at him now?"

"I think we'll carry on. You lead Brian. Let's see how long it takes to get under his skin again."

They waited silently side by side until the pair had drained their tea cups then entered the room and Brian switched the tape on.

"*Interview re-commenced 11:00 Wednesday 17th August 2016.* Those present: D.C.I. Sally Benson, D.S Brian Mann, Doctor Christophe Schultz and Ms. Georgina Townsend introduced themselves.

"May I remind you Dr Schultz that you are still under Police Caution?"

On this occasion Brian sat opposite Christophe as they resumed they seats.

Christophe adjusted his position in his seat and looked at Brian before looking diagonally across at Sally: sensing what was to come with the change of seating arrangements. *He resolved to stay calm.*

"So do you prefer the company of women Dr Schultz?"

"You mean compared to men?"

"*Sometimes, yes; they're often more cultured.*" He cast a brief look at Sally as he made the comment.

"And your relationships; how do you feel when they are over: those *one night stands that constitute your sex life*?"

His comment was calculated to sound derisive.

Georgina flashed him a dirty look and opened her mouth but Christophe flashed back in an instant.

"Hardly relationships if they last *one night*." Christophe replied dryly: echoing the inflection in his opponent's voice.

"*That's my point, exactly.*" Brian responded with a slight smile.

Georgina leaned slightly towards Brian as she spoke; looking him directly in the eyes.

"And what is your point, *precisely*, D.S. Mann? Are you trying to provoke my client?"

"Dr Schultz how did you feel when you knew Professor Justin wouldn't see you again?"

"*We had an understanding.* We enjoyed no strings attached fun on Boxing Day; nothing more."

"So....who *proposed* the *understanding*.....was that your idea?"

"No it was Edwina's proposal."

"Mmmmmmmmmm" responded Brian, appearing thoughtful and nodding his head sagely:

"And you were *happy* with that arrangement?" He wore a sceptical face as he posed the question, tilting his head and raising an eyebrow.

"Yes."

"You didn't want to repeat the "fun"?"

"Sure, I wouldn't have minded; but our lives were very different."

"She was a successful Leader in her Field and you are, well, a Medical Director in the *Industry*?"

"What are you trying to ask Detective Sergeant Mann...or *imply*?" Georgina interrupted.

"Are you trying to intimidate my client or to belittle his achievements?"

(She's a feisty one thought Brian, young but fiery...)

Sally watched Georgina carefully; her body posture composed and her interruption well timed.

She was calm and her objections appropriate. No game play.

"*I will re-phrase my question Doctor*. Why do you think Professor Justin invited you to her Apartment?"

Christophe sat quietly for a moment and didn't respond.

"Perhaps despite the differences in our Social standing and Academic standing; *she like me was simply lonely.*"

His response was disarmingly simple: Sally had to admit. Georgina sat quietly, watching Brian.

"So what did you talk about when Professor Justin called you on Tuesday 9th August at 10:15 a.m.?"

"*Earlier last week: in fact the very day upon which Professor Justin may well have been Murdered in her own Apartment?*

"You *lied* to us again Dr Schultz didn't you?"

Brian's intonation was deep and guttural.

"How many more lies Doctor?"

Christophe hesitated and looked at Georgina.

"The call was work related."

"It concerned U0008?"

"Yes."

"In what way: new results?"

Brian's questions flowed quickly and effortlessly.

"No, we discussed the timing of the Press Release."

"What time was it due to be released?"

"2pm CET that day."

"'And?" Brian asked with a an open gesture of his hands.

"Were there any problems with the content of the statement?"

"No"

"So why the second call?"

"I don't see what..." Christophe looked undecided and bit his lower lip.

"No comment."

"And the third call that day?"

"No comment."

"You're not helping yourself Dr Schultz." Sally sat impassively as she commented. She continued:

"You have had plenty of opportunity to disclose the calls you made and explain in detail the reasons for your calls."

"What are you not telling us Christophe? *Please start helping yourself.*"

Georgina looked directly at Sally as she made her comments and held her gaze before looking at Brian. She remained silent, as did Christophe.

"*Dr Schultz we have forensic evidence which puts you at the scene of Professor Justin's death on..*"

"*Why has this evidence not been disclosed.*" protested Georgina looking indignant: eyes wide open.

"We have only just received the update from Forensics." Brian retorted.

Georgina looked sceptical and huffed.

"*We have matched your fingerprints to the bedroom where the Murder took place.*"

Georgina touched Christophe's right arm as she spoke; just a momentary contact on his right upper arm. Sally watched her body posture intently now as she spoke.

"And my client has already explained that he was at Edwina Justin's Apartment on 26th December 2015. Where *exactly* were the supposed finger prints located?"

"One was lifted from the left hand bed-side table; and a second partial print from bed frame."

Brian opened a plain brown A3 envelope and selected two 8x10 inch photographs; he placed them on the table in front of Georgina and Christophe.

"I am showing the suspect exhibits labelled B138 and B140.

"The prints taken from here and here; are a direct match for your finger-prints taken from our Custody Records."

"This evidence only proves that my client was in the Apartment at *some* time; it does not link him to the day or days in question: or the Murder of Professor Justin."

Christophe looked down at his finger nails.

Brian looked directly at Christophe and leaned forward a few inches as he spoke.

"You've been in trouble with the Police before, haven't you Doctor Schultz?"

Georgina glanced across at her client. Sally noted the element of surprise in her expression; Georgina drew a swift deep breath through slightly parted lips.

"What do you mean?" Christophe response was flat, vacant of surprise.

"You've visited Sweden I understand; as a teenager?"

Christophe looked hard at his nails.

"I understand. I was arrested for driving after I had been drinking. I was just *nineteen* at the time."

He glanced across at Georgina. She made a note in her brown leather notepad before closing the fastening.

"You were charged?"

"Yes. I lost my license for a year and then re-sat my Driving Evaluation."

"Any other Police Arrests you want to share with us?"

Christophe shook his head.

"For the benefit of the tape please Dr Schultz."

"No: nothing else."

Sally's mobile phone buzzed against her inside pocket of her jacket.

She stood and walked towards the door.

"For the benefit of the tape; D.C.I. Benson is leaving the room at 11:45 a.m.: Recorder left running."

Brian sat squarely looking at Christophe as he in turn; looked down at his finger nails. He'd topped up the oil on the BMW the previous evening and could see oil remnants deep underneath the cuticle on his right mid-finger. By contrast, Christophe Schultz nails looked clinically clean; not a blemish in sight.

Georgina sat quietly making notes with a gold slim-line pen having re-opened her note-pad.

Two minutes later, Sally re-entered the room with an A3 envelope.

"11:48 a.m. For the benefit of the tape D.C.I. Sally Benson has re-entered the room."

Sally sat and looked at Christophe for a moment.

"Dr Schultz: are there any *further* aspects of your Statement you wish to amend?"

"No."

"I am showing the suspect exhibits labelled B98 and B99."

Sally spoke slowly and deliberately.

"These photographs were taken from the scene of Professor Justin's Death and show Edwina Justin's body."

She placed two photographs on the table in front of Christophe.

He looked up to the ceiling and didn't look down for a few moments; as if composing himself.

"Please look at the photographs Dr Schultz." Sally's voice was firm, unemotional.

Christophe looked down; his eyes tightly shut.

He started at the exposed body of Edwina; an unnatural, explicit pose: one he could barely have imagined. He looked away and suddenly dry retched. He stood up and Brian was quick to his feet.

"Sit back down please Doctor Schultz." his tone was firm.

Georgina ran her fingers around the ring on her hand as she looked over her shoulder at Christophe. She remained silent.

"I need air...please take them away."

"Please sit down Dr Schultz." Brian's tone was measured and unyielding.

"I can't look at those pictures."

His speech was tremulous and he began to shake visibly.

Chapter 16

""*He's a strange one*." remarked Edward Ballard to Louise who stood next to him one the other side of the two way mirror.

"He certainly fits the profile Sir." Louise responded.

"What do you think remorse, self-recrimination or just a good actor?"

"It's difficult to say, Sir. His physical reaction looks real enough."

"I think he's in Denial: he's distanced himself from the memory and this reaction is only partly for our benefit."

"I presume you'd like to be in there?"

Not wanting to walk into an awkward conversation her response was non-committal.

"*I think the Boss and Brian have done all the leg-work on this one Sir.*"

"Quite so: the spoils of war Louise."

"So to speak: Yes Sir."

Louise felt a sense of relief as *Gloria* approached them along the short corridor; which lead from the main Murder Unit office. She appeared a little breathless despite the short distance.

"*Keep me posted please Louise.*"

"Yes Sir." Louise watched Edward Ballard as he exited via the double doors back to the Murder Unit main corridor.

Christophe rubbed his right forearm and bit his lip as he paced forward and backward behind Georgina's chair. Sally nodded quickly to Brian; who stood behind his chair. He wanted to be ready if Christophe upped the ante.

Sally watched him closely. He hugged himself as he paced up and down like a caged tiger at the zoo; but with none of the Pride or Presence. Instead, she saw a frightened and vulnerable adult.

"Sit down please Dr Schultz." Instructed Brian: to no avail.

She thought about the fading marks on his Christophe Schultz right forearm; a probable history of Self-Harm.

The elements of her *Duty of Care* they owed to him legally; ran through her mind. 'Schultz had been pacing for nearly five minutes and showed no signs of abating. Georgina looked her in the eye and frowned as if to say, what are you going to do?

Georgina stepped up to the mark.

"D.C.I. Benson, I'd like to suggest we take a break; I'm worried about my Client."

"I agree: Dr Schultz I would like the Duty Doctor to talk to you."

Christophe either didn't hear her or didn't respond.

"Interview suspended at twelve-fifteen."

"I'll arrange for some more tea." Sally smiled briefly at Georgina as she left; Georgina nodded and reciprocated."

"Keep a close eye on them Brian." Sally joined Louise and Gloria on the other side of the wall; Brian at her side.

"What do you think Boss?" asked Louise; frowning as she spoke.

"Psychiatric issues: depression?"

"Could be, given the likely Self-Injury: I'm going to speak to the Duty Medic. *Something is not right here."*

"Your gut instinct again, Boss?"

Sally shot Brian a look and he broke eye contact; watching Christophe pacing up and down.

Chapter 17

20:10

"So what are you saying Sally?

"Why the hesitation?"

As he rose to his feet, he towered above Sally and she was acutely aware of his overbearing demeanour and his icy stare.

Edward Ballard sat motionless behind his desk, content to let the dialogue play out.

"It's just that he's a highly trained Medic and he leaves the Scene of the Crime having had unprotected sex; leaving behind his DNA which he surely must realise will eventually incriminate him."

"What's more he had *previously* used a condom Sir, on Boxing Day 2015."

Henry Curzon stood dispassionately as she argued her case.

"Furthermore he made *no attempt* to remove the deceased' mobile phone to cover up their telephone conversations which...."

"Which as I understand it: he lied about in the first instance, denying any contact!" Henry cut in. "In the heat of the moment having killed her he simply didn't cover his tracks."

"The contemptuous staging of her naked body demonstrates he had other preoccupations: mobile phones were the furthest thing from his mind having committed murder."

"His reaction to the photos of her body looked genuine enough."

"So he's in a state of denial! Can't believe his loss of control: a sexual encounter where he finally lost control, then attempts to demonstrate his omnipotence by his contemptuous staging of her naked body."

He sat back down again, sighed and regained his composure.

"Let the Duty Police Surgeon assess him. If he's deemed not fit to continue with further questioning then Charge him and let him sleep."

"For Christ's sake you've got his DNA which no doubt will be matched to the semen sample and his fingerprints are all over the Scene." He let out another sigh: even he was tiring of the high level Political interest Professor Justin's murder had created.

"Speak to the C.P.S. He knew the victim; he pre-emptively covered his tracks by admitting to sexual relations last year. He had means and opportunity…"

"What about motive Sir?"

"You've read the mobile transcripts: Professor Justin's unequivocal stance and instructions relating to the drug's safety profile."

"She was about to quash all his hard work and jeopardise the future revenue stream of a potentially very lucrative drug launch: in so doing she would have exposed his reckless behaviour in authorising the Press Release in contravention of her direct instructions."

"That's surely motive enough Sally?"

"Just a case of good old fashioned greed. Don't let the sexual aspect of the case cloud your judgement."

"Speak to the C.P.S. I want this one cleared up. It's a good result."

Henry Curzon stood up, straightened his uniform and strode out of the door without looking back.

Edward Ballard nodded. *"Goodnight Sir."*

He closed the office door behind the A.C.C. and spoke as he leaned back in his black leather chair.

"Look Sally: you've done a great job. It's been a long day. Let the Police Surgeon do his job. Keep 'Schultz under constant supervision and re-interview him tomorrow morning."

"We don't expect Dr Arnold to attend for the next couple of hours. He's snowed under apparently. When I spoke to him he said it's worse than A&E on a Friday night." Sally stated pragmatically.

Sally looked Edward Ballard directly in the eye as she spoke.

"Can I talk frankly Sir?"

Edward nodded.

"It doesn't *feel* right. You've known me for how long? Twelve or is it thirteen years?"

"Sleep on it Sally. Have a stiff G&T and get a good nights' sleep. Brian can...."

"With respect Sir....I'll speak to the Duty Medic first after he's assessed Schultz."

"Of course: as you wish."

"Let's catch up tomorrow morning."

"Goodnight Sally." He didn't look up as he typed his password and unlocked the file entitled "Justin murder."

Sally headed outside and lit up a cigarette. The rain started to pelt around her as she huddled under the smokers' shelter which was otherwise deserted.

She had a deep sickening feeling in the pit of her stomach which wouldn't go away.

Chapter 18

23:30 August 17th 2016

25 hours after Arrest

Peter Arnold was a softly spoken man; a G.P. with a special interest in Forensics. Having trained initially in Pathology, he switched trajectories after five years to re-train in General Practice. Though some days, he missed the mysteries that only the deceased could decipher; the majority of the time he preferred to be surrounded by living testimony.

Fifty-five years of age with a mop of poorly combed snow-white hair, he portrayed a relaxed demeanour which concealed an eagle-eyed attention to detail.

It was 11:30 p.m. by the time he arrived at the entrance to the Murder Unit; wearing his Police Visitor lanyard around the open collar of his blue cotton shirt.

Brian released the security door for him.

"Hi Brian: how's business." Peter yawned and held an outstretched hand as he walked towards Brian; an aged leather Gladstone bag (a hand-me-down from his late father); in his left hand.

"Thanks for coming Peter. Busy one?"

"Non-stop since I came on shift at 'Seven. Busy day at the Practice, looking forward to my bed tonight; or should I say tomorrow morning?"

"So tell me about Dr Schultz: I'm intrigued."

"He's been like it all evening; ever since he saw the photographs from the Crime Scene earlier this afternoon. Hasn't sat down: he can't settle. We've had him on fifteen minute observations. Solicitor can't seem to reason with him. He seems to have closed off to us all. *The Boss is very concerned."*

"And there's no Psychiatric history; that we know of, apart from the possible self-inflicted injury? Anyone speak to him about this yet, during interview?"

"*Let me get you a cup of tea and I'll give you a bit more background.*"

The klaxon came without warning and took no prisoners as the wailing would have woken the dead.

"*SHIT*!" Brian exclaimed and dropped the teas in the vending grill as he raced towards the holding cells.

Peter heard the klaxon as he was washing his hands in the Gents' toilet.

He grabbed his bag and ran out into the corridor; instinctively heading for the Cells.

Sally was kneeling on the floor and had hold of Christophe's legs and was struggling to restrain him as Brian and Dave held his flailing arms. Christophe's face was ashen and his lips blue; his eyes were rolling up into his sockets; exposing his white corneas. They assumed he was fitting.

"*Quick he's ASPIRATED!*" Peter yelled from the doorway as he took in the scene and the plate of barely touched meat balls and spaghetti cast to one side of the cell. He dropped his bag and dashed across the cell and dropped to his knees as he gripped Christophe under the arms and began to drag him up by his torso; struggling to grip him.

"We need to do a *Heimlich manoeuvre* STAT!"

He interlaced his fingers under Christophe's sternum and heaved upwards and backwards burying his thumbs under Christophe's xiphisternum and using an upward thrusting movement: trying to force the air out of his lungs to displace whatever was obstructing his trachea and preventing air entry.

Struggling with Christophe's weight he forced up a second and finally a third time. Christophe made an odd gurgling sound, coughed explosively and a bolus of brown food flew out of his trachea, mouth and hit the wall across the cell; narrowly missing Sally's head.

A loud series fog horn style inspiratory gasps [stridor] filled the cell as Christophe finally took in air. He gulped and vomited pasta down his white jump suit and stopped thrashing. He lay motionless; staring up at the ceiling; eyes blood shot, his carotid pulse racing.

Brian and Dave stood upright as Peter calmly said: *"Okay let's give him some space."*

Christophe bent his knees up to his chest and put his arms around his lower legs.

He whispered something inaudible.

Peter knelt beside him; still behind his head at the far end of the windowless cell.

"I'm Doctor Arnold, Christophe. What can I do to help you?"

Christophe's reply was barely audible.

Peter leaned down next to Christophe's face; smelling sickly vomit.

Christophe's eyes were vacant as he looked up at Peter Arnold.

"Let me die next time."

Chapter 19

01:55 Thursday 18th August 2016

"It was a serious attempt you say?"

"Yes Sir. Peter Arnold believes he aspirated on purpose."

"He's already liaising with a local secure unit to get him admitted overnight. He needs a full Psychiatric Assessment before we can proceed further with our investigation."

"The A.C.C. won't be impressed." Edward Ballard was set in his favourite leather brown arm chair at home as he spoke; *"Rusty"* his beloved Spaniel at his feet. He swirled a Single Malt in his crystal glass. No ice: just the way he liked it.

Sally rolled her eyes as she sat in her office, hugging a mug of freshly brewed coffee. She glanced at her watch: 1:55 a.m.

"With all due respect Sir, we should be thankful he didn't *die in custody."*

The phone was silent at the other end as Edward Ballard took a gulp of whisky; not Dutch courage: more a daily ritual.

"Yes, yes. You did well to retrieve the situation Sally. I'll update the A.C.C. myself. Will you initiate the C.A.P.A. in the morning?

"Yes Sir, though I don't think we could have done anything more or differently."

"'Understood. We'll speak tomorrow. Goodnight Sally."

The line went dead. So we almost lose a suspect and all 'Ballard can think about is the "Corrective Action, Preventative Action [C.A.P.A.] Protocol: *seriously?"*

Sally felt thoroughly pissed off.

Edward Ballard emptied his glass and retrieved Henry Curzon's number on speed-dial.

"Good morning Sir: I'm sorry to wake you. There's been a development in the 'Justin case."

Brian drew up a chair alongside Sally. She looked down-hearted.

"How are you Sally?" He rarely called her anything other than *Boss*. But right now she looked like she needed a friend; not a subordinate.

"Bloody relieved Brian; glad we're not facing a Death in Custody Investigation. All 'Ballard can think about is running a bloody C.A.P.A. to cover our asses with the A.C.C. I hate the bloody Politics. There was a time when this job was about lives, people and doing the right thing."

She sighed and took a long gulp from her coffee cup, burning her lower lip in the process.

She turned to Brian again and asked:

"How's 'Schultz?".

"Dave has just rung me. 'Schultz has been admitted straight from A&E to the *Eden secure unit* where he can rest before he's formally assessed tomorrow; that's to say later today."

Brian glanced at his watch as he corrected himself.

"So Dave didn't leave his side?"

"No, even followed him to the X-ray unit: his chest X-ray was normal."

"No sign of him having aspirated any of the food he choked on."

"Peter Arnold did a good job: arrived just in time." Brian looked relieved and exhausted in equal measure thought Sally as she looked across at his crumpled shirt.

"I need to buy that man a good Single Malt Whisky; he saved our bacon tonight Brian."

Sally had always liked Peter; Professional, caring and good at his job; not in it for the overtime payments like some of the Medics she'd met.

They sat in silence for a few minutes drinking coffee. Sally could feel the urge for a cigarette increasing; she hated herself for having given into the craving again.

"So what do you think of him, Schultz: *you think that attempt was out of guilt for what he'd done*?"

"You still have your doubts Sally?"

She stared vacantly for a moment as she contemplated.

"Let's sleep on it Brian."

"For now, I'm going to get a few hours sleep in my office."

"Camp bed again?"

"Doubt I'll sleep much to be honest with you; too much going around in my head."

"Okay Boss, I'm heading home for a few hours; see you tomorrow."

Sally smiled. *"Good night Brian. Sweet dreams."*

"I wish." He gave a faint smile as he closed the door quietly behind him.

Sally replayed the interview over and over in her mind as she tossed and turned on the camp bed, hastily erected behind her office table; venetian blinds turned down on the office window and the door locked for good measure.

Sleep denied her: she couldn't get Christophe Schultz out of her mind. Something didn't feel right.

Ten miles away Brian sat in bed watching a late night suspense movie. As his eyelids closed, seduced by REM sleep; he replayed another twisted tragic movie scene, a dead suspect in a custody cell.

Chapter 20

9 a.m. Tuesday 23rd August 2016

"Right team: let's kick off!"

Sally stood immaculately dressed in a dark grey two-piece suit with light blue blouse and unusually, was sporting a moderate heel to her matching grey suede shoes. Her hair was pulled tightly back in a single bunch; held in place by a toothed brown hair claw which matched her freshly dyed hair colour.

She stood with her shoulders braced back and was holding a dark green manilla filing folder with a sheaf of paperwork clipped together in her left hand. She placed the file onto the small white table to the left of the display boards which were covered in a variety of forensic photographs and a Police Custody photograph of Dr Christophe Schultz.

Louise sat directly in front of Sally as she opened the meeting.

By way of contrast, Louise looked relaxed wearing a full-length beige cotton dress and her blond hair was held neatly back in place with a black scrunchy. She'd taken an early morning run, followed by forty five minutes of on-line yoga training at 5.30 a.m. so felt chilled and focused.

"This morning, we've formally charged Christophe Schultz with the Murder of Professor Edwina Justin."

The news was greeted with a veritable buzz of verbal approval around the briefing room.

Edward Ballard stood at the back of the room; he had an unusually broad smile which emphasised the crows feet at the corner of his eyelids. He stood proudly erect with his arms loosely folded across his chest; watching Sally intently.

"Good Job Boss." Dave was the first to say what they all felt: she'd led the Investigation from the front. Everyone tapped on the side arms of their chairs in unison.

Sally blushed and raised he right hand in appreciation but behind the smiles and the gracious acknowledgement: she felt drained and exhausted. She dreaded Press Conferences at the best of times.

The real celebration would come later; long after the barrage of Press questions had subsided and without the esteemed company of the Chief Superintendent. Odds on though, he would make an appearance at the Rose and Crown, later' that evening.

Sally had barely managed fours hours of sleep during any night for the previous fortnight and was beginning to feel the strain of sleep deprivation. She was smoking more and surviving on coffee and carbs'.

Louise noticed the dark half-moons under Sally's eyes that she'd barely disguised with make-up at 6:30 a.m. that morning, after dragging herself out of bed for a shower.

Brian stood next to Sally looking chipper and altogether more rested. He'd resumed his old habit of extended late evening walks before reading deeper into the history of Elizabethan England for the previous three nights: one his favourite ways of chilling down as things came to a head in what had proved a challenging investigation.

Brian caught Ballard's eye as he noted that unusually, Edward Ballard was wearing his Queen's Medal awarded for Gallantry in the line of duty, adorning his immaculate uniform; doubtless in readiness for the forthcoming Press Conference Brian presumed.

"This is no time to relax..." continued Sally

Mock groans from Jock.

"And there was me about to book another fishing trip in the outer Hebrides Boss."

"And I've scheduled a full facial." chimed in Louise.

"Aye but I'm handsome enough." retorted Jock with a hearty chuckle; thereby reddening his deep rugged facial features.

"Okay you lot, let's save the banter for later." Brian interrupted, benevolently gesturing with his right arm to calm exuberant spirits. There was a palpable sense of relief around the room.

"The C.P.S. has given the green light to proceed based on the Forensic Evidence which now unequivocally places 'Schultz at the Scene of the Murder."

"In addition to the original DNA semen samples obtained from Professor Justin's body and the Crime Scene finger prints; the anonymous tip off which led to the Forensic recovery of a single surgical glove from a Westminster house-hold recycling bin was *pivotal."*

"Christophe Schultz' finger prints were readily recovered from the inside of the fingers of the glove; and significant semen residue was recovered from the outer surfaces of the latex glove."

"The rectal DNA semen sample extracted post mortem is identical to that recovered from the discarded glove."

"It seems likely that Christophe Schultz disposed of the glove after leaving the Crime Scene and assumed it would never be found."

"Unfortunately as yet, we haven't recovered any CCTV footage from that area linking Christophe to the location by way of tracking his homeward journey. In any event, the bins themselves are in a blind spot as they are positioned behind a series of garages."

"Moving on…"

Sally gestured to the mobile phone extracts on the display board:

"Schultz' mobile phone records and those of Edwina Justin tally up. They had a series of phone conversations initiated by Professor Justin on the day of her Murder." The final message from his phone at 20:15 was made a few minutes after Christophe arrived at Waterloo station at 20:09 on Tuesday 9th August; after which his mobile was turned off. His phone could therefore not be tracked after he left Waterloo station. His signal came back on the grid the next morning at 5:45 a.m."

"Professor Justin agreed to meet 'Schultz at her Apartment and he purchased a train ticket from First Southern Train Company and took his bicycle with him to cycle the route to her Apartment. Records from his Credit Card Company document the date and time of the online purchase of the single journey ticket: directly into Waterloo Train Station."

"The CCTV footage from the First Southern train clearly identifies him on route and he's captured on the station security CCTV cameras, arriving at Waterloo'."

"There is piecemeal, incomplete, street camera CCTV depicting him cycling from Waterloo Station heading towards *Melway Mews* in Mayfair."

"Overall, the travel timelines tie up with the SMS messages and the likely time of death."

Sally moved to her right and pointed at the horizontal timeline depiction which was placed centrally across the middle crime scene evidence board with corresponding annotations written in black marker pen.

"I must emphasise that the CCTV footage is incomplete and that will be a clear priority: *Dave and Karl I want you to share the lead on this task.*"

"We need the complete journey documentation: if at all possible.

"If you need extra resources, speak up."

"Bear in mind of course, that 'Schultz may have left his fold-up bike hidden discreetly somewhere on route and either walked or taken a taxi to the Mews to complete the final segment of his journey. Given that we got a lucky break with the surgical glove: make sure you survey all the traffic CCTV: start within a three mile radius of Westminster and enlarge the survey area accordingly....."

"Keep an open mind and check with all taxi and minicab companies to locate any fares which dropped off or picked up in the region of the Mews during the timeframe after Schultz' arrival at Waterloo. I would start within a three mile radius of the Mews and look at pick-ups through the night from his arrival time at 8:11 p.m. onwards."

Dave and Karl sat shoulder to shoulder and were both taking careful notes as Sally made her instructions clear.

"There's no CCTV footage of 'Schultz entering the area around Mayfair at the front entrance to the Mews and it's likely he went in via the rear, underground garage entrance for which there is no *functional* CCTV monitoring at the time of the crime: though that has since been rectified by the management Company."

"Furthermore, Schultz' knew the six-digit underground entry code, having been back to Edwina Justin's Apartment previously in December 2015."

"By way of background, as you're aware from Dave's work: the Mew's CCTV footage is overwritten every two months so we don't have footage from his Christmas visit."

"Once inside the Mews on the night of the murder, he clearly didn't take the lift, which he would have known has an integral CCTV camera: instead opting for the Fire Escape and stairwell."

"There was no sign of forced entry at the Apartment: *Edwina Justin was expecting him at around 9pm: reference his final text to her* which she read at 8:15 p.m."

"In the event he did arrive on four wheels as opposed to two: he could have arrived at anytime from around 8:30 p.m..." So let's keep in mind the flexibility around the Mew's arrival time-frame."

"If there are no questions around what I've stated so far...." Sally scanned face....then took a pause.

Louise looked perplexed and Sally sensed Louise had a question and she raised her eyebrows.

"Boss can I just clarify the *motive* for the killing at this point?"

"*Yes, thank you Louise: this is the more contentious area of our Case.*"

Sally was well aware of Louise misgivings' around the case and had shared many herself: much to the annoyance of the A.C.C.

"As you're all aware 'Schultz *flatly denies* having entered the Mew's Apartment after their meeting on Boxing Day 2015: claiming he went into London on the 9th August as documented, *but claims to have abandoned his journey after just ten minutes of cycling.*"

"He claims he realised, rather late in the day, it was pointless to argue his case for the drug safety database with Professor Justin and that he decided to accept the consequences of the adverse publicity."

"His journey to her Mews was obviously a private arrangement without the knowledge or sanction of UPL his employers: so he was taking a considerable personal career limiting risk by visiting her at home with an intention to use coercion to change her Professional opinion."

"Hardly a visit likely to be sanctioned by any Doctors' Ethics Committee or the Pharma' Industry Code of Practice handbooks!" Remarked Brian; raising his eyebrows and a wearing a wry smile as he did so.

"Absolutely." Replied Sally succinctly; casting a knowing look at Brian who had taken a rather dim view of Christophe Schultz: given his misguided economic approach to the truth from Day One of their investigation.

"He claims to have hailed a cab and was driven back home." Continued Sally. We have never managed to identify a cab firm with whom the journey was logged so it seems likely it was a freelancer who struck lucky with a journey from Central London out to Surrey."

"Moving onto the time 'Schultz spent in custody and thereafter under psychiatric assessment:"

"Schultz' response to the Crime Scene photographs was dramatic to say the least."

Her mind flashed back to his grey figure lying on the concrete floor as the three of them held him securely; based on the supposition he was having an epileptic fit on the cold concrete floor of the holding cell.

Sally reached across and drew a grey folder out of the green filing sleeve. She flicked open at the page marked with a red place marker stuck to the outer upper edge of the page.

Sally delivered a pre-amble in readiness to read verbatim from a line within the body of the medical report:

"The Forensic Psychiatrist who interviewed him on the Eden Unit regarded him as having entered some kind of "Fugue."

Dr Morrison's report provided the background. Sally read allowed.

"We can characterise a *Fugue* as a Psychologically Defensive state, characterised in the instant case by amnesia for recent [traumatic] events: *given that Christophe Schultz is in total Denial about his [alleged] murder of Professor Edwina Justin.*"

Sally looked up from her paperwork and gave her own brief interpretation of events:

"The Fugue state is rare, but medically well-documented in individuals who suffer an extreme emotional disturbance."

"The dramatic turn of events in respect of the Press Release, which Edwina Justin refused to sanction, given the emerging Safety Signals for U0008 and the possibility of Criminal alteration of patients' blood results: suggests that 'Schultz was under huge personal pressure to *change Edwina Justin's* opinion and management of the Company claims.

"His statement in relation to the Company's Legal response after hearing of Schultz conversation with Edwina Justin pays lip service to those pressures."

"So….his suppressed anger at his treatment by his peers and his personal frustration with his invidious predicament in which he found himself: *may ultimately have triggered his violent response*."

Sally looked thoughtful for a moment and stroked her chin before continuing.

"The mobile phone transcripts and Edwina Justin's critical, bordering aggressive view of his actions; adds further weight to the concept that he reached a tipping point in his state of mind: especially as he seemed to have developed feelings for her which were maybe disproportionate to the time they'd spent together."

"The notion that he just had a change of heart whilst on route to her Apartment stretches the imagination and really doesn't stack up to my mind."

Sally noted that Edward Ballard was nodding his head in agreement with her thinking.

Louise looked thoughtful again and caught held Sally's eye once more.

"Taking on board everything you say about the Forensic evidence and psychiatric opinion though Boss: it's the transition from a serious discussion around the safety of U0008 to the idea of indulging in sex"….

Louise hesitated then thinking aloud continued….."and then transitioning from consensual sex to strangulation and murder…. that's challenging however much strain he was under…."

She used her hands spread out in front of her to convey the transition as she spoke and exemplify her open mindedness.

"I understand your misgivings Louise and you're absolutely right to question the evidence; the Psychiatrists couldn't make progress on those points either."

"However, it is clear that 'Schultz manifested strong feelings for Edwina Justin; despite their limited contact and sexual history."

"Strong feelings bordering on obsession..." added Brian.

This aspect of the case had given Sally sleepless nights and even as she argued the case; she had grave misgivings.

"I think we will face aggressive questioning from his Defence lawyers in due course, under Cross Examination: but the means and opportunity are clear, as are the Forensics; even if the motive appears less easy to substantiate." Sally concluded as she glanced at her wrist watch.

Edward Ballard walked forward as he spoke; mindful that Sally had other commitments pending, including a meeting with the A.C.C that he would also attend.

"You've all done an *excellent job* under D.C.I. Benson's Leadership and as she's already said, the real work continues up to his trial: which may be fast-tracked given the Political ramifications of the murder."

"It's essential with the time-line in place that you review and collate all the CCTV evidence to ensure a smooth documented sequence of events."

"Make sure that all the external and internal CCTV at the Mews is reviewed; we don't want any surprises."

He strode across to the middle display board before continuing.

"I want statements from everyone in the building; I don't care if they're filming in LA or cliff diving in Acapulco: build a clear profile of Professor Justin's public and more importantly, her private life. You did well to track down her remaining distant family in China. I don't want some smart arse Journalist digging up something we've missed; so tie up the loose ends."

"Thank you D.C.I. Benson; I'll see you at 11 a.m."

"Right you heard the 'Chief Super. Let's get back to it. Brian will assign further tasks...."

"Finally, I expect you all at the Rose and Crown for 8 p.m. *The first round is on Brian!*"

She gave him a pat on the back as she left the briefing room; which was already buzzing with lively banter. Her mind was focused on the Press Briefing. She headed for Clare Simpson's office with a strident step.

Chapter 21

12:55 Tuesday 23rd August 2016

Lake Road, Cardiff

Professor Roger Ennis had just finished the ritual dead-heading of the Rhododendron shrubs in his garden as he headed back into the stone-floored kitchen in his oversized green muddy boots. His wife had gone to visit her sister in Carmarthen for the day; so he could please himself. Wearing his tatty old brown check shirt and green corduroy trousers he was happy to potter around the garden all day at leisure.

The Grand-Father clock in the hallway chimed *One o'clock* and he flicked the small red button on the remote control; just in time to catch the BBC lunch-time News as he switched on the kettle.

A hot cup of builders' tea was top of his agenda and Rose had left him scones and an assortment of cheese and pickles for his lunch. She'd reminded him to finish up the celery too; didn't want it going out of date and heading for the composting bin. She needn't have worried; he'd have consumed it a week out of date without any undue concern.

"And we'll be bringing you the latest news concerning the ongoing Brexit negotiations in Brussels; since the triggering of Article 50. But first back to our top story; *here's John Temple with the latest on the Murder of Professor Edwina Justin."*

Using the remote control, Roger Ennis turned up the volume on the small TV sat in the far corner of the kitchen; strategically elevated on a small shelving unit and positioned so that Rose could watch it in the evening whilst she was cooking.

"Thank you. We're taking you live to the Murder Unit in Central London where we're about to hear a statement from *D.C.I. Sally Benson* who had led the investigation into the murder of Professor Edwina Justin; Chair of the prestigious National Institute of Cancer and Oncology: based here in London."

The cameraman framed the face and shoulders of the Detective who read a carefully prepared statement from a set of notes in front of her.

"I am pleased to announce that we have charged a man in connection with the Murder of the late Professor Edwina Justin who was found dead at her London Apartment on Friday 12th August."

"Dr Christophe Schultz a Medical Director from the Pharmaceutical Industry.."

Roger Ennis caught his breath. His stopped mid-crunch and dropped the remaining half of the celery stick he was holding as he grabbed the remote control and turned the volume up louder. Had he heard correctly: *Christophe Schultz*; his former Senior House Officer?

A barrage of questions greeted the closing of the Statement and the Detective raised her right hand.

"At this time, I have no further comment to make."

The questions continued as the cameraman panned to the audience of Journalists: cameras were focused from every available vantage point on the three Participants who sat behind the small desk in front of the Worlds' media.

"Chief Superintendent Ballard: you must be very relieved to have charged the Suspect so quickly in your Investigation?"

Clare Simpson sat on the left hand side of Sally and she looked across at Edward Ballard as he spoke.

"Our first thoughts are of course with Professor Justin's Family, Friends, Colleagues and Loved Ones. I am sure this has and will continue to be a very difficult and painful time for all of them. The Investigation is ongoing and as D.C.I Benson has stated, we have no further comment to make at this time. *Thank you all Ladies and Gentlemen*."

Edward Ballard stood whilst Sally and Clare filed past him out of the glare of the lime-light as questions continued unabated and remained unanswered.

Roger Ennis sat down at the solid oak kitchen table, staring at the TV; *disbelief was putting it mildly.*

The footage cut to *John Temple* again.

"So to confirm the emerging news and today's top story: Police have charged Dr Christophe Schultz in connection with the murder of Professor Edwina Justin at her London Mews: two weeks ago."

Back at the Studio, the Anchorman *Peter Elliot* spoke to *John Temple* by satellite link and posed questions as he spoke.

"*So John*: what do we know about the charged man: Dr Schultz?"

"Well Peter, he'll appear before Magistrates later today and is expected to be remanded in Custody Pending Trial."

"And is it likely that the recent changes in Legislation which have been *driven by the Home Secretary* will impact the timing of the Trial?"

"Yes I believe that's the aim of the new recent Legislative amendments Peter. The Home Secretary made it very clear that with the recent Parliamentary Debate on the adoption of the American System of Justice encompassing a hierarchy of charges for Murder: *those accused of Pre-meditated or First Degree murder*: could see their trials expedited. The length of Mandatory Life Sentences might also increase, equating more closely to those seen in America."

"John do we know anything further about the Suspect?"

"Sources have revealed that a man was taken from Police Custody to a Local A&E Department shortly after his Arrest a week ago."

"And do we know whether it was the Accused; Dr Schultz?"

"We don't Peter; the Murder Unit have refused to comment."

"Thank you John." Turning back to Camera One: Peter Elliot moved onto the next story.

"*Discussions in Brussels today have continued amidst the growing tensions over Article 50*, which has now been triggered and signals the start of what many experts now see as a protracted period of negotiations as the UK disentangles itself from the remaining Twenty-Seven Member States of The European Union."

"*What bloody sources is that TV reporter talking about Edward*?" yelled the A.C.C. at Edward Ballard; his face crimson. Even *Jocelyn Wilson* stopped what she was doing on her computer and thought it politic to take a coffee break in the canteen; no matter she'd just eaten her lunch at her work station. There were some conversations which were well above her pay grade.

"*I'm sure the leak would not have come from my Team Sir.*" Edward stood his ground.

"Well they've got it from someone. *And I want his balls in a vice* if we find any evidence of pillow-talk. The Home Secretary has already spoken to me. If there's a leak: *plug it now*."

"I want the evidence on 'Schultz tied up and the Trial dates in place ASAP."

"I think that's a matter for the C.P.S...." Edward Ballard was stopped mid-sentence.

"*ASAP Edward: 'you hear me?*"

Edward nodded as 'Curzon left; banging the door loudly behind him.

Roger Ennis turned the TV off. He wandered in a daze to the fridge to retrieve the cheese. He chose some low calorie crackers and absent-mindedly discarded the celery in the recycling bin; as he sat down to think.

How on earth could Christophe Schultz be guilty of Murder? *It was unfathomable*. Could his judgement have been so wrong about the character of the young Doctor under his charge: his Mentorship?

What could have gone so radically wrong in the young man's life?

Chapter 22

13:10 Tuesday 23rd August 2016

Molly Hull sat staring at the TV screen. The stuff about the EU went right over her head like a flock of seagulls in her beloved Margate.

She'd watched the lunch-time news with considerable relief to know that someone was to be charged with Edwina's murder; but then in disbelief when she realised it was Dr Schultz who'd been charged. The same handsome and polite young man who'd had lunch with Edwina in her office; just four months ago. And how could he have.....she closed her eyes tightly and willed the images to go away; just as she did every night before darkness enveloped her room at night and terror invaded her dreams.

What had the doctor and counsellor called it: PTSD: *Post Traumatic Stress Disorder*?

"That's what those brave young men and women suffer from that go off to War." she'd said in response to the suggestion.

"I just saw something I should never have witnessed; but now it won't go away."

"And the scene will probably never leave you Molly." the Counsellor had revealed.

He's doing his best she thought as she'd listened to him; but how could he know? He looked barely twenty-five and what did he know about life and more to the point....*death*?"

Chapter 23

13:20 Tuesday 23rd August 2016

Sally could see Edward Ballard smoking in his office behind the desk as she walked towards his office; *Jocelyn Wilson* conspicuously absent from her desk.

He looked fractious as she knocked on his door and he beckoned her in.

"Is that a good idea Sir? In here I mean...the cigarette?"

He took a long slow inhalation; leaned back and exhaled a smoke ring before stubbing out the butt in his saucer.

"Probably not but it's the least of my worries; *our* worries."

Sally could feel it; *shit storm about to hit.*

"You've heard the comments about the leak?"

"The suspect taken to hospital you mean?"

"Yes: *that bloody news reporter.* What else?"

As an after-thought he added:

"Why, Is there something else I should also be made aware of?"

Now it was Sally's turn to look and sound pissed off.

"No Sir and I bitterly resent the implication that my team have been gossiping!"

"Well let me tell you..." he pointed his finger as he spoke..."I *bitterly resent having the A.C.C. chew my bloody ear off!"*

Sally regained her composure; she knew he had a short fuse and she had more important things to be worried about than his pride.

"Isn't it more likely a Journalist or Ambulance chaser made a few pounds on the side?"

"Why would one of *our team* jeopardise all our hard work and put a Prosecution at risk by giving away valuable information?"

Edward Ballard knew she was right.

"Drink?" he asked, removing a bottle of Malt from his left bottom drawer.

"No thank you Sir."

He thought better of it and replaced the bottle; but lit up a second cigarette.

He proffered one to Sally and she took it and pocketed it. She didn't want to appear wounded or churlish.

"Thank you; I'll smoke it later."

He lit up and they sat in silence as he took four deep inhalations before snubbing out the remainder.

"Sally we're a good team. We work well together."

She watched him carefully; noting he'd now broken eye contact as he spoke.

"I wouldn't like to see anything upset the symbiotic relationship we share."

(What am I now some bloody limpet she thought; tethered to your immovable rock. *Fuck you*!)

She stayed silent.

"The A.C.C. has powerful connections as you know. The outcome of this investigation is crucial to our continued success as a team."

(It's for the Judge and Jury to decide the outcome having reviewed the evidence thought Sally; but continued to stay silent).

"If there's nothing more: Sir?" Sally stood up as she spoke. What she really wanted to say was: "And do I give a flying fuck if he plays golf with the P.M.?

He shook his head and she left without comment. *"Fucker!"* she thought.

Chapter 24

13:30: Central London Apartment

"Twelve Good Men and Women: of course they'll make the right decision Molly. *Now don't you worry yourself* about the Investigation and Trial. Let the Police do their job. Try and get some rest."

"But Frank.." protested Molly on the other end of the phone.

"He seemed such a lovely young man."

"Well Molly, we both know appearances can be deceptive."

"Is there anything I can do to help you at the moment?"

"No Frank. Thanks for just.... *being there.*"

"Day or night Molly; I've told you that. If you need me: just ring."

She knew he must be busy; a man down at work and the staff trying to manage with all the Journalists and busy-bodies; to say nothing of the work-load without......Edwina.

"Thank you Frank; take care." Molly ended the call.

Chapter 25

14:20 Wednesday 24th August 2016

"What are you proposing Edward?" asked Sally pointedly as he signed the overtime sheets she'd hand-delivered.

He looked back at her; his poker face firmly in place.

"Let's make sure now that we have our Man, we tie up the loose ends and nail him: *simple as that.*"

He pushed the Manilla file across the desk to her.

Sally thought about the phrase. She didn't like the connotation which for some reason struck her as oddly Biblical. She had a flash-back to Christophe on the floor of his cell; turning grey and close to death.

"I trust your concerns about the case have subsided?"

Sally contemplated her answer carefully; feeling his eyes scrutinising her as she looked over his shoulder to his commendation for bravery; *'Curzon handing him a plaque.*

"I'm sure Justice will be served Sir."

Wrong-footed; he let the comment go.

"Okay Sally; keep me updated."

He opened a thick lever arch file on his desk as she stood up to leave.

"And Sally: no cock-ups on this one." He didn't look up as he spoke.

She left without comment and headed for the smoking shelter for a nicotine fix; Sally text Brian on route.

"He's a heartless bastard."

Brian listened, he knew when she needed to off-load; his ex-wife Annie had been the same.

(Annie would smoulder for days or even weeks; then came the explosion. Totally unpredictable; a plume of smoke if you were lucky, then bang: all the power and ferocity of Mount Etna; followed by days of dark skies; waiting for the metaphorical dust to settle.)

(*Thank God Sally was predictable* and didn't pass the buck unlike his ex'; always playing the blame game with him as the fall guy. *Still every cloud*: she'd been swept off her feet three years ago by an unsuspecting car salesman from Lewisham. He sure wished him luck. Poor unsuspecting sod; *lamb to the slaughter.*)

"*Nail him:* those were his precise words."

"It made me think of The Bible for some reason: right back to good old care-free school days and assemblies. Mr Jones reading from the *Old Testament.*"

"*It bothers me though Brian; this case.* There's something amiss. Something doesn't feel right. It's all too easy."

"Is it the *motive* Sally; is that what's really bothering you?"

"Maybe......It's just...he doesn't fit the mould. I can tell Louise is not convinced either."

"*If the Psychiatrists couldn't unravel him; why should you beat yourself up about it Boss?*"

There was something else she wanted to say; but she was holding back; his intuition meter was at Red Alert.

"*Boss: is there something else?*"

Sally exhaled slowly and pursed her lips.

She knew how perceptive Brian was.

Sally stubbed out the cigarette and turned and stood looking directly at Brian in the shelter; her face like stone.

"This stays between us understand?"

"Sure; of course."

"His lawyer: Georgina. I met with her. We had a coffee"

Brian raised his eyebrows as his eyes widened and his jaw dropped: but he stayed silent.

"Two days after he'd been admitted. She'd seen him in Hospital, on the Eden Psychiatric Unit. Took him some fruit and had a chat with him. He told her something; I don't know what exactly: client confidentiality..."

"She told me there was *no way* he could have committed the Crime."

Brian replied pragmatically, slowly and deliberately; as though grappling with an English comprehension question in a mock exam.

"So, we don't know why but we're supposed to take *her word* for it; the word of an inexperienced lawyer, that he's innocent?"

Brian looked and indeed sounded incredulous at the prospect thought Sally as she read his expression.

"She trained in Medicine before Law. She knows something Brian."

"But the Lord alone knows what he was thinking or saying. He'd just tried to kill himself. How can we take that as meaningful evidence?"

"I know how it sounds."

"Do you think the Evidence will be disclosed?"

"Hard to say, without knowing what he's told her: Doctor to Doctor: Client to Lawyer.

"'Christ I wish I'd not asked." Brian looked deflated. He shook his head and looked heavenward as he spoke.

He lit up another cigarette and proffered another to Sally. She declined.

"Well for *fuck sake* don't take this to Ballard. *He'll take you off the case.*"

"Don't I know it? I guess that's why it was so hard to listen to his bull-shit this afternoon."

"Boss, if there's any doubt when we've looked the entirety of the evidence you know I'll stand shoulder to shoulder with you on this one."

Sally smiled briefly and raised her hand a little in appreciation of his unconditional support.

"Thanks Brian. I appreciate your support. But if the shit hits the proverbial fan; I will take the blast. You keep out of the picture."

She looked him directly in the eye as she spoke.

"We never had this conversation."

He nodded sagely and watched as she walked back to the office; head bowed.

Part Three

Chapter 1

22nd September 2002

"*Earth to Dr Schultz* – are you with us this morning Doctor?"

Professor Ennis stared at Dr Christophe Schultz over his silver horn rimmed spectacles; whilst the attendant Medical, Nursing and Student entourage looked on in complete silence. A moment later, Christophe gathered his thoughts and snapped back into his polished routine.

"*My apologies: Professor Ennis.*"

"This sixty-seven year old retired gentleman was admitted at 11p.m. last night with a two-hour *history of retro-sternal chest pain, radiating to his neck and arms bilaterally*. Mr Hewitt is a former solicitor and ex-smoker with a paternal history of Ischaemic Heart Disease. His GP has treated him for Hypertension for the last five years and diagnosed with *Type 2 diabetes* three years ago; he is currently treated with mini-aspirin, simvastatin, metformin and atenolol."

(Christophe placed tonal emphasis on the site of the chest pain and the recent diagnosis of diabetes: both of which were key indicators of the likely diagnosis. During medical ward rounds, it is routine practice to highlight important markers of past and current disease markers prior to presenting clinical findings. Carefully considered *intonation*, guides the team towards your final conclusion which may be a definitive diagnosis: or range of likely *differential diagnoses*.)

"*On examination*: Mr Hewitt was pale and looked anxious with a tachycardia of 110 beats per minute; and a blood pressure recording of 170 (systolic) over 90 (diastolic). His cardio-respiratory examination was otherwise unremarkable with peripheral pulses present and equal and no signs cardiac failure.

His ECG [*electrocardiogram: in USA EKG*] revealed *mild ST segment depression* in the lateral leads but his cardiac enzymes were unremarkable and his repeat ECG this morning was normal; post GTN sublingual [*glyceryl-trinitrate*] and long-acting intravenous nitrate: both given last night and overnight, respectively.

This morning's haematology and biochemical profiles reveal: a *fasting* blood glucose of 8.6mmol and his blood pressure is 150 over 82."

"Thank you Dr Schultz", replied Professor Ennis with a warm smile as he stretched out his right hand to greet his latest patient.

"*Good morning Mr Hewitt – how are you feeling this morning*?"

Mr Hewitt smiled and responded: "Much better, thank you Professor. My pain has completely settled."

"*Excellent*. We'll take some time to explain the science behind your admission in a while but in the meantime with your permission, I would like one of our medical students to assess your heart? As you're aware, we are a teaching hospital and it's vital that our trainee doctors are able to assess patients soon after admission to prepare them for their future practice."

"*We all have to learn - happy to help*."

Without being asked *Staff Nurse Martin* promptly adjusted the backrest behind the patient's upper body and neatly re-positioned the sheets level with his umbilicus and then returned to join the ensemble of students.

George Hewitt, a retired Commercial Lawyer, lay back in bed with his back rest and pillow inclined at 45 degrees from the horizontal plane. With an ear for detail and an avid follower of medical dramas; Colin Hewitt had already deduced that his blood pressure had been raised on admission and Dr Schultz had explained that the ECG pattern belied a possible indication of heart damage due to lack of oxygen supply as a consequence of coronary artery narrowing; likely to be related to his underlying diabetes.

"*Mr Jones*" instructed Professor Ennis.

 "Please examine Mr Hewitt's cardiovascular system and talk us through your findings; positive and negative."

Christopher Jones' cheeks blushed visibly as he shuffled between his Colleagues towards Mr Hewitt' bed.

Weighing in at eighty-two kilograms and standing just one hundred and seventy-five centres tall; Chris' Jones had earned himself the nick-name "*Animal*"; bestowed by his Welsh friends.

 Chris' had a friendly demeanour which belied his uncompromising and aggressive nature on the rugby pitch.

He greeted most people with the phrase: "Hi Buddy": (which sounded like "*Hi Butty*" by virtue of his Welsh accent).

 Sister Richards who ran ward H7 with near Military precision had once reprimanded him for greeting a patient in such a colloquial and as she viewed it: *unprofessional* fashion; much to the amusement of the other five fourth year medical students seconded to Professor Ennis' team for the duration of their *Block*: (a "block"- literally a twelve week segment of time spent studying the relevant speciality of either Medicine, Surgery as *major blocks* or Psychiatry, Obstetrics, ENT [Ear, Nose and Throat], Anaesthetics or Paediatrics).

As "Animal" picked up Mr Hewitt's hand he began his examination by feeling for the radial pulse on his right wrist (the arterial pulse *palpated* where the radial artery is in close contact with the head of the radial bone on the lateral/outer portion of the forearm): Professor Ennis began his Tuesday morning teaching round with his characteristic enthusiasm.

"Now whilst your colleague examines the *rate, rhythm, volume and character* of the patient's pulse I would like you all to observe Mr Hewitt from the end of the bed, remembering that inspection precedes palpation: *we look before we touch – especially* when examining the abdomen."

"Under examination conditions: *always ask the patient's permission before touching:* remember the patient must consent to your examination despite implicit consent by volunteering their presence in the Hospital in order to assist with students' formal assessment. This is especially important to demonstrate in your *final examinations.*"

"Remember, if you suspect a diagnosis of Rheumatoid Arthritis for example, from *observation* alone: if you provoke pain during a finals exam and certainly at *Membership level of Post-Graduate examination: you may well fail the entire examination!*"

Professor Ennis turned to face 'Animal.

"Your initial findings please *Mr Jones*?"

"The patient shows no signs of distress at rest; his respiratory rate is sixteen breaths per minute and he is not cyanosed." (Distressed in this context is given its *literal* meaning and refers to any perceived difficulty the patient might have when breathing).

"*And would you expect him to be cyanosed*?" interjected Professor Ennis with a slight turn of his head to the right and a narrowing of his eyes as he turned inquisitor.

"*Well no, not from the history..but.*"

Animal crossed his arms and looked defensive as his body posture became suddenly more closed. He hunched his shoulders and shuffled from one foot to the other.

George Hewitt who had always been fascinated by body posture having initially shown an interest in criminal law as a young Graduate Law Student; was watching *Animal* intently.

"Okay, but what clinical feature may well prove to be of *particular relevance* to his presentation? *Remember*... don't fall into the examiner's trap by refining your search to a specific organ system whilst neglecting to mention a key clinical sign *which may pivotal to the diagnosis.*"

Animal fell silent and pursed his lips.

"*Anyone*?" asked Professor Ennis referring the question to the huddled team of Medical students and the three final year Degree Level Nurses who stood alongside.

"Mr Ennis has an enlarged thyroid gland Professor." interjected *Julia* without a moment's hesitation.

"*Exactly*" responded Professor Ennis with a satisfied smile.

"We can forgive Dr Schultz for not mentioning this fact in his otherwise excellent synopsis; particularly given the cardiovascular focus regarding Mr Hewitt's presenting complaint. As you know, a *thyroid disorder* could contribute to a raised blood pressure and might be linked *genetically* to the presentation of diabetes mellitus. An overactive thyroid' might also precipitate angina."

"Central cyanosis evidenced by a blue tinge to the lips, might of course be apparent if the patient had presented with a *congenital heart condition* or significant compromise in oxygenation of his blood by virtue of *chronic lung disease*."

(Cyanosis may be subdivided into *central cyanosis*: a blue discolouration of the lips caused by a de-saturation: a reduction in the oxygen content of the blood; or *peripheral cyanosis*: which might be triggered by simple spasm of the digital arteries to the fingers or toes; [the latter always present if the former is evident.])

Conscious of his nursing contingent on the teaching round, Professor Ennis added:

"I would like you *all* to make a list of the conditions which might present with cyanosis for our next ward round."

"*Miss Simmons*: you can take over the examination once we have finished examining Mr Hewitt's cardiovascular system."

The "*Royal We*" denoted the fact that this was a team effort in

establishing diagnosis, contributing co-morbidities and relevant clinical findings which might or might not be relevant to the presenting complaint of chest pain.

"Please continue." instructed Professor Ennis with a cursory nod towards *Animal.*

"The patient is angled at forty-five degrees in his bed and inspection reveals that his Jugular Venous Pulse is not raised....examination of his radial and brachial pulse reveals a pulse rate of seventy-six beats per minute, with no irregularity of rate, rhythm or character".

(The Jugular Venous Pulse - JVP – is a representation of the filling pressure in the right side of the heart, which receives *deoxygenated* blood from the body via the large veins which empty into the *right atrium*. It is traditionally examined with the patient inclined at 45 degrees from the horizontal or flat position...in order to both visualise the pulse and provide *standardisation.* If a patient has signs of heart *bi-ventricular or isolated right sided* failure, the JVP will be raised and a patient will typically have swollen ankles and may have an enlarged and/or tender liver edge. Other signs of heart failure, particularly if there is left heart failure [left and right=bi-ventricular failure]: will include shortness of breath, which may be acute and severe.)

At this point *Animal* proceeded to expose Mr Hewitt's chest and began examining his thorax, using his hand to "palpate" and locate the apex of the heart beat and then with his stethoscope to listen to the "*Lub-Dub*" of his heart sounds. As he did so Professor Ennis resumed his teaching session.

"Each of you should ensure that you develop an examination routine which is second nature to your practice."

"Remember the routine; inspection, palpation, percussion and auscultation: look, feel, *percuss* the chest to detect fluid or consolidation. *Many students find percussion challenging: practice on a friend or loved one, or each other!*" The students laughed as he raised his eyebrows and gave a little chuckle.

"Remember," Professor Ennis demonstrated in the air with his own fingers as he enunciated his instructions: tapping the middle phalanx of his right middle finger with his left middle finger.

"You're using your fingers to create resonance on the chest wall: so just as a hollow drum if the chest cavity is filled with air, as in normal circumstances, the feeling imparted to your fingers is one of resonance. By contrast, if the lung contains fluid, the chest will be dull to percussion: in this particular instance – stony dull. You and colleagues next to you will hear the difference once your technique is perfected."

"Finally listen. Adopting this step-wise approach you will not overlook significant clues to cardiovascular or respiratory disease, even before you use your *guessing stick*!"

At this point Professor Ennis waved his old stethoscope, his personal "guessing stick"; in the air to emphasise his point. The assembled team gave a light ripple of laughter, attesting to the huge experience and expressly humble nature of Professor Ennis' approach to his Discipline.

He made the point repeatedly, that auscultation, listening to the heart sounds for example; was all about preparing one-self for the extra vibrations from the heart which indicated malfunction of the valves or chambers of the heart, or aberrant blood flow across congenital malformations of the heart structure. *"Learn to anticipate what to expect from the initial steps of your examination!"*

(Professor Roger Ennis MBE [The *Most Excellent Order of the British Empire*: rewarding his contribution to Science: awarded by The Sovereign]; had practiced General Medicine for over thirty years.)

(The son of a coal miner he stood tall amongst his Peers, both literally at one metre eighty-nine centimetres and in Academic Achievement. He had advised the Government of the day for a decade on health initiatives and the delivery of Patient Care; such was the strategic rigour of his approach to the delivery of limited resources.)

(During his brief moments of reflection Roger Ennis missed his student days, not the supposed drunken nights of debauchery experienced by all University students, so much as the camaraderie; with friendships forged during long hours of student "blocks": ward placements which were the true preparation for a life-time of Clinical Practice.)

(Roger Ennis never forgot his roots, his father's face ingrained with coal tattoos when he returned home after his work deep underground; the smell of coal dust clinging in the air of their modest home in Merthyr Tydfil, where his mother toiled in vain to maintain a dust free house.)

(Roger had specialised in Endocrinology early in his Post-Graduate career and chosen the amelioration of the impact of the emergent ticking time-bomb of *Diabetes Mellitus*, as his life's Mission. His father had been justly proud of his son's decision to Practice Medicine, but sadly died of Pneumoconiosis - a coal dust related lung condition - in his sixth decade; long before Roger had entered the highly influential world of Political Medicine. The coal pits of South Wales had claimed many casualties, both young men in pit explosions, which disseminated families; and men in their prime, who died after many years of enduring daily breathlessness; Roger's father had been in the latter cohort.)

Chapter 3

Christopher a.k.a. *Animal* stood like a proud father as he prepared to deliver his definitive summary of his findings arising from the palpation and auscultation of *Mr Hewitt* who lay propped up in bed; studying the young burly Medical Student intently as he prepared to speak.

With a brief nod from his Professor, the stage was his:

"On palpation the apex beat is not displaced, there are no heaves or thrusts and auscultation reveals a *soft mid-systolic murmur*. I would like to inspect the patient's ankles for signs of oedema, palpate his peripheral pulses, in light of his diabetes and exclude an aortic aneurysm by abdominal palpation". Finally, it would be desirable to examine *the retinae of his eyes*, for signs of diabetic retinopathy. Given the murmur, I would request echocardiography."

"*Bravo Mr Jones!*" exclaimed Professor Ennis, with genuine satisfaction.

The progress his penultimate year students made under his guidance; was always a source of great reward to him and his team of clinicians.

"*So Mr Chapman*, please explain the possible significance of the murmur in the light of the patient's history."

He turned to Mr Hewitt and added succinctly:

"We care talking *generally* Mr Hewitt and our comments reference patients as a whole and *not to you in particular*".

Mr Hewitt nodded his appreciation for the thoughtful clarification and smiled.

Taken aback by the question *Gordon Chapman* still looked a bemused and hesitatingly replied:

"Well the murmur could be caused by.."

Christophe's bleep [pager – known colloquially as a *"bleep"*; resonated loudly in the pocket of his white coat as the electronically enhanced female voice announced:

 "CARDIAC ARREST G4, CARDIAC ARREST G4"!!

Christophe leaped around the assembled team, closely followed by his burly Registrar *Dave*, whose bleep had sounded in concert; alerting them both to the unfolding drama three floors below them.

Staff and patients on route to the bathroom or returning from the dayroom parted likes the waves before a ship's bow as Christophe ran the short distance from the four bedded bay into the main foyer of Ward H7. He raced through the double doors into the short corridor which led to the main lobby and by passing the lifts completely he headed for the stairwell; taking stairs two or three at a time. He emerged on floor four and turned sharp right into the G4 link corridor and on into the ward where the receptionist stood open mouthed and gesticulated left with her outstretched arm. He continued on into a side-room already equipped with a portable electrocardiogram and defibrillation trolley. Two nurses were already hard at work: *Gloria* the Ward Sister, firmly barking orders to *Linda*, her Staff Nurse.

Christophe drew breath momentarily as he recognised the seventeen year old patient his Registrar had admitted the night before during their medical "take".

Chapter 4

Robbie De Sanchez was lying deeply unconscious; Sister Gloria Steadman had swiftly inserted a green eighty millimetre *"Guedel"* [oropharyngeal] airway into the patient's mouth to prevent the patient's tongue from falling backwards and obstructing his airway.

Christophe noted the blood stained sputum draining from the corner of the patient's mouth and his blue, cyanotic lips. His chest showed no respiratory effort and *Gloria* began bagging Mr 'Sanchez: intermittently delivering air through the mask applied directly over his mouth and lips; in between chest compressions delivered by *Linda*.

As Christophe moved to the head of the bed to take over the manual ventilation of the patient, *Dave* entered the room, breathing heavily.

 "You must have wings Christophe you flew down here: J-E-E-Z' what's happened to this lad, he only came in last night with a fever and shortness of breath..."

Gloria was quick to interject: "At handover, night-staff noted persistent fever, dry cough and.."

Christophe had seen all he needed and called for *suction, a tube and laryngoscope*.

VF Christophe! Called out Janice as she watched the *saw-tooth* pattern of the ECG trace.

The patient needed intubation stat: he was making no respiratory effort and *Robbie's* pupils were bilaterally dilating. His brain was beginning to starve from the lack of oxygenated blood supply.

Gloria rapidly transferred the suction tube to Linda and took over *chest compressions*; it would be good practice for her junior Staff Nurse to be involved in resuscitation alongside Christophe; he was calm, methodical and intubated patients with all the professionalism of an anaesthetist.

Dave interjected again, gathering his composure as his own respiratory rate slowed (vowing mentally to take up his jogging again):

"Glo', what happened before we arrived?"

Sister Gloria Steadman winced at the acronym *"Glo'"* replacing her full name; or at the very least *Sister Gloria*: in front of her Junior Staff. Although she wouldn't have tolerated the shortening ordinarily; she'd spent a couple of nights with *Dave Dickens* after Doctors' Mess parties at Christmas and New Year at the hospital.

(Despite being married, or perhaps because of it; she enjoyed Dave's attention and didn't want to spoil her infatuation with him only to lose his affections to one of her Staff Nurses: she dreaded the thought of *pillow talk* and what it might do to her reputation in the hospital.)

"Julie was doing his obs' [observations] earlier when he suddenly stared vacantly and collapsed, losing consciousness; she thinks he may have twitched a bit or had a short *convulsion..*"

Gloria had witnessed many cardiac arrests; but few afflicting in-patients as young as this lad. He was barely as old as her beloved son *Mathew*. She looked down at *Robbie* as she spoke; with the caring eyes of both a mother and an experienced nurse.

"Now that would explain the blood stained sputum." Christophe muttered as he gently extended the patient's neck and inserted the angled blade of the laryngoscope scooping the tongue to one side and guiding the 6.5mm Endo-Tracheal-Tube [ETT] into the trachea; *Linda* clearing blood-stained saliva as he did so.

Tube in place; *Dave* used auscultation and checked for air entry in both sides of the chest with his stethoscope, whilst *Christophe* inflated *Robbie's* lungs with the Ambu-bag™; which was connected to an oxygen source on the wall of the cubicle.

"Air entry bilaterally and symmetrical chest expansion!" shouted Dave; above the noise generated by the increasing throng of staff gathering in the small side-room.

Janice, a Senior Staff Nurse was positioning the defibrillator paddles as the monitor confirmed the patient was in Ventricular Fibrillation [VF]: *"All clear, shocking at 200 Joules". Still VF."*

Janice carefully palpated Robbie's left groin for a femoral pulse: a sign that his heart was circulating blood. None was forthcoming. She shook her head at Christophe. *"Absent femoral pulse"* she declared.

"Carry on with CPR - 2 minutes please." Christophe instructed; now firmly in control at the head of the patient and surveying *Robbie* and the team' effort as the crisis unfolded.

Christophe was acutely aware that speed and intervention was of utmost importance in ensuring that *Robbie's* brain received oxygen via his manual efforts of "breathing for him" by inflating his lungs; and *Gloria's* efforts in mimicking the normal pumping function of the heart by external chest compression. The use of the external defibrillator to deliver measured electrical shocks across the axis of the heart would allow the heart to restart a productive rhythm if the team managed to effectively resuscitate the patient.

Dave was busy cannulating the *Robbie's* right forearm with a grey Venflon™: large bore, ideal for fluid replacement and drug delivery. The patient was young and his veins although constricted by virtue of his acute cardiovascular collapse and low blood pressure; were no match for Dave's manual dexterity.

"Okay I'm in, time for blood gasses Christophe?" A rhetorical question but Dave enjoyed empowering Christophe during cardiac resuscitation: he could see he had all the hallmarks of a competent Medical Registrar, and knew he had caught the eye of several of the Consultants on the Professorial team to which they both belonged.

(Although senior in training and years qualified; Dave deferred the final decision to Christophe during this acute resuscitation as he was currently competently "leading" the team; a role typically occupied by a Senior Medical Colleague [or Accident and Emergency Consultant] who traditionally was *"hands on"* with the team effort rather than acting as a

Director of Operations in *a hands' off capacity which is the current vogue).*

"Go for it, you've got less than a minute." Christophe sounded calm, though the beads of sweat on his forehead disclosed his underlying determination to get the job done quickly and effectively.

The Pre-heparinised syringe was quickly full of arterial blood taken from the patient's left radial artery: (ordinarily a painful procedure as the needle is advanced until the distal end of the radial bone is pricked, before pulling back slightly and puncturing the artery).

"Job's a good 'un." announced Dave pragmatically. He handed the syringe to *Julia;* the fourth year medical students who'd arrived to observe process and report back to the rest of the team on G7.

Dave smiled radiantly at her as he noted she'd already filled out the request form and was ready to hand-deliver the sample to the biochemistry laboratory where the blood gas analysis would guide the correction of any *primary or secondary disturbance in pH of the patients' blood.* [The patient's blood would typically show an acidotic pattern due to the paralysis of respiration following a cardiac arrest or respiratory arrest.]

"All clear: shocking 200J."

Everyone stopped momentarily and stood back from the bed as *Janice* delivered another electrical shock via the two paddles placed across *Robbie's* chest. His body leaped momentarily off the bed as the shock was delivered.

 "Still in VF!" Janice announced; her voice having risen an octave from her normal speaking voice.

She felt again for a femoral pulse; but none was palpable. *"Still no pulse!"*

"Okay, Adrenaline please Dave." instructed Christophe; feeling calmer and all the while continuing to ventilate the Patient's lungs with his

manual compressions via the Ambu' Bag™ with his left hand; as he stabilised the patients jaw with his right hand.

"Adrenaline delivered. Now 9:05 a.m." Dave recounted; noting with approval that Janice was dutifully scribing on the Patient's drug chart: recording all administered medication in preparation for the doctors' completion of the medical notes and to ensure all treatments were duly recorded.

"Shock 400 Joules Janice." Christophe instructed and Robbie De Sanchez body leaped involuntarily for a third time from the bed as everyone stood clear.

"Sinus Rhythm: Christophe!"

"Yep I've got a pulse mate!" announced Dave excitedly.

Janice's shout was exuberant as she watched the monitor switch from the saw-tooth pattern of ventricular fibrillation: back into a sinus rhythm of eighty beats per minute. She shot him a quick glance and a warm smile of admiration; reciprocated by Christophe's transient grin as he confirmed the patients' pupils were less dilated.

At that moment *Dr Anil Sharma* arrived, weaving through the throng, wearing theatre blues and "white" theatre clogs, discoloured brown by heavy use in Theatre emergencies over the years of his work.

Seeing Christophe at the head of the bed he smiled broadly showing two rows of immaculately polished white teeth and greeted Christophe:

"Hello mate: doing MY job for me again? What have we got?"

Dave interjected:

"Seventeen year-old – *Robbie De Sanchez* flew into Cardiff Airport last night; 'Paramedics brought him directly from the 'Plane. He had complained of fever and shortness of breath during the five hour flight from Cyprus. No known previous' history; febrile thirty-eight (degrees Centigrade) on arrival, with tachypnoea, rate of eighteen to twenty breaths per minute; a few isolated rales in his chest. His sats' (*blood oxygen saturation percentage*), were ninety-eight percent on 100 percent oxygen which the Paramedics had administered during transfer."

"ECG on route was normal; twelve lead (ECG) on the ward was equally unremarkable, as were his blood gasses. We did the usual bloods, including three sets of cultures."

"Chest x-ray showed bilateral diffuse infiltrates, suggesting infection but nothing specific to hang your hat on...."

Sister Gloria took up the story:

"Night staff said Robbie was pyrexial; 37.8 degrees Centigrade this morning despite four hourly doses of One Gram of Oral Paracetamol last night. He felt nauseated and refused breakfast."

"Whilst having his obs' done this morning he suddenly stopped talking, and promptly lost consciousness; his eyes rolled and he started twitching and *may have had a seizure*..."

"That would fit with what we found when we arrived at about 9 o'clock.." *Christophe added* as he stood to the left of Anil who had seamlessly taken over control of the Patient's airway and was pumping the Ambu' bag™.

"I noted he had blood stained saliva prior to intubation, he has a small laceration on the right side of his tongue and as I put the tube down I could see ulceration of his pharynx....we've shocked him twice at 200 and once at 400J which brought him out of VF; second time we gave him adrenaline IV through his ante-cubital vein. Blood gases are on route."

"Okey dokey, that's brill' team." said Anil. "Thanks everyone. *Grrrreat team work*!"

He roared the *Great* like an affable lion for maximum effect.

"It's his lucky day: we've actually got a bed *free* on ICU [Intensive Care Unit].

He gestured to Dave with a nod of his head then he checked the Endo-Tracheal tube was well secured and ensured bilateral air-entry in the Robbie's chest; listening to the Patient's chest with his own stethoscope. He looked up at the monitor and checked that the patient remained in sinus rhythm then instructed:

"OK: *Lead on McDuff*!"

Working under the directive of the ever popular *"Dr Anil"* as the team called him; the assembled group cautiously wheeled the Patient's trolley to the lifts and transported him to the Intensive Care Unit; where he would remain' under the watchful eye of the Unit's brightest Anaesthetics' Registrar: until he regained consciousness.

Chapter 5

Friday 8th July 2016

The pungent odour of burnt popcorn clung to the early evening air as *Dan Ennis* left the crowded entrance hall of the Central Railway Station in Amsterdam [NL]. He adored the city with its eclectic mix of cultures, food, clubs, galleries and people and especially the evening scent of marijuana; which invariably clung to the back of his throat on even the shortest of walks in the nightclub area of the City.

Trams, bicycles and cars intermingled imperceptibly around him; not like the snarling mass of congested traffic he had left behind in London a few hours previously.

His flight from London Heathrow Terminal 5 had been on time and the Sprinter™ train journey from Schiphol Airport had been a breeze; he had a few hours yet before *Archie's flight* arrived from *New York*.

The bicycle bay was crammed outside the Hotel and Dan made a mental note to book a leisurely city tour for Saturday afternoon. Archie would relish the opportunity of ambling alongside the network of canals and coffee houses whilst accumulating some mood enhancing exercise on two wheels. Archie was just as addicted to his endogenous dopamine release inside the *amygdala* of his brain's *limbic system:* the core of the emotional and behavioural centre of the brain.

(*Dopamine: "the feel good neurotransmitter". That's how his father had explained it to him years before he discovered Google™ and realised that dopamine underpinned everything from his craving for food and his reward directed sexual behaviour!*).

"Good evening Mr Ennis, welcome back to Amsterdam, how was your flight?"

"Effortless thank you: *Ingrid*." replied Dan flashing a look at the receptionist's name badge.

Handing her his pre-paid hotel voucher supplied by his airline and his Charge Card for "extras", he retrieved his Passport and waited patiently whilst Ingrid completed his electronic Registration.

Handing him two key-cards to the fourth floor she smiled as she added:

"Enjoy your stay: *both of you!*"

With a broad grin Dan nodded and headed straight for the bank of lifts immediately behind him which whisked him effortlessly to the fourth floor.

Twin beds were neatly folded down and a small Belgian Chocolate offering was carefully perched on each freshly starched white pillowcase. Dan turned on his electronic tablet and selected a Greatest Hits album by his male idol. Familiar lyrics danced around the room, interrupted only by the distant noise of trains rumbling through the nearby station.

Chilling on the bed, Dan's thoughts switched straight to his handsome Archie and their plans for the weeks ahead. Three days in Amsterdam then a flight to Berlin and back to London for their final week. It felt like forever since he had held Archie and he could feel the mounting anticipation in his denim Jeans as he grew hard.

Archie had returned to New Jersey a year ago to be with his family after his dad had been diagnosed with Alzheimer's disease. At just fifty-nine the disease had been rapidly progressive and Archie knew at once that he must support his Mother during what was likely to be a difficult year; and so it had proved, *for all of them*.

Alfred had died three months ago, since which Dan's conversations with Archie had felt increasingly strained; some-times Archie felt far more distant than the thousands of miles which separated them.

Dan had convinced himself that this chain of events would put a strain on any relationship and tried to put negative thoughts to one side; 'all that would be forgotten tonight. Reaching for the half-bottle of vodka he had in his shoulder bag Dan took a big swig from the bottle as he settled back on the bed humming along to the words cascading across the room from his tablet.

The rumble of a passing train woke Dan and flicking a look at his watch he realised it was already half past seven. He stretched and yawned, grateful for the impromptu rest. Archie should have landed in Schiphol Airport by now.

He checked his phone. Two new text messages; one from his mother wanting to know how his flight had gone, and a voicemail prompt.

 "Ah finally; he said excitedly, doubtless he's in the taxi right now!"

Reclining against two pillows, he speed-dialled Archie.

After what seemed an endless wait, Archie picked up.

"Hello Dan, how are you?" said Archie, tension palpable in his greeting.

"Hi Archie mwah! *Great to hear your voice finally! How long before you get here fella*?"

"The beds are lush! The clean white cotton smells heavenly."

Silence greeted his question.

"Archie, 'you okay?"

"Dan, it's not easy to speak right now...."

"No worries, call me back Archie, is the traffic bad or is your signal poor?"

"No, nothing like that...I....*I won't be coming* Dan"

"Not coming; are you held up...at the airport...?

For a moment Dan's thoughts were racing, surely Archie hadn't put a joint in his hand luggage, *like the time in Australia when he was a teenager when*...

"No mate, I mean I won't be coming to Europe".

Dan sat open mouthed – stunned by the revelation; unusually, completely lost for words. The sentence bounded backward and forward between his auditory and frontal cortices of his brain as he tried to process what he had heard.

"Dan: you there?"

"Yes – *I'M HERE,....*" snapped Dan; suddenly feeling hurt and bewildered....he could feel his cheeks flushing and his heart beating ten to the dozen; so had his instincts been right?"

"*Archie what the HELL is going on*?" continued Dan, sounding more assertive than he felt; swallowing hard he cleared his throat and continued, less assertively and trying his best to be empathetic and hide his disappointment:

"*Is it your mum, do you both need more time to get over your dad...together*?"

"Sure more time would be good Dan; *but it's more than that..*"

Archie's voice drifted off and Dan thought he could hear him quietly sobbing. He waited, put his phone on speaker mode and lay back ready to listen: *focusing as much on what Archie didn't did say as much as what he was actually revealing...*

"Dad, all that time at the hospital it was hard on us both, on everyone. Watching him day after day, some days like the old days talking about cars, fishing, holidays when I was a kid and then other times...he was so...*so..bloody angry* and *hostile*, lashing out at us". More gentle sobbing.

"*It's been shit, shit man, total SHIT.*"

Archie was now openly crying at the end of the phone, his words staccato; followed by more silence.

After a long pause Archie seemed more composed.

He sighed heavily and Dan could picture him drying away his tear stains on his lightly tanned soft white cheeks.

"We' been pretty strung out, mum, me, crying a lot, Counselling was good for her..but....well I couldn't, not with a stranger; Nurses' were great though, couldn't do enough for us..."

Dan waited, knowing there was more to come and Archie needed to let it all out.

 "Guy was Dad's Lead Nurse he took real good care of him, like one of his own, we talked a lot; at night especially when he was on shift. I did part time work at a cash and carry; you know, bit of money for the car and stuff. So at night I spent time there, that was the worst time for dad, he was always worse at night: sun-downing they call it. The combination of the dark and literally the sun going down aggravates their confusion.."

A deep rooted feeling told him the sun was definitely starting to set for one of them...both of them...

"That is normal in dementia" Guy told us; "whatever normal is: sometimes I wonder about frigging normal."

"YOLO" says Guy – "you only live once". He uttered an embarrassed laugh at the end of the 'phone; trying to lift his own spirits as he narrated his story, emotions flooding back into his twenty-two year old heart.

"Too true Archie, too true." interjected Dan.

"So how are things with your mum?"

"We're closer, we talk a lot about Dad and the old days, before he got sick; even Guy says..."

"So Guy....he was dad's Nurse yeah - he's...still in touch, supporting you both?"

Dan prompted quietly and slowly. His mind was now buzzing.

No reply, just the sound of Archie gently sobbing again.

It was now beginning to make sense to Dan; nights' together, emotional support becoming something more...intimate.

Dan waited, saying nothing; but he needed to know the truth.

"*Okay Archie, take a deep breath*; I am not angry, I just need you to be straight with me."

"Are we still *together*, I mean, a couple....or..."

Clearing his throat, Archie was summoning his strength; Dan could feel it.

"*Dan, I'm real' sorry....*"

Silence again.

"It just happened sort of *naturally*...."

"*Guy was here, you weren't and I needed.......*needed support and well you know... we are just good friends, *really*."

"*I didn't know how to tell you..Dan....hardest thing.....*" his voice trailed off.

Silence on the end of the phone.

 "Good friends, like we're *just good friends* you mean?"

 "*Isn't that what you used to tell your mum and dad and friends at home Archie?*"

"*Just EXACTLY how close are you with Guy, Archie?*"

"Level with me *please*?"

The sound of silence at the other end of the phone now grew deafening loud to Dan.

 "*Archie I need to go now*" said Dan quietly but decisively. "*I need time to think and ...*"

Dan ended the call and sat staring at his phone on the bed.

His screensaver showed happier days for the two of them, arms wrapped around each other, cheeks touching, with *Notre-Dam Cathedral* looming large in the background.

Paris had been - special: a city made for *good friends* who were also *lovers*.

Archie slumped back and took several gulps of vodka.

A text message read: "*Sorry: Guy and I are together. I'm so sorry Dan.*"

"*FUCK, FUCK, FUCK!*" echoed Dan as he re-read the message over and over.

Chapter 6

Dan hardly noticed the moist frosty evening air as he exited the Hotel through the revolving doorway just after 9 p.m. He replayed his Trans-Atlantic conversation over and over in his head; his mood darkening with each iteration. Perhaps he should have been more understanding, more compassionate; but he was the one *here* in Amsterdam, alone, rejected and pissed off. And Archie, well he had a new love in his life.

Dan headed across the ornate stone bridge directly outside his hotel and turned right towards the main traffic intersection opposite the Central Railway Station; heading south in the general direction of the infamous Dam Square. The thought of throngs of Friday night revellers enjoying beer, puff, and exchanging travel stories and banter helped lift his ailing spirits.

Trams and taxis were whisking travellers to the four corners of the City but Dan always preferred the hub of European cities for his entertainment; why travel miles back to your Hotel after a good meal and bottle or six, of great *Dutch beer*?

As he walked purposely towards his destination, he rubbed shoulders with backpackers with an abundance of American and English voices vying to make themselves heard, many heading towards the notorious Red Light District, sharing bawdy stories of Night Club antics and working girls' tricks of the Trade.

Dan knew the back streets well and soon found himself in a narrower cobbled street, full of ruts, meandering cyclists and small outlets displaying rubber paraphernalia and wet-look sado-masochistic outfits. These were not his thing but he stopped to take a look, none the less, as he was in no particular hurry.

A small red lamp hung above a dimly lit narrow entrance and he entered the smoke-filled aptly named *"Guys Bar"*. His eyes smarted at the intensity of the marijuana fumes, coughing slightly as he navigated through the intimate huddles of drinkers.

"Pint of lager please Fella!" he called to the olive-skinned barman who had immediately caught his eye as he snaked his way to the bar.

Dan found a cosy area next to the roaring log fire; momentarily bumping into a couple of ripped guys in complementary skinny white tee-shirts. They were exchanging mobile numbers.

"Sorry Guys." nodded Dan.

"No worries Limey!"

The Australian guy's response was as warm as the fire Dan was now using to defrost his chilly buttocks.

Thank God I'm out of London, thought Dan, his mind wandering back to the coffee bar in Bangkok where he had first met Archie; Thailand the *"Land of Smiles"* where a smile came from the heart:

"Jai dee kab": in Central Thai dialect: literally a warm heart.

All too often if you could procure a smile from a stranger in London it was at best a contraction of facial muscles thought Dan; his mood darkening again as his spat with Archie came back into his thoughts.

"Weight of the world, mate?"

"Sorry?" snapped back Dan, sounding unintentionally brusque as he turned and looked up to the stranger now at his right side.

"You looked, what do you English say, *melancholy?"*

"Long day that's all." muttered Dan, softening his tone and dropping his tight shoulders.

"Is that a Russian accent I detect?" asked Dan with a smile.

"Ah a comrade in arms!" came the animated reply.

"Sergei: *'at your service!"*

With a mock bow the blond figure now ahead of him came closer to Dan and held an outstretched hand.

Dan returned the Russian's smile, this time from the heart. He immediately noticed Sergei's vice-like handshake.

(*"You can tell a lot by a man's handshake Dan."* His father had constantly reminded him when Dan was a teenager.)

Sergei held up his pint and Dan met his with an enthusiastic: *"Dastroviya!"*

"Dan – from London"

"So *Dan from London*, what brings you to Amsterdam?"

Dan hesitated for a moment, thinking of his last visit with Archie and he suddenly felt a sickening wrench in the pit of his stomach.

Sergei stood silently, fixing his gaze upon Dan, as if sensing his vulnerability.

A roar of laughter exploded at the bar as one of a young group of lads produced an oversized black dildo on which he began to demonstrate his skills with his left hand. Dan and Sergei joined in the laughter and as Sergei shouted his approval Dan looked at the well built Russian who was dressed in a black tee-shirt and blue jeans. His chiselled features, muscular forearms and short cropped blond hair certainly labelled him a *"Catch"*; as Archie would doubtless have said.

As they continued to watch the group it seemed to Dan that the night might not be so dire after all.

As Sergei turned to Dan he finally responded.

"Sorry Sergei, I don't mean to be a wet blanket, I was let down by a good friend".

Sergei looked puzzled. "You have a..., *wet blanket*?"

"No, No, I mean, oh Jeez, sorry...I..."

"What is it with you English boys, always *sorry* about something?"

Sergei looked Dan straight in the eye and then began to smile, then laugh, first quietly and then with a roar like the powerful, perfect Russian bear he resembled.

"Now you're taking the piss!" retorted Dan with mock indignation.

"Yes now I see you smile *Dan from England*; come we drink more of this "Dutch piss": *sorry* here you say *beer* I think".

As Sergei headed for the bar the group of teenagers ahead of him parted, giving him a friendly pat on the back and triggering another round of laughter as the dildo made a re-appearance.

The fire was now defrosting both Dan's taught buttocks and his spirits, *or maybe that was Sergei*; either way a couple more pints would fit the bill; though he started to feel the first pangs of hunger as a pint of the local brew and a glass of vodka were thrust into his hands.

"Bums up!" exalted Sergei.

"I think you mean bottoms." corrected Dan.

"*Yes, up your bottom*," replied Sergei with a mischievous wink of his right eye.

They laughed in unison and Sergei downed his vodka in one and Dan followed suit.

Replete with the spiced chicken kebabs they had shared an hour before, Dan and Sergei swayed along together in alcohol-fuelled banter; and the security guard outside the revolving door paid them scant attention as they entered the Hotel Foyer.

Dan directed Sergei to the left of the lobby and the Russian appeared to stumble a bit as they entered the lift alongside a middle-aged German couple. As the couple exited hand-in-hand, they waved goodbye with a cheery salutation and knowing smile:

"Guten Nacht!"

"What'd 'ee saay?" asked Sergei, slurring his words.

"They said "*Good Night*" to us." responded Dan.

As they left the lift and turned towards room Four-Seventeen; Sergei wrapped himself around Dan's shoulder.

Once inside Sergei headed swiftly into the bathroom and was evidently trying to compete with the *Niagara Falls*; judging from the noise of cascading water emanating from the bathroom.

Dan switched on his tablet and shuffled through to an easy listening compilation from the Nineteen-Eighties' and riffled through the mini bar which had been stocked following his request to Reception earlier in the evening.

He retrieved and emptied four bottles of Smirnoff Vodka® and offered Sergei a glass. Without hesitation they both emptied the contents with a salutary clink of glasses, whilst making a futile attempt at a karaoke sing along.

Sergei slumped back on the bed nearest the mini-bar pulling Dan alongside him with a single sweep of his powerful right arm. A classic rock salad played in the background and Dan smiled and thought of

Archie as the words filled the room. He heard only the positive encouraging vibes of *"you're indestructible..."* sung with a Russian accent by Sergei, who was engulfing him as a bear does it cub: just as his mother had done as a child.

Dan felt Sergei's left hand stroking his face as he drifted into a deep sleep; filled with vivid lurid dreams.

Chapter 8

Saturday 9th July 2016

The shrill hotel telephone ring woke Dan with a start.

Instinctively he reached right and then correctly chose left, and retrieved the receiver from the hotel telephone which rested on the small cabinet between the two single beds.

"*Good Morning Mr Ennis*, this is Natalie from Reception. *Do you wish to extend your stay Sir*?"

Dan tried to take in the words, feeling disoriented:

"*No why would I need..... Sorry. What time is it*"?

"12:30 Sir: I think you oversleep *maybe*?"

"Yes, sorry, yes I must have...can I call you back please?"

"Of course Sir, just ask for Natalie." The phone went dead.

Dan sat up: too quickly. The room span around a little; the mini-bar looked out of focus for a moment. Dan rubbed his eyes feeling distinctly jaded; his mouth as dry as an archaeological bone. He slumped back down on the bed.

The room was silent. With the distant rumble from a nearby train he began to orientate his mind.

Dan stood up slowly, leaning forward a little; steadying himself on the mini-bar and coffee bureau adjacent to the bed as he did so. He headed toward the bathroom and the bed next to him was tidy with the corner turned back and the chocolate where he'd left it...*where was Sergei*?

His body ached and he felt discomfort in his jaw and lower back; he needed to pee desperately.

Alarm bells started to ring in his head: had Sergei robbed him?

He turned around, maybe a little too quickly as he head began to spin once again: his tablet lay on the writing table where he'd left it the night before.

He explored the room at a more hesitant pace: his hold all was on the luggage rack just where he'd unpacked it and he went to the wardrobe where his shirts hung. His wallet was still in his jacket pocket, with his bank cards and a wad of Euros.

He took a pee, then Dan sat on the unused bed nearest the bathroom and tried to gather his thoughts.

"I need to rehydrate," he heard himself say out loud; wasn't that what his father had always said before he packed his son off to University?

"We're all two-thirds water Daniel. Rehydrate your brain; *especially* when you've been drinking alcohol."* He recalled the worldly-wise looks his father would give him over the rim of his silver framed spectacles.

The large bottle of sparkling water from the mini-bar brought a welcome relief to his parched mouth and he cleaned his teeth with the remnants before calling reception and thereafter; climbing gratefully into the hot power-shower. The steam rose in billows around him like cumulus clouds as he tried to piece together the events of Friday night.

Towelling down he donned a fresh white cotton shirt and changed into his dark brown jeans and put his Nike trainers back on without socks. He wolfed down the complementary chocolate from the spare bed.

It was 1.30 p.m. on the dot.

He had returned Natalie's call and agreed a late departure for 2 p.m. He checked his mobile. Two texts from his mum; *how were his Flight, Hotel and Dinner with Archie*?

He reciprocated with a brief text: *"everything's fine; call you in a few days"*.

But everything was far from being fine; at that moment in time his entire World seemed to be spinning out of control; rather the way his head had been when he first woke to the noise of the telephone.

First Archie's *betrayal; now Sergei*?

'Christ' so much had happened; had he really been that pissed last night that he couldn't even remember getting back to the Hotel?

Dan packed his bag and checked out; neither Natalie nor her assistant Kelly; could recall seeing anyone resembling Sergei leave the hotel earlier in the day. That said, both of them had started work at 7.30 a.m.

So maybe Sergei simply had an early start, a flight or a train. But surely he'd have left a note or something?

The sun felt warm on Dan's skin and he began to feel calmer as he chose a white sofa style seat in the Cafe outside the Hotel; strategically positioned under the awning of a large plum-red coloured umbrella. The deep white cushion and pillow felt sumptuous as he relaxed back and thought of Archie.

The young dark-haired waitress smiled obligingly looking him directly in the eye as he ordered a double espresso, sparkling mineral water and two warm croissants with raspberry jam. Her warm smile complemented the bright afternoon sun as she recorded his order on her smart pad.

Dan sat looking at the buzz of activity as groups of all ages cycled along the road outside the cafe and trams hummed past the Central Station in the distance; gently clanging like the metal workers in an old forge, as they crossed tracks on the nearby exit roads.

He was deep in thought when his order arrived and he wolfed the food like a half-starved prisoner whilst he swilled down the espresso in three gulps.

Dan slowly sipped the sparkling mineral water, closing his eyes as he felt enveloped in the warmth of the early afternoon sun. But try as he did, he still couldn't piece together the jigsaw of events of the previous night. His conversation with Archie came back in fragments....his emotional reaction to Archie's new *friend...what was his name*?

Dan moved his eyes repeatedly left to right and back again in a horizontal plane - recalling that this manoeuvre stimulated the retrieval of long-term memory: though the neuro-physiological basis of the activity evaded his non-scientific brain.

"*Can I bring you more coffee Sir*?" asked the blonde waitress hovering at his right shoulder.

"*Yes please, better make that another double espresso*." replied Dan

As she started to walk away he called after her:

"*Oh sorry... and a large freshly squeezed orange juice... and another croissant please*?"

"*Definitely a case of the post-hash munchies*": thought the waitress as she headed for the kitchen. '*Bet he had a good night last night*. She looked at her watch anticipating her early finish and her date with *Antonio*: well endowed and an apartment in Central Amsterdam. She licked her lips in sexual anticipation: what more could a girl ask for on a Saturday night?

Dan checked his phone for new messages: none. As an afterthought, he clicked into contacts and rapidly scrolled down the entries; none for Sergei. It was as though he'd never existed.

It seemed the more he thought about the night before, the less he could remember. Most troubling was whether he brought Sergei back to the Hotel with him or did he simply dream that part of this.... *empty nightmare*?

The Restaurant section of the Cafe started to fill up with guests as the late-afternoon tea brigade began arriving, which Dan took has his cue to leave for a more tranquil spot to contemplate his next move: he needed to find answers to the growing list of questions in his head.

Part 4

Chapter 1

Old Bailey

Central Criminal Court: Day 57

Wednesday November 23rd 2016

Cooke L.J. Presiding Judge:

"*Mr Sudeck*, the closing case for the Prosecution if you please."

Mr Sudeck Q.C. Counsel for the Prosecution rose to his feet and adjusted his robes momentarily, nodded briefly and in his mind's eye he approached the Members of the Jury with long deliberate strides and positioned himself majestically before them.

"Thank You. Your Lordship, May it please the Court: *Members of the Jury:*"

He spoke slowly and deliberately without pause or hesitation: his voice unwavering with pre-determined intonation. His eyes passed slowly and methodically from one juror to another as he spoke from the lawyers bench. He surveyed their individual faces: his dark hazelnut-brown eyes burning with passion and unyielding determination.

"Professor Edwina Justin held two prestigious appointments in Society: she was Deputy Chair of the Pan European Pharmacovigilance Evaluation Unit and she implemented, chaired and nurtured the National Institute of Cancer and Oncology."

"As you heard from Professor Stanley's eminent testimony, N.I.C.O is a charitable organisation which formulates, implements and independently funds studies in cancer; all around the World.

"In her capacity as Chairman of the Organisation, and unlike many of her contemporaries; Professor Justin's remit extended far beyond Country barriers and subordinated regional political considerations."

"In short, she was a respected World Renowned *Thought Leader* who evaluated the risk of novel drug treatments developed by Government departments, University institutions, Hospitals and Pharmaceutical Companies: for the *benefit of Mankind*."

He spread his long slim fingers and arms wide as he spoke, embracing the World around him as many a World Leader would do: omnipotence at his finger tips. His aged grey wig sat perfectly positioned atop his slick coal-black immaculately combed back hair; peppered with flecks of grey upon his side-burns.

Adam Sudeck Q.C looked distinguished and resilient in equal measure: a Preacher, Politician and Orator rolled proportionately into one.

"Professor Justin *judiciously and slavishly* balanced the risks versus benefits of *new drug treatments*, to ensure that the pendulum swung compellingly in *Our Direction*; that *we*: that's *you and me*, members of the Jury........."

(He dorsiflexed his wrists [backwards] so capturing his twelve member audience, then flexed his writs towards himself as he delivered the *"you" and "me"* respectively; then continued:)

"Might benefit from such medical breakthroughs..... without the undue burden of "Adverse Events", colloquially known as side-effects."

He momentarily returned his arms to his side, then he placed his right hand across his cardiac area and paused: a look of longing and hurt crossed his face as he looked from left to right at the faces of the Jury: darting between the rear and forward row respectively.

"Her untimely death was nothing short of a tragedy for her family, friends and the Medical Community as a whole...*for you and me...and our families, present and future.*"

(He repeated the movement of his wrists and hands as he spoke: emphasising ownership.)

A fiery look flashed across his features..

"But a calculated risk for the Perpetrator of this heinous crime."

He widened his eyelids, inhaled and turned his whole body around to the right....keeping his feet pointed toward the Jurors..

He pointed directly at Dr Christophe Schultz who sat impassively in the dock: flanked either side by a Policeman.

"The accused stands before you: a brilliant but M-A-L-E-V-O-L-E-N-T MIND."

He turned back to the Jury in a calm and pragmatic manner, he continued to instruct.

"Dr Christophe Schultz trained in all aspects of drug development. He excelled in a Commercial environment spending his days *manipulating risk* for Company Profit."

He looked indignant as he continued his derision. His shook his head and exhaled.

"In his eyes, Patients became mere "subjects": de-humanised and data rich mines, ripe for exploitation."

Then he started slowly with a steady eye and firm jaw-line poised to deliver his damning testimony.

"The Prosecution has described how Dr Schultz *meticulously planned* the murder of Professor Justin: visiting her London apartment under cover of darkness, subjecting her to a barbaric and tortuous series of sexual assaults whilst she was under the influence of an *unlicensed sedative drug*. A drug so unusual that it took a small team of expert medicinal scientists to evaluate its potential for harm."

"His final callous act was to strangle his helpless victim: then stage her body in a grotesque and dehumanised fashion: before he *cowardly* made good his escape into the night."

"But as Professor McKinnon so expertly enunciated, the Accused left two *unequivocal* pieces of forensic evidence at the scene of the crime: his finger prints and his semen; the latter taken from the most intimate of human orifices – the *rectum* of the deceased…. and the oral cavity."

Mrs Jenny Patterson, mother of three, the third Juror from the left; looked down into her lap as he continued. For her he detail was still too vivid, too painful and the forensic pictures too grotesque for her to contemplate in the cold light of day.

"Post-Mortem Evidence, photographs and the graphic details presented by the Prosecution has at times, I am sure, been traumatic and extremely distressing to *you all,* Members of the Jury."

He softened his cultured tone as he spoke; looking at Mrs Patterson with empathy; she caught his eye for a moment then looked down into her lap and avoided his glance.

"The full extent of the Victim's suffering on the night in question is *not one for the Jury to debate*."

"For her extended family however, the details will haunt their sleeping hours; of that I have NO doubt."

He nodded his head and took at deep breath.

Mr Sudeck raised his voice again as he stood fully erect with his shoulders braced back and looked from Juror to Juror sequentially; his eyes wide and filled with the determination and vigour of youth.

"The *simple question*, having heard the expert testimony before this Court: is whether *YOU BELIEVE* that the *Doctor* in the dock before you, cold-bloodedly *Murdered* Edwina Justin."

"I am supremely confident that you will reach the only viable conclusion possible in this grizzly Epitaph to a World Leader so savagely taken from us *all*: *GUILTY AS CHARGED!*

"Thank you ALL for your fortitude and strength during this ordeal."

He nodded pragmatically with one last glance at Mrs Patterson and then looked at the Spokesman of the Jury and held his eye momentarily.

He turned to face Lord Justice Cooke; and bowed gracefully:

"The Prosecution Rests My Lord".

Chapter 2

Old Bailey

Central Criminal Court: Day 58

Thursday 24th November 2016

Cooke L.J. Presiding [closing remarks]

Francis Ledbetter Q.C. Defence Counsel:

"And so Members of The Jury to summarise this most *distressing case* succinctly: the whole case against Dr Christophe Schultz hinges on just two pieces of forensic evidence gathered from the tragic Scene of Professor Edwina Justin's death."

"There were two *partial* sets of finger prints which were recovered from the bedside lamp and the bed frame in Professor Justin's bedroom."

"Dr Christophe Schultz was forthright and very detailed in his account of his visit to Professor Justin's apartment on December 26th 2015 *at her invitation: on the occasion of her fifty-third birthday.*"

"As Professor McKinnon pointed out: we might expect Dr Schultz' partial finger prints to be present on the bed frame and bedside lamp: finger prints may be recovered after an extended period of time unless specifically erased or cleaned from the surface."

"We know that Professor Justin was a very private person and cleaned her own apartment: it was not professionally managed; not regularly deep cleaned by an agency."

"The second piece of forensic evidence is highly contentious: *microscopic*, as opposed to *macroscopic;* residues of semen. Very small amounts not visible to the naked eye."

"The samples were a close , but imperfect match for DNA extracted from buccal samples taken from Dr Schultz whilst he was held in custody."

"However the residues appeared to match samples taken from the single surgical glove: *rather conveniently found in a recycling bin in Westminster: after an anonymous tip off to the Police.*"

"Despite requests from the Police, no one ever came forward to link Dr Schultz to the disposal of the glove……a single glove: begging the question - why dispose of a matching pair separately?"

"The defence absolutely refute the Prosecution' claim that the DNA evidence from the crime scene and a single surgical glove,: prove that Dr Schultz committed the murder of Professor Justin."

"Members of the Jury…"

"*The Central Tenet of every Criminal Prosecution;* the backbone of every criminal case brought by the Crown Prosecution Service: is that the accused had *means, opportunity and….motive.*"

Francis Ledbetter stood completely silently for a moment and surveyed the Juror's faces: watching their eye movements and facial expressions very carefully as he spoke. He stood bolt upright and used his hands to gesture; rather more conservatively than his learned friend on the Counsel for the Prosecution.

"Where the case against Dr Schultz lacks *any credibility*, is on the *pivotal* question of a *motive*."

He held his hands wide open as he spoke. He brought his hands together and interlaced his fingers; as a priest might do in contemplation.

"The Prosecution were completely unable to provide a sound motive for the murder of Professor Justin."

"The murder of a Colleague with whom Dr Schultz' had a relationship: a relationship which blossomed into that most tender expression of human feeling when Dr Schultz' and Professor Justin…*made love*..on December 26th 2015 at Professor Justin's apartment."

"You heard the testimony of Mrs Molly Wright, who suffered a Heart Attack no less; having discovered the body of her employer on Friday

12th August 2016. They'd worked together for a decade; if anyone knew *Edwina Justin: it was Molly."*

(*Francis Ledbetter dropped Edwina Justin's title purposely at this point: to demonstrate the human bond they shared: a friendship..*)

"After all, she was one of the chosen few, given access to her employer's private abode; *her personal sanctuary no less:* a privilege bestowed on few of Edwina Justin's Colleagues or even close friends."

"Molly Wright was trusted as a confidante of Professor Justin and a lady of impeccable character who testified that she found it *"Inconceivable" that Dr Schultz could have murdered Professor Justin."*

"Are we *truly to believe that Dr Schultz somehow transformed from a lover into a killer over the course of just eight months?"*

"*A man who himself had an untarnished record of patient care?"*

He sounded incredulous as he raised his open palms to the jury and shook his head and turned to look at Mr Sudheck who sat impassively on the Prosecution Bench.

"Indeed but for, the quick thinking Police Detectives and the skills of Dr Arnold; Christophe Schultz would not be sat before you today. Such was the overwhelming distress he experienced when showed the horrendous Forensic photographs of Professor Justin's body…….."

He swallowed hard; theatrically, as if finding the words were stuck in his throat: a flash-back to Christophe choking on the floor of the holding cell in Police custody….

"*That Christophe Schultz attempted to take his own life by choking on food delivered to him in a Police cell…..it beggars belief."*

He stood silently for a moment and then looked at two of the lady jurors who hung on his every word: sat shoulder to shoulder as he spoke on the back row of the Jury' benches. They mirrored each others body language as they sat forward deep in concentration.

"Expert Psychiatric evaluations on Eden Ward revealed none of the Hallmarks of a Psychopath or Personality Disordered Individual."

His eyes locked with the Foreman who's shepherding role would be pivotal during the forthcoming deliberations of the Jury: consciously trying tho read his reaction as he progressed.

"Quite the opposite: *he entered a Fugue*: a state of absolute denial; that such a horrendous and callous act could have happened at all: a crime which ended their relationship and any prospect of sharing the warmth of human contact together, a closeness they both craved: *such was the individual loneliness of their work-focused lives.*"

Edward Ledbetter sighed and shook his head theatrically.

"You heard the Testimony of Colleagues such as *Professor Ennis* who attested to *Christophe Schultz* calm, resourceful demeanour and ethical approach to his work and lifestyle."

"*Members of the Jury*, the Prosecution are asking you to accept what amounts to a *construct*: *not* a motive."

"The notion that Professor Justin's *refusal* to sign a *Press Release*: a Company Document, could have *so enraged Dr Schultz*: that in a moment of pique, of uncontrolled anger.......*he drugged and raped Professor Justin.*"

He stood shaking his head with an incredulous look on his face.

"Furthermore even if you accept that construct: you will need to conclude that Dr Schultz went equipped for murder...that he somehow *anticipated that at some stage in his life he would need access to and have had about his person an unlicensed sedative. Procured from where, from whom?*"

"*It was perfectly clear from Forensic evidence...*that there were no signs of a struggle at the Scene of the Crime: *no indication that a tender act of love making had turned sour.*"

"Indeed...the final act of the *true Perpetrator of this crime, whom so ever that might be*: in order to demonstrate *his utter scorn* for Professor Justin....was to compose a depraved crime scene that Molly Wright will continue to visualise for the rest of her life."

"To return to the question of forensics...."

"Are we seriously to believe that Dr Schultz would have left his own semen at the scene of such a murder and thereby incriminate himself?"

Edward Ledbetter looked directly at Mrs Patterson and surveyed the faces of the adjacent Jurors: Jenny Patterson looked directly back at him as he spoke.

"Are we truly to believe as the Prosecution have alleged..."

"That such a cruel and utter contempt could have simmered throughout Tuesday 9th August and exploded so savagely, so unexpectedly..."

"That Dr Schultz could have murdered the woman he had held in his tender embrace eight months prior to her killing?"

"Members of the Jury, *I ask you in all humility*:"

"Does this *truly* stand the test of probability...or stretch the imagination to breaking point?"

"Members of the Jury, you have had ample time to observe Dr Christophe Schultz during the course of this trial: to witness the pain and suffering he has experienced."

"I ask you to examine the existing evidence very carefully and consider whether the case made by the Prosecution would permit you to find Dr Schultz guilty beyond *all reasonable doubt*."

"We contend that it most certainly does not."

Francis Ledbetter bowed slowly to Lord Justice Cooke.

For the first time in many years of Legal Practice; his heart felt heavy and his mouth dry as he sat down and took a sip of water.

Chapter 3

Old Bailey:

Central Criminal Court: Day 65

Thursday 1st December 2016 10 a.m.

Cooke L.J. Presiding.

Clerk to the Court, *Mrs Olivia Simpson*:

"Chairman of The Jury: have you reached a verdict on which at least nine of you are agreed?"

Jury spokesperson, Mr Kenneth Down: *"Yes my Lord."*

Kenneth Down looked the judge squarely in the eye as he spoke, then bowed his head respectfully; just as he'd seen both counsels do over his long period in court.

Court Clerk: "On the single count of the Murder of Professor Edwina Justin...."

"How do you find the defendant, *guilty or not guilty*?"

Spokesperson: "Guilty: My Lord."

He locked eyes and then nodded to Mrs Simpson as he delivered the verdict of the entire Jury: they had started their deliberations with an eight to two majority and thereafter settled within twenty-four hours upon an unanimous verdict.

(The finding of the discarded surgical glove in a recycling bin in Westminster had been pivotal in the decision making of dissenting members of the Jury.)

Cooke L.J. *"Will the Defendant please rise."*

Cooke L.J. "Christophe Schultz: The Jury has found you Guilty of the Murder of Professor Edwina Justin.

"The Sentence of this Court will be adjourned to a later date: pending a full Psychiatric Re-Evaluation."

"You may take the Prisoner down."

Chapter 4

10:05 a.m.

Christophe listened but could not speak. The beating of the cerebral metronome in his ears grew louder, the whirlpool of solemn court-room colours swirled before his eyes, then darkened; lit only by the twinkling of distant silvery stars.

Then an unseen shroud of darkness descended.

Images played before his eyes like a retro movie in slow motion.

A distant unfamiliar voice, then several: suddenly moving closer, louder.

Clarity returned in an instant, light returned to illuminate his darkened World.

"Dr Schultz, wake up Doctor; open your eyes please. "

Knuckles rubbed forcefully over his white shirt covering his sternum.

Faces looked down at him: the familiar Police Guards and his Barrister.

"Dr Schultz, are you okay?" *Mrs Simpson*, the Clerk to the Court, smiled down at him.

Do you have any pain anywhere?" asked Francis Ledbetter Q.C., concern audible in his tone of voice; his glasses perched precariously across the bridge of his nose as he leaned down towards Christophe's face.

All residual colour had drained from Christophe's typically pale complexion. He looked as white as freshly fallen snow.

Perspiration condensed on his brow and he felt cold and shivered involuntarily for a moment.

"I'm okay, I can sit now." responded Christophe; sounding more in control than he felt.

"I don't have any pain. Thank you."

"I'm sorry.....I....."

His voice trailed off as he continued to compose himself.

The courtroom continued to slowly waver in front of his eyes; a cool glass of water appeared in his left hand. The Clerk to the Court steadied his hand as he grasped the tumbler.

"Stand when you feel steady lad." instructed *Ted* the Police Guard, in a tone more strict than his colleagues; yet looking down with fatherly concern rather than harsh judgement.

Christophe emptied the glass and rose cautiously to his feet; in time to see the last of the jurors leaving the courtroom. She looked back over her left shoulder; Christophe thought he detected a slight smirk momentarily pass across her lips before she was gone.

"*What happened to me*?" asked Christophe; feeling embarrassed and vulnerable in equal measure.

The guard pragmatically described how Christophe had heard the verdict, turned as white as a ghost and then slowly slid down to his seat and progressively onto the floor of the Dock; momentarily losing awareness before regaining full consciousness. The whole incident had taken less than two minutes to unfold.

"*That'll be the shock of the Sentence lad.*" announced Ted with an air of finality.

Pronounced fit to walk, Christophe was taken down to the holding cells of the infamous Old Bailey.

Chapter 5

Friday 2nd December 2016 10:15

Francis Ledbetter Q.C. reiterated the Judge's final comments for Christophe's clarification: his sentencing would be adjourned pending full Psychiatric Assessment. A conviction for Murder carried a Mandatory Life Sentence but a Psychiatric Report might impact the Judge's recommendation on his term of imprisonment or dictate further recommendations for his internment.

In all probability: Christophe faced a sentence of Imprisonment for Life.

Francis Ledbetter's spectacles were finely balanced on the bridge of his lightly freckled nose; exquisitely framing his small piercingly blue eyes. He fixed his gaze on Christophe whilst speaking; quietly and deliberating emphasising certain key words. His greying hair was cut to within a centimetre of his scalp.

As his Barrister spoke, it seemed to Christophe that Francis Ledbetter could track even the slightest deviation of his own eyes, as he tried in vain; to maintain his Barrister's eye contact.

Sometimes during their preparation for his appearances in court, Christophe had felt that their conversation was akin to a one-sided tennis match. Questions were mercilessly served by Ledbetter, answers returned by Christophe, only to be smashed back into his court with a crushing volley; all without any change in eye contact or body movement on the part of his formidable opponent.

Francis Ledbetter outlined the process ahead for their Appeal against Christophe's conviction.

Chapter 6

Monday 5th December 2016

Francis Ledbetter had an enviable reputation for successfully defending clients to the best of his ability and he had rarely lost a case; even before he'd joined the Elite Barristers of the Queen's Counsel [Q.C.] : *The Learned in Law.*

Throughout preparation for the Trial of Christophe Schultz, he had rarely let slip his mantle of emotional detachment when discussing Christophe's case with the Legal Team. He constantly grilled them with an array of questions and observations which threatened to annihilate all but the most skilled of his Legal Protégées.

In the instant case, however, the Prosecution had provided clear CCTV footage of Christophe boarding a First Southern Railway train and thereafter travelling into London Waterloo Railway Station with his fold-up bicycle. Wearing his branded black cycle outfit with fluorescent high visibility vest over his jacket, it had been possible for the Police to provide footage of him completing his train journey at 8.09 p.m. before riding through parts of Westminster on route to the Scene of Professor Justin's death on the night in question.

A hidden external wall-mounted camera near the entrance to the Apartment Block in which Professor Justin resided had failed to capture footage of Christophe entering 'The Mews on Tuesday 9th August: the night when Professor Justin was highly likely to have been murdered. Christophe Schultz was judged to be the last person to have seen her alive.

Entrance to all fourteen of the Apartments in the four storey Apartment Block, was ordinarily via an internal lift.

The Prosecution successfully adduced evidence that Christophe gained entrance to The Mews via the rear Underground Parking Bay, having first entered in a six digit PIN into the external keypad: the Code was known to him as he had visited the 'Mews on Boxing Day 2015.

They successfully claimed he had used the fire escape stairwell to enter the fourth floor and thereafter taken the short walk to her Apartment; to avoid being captured on the CCTV camera within the lift.

In addition to the DNA Evidence of Christophe's seminal DNA gathered from her oral and rectal body cavities; the Prosecution Forensic Scientists had discovered a discarded surgical rubber glove, size 8: a right hand glove which had revealed finger prints which matched the fingerprints found at the Scene of the Crime taken from the bed frame and bedside lamp within Professor Justin's Apartment.

An anonymous tip off had lead the Police to the discarded surgical glove which had been procured from the top of a recycling bin in Westminster; found wrapped in a small plastic bin bag.

This item had been a hugely influential piece of evidence and Francis Ledbetter had argued unsuccessfully that this item pointed towards Christophe having been framed for the Murder of Professor Justin.

Furthermore, the presence of a drug not previously documented in European Pharmacopoeia Literature had been found in blood samples taken from Professor Justin's deceased body and the Prosecution had successfully argued that Christophe would have had access to such non-Prescription Medicines, though they offered no evidence as to source of the chemical entity which had been characterised using Mass Spectrometry; effectively arguing *Res Ipsa Loquitur*: literally *the "evidence"[the thing]; speaks for itself.*

[Mr Sudhek had introduced the rule explaining that The *Res Ipsa Loquitur* rule is typically used in medical malpractice when by way of example: in the case of a patient with abdominal pain arising at the site of previous surgery... the abdominal pain would not have arisen... *but for* the presence of a surgical instrument left inside the abdomen of the patient by a grossly incompetent surgeon.]

{The evidence speaks for itself and forms the basis of the claim in negligence.]

In the instant case: were it not for the novel chemical entity found in the blood stream of Professor Justin, she might have struggled with her murderer and may have fought off his attempts to rape her orally and rectally; and ultimately strangle her to death.

Edward Ledbetter had argued that the murderer used the chemical to sedate her and therefore there were no signs of a struggle; whereas the prosecution argued that Christophe Schultz used the sedative to pacify her so that he could rape her.

The testimony of a highly respected Pharmacologist: Professor Adam McNamara: adduced that Compound X; "Exhibit 9166" was contributory to the cause and manner, of Edwina Justin's death.

Chapter 7

9a.m. Monday 5th December 2016

The Legal Team was assembled in a tight arc in Francis Ledbetter's Office. The dark wood panels covering three walls made the room feel smaller than the real dimensions. They did however, contribute to an air of Academia, displaying over one hundred and fifty years of Legal Memorabilia; matched only by the extensive library of books and journals which adorned the wall at the North end of the room.

Pupil barrister Georgina Townsend took a lead in the discussion and had been instructed to recap' on all the salient points related to Professor Justin's commitments: as the painstaking process of evidence review started afresh with view to an Appeal against Christophe Schultz' Sentence for Murder.

"Professor Edwina Justin had an *awesome* reputation amongst her Peers. Having graduated with Honours in her year at Medical School she sailed through post-graduate training in General Medicine before specialising in Therapeutics and thereafter Oncology, working at several large Teaching Hospitals in London."

"Continue" instructed Francis, without shifting his gaze from Georgina's brow.

"Her expertise, networking skills and leadership quickly marked her as a potential recruiting target for Pharmaceutical Company Sponsored Drug Trials. However despite the unrelenting efforts of the Big Ten Companies, she always resisted Commercial Alliances and worked increasingly in European Consortia of Teaching Hospitals; focusing her attention on novel treatments for liver cancer and acting as Vice Chair to the European Council for Pharmacovigilance: collating, categorising and analysing safety data for drugs in development for the treatment of cancer."

"We sourced numerous letters and emails over a ten year period from her two laptop computers; mostly inviting her to participate in Clinical Trials and Advisory Boards: *she politely declined all*."

"So that made her an even bigger prize to bag for Pharma,' given the progression of patients with chronic Hepatitis C infection to cirrhosis and liver cancer; particularly when UPL came knocking at her door!" chimed in Gregory Tanner; her fellow Pupil Barrister.

"The progression of *some* patients;" corrected Georgina, irritated by Gregory's blatant point scoring in front of Francis.

Francis had noted the repetitive momentary double-blink of Georgina's eyelids as she responded to Gregory's point: this was her "tell" and revealed her irritation, even when her tone of voice remained even.

Georgina's training as a Junior Doctor before taking the Graduate Diploma in Law and switching career trajectory, separated her from most of her contemporaries. She stepped adeptly back and forth between the two disciplines of Law and Medicine, with the ease of a tennis player at Wimbledon; changing ends between games. What's more in Francis' estimation; *Georgina rarely dropped the ball*.

"As an aide memoire, here are the Progression Data for patients with Chronic HCV. Of those who progress to through to irreversible liver damage which the clinicians describe as cirrhosis; a significant number of patients go on to develop liver cancer."

As usual Georgina had prepared a colour coded spreadsheet which was broken down into those patients who despite a diagnosis of past viral infection, showed no evidence of ongoing inflammation within the liver.

By contrast, a larger proportion of patients revealed evidence of *active* cell destruction and as a consequence of the body's attempt at repair within the liver; had developed a chronic fibrous tissue destruction of liver tissue which resulted in cirrhosis.

Georgina walked the team through the Data and the patients' possible pathways in disease progression.

"So around fifteen percent of patients with a past exposure to Hepatitis C virus, whether through needle sharing during intravenous drug abuse, contaminated blood transfusions or potentially through blood contamination during sexual practice; show evidence of *exposure*, through the body's production of tell-tale "antibodies": but have no evidence of virus in the blood samples."

"So if I understand correctly", interjected Nadia, "The patient's body has mounted an immune response which has destroyed the original virus completely?"

As an experienced paralegal secretary, Nadia Mason was busily taking extensive notes from the meeting and was determined to understand the Science behind the Case; an approach which Francis invariably nurtured. He was content to wait whilst Georgina brought the Team up to speed before moving onto the final detail and digging into the evidence.

"Exactly." responded Georgina succinctly; with an encouraging nod and smile.

 "Much the same as a lock and a key: the lock is the original virus and the key is the antibody. The body manufactures a specific key which is able to unlock the secrets of the virus' structure and the body's defences after which it will enable the body to combat the infection. The presence of the original *keys* in the body's circulation, which we call *antibodies*: provide evidence of the original infection which may remain dormant for years or trigger early inflammation if the virus re-surfaces or the Patient is re-infected."

"So sometimes the keys are the wrong shape to fit the lock and the virus carries on reproducing?"

"In simple terms, the keys are manufactured by the body but the configuration of the locks may change so that the body is unable to destroy the virus; simple changes in the viral configuration can lead to unchecked viral reproduction. That's what viruses do well, they *mutate: they change their appearance so to speak;* and thereby avoid destruction by the body's immune system."

"The presence of the virus in the patient's body can lead to a long period of inflammation; *a slow burning fire if you like*. The liver is actively involved in fighting the fire but in so doing becomes damaged. The damage causes the release of chemical markers in the patient's blood which evidence the ongoing damage, but are a poor guide to prognosis".

"Doctor's take a series of small samples of the Patients' liver, either through a small puncture made in the skin using a long needle or through a vein in the patients' neck. "

Georgina gestured to the anatomical areas on her own body; watching Nadia grimace visibly at the thought of a needle inserted into her neck. She looked relieved by Francis' intervention.

"Remind us all again please Georgina of the significance of the different types of HCV and thus the attendant proclivity to produce liver damage and resist conventional treatment."

Chapter 8

10 a.m. Monday 5th December 2016

Having trained in Medicine like Christophe, Georgina had been given a unique opportunity to interrogate Christophe's in gathering evidence for the Defence. She had felt the sense of failure as acutely as anybody when the Defence case had been crushed by the Jury's decision in Court.

Georgina went on to explain that there were six different viral strains which she called *Genotypes*. Prior to the novel treatment pioneered by UPL, there was no tablet single oral agent which could effectively eradicate all viral strains.

There was no evidence of "resistance to treatment" on the part of any of the viral genotypes, which might otherwise result in treatment failure. Furthermore, unlike historical treatment combinations there was no need to add in drugs which targeted the immune system and which thereby caused patients flu-like symptoms which were often debilitating.

"Of key consideration to decision makers is the short treatment period with the new medication. Just four weeks and without the astronomical price tag of some combination treatments; a unique selling point which the Company had used to differentiate its Product from Competitors; especially in the eyes of Government Departments who held the purse strings for ring fenced budgets".

At this point Georgina could see Gregory itching to comment so she sat back in the leather chair and took a sip of spring water from the ornate ebony table to her left.

"So in short – a Blockbuster!" exclaimed Gregory, never one to miss a one liner.

Despite his outward portrayal of a relaxed demeanour, Gregory was fiercely competitive and never missed an opportunity to challenge Georgina.

During Christophe's Defence, Gregory had spearheaded the gathering and sifting of evidence and thereafter systematically catalogued the Prosecution's disclosure documents and Witness Statements; he rigorously cross-referenced and re-checked the facts of the case.

Francis looked thoughtful. Unusually he began leafing through his file of hand-written notes and the room fell silent, awaiting his directive. The Team had grown accustom to Francis' *modus operandi*: they had no way of knowing where his line of questioning would go, but they'd best be ready with the detail when asked. After a few minutes Francis looked up, focused squarely on Gregory and asked his question.

"When did the serious safety issues concerning the new drug treatment begin to surface?"

Knowing better than to recall a date from memory, Gregory flipped up the lid on his laptop and it whirled into action; having been left in sleep mode during their meeting. Gregory responded by recounting a list of dates when a series of reports of bone marrow failure had been communicated to the Regulatory Authorities by Elizabeth Tully; sensing the need, he continued with some background detail.

"As we have previously discussed, both the Clinical Trial Investigators and the Sponsoring Company have clear and legally enforceable timelines for the submission of reports for the Serious Adverse Events which Patients experience when participating in the Clinical Trials. The Company submits a full report on the outcome and..

"Yes thank you – now to be crystal clear, when was Dr Schultz first aware of the serious safety concerns for the drug U0008?"

"That's more difficult to quantify." responded Gregory slowly...

"And that's an evasive answer." Volleyed Francis.

Georgina cut in; keen to rescue the match.

"The first email which documents Christophe's concern as UK Medical Director was sent to the Head of Drug Safety: *Dr Josh Herbert-Lane* in the U.S.A.... on Tuesday 9th August 2016: logged at 10:30 a.m. U.K. time: the same morning as Christophe' received notification from Elizabeth Tully during an internal meeting."

"George Latimer was updated *unilaterally* on 9th August 2016: but the email was sent by *Legal Counsel Clive McGregor*: logged at 10:55 a.m. on 9th August 2016: UK time."

Francis removed his spectacles and rubbed his eyes. His gold cufflinks glinted as the morning sun caught their edge and created a sword beam of light which scattered across the meeting room as the reflections danced around the ceiling and walls; Gregory's concentration wavered momentarily as he watched the display.

"So what have we missed Gregory – clearly not the light show?" came Francis' acerbic question out of the shadows.

Gregory was caught unawares and sucked in his lower lip; looking deflated.

"Police interviews with Company personnel at UPL suggest all procedures followed by the Company were agreed with Christophe Schultz and the safety team but the documented conversation with Edwina Justin obtained from mobile phone records suggests otherwise and casts doubt on the veracity of the Press Release. However that's outside of our current remit." Concluded Francis.

"Okay Miss Townsend; revert to our defence strategy and review steps please."

As instructed, Georgina changed the course of the discussion abruptly.

"As to the third or *unknown Party or Parties*......." gestured Georgina using the three outstretched middle fingers of her left hand; reflecting on one Defence strands which even the judge had mentioned and dismissed in his closing speech....she hesitated and glanced across at Francis...

"You have our attention Miss Townsend." replied Francis.

Georgina began choosing her words carefully as if preparing for a surgical procedure, knowing Francis would watch every move of her scalpel; every part of the dissection of their case for the defence; which had failed only a few agonising days before their meeting.

"We could not determine the existence of a *third party* but the evidence culled from the Scene of the crime renders that Conclusion *unavoidable*; if Dr Schultz is indeed innocent of the murder of Professor Justin."

The room fell silent as that premise was accepted by the whole Team without reservation and they nodded their collective acquiescence.

"The Prosecution provided unequivocal CCTV digital footage of Dr Schultz captured from a First Southern Train on-board camera, on route to London. Furthermore, they provided very dark fragmented CCTV of someone cycling through Westminster and selected side streets between Westminster and Mayfair but they were unable to provide footage of anyone either in or around the Mayfair location of the Mews' Apartment; or within the Mews' lift or internal buildings and that includes the rear entrance to the garage: on the night of the murder."

"In point of fact, *no one witnessed* his alleged presence in the Apartment on the night of the murder."

"The presence of Christophe's partial finger prints in the bedroom could reflect his previous visit to Professor Justin's apartment."

"The DNA evidence, specifically the finger prints inside the discarded latex glove and the DNA evidence of semen deposits in the deceased rectum and oral cavity was not contested by our Independent Experts."

"The DNA evidence ultimately convicted Dr Schultz."

"The Prosecution claimed that the discarded glove is consistent with Christophe having worn gloves during the sexual assaults and rape if the actions had been non-consensual, as seems likely."

"But the single size 8 surgical glove which was reported to the Police anonymously could have been planted by whoever *extracted DNA via seminal fluid deposits from the glove.* The police could not explain why only one glove was recovered and argued that given the passage of time: the matching glove is unlikely to be recovered."

"So if Christophe is innocent, someone else entered the Mews Apartment and took a sample from said *undiscovered* latex glove and inserted a *semen sample* into the deceased' rectum."

"Continue" said Francis without averting his gaze from Georgina.

The third party entered the Apartment, committed the murder, *inserted* the semen evidence and was unseen and undetected."

"*Go back in time.*" suggested Francis thinking aloud.

Pausing for thought, Georgina re-wound her hypotheses to Waterloo railway station.

"The Prosecution provided unequivocal evidence of Dr Schultz boarding the train to Waterloo and travelling into London: he is clearly identifiable in the train carriage. CCTV at Waterloo station clearly showed Dr Schultz leaving platform Ten and exiting the station.

"Part of the onward journey from Waterloo to Professor Justin's apartment was allegedly captured; albeit in a fragmented sequence, to the apartment block".

"Unless..." interjected Gregory, "*he* was captured on Police Surveillance Cameras and we missed it!"

Francis transfixed Gregory for a moment: "Explain Mr Hughes"

"Well, in light of the cumulative evidence taken from the train journey, arrival at Waterloo and the appearance of Christophe in segments of CCTV footage from Waterloo' to Melway Mews where Professor Justin lived; the Prosecution convinced the jury that Dr Schultz completed the journey. Suppose *he* didn't!"

"So you're suggesting that Christophe was definitely not the Person on the bicycle seen travelling through Westminster?" responded Georgina.

"Sure: that Christophe was *impersonated* by someone else".

Gregory opened his mouth for a moment, bit his lower lip; and waited; sensing Georgina's mounting assault from the way she now sat forward in her chair.

"Somebody wearing exactly the same outfit, looking every inch like Christophe, arrived at the Apartment; knew the security code for the underground entry, planted the evidence on the deceased' and thereby framed Christophe?"

Georgina continued with a series of questions.

"So what was the *motive*?"

"How did the real murderer *acquire the DNA evidence extracted from the surgical glove....*?"

"How did he..."

"*Or she*" interjected Gregory ready to return the ball in play.

"It's true we have poor images of a person riding a bicycle which looks like Christophe's but no facial recognition evidence which directly identifies the rider *definitively* as Christophe."

Georgina was on the forefoot again as she spoke and they jousted as adversaries in a mock battle: just as they would in their future roles as Barristers in Criminal Cases……

"But the Judgment of the Courts to dismiss this kind of approach as without foundation." Francis reminded the young advocates who were now beginning to lock horns.

"*Understood*." responded Gregory with a respectful nod to Francis, yet sensing he still might regain the upper hand, he continued:

"The fragmented CCTV from street cameras revealed only indistinct images where the perpetrator's facial features were obscured throughout the journey by *his or her*, cycle helmet."

"Why your sudden doubt concerning *gender of the third party*; the lean body outline?" asked Francis. He didn't wait for conjecture before he pressed on:

"I agree that given the dark images, only the DNA evidence places Christophe on the First Southern Train and thereafter *at the scene*".

"However the data from the CCTV during his train journey is *unequivocal*; it places Christophe in Waterloo on the night of the murder and sets the timeframe for the subsequent journey..."

"I know all that." responded Gregory in an even tone.

"But what really happened to Christophe once he arrived at Waterloo and left the Station?"

"I think that's a good place to stop for today." interjected Francis definitively; glancing at his watch and sensing they were now moving into the realm of pure speculation once more.

"We must continue to question and dissect all the details pertaining to this case until we expose a *critical* piece of evidence which has thus far been overlooked."

Chapter 9

Wednesday 7th December 2016 9 a.m.

Georgina sat opposite Christophe: a metal table, bolted to the floor; separating them. But there was more than a physical gulf between them. Christophe looked tired and drawn, with dark half-moon circles beneath his eyes. It was the first time she had seen him since his sentencing, he looked shell-shocked: drifting in a sea of despair with no land in sight.

"Christophe, I cannot imagine how it feels to be you, locked up, day after day; for a crime you *didn't commit*. That's why I am here; to help you move on, away from this nightmare."

She injected as much sincerity into her voice as she could: she did not doubt his innocence, but as yet, she had been unable to prove it.

Christophe was silent. He stared ahead, beyond Georgina; at some distant safe unattainable, intangible haven.

His grey shirt and jeans matched the mood which engulfed his body language.

"Christophe, we need to work *together* to understand who could have masqueraded as you and committed this crime; *who could have killed Professor Justin.*"

He remained silent, impassive to her attempts to bridge the abyss between them. Sensing a need to make progress, Georgina elected to press on with open questions.

"Christophe, can we talk more about your Personal life; before this nightmare began?

Christophe turned towards her, but did not make eye contact. He felt ashamed and could not hide his disgust at the placard which he felt had been hung around his neck for all to see: *Murderer.*

"Work dominated my life; for the last seven years at least; whilst I was with Utopia'. My personal life was... limited; mostly to work contacts." He shrugged his shoulders and studied his hands.

She could see lines of ingrained dirt underneath his short fingernails; a stark contrast to his previously well manicured nails and sensed how he must hate to look at himself in such a poor physical state: let alone his shattered self-esteem.

"Was there anyone else important in your life?"

"There were no regular girl friends if that's where your question is leading."

"What about other *regular* contacts? What about any.. *platonic..* relationships?" Responded Georgina; choosing her words carefully and emphasising key words; anything to hook his interest.

"No." came Christophe's curt response.

"Anyone *online* you might have met or corresponded with?"

"On-line dating you mean?" said Christophe his eyes widening and his expression incredulous.

"Not my style." He smiled for the first time, albeit fleetingly. That's a start, thought Georgina, pressing on.

"Anyone who you turned to when life was difficult; or work pressures, mounted?"

Christophe looked indecisive for a moment; then looked directly at Georgina.

"What is it you think you know?" asked Christophe, his brow furrowed, searching her face for answers; his interest piqued.

Georgina remained silent and spread her fingers out on the desk ahead of her; she could feel she touched a nerve.

"Christophe, to be successful in your Appeal we need to dig deeper than we have done before; *understand who and why anyone would have wanted to have you convicted of murder.*"

She looked him steadfastly in the eyes and fell silent. She looked down at her notepad which remained closed, giving him time; sensing he was now wrestling with an unspoken decision.

"There's only one person we haven't talked about. Not a relationship *exactly. Barbara Turner. She was my counsellor.*" Christophe looked at his fingers, examining his nails.

A loud knock was followed by the guard's gruff voice announcing: "Time's up".

"One minute please." responded Georgina hurriedly.

She reached forward touching Christophe's right finger tips momentarily.

"Christophe I need to understand your relationship with Barbara; please help *me* to help *you*".

Christophe was escorted from the room. Minutes later Georgina took several deep breaths as she looked up at the early morning sun in the perimeter car park and counted her blessings.

Chapter 10

Wednesday 14th December 2016

Georgina stoop up as Christophe entered the room and he smiled as he gazed at her; she watched his eyes course down her slim body. He waited momentarily and then sat down opposite Georgina; establishing eye contact immediately. She was wearing a white blouse and dark blue two-piece suit and Christophe's reaction was exactly what she'd hoped for as she had carefully dressed that morning; before her visit to the prison.

It was 9 a.m., a week since they had last spoken and Georgina needed to make progress with Christophe, but she knew he must dictate the pace of their conversation today. She sat with her hands in her lap, upright, focusing her full attention on Christophe. He still looked tired, but less hopeless; less resigned to his fate than he had a week ago.

She had placed a small black tape recorder on the table to the right of her and she pressed the red button to initiate the recording. Nadia would prepare a transcript of their conversation when she returned to Chambers later that morning.

"How are you Christophe?" asked Georgina with a warm smile.

"Better; ready to talk to you today...I think."

"Take your time." encouraged Georgina.

"I discovered Barbara Turner whilst researching a Counselling Network on-line. She had excellent on-line testimonials. We emailed a few times and she outlined her experience in managing Obsessive Compulsive Disorders and I read a couple of Publications she had contributed to; including two as Lead Author."

"We agreed an on-line payment schedule and talked, usually once every two weeks, unless I felt very stressed or my habits were becoming intrusive to my daily life."

"Our discussions were mostly about my *rituals*: repetitive hand washing, obsessing over bodily cleanliness, and the like." His voice trailed off for a moment and he studied his hands.

"I often just talked about, work issues, pressures and the stresses of my job with Utopia; the triggers for my rituals. Barbara helped me to understand how stress often triggered or exacerbated my habits. As we made more progress, we talked about coping strategies and relaxation exercises, including meditation. Sometimes we practiced these on-line *together*. It felt good to share; I 'never spoke to anyone about this stuff before Barbara."

Georgina waited; Christophe fell silent. "*Go on, please Christophe.*"

"We talked about my childhood a lot, my family, my father." More silence.

Georgina put her hands onto the table, her fingers interlaced. She mirrored Christophe's body posture with her own.

Christophe continued looking at his hands. "My father was a dentist; well connected in the German Dental Association, which he Chaired. He often travelled to regional meetings. I spent more time with my mom in my early teens, until she took up work in the evenings."

"And were you close?"

"Closer to my mother." said Christophe.

"And did you get along with your father?"

"He could be...distant....in both senses...physically and metaphorically." joked Christophe, without smiling, but looking back at Georgina.

"So you spent a lot of time alone?" clarified Georgina, in a softer tone of voice.

"At times....when I was older...sometimes my Uncle helped out". replied Christophe; breaking eye contact again.

Georgina opened her hands and spread her fingers, rolling a sapphire encrusted ring on her right middle finger; sensing the need to share.

"This was my Grandmother's ring; she gave it to me when my father died. I never take it off; it reminds me of happier times, before he died."

Christophe remained silent; Georgina sensed his unease.

'Sometimes, when I have dark thoughts, I find it very comforting, it somehow seems to anchor me; I suppose that makes me sound a bit childish?"

"No, not at all, I understand. I don't have any touchstones or *anchors* for some parts of my life; and no keepsakes either."

Christophe sighed and shrugged his shoulders.

"I had my Grandmother when things were difficult with my dad; she was a rock when my mother was tired and worn down with my father's illness. Did you have anyone like that, anyone you could turn to when life was hard?"

"No, not really." was Christophe's simple reply.

"What about your Uncle, did he look after you?"

Christophe averted from her gaze and did not reply immediately.

"My uncle did take an interest in me; at first I thought I might be able to trust him."

Georgina waited; Christophe's brow was furrowed again and he bit his lower lip; looking pensive. She watched as he took a number of slow deep breaths; he was preparing himself.

Georgina spread her fingers on the table, edging her left hand closer to Christophe's right hand. As she spoke she touched the back of his hand.

"Christophe, you're doing great, take your time. I think I understand..."

A loud knock broke the silence. Georgina stood up and walked briskly to the door. She spoke through the tiny grill to the guard and sat back down; grasping the initiative.

Christophe sat motionless.

"Barbara opened doors that I had closed many years ago; looking inside those dark rooms was painful. We closed them and...I guess I would rather they stayed *locked*."

"*My mother re-married four years after my father died.*" said Georgina in a soft voice; she hesitated then added in a barely audible voice:

"My step-father became....*over-familiar*...I left home and never went back. "

A second loud knock on the door interrupted the conversation. Christophe touched the back of Georgina's hand almost imperceptibly; leaving his hand next to hers. They sat momentarily, each exploring the other's faces, each looking back at inescapable bleak memories.

As the guard entered the room Christophe walked towards the open door; turning briefly as he exited: unsure whether he had seen tears in Georgina's eyes as she him gave a fleeting smile.

Georgina sat in her car and sobbed, twisting the emerald ring on her finger forward and backwards as she did so. The early morning drizzle did nothing to lift her sombre mood as she drove back to Chambers. She was now sure they had shared a common unspeakable experience as children.

Chapter 11

Wednesday 21st December 2016 9 a.m.

Christophe sat motionless in his solitary cell waiting for the guard to escort him to the Interview Room. He had positioned his feet flat on the cold stone floor, his hands in his lap; his eyes closed. He tried in vain to block out the bedlam around him as he focused on his breathing pattern. He lowered his shoulders aware of the tension in his neck and started to take a long slow deep inhalation before breathing out slowly and deliberately; lips pursed. He visualised himself walking in the early morning mist, peaceful, only the sound of the early morning birdcall.

"Visitor 'Schultz." Called a harsh voice through the open door.

He stood, stretched his arms and neck momentarily and followed the guard through the throng of prisoners, followed by the usual jeers and personal insults as several inmates spat at him.

"*How are you Christophe*?" enquired Georgina; as he sat down opposite her.

The guard closed the door with a heavy merciless clank, which felt as if it reverberated through Christophe's entire body. He shivered visibly.

"*I'm sick of the constant noise*!" responded Christophe; visibly irritated; stubble on his ordinarily clean shaven chin.

Georgina looked concerned, opened her mouth to speak, but said nothing; she looked slightly awkward, thought Christophe. She toyed with her hair as she spoke, quietly.

"I am sorry if I...made you feel at all awkward at our last visit..." said Georgina; her eyes averted from Christophe's gaze as she spoke.

"Sometimes it's hard *not to share*...particularly when...." she sat looking down at her hands. She had put the dicta-phone on the table but it was not switched on.

"*When you've had a similar experience*?" said Christophe, waiting for her to make eye contact.

"*Exactly*." responded Georgina, holding his gaze momentarily.

"But this is about *you*, not *me*." said Georgina sounding stronger, looking directly at him, lips tightly pursed. Christophe heard the tension in her voice and could feel her empathy.

"Georgina; I *am* ready to *share*." Christophe reached across the table picked up the dicta-phone and switched it to record.

Chapter 12

24 hours earlier....

18:30 Tuesday 20th December 2016

Francis removed his spectacles and replaced them in their worn black leather case.

"We'll reconvene in three days: let's explore this avenue further, review all the timelines and CCTV. Again please."

He pressed home his final point before they left:

"I want each of you to ask yourselves *what vital information have we missed*?" Check all forensics, every piece of evidence offered by the Prosecution: follow all paper trails." He nodded.

"Thank you." responded Gregory, looking over his shoulder: as the three of them shuffled out through the door, each carrying a stack of case-note files from the Trial.

Francis swivelled around in his fading brown leather chair to face the street outside his window, where visibility was hampered by the fading light heralding the onset of more heavy rain. A distant clap of thunder exacerbated the sense of urgency as the evening commute from Central London got underway.

Francis lifted his mobile phone to his left ear; he needed to call in a favour.

Jonathan Clarke was engrossed in an encryption programme on his laptop computer when his mobile phone began to vibrate on the table next to him. He always turned the ring tone off when working so that he could screen calls with a glance without breaking his concentration. This call he would take.

"Jonathan Good Afternoon, it's Francis Ledbetter."

"Hi Francis to what do I owe the pleasure?

"I need your Professional help Jon'; a client."

Jonathan could detect an earnest tone in Francis' voice.

"I'm all ears – shoot." He was flattered that Francis had called him and he was determined to help.

"Not on the 'phone Jonathan, our usual watering hole at 8:30 this evening?"

"Done." said Jonathan and ended the call.

Jonathan knew Francis well enough to recognise a note of urgency when he heard one. He was also conscious that a spate of phone hacking scams left mobile phones vulnerable and Francis' cautious approach was pragmatic.

Jonathan text' his wife to update her on his plans for the evening; ending the message:

 "Don't wait up." His euphemism for *"leave me something to warm up in* the microwave."

Jonathan was already half way through his first pint of Old English Ale when Francis walked briskly through the doors of the Huntsman's Arms, which clattered noisily behind him. Spotting his drinking partner near the ornate fireplace Francis was quick to catch the eye of the barmen who was stood at the far end of the bar replacing an optic. With a nod towards Jonathan and a hand gesture from Francis, George set about filling a pint glass with Ale for Jonathan and a large wine glass with Francis' favourite red tipple: a rich full-bodied Merlot.

The bar was busy with the usual medley of Journalists, fellow Barristers, Bankers and overseas' tourists who'd wandered off the beaten track and ended up in the City. Francis wore a dark grey pin-striped suit and Jonathan had been watching the room carefully before Francis arrived; wary of strangers and Journalists who might show any undue interest in their conversation. He already sensed that Francis had an important agenda and the recent news story concerning the conviction of a young Doctor for murder, only served to consolidate that conclusion.

Handing George a Twenty Pound Note Francis nodded appreciatively and was met with a broad smile from "Old George," as he was affectionately known to the regulars.

George had long since given up regular dental care and his smile could appear menacing to the uninitiated by virtue of several missing the incisors from his right upper mandible. Francis conjectured that it also explained his paucity of conversation as he tended to lisp or spit during the rare conversations in which he actively engaged in banter with his regular customers.

Jonathan watched as Francis weaved through the evening crowd of drinkers like a powerful grey shark stalking its prey with precise and measured movements. He imagined he would be a ferocious Adversary in Court and had followed recent events in the Old Bailey with more than a casual interest.

"Cheers Francis!" smiled Jonathan as he raised his glass and moved carefully backwards, retreating from a group of raucous young Merchant Bankers who stood adjacent to them near the fireplace. He took several large gulps from his second pint of Ale and waited patiently for Francis to speak.

"No doubt you've been following the recent case in the Old Bailey?"

He knew Jonathan always followed his big cases and the case of a Doctor from the Pharmaceutical Industry accused and convicted of murdering a public figure was high profile by any standards.

Bingo: Jonathan nodded affirmatively and waited.

"This is the Defendant's *private laptop*; it's been released to us as it's not thought to contain material evidence of relevance now the conviction has been secured. I want you to examine it for me."

"What am I *specifically* looking for Francis?"

Jonathan instinctively looked around as he asked the question but was satisfied that their conversation was buried in the throng created by the crowd of happy revellers.

"I'll be in touch when I am sure. For now, anything unusual for the three months preceding his Arrest; and then start working backwards: timeframe to be determined. 'Anything which suggests outside interference, monitoring, tracking or hacking: the clever algorithms you design and decipher. I'm working a hunch at this stage."

"I know your hunches Francis…" replied Jonathan; "…they usually end in acquittals."

For the first time since he'd arrived Francis smiled; he took a large swig of red wine and sighed before responding:

"With the emphasis firmly on…*usually.*"

They stood in silence absorbing the atmosphere, Jonathan recognising the distracted look on Francis' face and the puffy bags beginning to form underneath his eyes.

He finished his Ale and broke the silence with "another drink?"

"No, I must head off Jon' - work to do; I'll be in touch as soon as I know more."

Francis placed his glass on the mantelpiece and took Jonathan's hand firmly before drawing closer and fixing Jonathan squarely with his steely gaze and lowering his voice, adding to the sense of urgency he conveyed.

"*This case isn't over.*"

The computer handed to Jonathan; he left without looking back.

Jonathan waited for a moment, then text his wife; feeling pleased with himself.

"*Change of plan Lucy, working from home tonight; see you in thirty minutes.*"

He left the pub and hailed a cab. As the taxi driver meandered through the steady stream of evening traffic, Jonathan sat reflecting on the fact that a man's chance of freedom might lie in his hands; the evidence buried on the laptop he held. As his thoughts drifted he recalled the wise words often repeated by his late father: *"time waits for no man."*

Not for the first time, Jonathan realised the deep admiration he held for Francis and began mind mapping his strategy for the task ahead. Francis had given him no lead except for the suspicion of some form of outside interference; endless possibilities existed.

At mid-night Jonathan was deeply entrenched in Dr Schultz' life; his emails, his credit card transaction history, his favourite websites; a long night lay ahead. Next to his feet lay *Ginger*, Lucy's beloved cat; purring to his heart's content in front of the fading embers as they slowly contracted within the fireplace.

Chapter 13

Friday 23rd December 2016

Gregory sat pouring over the CCTV from First Southern trains. He was drinking his third cappuccino of the day and it was still only 9:30 a.m. As Christmas edged ever closer, Chambers was already bustling with activity around him.

He watched intently as Dr Christophe Schultz boarded the train wearing his black cycling outfit with a high visibility fluorescent jacket over the top of his cycling jacket. He stood directly opposite the CCTV camera and his identity was clearly visible when he removed his cycle helmet. He positioned his collapsible bicycle behind his legs, out of the way of other commuters.

Gregory took a screen shot record the bicycle in readiness to compare it to the version visible on the roads exiting Waterloo station: repeating a process he had previously enacted without spotting any apparent differences.

The manager of the local sports cycle shop, three miles away, held the same opinion: they were indeed of identical build and specification: if not the same collapsible cycle.

Gregory watched the footage of Christophe intently: frame by frame.

Christophe mopped his brow with his left hand and disposed of the tissue in the metal waste bin opposite him, in the passenger standing area between doors either side. He then took a wrapper from his left hand jacket pocket which he tore open before systematically cleaning his right, then his left hand with a moist disposable towel. He paid no attention to the CCTV and kept his bicycle next to him for the entire journey.

Passengers came and went and Christophe paid scant attention to most. The ticket inspector passed by without checking his ticket heading for the front of the train. Gregory began switching fast forward on the tape, checking the time and date log as he did so.

He re-referenced the on-line train timetable against the time periods between stops of the train; nothing unusual.

What are we missing? He sat thinking; looking at the footage of Christophe passing through Waterloo station.

He counter-referenced the timings on the Waterloo footage at exit number 10: his face obscured by his cycle helmet as it had been across the entire Station footage. He cycled along the Station Exit Road, past racks of parked bicycles.

Gregory re-ran the footage and watched again; and repeated the whole journey again.

Gregory sat back in his chair, then stretched and yawned.

"Keeping you up Mr Hughes?" asked a deep voice over Gregory's right shoulder. Francis circled the office hunting his prey: *"Where is Miss Townsend this morning"*?

"She's working in the library Mr Ledbetter" responded Gregory, placing all four legs of his chair back on the floor. *Typical thought Gregory, the moment I take a breather...*

"Follow me" instructed Francis with a theatrical flourish; without looking back at Gregory.

Gregory made a grab for his coffee, thought better of it; and hurried to catch up with Francis.

"Right, let's see where we are this morning" announced Francis as Gregory pulled up a chair to sit next to Georgina who was nestled at the far end of the library, her brow furrowed as she worked.

She brushed her right hand distractedly through her blonde hair as she stared intently at the laboratory reports in front of her.

"Looking for the missing evidence Miss Townsend?"

"*Precisely*" pronounced Georgina, with a certainty she did not feel.

"*Your thoughts*" asked Francis.

"Outside interference" responded Georgina; "How could the DNA samples found at the Crime Scene have been manipulated in the Chain of Evidence, and by whom….?"

"The Police Forensic Logs, Custody Records, Laboratory Reports; I have compiled a new list and am reviewing the entire Chain of Evidence, just as Gregory did pre-trial. So far: nothing to report.

"And I am reviewing the travel CCTV; responded Gregory, before being asked. This task had originally fallen to Georgina.

Francis nodded, showing no sign of surprise at their lack of progress.

"*I would like you both to review Dr Schultz' social activities*, starting with the three months before his arrest. Where did he go in his spare time, who did he meet, where and when precisely? Look for anything outside of his normal patterns of behaviour."

"He appears to be a reserved and measured man; with few external contacts beyond his Job."

"I have given his laptop to a colleague; an IT expert. *He will review his on-line activity.*"

"*Who did he meet who had something to gain from his conviction*? Was there anyone harbouring a grudge against him?"

"I know we have already explored these avenues, but we must do this with a *wide-angled lens*. Review his neighbours statements, his work colleagues; check his bank account details. What have we missed?"

Francis stood up, checked his watch and headed for the door.

"That's all for now, I am due in Court shortly."

He closed the library door behind him and Georgina turned to Gregory.

"How are you today Gregory'? Sorry it's been busy and you had your head down when I arrived; no doubt Nadia told you where I was?"

"Sure, no problem: glad of a break from the CCTV. Fancy a coffee to go?"

Without the need for persuasion, Georgina grabbed her coat and they headed off into the fresh morning air. Ten minutes later both were back in the library, sifting files and hunkering down over transcripts.

The Grandfather Clock in the corridor struck two o'clock before either spoke a word. Georgina looked up apparently startled by the sound of her own voice as she broke the silence: "the Pendulum!" she exclaimed excitedly.

Gregory looked up reacting quizzically to her suggestion and wondering whether her blood sugar was too low, interfering with her thought processes:

"Sorry, did you say *Pendulum*?"

"The Grandfather Clock: that's what made me think of it!"

Without waiting for Gregory's response Georgina was already heading to the desktop computer keyboard in the well lit corner of the library, nearest the window.

Georgina's fingers skipped over the keyboard as she entered; then re-entered, a series of key words. She began searching Legal Citations to procure previous Judgments on the admissibility of evidence culled from *"hypnotherapy"*. She was entirely oblivious to Gregory's wise-cracks about quackery as he looked over her shoulder, shaking his head from side-to-side and wondering what on Earth Francis' would make of her craziness.

Chapter 14

14:00 Tuesday 27th December 2016

"I want you to focus solely on my voice Christophe. Let me guide you as you begin the process of complete relaxation..... "

"Concentrate on any part of your body where you feel most relaxed and feel that sensation as it begins to radiate across your body up into your head, flowing down over your shoulders, radiating to your fingertips; onwards down through your abdomen and into your legs; as far as your toes."

As Dr Kleinberg continued to gently issue soothing instructions, inducing a state of hypnotic trance; the assembled team on the other side of the two way mirror watched in complete silence. Nadia captured the narrative and the digital recorder followed every word. A small CCTV camera captured the entire Consultation.

Georgina looked tense as she sat poised with her notepad and pencil rested on her knee. Gregory felt sceptical but concealed his feelings; at the same time hoping for a small miracle.

The Prison Guard in the corner of the room looked dispassionately at the Legal Team and the two players on the opposite side of the mirror in this emerging scene.

Chapter 15

18:30 Wednesday 28th December 2016

Gregory sat down and stared vacantly for a moment at the CCTV footage from First Southern trains; wondering where to go next with his review. He got up again and discarded his cold coffee in the sink at the far end of the room.

The holiday period between Christmas and the New Year was always a quiet time for Gregory since he'd lost both his parents so he was glad to be working. He'd enjoyed a busy day with friends on the 26th and was glad of a more sedate pace of life in the office, with most people having bridged the gap between Christmas festivities and the arrival of the New Year; with a few days of Annual Leave. He would certainly have done the same if he'd been blessed with kids or family at home.

As he sat back down he was mentally weighing his options from his list of things to do.

"Penny for them" said Nadia over his left shoulder.

"That maybe all they're worth today." responded Gregory. "Think I need more caffeine."

"What about something to eat instead?"

"Now you're talking. I could do with some Chinese food; how does that grab you?"

"Great idea; shall we say twenty minutes; give me time to clear my in tray?"

"Cool."

The platform entrance was heaving with tourists as they exited through the ticket barriers at Piccadilly Circus London Underground Station.

Shaftesbury Avenue was crowded with early evening theatre goers, dressed in their finery and heading off for long-awaited West End Productions.

The restaurant was already beginning to fill up as the younger waiter of the trio ushered them to a window seat. He held Nadia's chair for her as she sat down. She flashed him a broad smile and he nodded pragmatically before placing menus in front of each of them.

"*I do so love people watching*. They're hardly aware of us at all." Nadia looked in her element as she made the comment and was already studying a young couple walking arm-in-arm meandering through the throng of people ambling through China Town. Surrounded by spectacular brightly illuminated lanterns, neon signs and street performers vying for attention: they were far too engrossed in one another to even notice the distractions.

"That must be lovely Gregory don't you think? To be so tied up in one another, *that no one and nothing else matters*?"

Meanwhile Gregory sat absorbed in the serious business of studying the plastic laminated menu and weighing up the pros and cons of the fixed menu as opposed to ordering individual dishes.

"*How hungry are you tonight*?"

Nadia looked back at Gregory. He had planted a pair of black rimmed reading glasses on his nose.

"Since when do you wear reading glasses?"

"Shall we share a meal for two, or can you eat a three person menu?"

"*Gregory, are you listening to a word I am saying*?"

He looked up; diverting his gaze away from the menu and over the rim of the glasses.

"Of course dear, you know how much you matter to me, but food *always* comes first: *you know that*."

He gave her a playful wink and she reciprocated with a swift kick under the table.

Gregory winced and scrunched up his nose, feigning pain; his glasses slipping forward until they were balanced precariously close to the tip of his nose. He hyperextended his neck to keep them from falling off.

Nadia started to impersonate him, much to the amusement of a couple outside who were looking at the evening menu. Spotting their reflection she started to giggle, scrunching her nose up even more.

"Right, let's have option two; you can share my deep fried balls."

"*Oh can I indeed*? Well as long as you let me indulge in some 'weed."

The waiter arrived with his notepad at the ready and they eventually opted for option three which included seaweed; Nadia's favourite starter.

By the time the food arrived Gregory could hardly restrain himself. Armed with chopsticks he began demolishing the sesame toast, before indulging in chicken satay.

"Gorgeous." declared Gregory, mid-satay.

"That's what I love about you Gregory: *you're such a romantic*."

"You don't like my compliments? He responded as he secured a piece of duck and lifted it carefully to his eager lips.

"You're very special Nadia...but tonight you've got serious competition I'm afraid....mmmmmm....perfect balls..."

The second kick to his left shin had been entirely predictable and Gregory just started chortling as he sipped his Chardonnay.

"You know I love you really Nadia. Who else would put up with me?"

Gregory re-filled her glass and they chinked glasses playfully.

"*Merry Christmas*!" they independently declared without prompting.

"Gregory how long do you think you'll stay with 'Chambers?

"Where did that come from?" Gregory responded frowning intensely and sitting back in his chair.

"I just wondered that's all."

"Well, a lot depends on the Partners; whether they think I'm worth investing in."

Nadia fell silent for a moment.

"It's just, well, we enjoy having you around."

"We? *Is that The Royal We?"*

Well okay *I like having you around*; you're a bit mad and a lot of fun, not like some of the others."

"Are you *hitting on me* Nadia Mason?"

Nadia blushed and avoided eye contact and started to giggle again.

Chapter 16

23:30 Clapham

Gregory opened the taxi door and took Nadia's hand as she stepped across onto the kerb, avoiding a large puddle.

"Why thank you Sir Walter!"

Gregory burst into laughter at the historical reference.

"I always forget you studied Law and History at University."

"Brains and beauty."

"Careful, that was *almost* a complement Gregory."

They walked arm in arm up the slippery pathway to the Green ornate front door. The sign above the door said: "Broadway."

Gregory disarmed the security system whilst Nadia removed her coat and placed it on the nearest brass coat hook. She stood marvelling at the ornate cornicing around the ceiling and admiring the stained glass in the hallway window panels. Having been raised in a tired two-up, two-down; the elegance of Gregory's hallway did not escape her eye for a single moment.

As he turned on the kitchen lights and filled the kettle Nadia followed him into the long galley kitchen. She was surprised to see the orderly arrangement of condiments and the immaculately cleaned kitchen.

He put a spoonful of instant coffee into each mug and retrieved the semi-skimmed milk from the fridge.

"Wow, lovely house."

"My mother did all the hard work after my dad died."

"She immersed herself in the detail. It was her way of coping I think."

They stood hugging their mugs filled with steaming coffee as they began to thaw out from the chilly taxi journey.

"Were you close to your mum?"

"She was my best friend."

"That's lovely Gregory.

Gregory blushed and blew into his coffee cup. Nadia noticed how the warm kitchen light seemed to highlight the freckles on his nose. He looked deep in thought.

"You're full of surprises Gregory."

He looked up and caught her staring at him.

"You're not so bad yourself."

"Come on; let's take the weight off our feet."

They sat curled up on the old brown leather sofa next to each other; as a *Chill Out* CD album played quietly in the background.

"I could get used to this…."

"Hot coffee and chilling out on your sofa."

Gregory put his right arm around Nadia's shoulder and hugged her to his chest. She nuzzled into his neck and kissed him lightly.

"I can hear your heart beating." She whispered.

"Thank God for that!" Gregory exclaimed giggling as he did so.

"It's beating *very fast* Gregory."

"It must be the wine."

"Nothing to do with me being next to you then?"

He put his coffee mug down on the wooden side table next to hers on a coaster purchased from *Chesil Beach in Dorset* a decade before. He interlaced the podgy fingers of his left hand in-between Natalia's long slender fingers, stroking the palm of her right hand gently with circular movements of his thumb.

She kissed his neck again, parted her lips and gently licked the skin beneath his ear.

He gently moaned and pulled her closer; breathing in her fragrant perfume.

They locked hands and Gregory began to massage her wrist and forearm with his thumb.

Their lips gently met and they found each others tongues in perfect harmony.

"Take me upstairs Gregory."

Chapter 17

Thursday 29th December 2016 11.30 a.m.

"Whilst you were making breakfast this morning I was taking another look at this and I noticed something odd."

Nadia was sat in the rear reception room at the white circular breakfast bar with Gregory's Chambers' laptop: studying the all important CCTV footage from First Southern Trains. She was dressed in one of his long white tee-shirts and a pair of grey track suit bottoms. Her dark brown hair was brushed back over her shoulders. Gregory stood looking at her for a moment.

He pulled up a bar stool alongside her, gently lifted some wayward hairs from her face and kissed her right neck and cheek.

She giggled, pressed pause on the screen and turned to him:

"Look at this first!"

"I was looking at this lady's three quarter length blue coat as she boarded the train looking for a seat." She pointed directly at a young woman with short wavy dark hair.

"I couldn't help thinking; I could do with a coat like that for the cold morning commute."

"Not with me to keep you warm in the mornings."

Nadia grinned like a Cheshire cat and kissed Gregory lightly on the left cheek and he blushed noticeably.

"Anyway….." she responded widening her eyelids before she refocused her attention on the screen as she spoke:

"She initially turns left as she boards the train and goes towards the front of the train out of view of the CCTV. Then she walks back down the aisle, *past Christophe* who's standing to the left of her at this point."

"Okay, I can see that."

"She then disappears from view as she obviously heads towards the rear of the train looking for a seat. But here's the thing: less than thirty seconds later; there she is again but this time, she's sat down between these two men. Here, four rows behind Christophe." She pointed at the lady who's face was clearly discernible.

"If you rewind, you'll see that there were three passengers occupying this seat when she passes it the first time; so there was *nowhere* for her to sit in row four."

"That doesn't make sense at all."

Gregory frowned and moved even closer to the screen, looking puzzled.

"Let me get my reading glasses; hang on a moment."

Grabbing the remote control he turned down the music on the CD player and repositioned himself with his left arm around her waist whilst she took him through the CCTV footage again.

"I noted the time interval; here go back to *thirty four minutes and five seconds* and this row: *I'm calling it row 4.* The same two men but with a different women sat between them; this one has long blonde hair. As you go forward in time - Mrs Blue Coat enters the train, moves forward, back and voila at *thirty five minutes and ten seconds*, she's at down; opposite these three passengers who haven't moved."

"What I am missing?" asked Gregory as he stared intently at the screen.

"What you're saying is that within the space of one minute and five seconds, the two women have swapped seats, with nothing captured on the CCTV? That can't be right."

As they watched the replay in slow motion it was clear that the lady with long blonde hair had somehow suddenly disappeared from her seat which was newly occupied by the lady in the blue winter coat with short dark hair.

Gregory sat back, unable to comprehend what he was watching.

"I can only think that the train stopped and the original lady got off; or moved seats. Either way, why is that not captured on the tape unless....it's been *EDITED*?"

Nadia sat back in her chair; looking like the cat who discovered the cream.

"My God Nadia you're a bloody genius!"

She disentangled herself from his left arm, slid down off her bar stool and stood up in front of him; blocking the computer screen. She ran her hands through Gregory' ginger curly hair and removed his reading glasses.

He looked at her large dark brown eyes and she stood grinning at him.

"So can I have my *reward* now please?"

Gregory smiled and put his hands around her slim warm body, pulling her closer to him, gently massaging her shoulders and kissing her neckline as he nuzzled closer.

She leaned back over the breakfast bar arching her back as he raised her white tee-shirt slowly; flexing forward as he did so and kissing the exposed skin on her soft abdomen.

His tongue found her umbilicus and he kissed her gently then encircled her abdomen with long slow sweeping movements of his lips and tongue, moving slowly up towards her ribs. She began to breathe more deeply and kissed his head, pulling him closer.

"Lovely pussy, cat." Nadia imitated her cat purring as she whispered into his left ear.

Gregory lifted her tee shirt and nuzzled under her ample breasts as his fingers stroked the skin between her shoulders. She shivered and started to sway her hips from side to side as his hands moved down, resting on the waistline of her joggers.

She pulled her tee-shirt over his head and he moved upwards and gently blew over her right nipple before encircling her enlarging nipple with his eager wet tongue.

Nadia moaned and arched her back again, twisting her left shoulder towards him and gently nudging her left breast to his open mouth.

"Suck pussy cat." Nadia pushed her breasts together as Gregory alternated his affection, one to another. His hands moved down and began massaging her firm buttocks as she swayed her hips rhythmically in time with the music.

Nadia whispered into Gregory's ear again as he dropped to his knees.

"Lick pussy cat."

Chapter 18

Friday 30th December 2016

Gregory opened the team discussion at 8 a.m. as agreed.

"Okay to cut to the chase: we believe the CCTV footage showing Christophe's journey via First Southern Trains has been *edited*."

"That fits entirely with the updated evidence provided by the hypnotherapy session with Christophe; where under hypnosis, and without *any* prompting, he could recall stopping at Clapham Junction."

"On the video footage presented during the trial, the train did not make a stop at Clapham junction and the timelines on the footage and the recording would have been different had that stop been incorporated."

"The time table from the train operators confirms that a stop at Clapham Junction would have added an extra four or five minutes to the journey time: and at that time there were indeed intermittent ongoing *unscheduled* track repairs. That delay would have been sufficient to account for the "lady in blue", securing a seat."

"Even if the CCTV footage was not *purposely* edited, it is clearly *incomplete*."

"So this new finding suggests that whilst Christophe had clearly taken a trip into Waterloo via First Southern Trains at some time, on the night of the murder, the CCTV from Christophe's journey had been cropped to fit in with the timelines from the Waterloo footage; meaning that the individual seen crossing the station and the subsequent CCTV tracked image was NOT Christophe. He would have still been on the train: delayed at Clapham Junction."

"The CCTV recordings from Waterloo station are independently verifiable from several camera angles, both of which are security cameras not operated by the Railways, installed by National Security Services; so the veracity of captured footage is not in question."

"The station footage of an individual crossing from Platform Ten to the North exit at Waterloo station; clearly shows someone wearing a cycle helmet. Whilst his or her appearance and clothing are similar to that worn by Christophe's; no definitive identification is possible and in light of the edited footage; the evidence is no longer persuasive."

"We are agreed that the street footage from Westminster is fragmented at best and again the quality, captured in the dark and with light rain that night: a definitive identification of the rider is *impossible.*"

"Therefore, It is not possible to reliably place Christophe at the Scene of the murder on Tuesday 9th August 2016 and this fits with his contention that he cycled part way of the journey to Professor Justin's apartment before changing his mind and taking a taxi home."

"Although his knowledge of London fell a longways short of being able to give a full amount of his *exact journey*; its clear that someone knew that he headed off to London and judging from the edited footage from the train journey had decided to set him up for the murder and had the capacity to produce an image which was good enough to fool the Jury into wrongfully committing him to prison for murder."

"It is likely that this had been planned carefully and in that context Christophe's historical cycling trips into London to enjoy cycling around Richmond Park: are likely to have been previously monitored by *Persons Unknown*. They would be aware of his make and type of bicycle and his cycle gear."

"The journey from Waterloo to Richmond is around ten miles; given that Christophe spends an hour cycling around the park; he cycles around twenty five to thirty miles on a typical round trip."

"The distance from Waterloo to Melway Mews is barely three miles and the Prosecution held that on the night of the murder, this would have been an easy trip for an experienced cyclist and that he would be aware of short cuts and back streets; thereby avoiding traffic cameras."

"As we've said before, it seems likely that the cab which Christophe took home was *unlicensed*; that's presumably why the taxi driver never came forward to help our Defence plea in corroboration of Christophe's assertion that he made an early exit from London."

"By the same token, it was one piece of the Prosecution evidence that was lacking: they could not shed any light on his return journey home on the night of the killing; they weren't able to locate any CCTV from First Southern Trains or find evidence that he took a taxi home as he'd always claimed. He paid in cash unfortunately so couldn't furnish a receipt."

Georgina looked thoughtful for a moment then said:

"That's brilliant Gregory; but we still don't have a *motive* for placing Christophe in the frame for murder. Why go to all this trouble to frame him?"

"I guess we start with the usual motives of *money, sex or revenge.*" responded Gregory with a disingenuous smile.

"*Revenge..* What are the options do you think?" asked Nadia.

Georgina looked thoughtful as she considered Nadia's question.

"So are you suggesting we go back to the beginning and look at Professor Justin's life in more detail and her one night stand with Christophe, Nadia?"

"What if it was something which Professor Justin and Christophe *didn't do*, rather than something they *did do* Georgina?"

Gregory started taking notes as the two continued to speculate.

"That's interesting Nadia. Professor Justin's Committee work must have provided plenty of scope for not approving or even blocking decisions which impacted not only powerful Institutions or Companies; but also individuals."

"The prosecution case was based on her failure to provide backing for Utopia's breakthrough therapy in HCV; thereby stealing Christophe's crowning glory and depriving the Company of a blockbuster treatment. But that motive was flimsy at best."

"We certainly didn't find any evidence of a Company conspiracy against Christophe." Georgina added.

Gregory had circled the word *individual* on his page. He spoke up:

"Suppose Nadia is right and this is vengeance. *We need to scrutinise the late Professor Justin's life more closely....*

Chapter 19

07:30: Saturday 31st December 2016

Georgina and Nadia had travelled into Central London together that morning, trudging their way through the early morning throng of bargain hunters already making the most of the New Year Sales and they'd negotiated congested escalators; before emerging into the breath-taking icy cold morning air at the Tube Exit.

They sat side by side defrosting in the library, each hugging a revitalising cup of early morning coffee; waiting for the rest of the team to convene.

Gregory arrived at seven forty-five evidently enjoying lively banter with Jonathan; both wearing healthy glows and sporting large latte coffees: the milky additives a substitute for breakfast in both cases. Jonathan had eaten in the early hours of the morning and Gregory often skipped the most important meal of the day.

"Good morning ladies" beamed Gregory, wiping the coffee froth from his upper lip onto his woollen overcoat sleeve: *"You both know Jonathan."*

The foursome sat exchanging small talk waiting for Francis, who was seldom late for team meetings. At seven fifty eight Nadia received a text from Francis instructing them to press on with their updates as his taxi was snarled up in traffic after an early morning Road Traffic Accident near his home in Chigwell.

"Okay team so we now have a number of leads arising from the Jonathan's detailed analysis of Christophe's laptop:" explained Gregory, *"Over to you Jonathan."*

Jonathan stood up and made his way over to the whiteboard and used a Blue-tooth device to operate his computer as he spoke.

"*Thank you Gregory*. As you already know from our previous *Skype meeting*, my brief was to look retrospectively, for any unusual online activity associated activity on Dr Schultz' Personal Computer."

"His email and browsing history was largely confined to online banking, clothes shopping and music downloads; so one particular email caught my attention early in the search: it's entitled "*investment opportunity*.""

Jonathan scanned the folders and opened the relevant email on the electronic smart white board, so that the team could focus on the detail; as he spoke he highlighted the key points with a laser pointer.

"It stood out because it was sent from *Daniel Ennis' tablet* on *9th July 2016* at two-thirty in the morning; whilst he was taking a holiday in Amsterdam."

Jonathan looked across the table to Gregory and nodded.

"*Jonathan and I spoke to him late last night.*"

"We know from Daniel's account that he had arrived in Amsterdam on *8th July*; the evening before the email was sent. Daniel had planned to spend the evening and weeks ahead with a close friend from America; but *Archie* had cancelled his flight from New York at the last minute. Daniel was therefore alone in Amsterdam."

"Daniel spent the evening in a Bar in Amsterdam, within walking distance from his Hotel, where he met a Russian, who called himself *Sergei*. They spent the evening drinking and had a meal before they returned to Daniel's hotel around one-thirty in the morning."

"Was it a chance meeting with the Russian?" asked Georgina.

"At the time, Daniel had no reason to assume otherwise. They had quite a banter going by the end of the evening; Daniel studied languages at University, he's quite the polyglot, but they mostly conversed in English. The Bar was full and they stayed there until around midnight, drinking and mingling with the locals before going for a kebab at a nearby take-away."

"When Daniel returned to his Hotel with Sergei, *if that's his real name*; he had no reason to suspect the Russian had any other motives or that the meeting was anything other than by chance. In retrospect of course, he's not so sure…"

"*Did they plan to have sex*?" asked Georgina.

"Daniel recalls little in the way of detail and any activity which did take place, *was not consensual*." Gregory answered pragmatically; 'bear with me Georgina and I will come to the detail."

"So moving swiftly on…. The next morning, *9th July* Dan awoke to find no sign of *Sergei*. Furthermore, it is entirely possible that Daniel had been given some kind of tranquilliser by the Russian. He felt disoriented, dizzy and had a poor recollection for the events of the preceding night."

"He'd been drinking but nothing out of the ordinary and only a mixture of beer and vodka; they had not consumed any "shots" or used any drugs."

"*What about marijuana?*" Georgina interjected.

"Sure good point Georgina; Daniel admits to having used weed recreationally on his previous visit to Amsterdam in 2014, but not during this particular visit. It means that he was well aware of the side-effects of weed as well, and equally sure that his symptoms were entirely different to *anything* he'd experience before."

"He did recall that the Russian had appeared to be very drunk on their return to the Hotel: Daniel wonders in retrospect whether that was a ploy to disarm him and put him at his ease. The Russian was a big muscular guy and appeared from Dan's perspective, to be a regular drinker…."

"Was Daniel tested for benzodiazepines; Rohypnol in particular?" clarified Georgina; "*Given his suspicions about being drugged*?"

"Rohypnol, is that the "date rape drug"?" Interrupted Nadia; cutting in on the conversation. Georgina nodded and Nadia looked thoughtful as she continued taking notes.

"*Unfortunately not*; but on return to the UK he discussed his memory loss and other symptoms with a Private Consultant at a Sexual Health Clinic in Harley Street, London. She also put Rohypnol in the frame, as the most likely candidate drug, which when mixed with alcohol would have readily produced Daniel's symptoms and contributed to his amnesia." As a full week' had elapsed since his drinking episode with Sergei; Rohypnol would not have been detected."

Georgina nodded: "it's detectable for up to seventy-two hours ordinarily."

"So why the visit to the Clinic in Harley Street Gregory; was Daniel worried about his HIV status? I assume from what you say he is gay?"

"Yes on both counts after his night out with the Russian: on *11th July specifically*, Dan began to receive a series of *anonymous* emails with graphic images from his night spent with Sergei. They depicted him with a variety of toys and used vodka bottles from the mini-bar, *inserted rectally*."

Nadia winced as she looked up from her note taking and caught Gregory's eye momentarily.

"Daniel could recount the images in some detail and although many were extreme close ups; some were full length and clearly identified him."

"*So the motive was some kind of blackmail*? *Did he contact the Police*?" Georgina asked; looking horrified by the revelation of the graphic detail.

"We assume so; though no demands have ever made. He didn't contact the Police. He simply deleted the images and tried to forget the incident, realising how it would look having invited the Russian back to his Hotel and having spent the night with him."

"*To return to your previous question Georgina*, Dan wanted to check his HIV status and understand the risks posed by the insertions he had been subjected to. His Consultant also ensured that he was free of Hepatitis B

& C infections, given the possibility of Daniel having been Penile raped by the Russian."

"I should add that he has never disclosed his sexual orientation to his Parents and whilst the emails were unnerving, he received no further contact." He had no discussion with anyone else about the whole experience, apart from the Doctor he Consulted."

"So Christophe was completely unaware of the events?" clarified Georgina.

"Absolutely; although they regularly communicated by email ordinarily, they hadn't heard from each other since around April this year: both busy with travel, and launch plans for U0008 in Christophe's case."

"We could almost certainly have recovered the images from Daniel's tablet; unfortunately he burnt the device, destroying the evidence and severing any further email link with the Russian."

"Any more questions at this time team?"

Gregory gestured with a smile and a nod to Jonathan, who continued with his presentation.

"The email in question was sent *only* to Dr Schultz. He opened it on the *10th July* and followed the hyper-link which took him to a Website which looked like this."

Jonathan opened a fresh tab on the screen.

"As you can see there are a number of grammatical errors and the Advertisement claims to be a *"sure-fire investment"* with guaranteed high returns. It reeks of a scam in the current economic climate and if you click on this link for further details; the next page invites the unwary to provide contact and financial details."

"The web-link is no longer live and I have traced the link to a server in one of the more run down suburbs of Moscow. The location is not associated with any investment bank, broker or legitimate Business concern which I could trace."

"*I presume Dr Schultz relegated the email to trash*?" asked Georgina.

"*Correct; he then deleted it.*" confirmed Jonathan.

"But as you are aware the damage had already been done and the computer virus had already infected Christophe's computer. I'll spare you the technical stuff, but effectively the technology behind this virus protocol allowed someone to *actively monitor Dr Schultz' browsing activity; all keystrokes, credit card details, passwords: you name it. His identity and personal details were no longer protected by his firewall; his computerised front door was wide open!*"

"Did Christophe have anti-spyware?" interjected Gregory.

"He did and I reviewed his entire security log from the commercial anti-spyware installed on his system. It provided no alerts and the software failed to recognise the threat from the encryption."

"This form of viral algorithm is quite sophisticated but is increasingly prevalent in security breaches; even in large Companies."

"*Dr Schultz would have been totally unaware of the snoopers' activity.*"

Gregory waited for Jonathan's nod then spoke:

"So we now have clear evidence of an incursion into Christophe's private life. Jonathan and I have already updated Francis on these details."

"Georgina: over to you."

"Thanks Gregory. We know that Christophe was participating in regular on-line counselling with Barbara Turner. She is a fully Accredited Counsellor, whom he sourced on-line and they met bi-weekly in *virtual face-to-face discussion on Zoom.*"

"*They never met in person?*"

"No Gregory. Christophe wanted the *physical* separation. I think he found it easier somehow, to distance himself from the reality of his ongoing symptoms; and in particular from his past experiences." Georgina paused momentarily.

"He was sexually abused by his uncle as a child."

Jonathan looked sombre, furrowing his brow. The team waited patiently whilst Georgina gathered her thoughts; she appeared distracted for a moment.

Nadia broke the silence: *"Do we know why Dr Schultz did not reveal these details prior to his trial?"*

"I believe the answer is that he didn't want to open up his past life for everyone to pore over. As you know he's an intensely private individual where his personal life is concerned. Despite the Pre-Trial time I spent with Christophe, he never gave any clue that he was receiving any form of Counselling, and certainly never hinted at a history of abuse."

"He never ever expected to be convicted of murder and therefore never wished to expose his past."

Nadia's phone pinged announcing Francis' imminent arrival at the meeting.

The door to the library opened and Francis entered the room with a flourish and an unusually buoyant and cheerful Greeting:

"Good Morning, team!"

He strode across the room, and firmly shook Jonathan's hand before taking the seat vacant seat on the other side of him, as they both sat down in unison.

Each of Francis' young protégées had updated him individually on progress on the previous evening by email and subsequent telephone conversation, and the new evidence from Christophe's laptop provided by Jonathan.

Gregory gave a quick resume as to their progress in the meeting.

Francis half turned to Jonathan and asked:

"Jonathan, do you have any more information beyond the transmitted email from Daniel Ennis' tablet and the possible Russian link?"

"*Yes indeed Francis*. Having cross-referenced Dr Schultz' personal diary with his work schedule; I checked his flight itineraries. He invariably booked his own flights and printed his Boarding Passes on line at home. He also *ordinarily* booked his Railway or taxi cabs on-line; so that's pertinent to his journey into London on the night of Professor Justin's Murder. He filed all of his receipts meticulously."

"I can confirm that he made two scheduled flights after *July 10th;* the date his computer was hacked."

"Through a mutual friend in security, I gained access to the airlines' manifest for the two scheduled flights."

"During the time he would have been flying from London Heathrow to New York on *July 12th 2016, the personal files on his computer were remotely accessed; by persons unknown in Russia.*"

"*The same server location as the original email link?*" asked Francis.

"Precisely." responded Jonathan and hovered his cursor over the files on the smart board display.

"Of particular interest is this file labelled "*BT*"; it contained the appointment schedule for his counsellor – Barbara Turner. The file was copied and extracted remotely.

Gregory looked puzzled and asked: "*How do we know Christophe didn't have his computer onboard at the time?*"

"Good question Gregory. When away he left his computer plugged in and connected to the internet so updates were routinely installed and the ISP records and use of cookies, in addition to other systems we have in place: confirm the exact location of his computer. *There is no doubt: he was not present in his apartment when the files were accessed.*"

"*You said files – pleural?*" clarified Francis.

Jonathan paused for a moment smiled, then presented his final *piece de resistance*:

"Dr Schultz also had an encrypted file."

With a few keystrokes he projected the specified file contents.

The address was all too familiar to the assembled team: the address of Professor Justin's apartment in London.

"This file was accessed, copied and extracted on Wednesday *July 13th at ten o'clock* in the evening: around four weeks *before Professor Justin's Murder.*"

Jonathan double clicked on a second file and projected a series of eight digit numbers aligned vertically with corresponding six digit numbers arranged horizontally.

"As you can see: these are Bank Account numbers and matching Sort Codes for Dr Schultz' on-line banking." Jonathan then used his cursor to highlight a six digit number in the middle of the list.

"This number will be less familiar to you all than Professor Justin's Address: it is the six digit pass-code for the underground car park used to gain entry to the late Professor's apartment."

"This code was also accessed, copied and extracted on the same date as her address details."

"*Wow*" exclaimed Georgina; "*result Jonathan*!"

"*Is it too early for a round at the Feathers*?" asked Gregory. Georgina and Nadia beamed at one another and a sense of relief was palpable throughout the Team.

 Francis grasped Jonathan's hand and quietly added *"Bravo Dear Friend."*

Chapter 20

Georgina perched unusually far forward on her chair and shifted uneasily as Francis and the Partners entered the library ready to hear the proposed *Grounds for Appeal* against Christophe's Sentence for Murder.

Georgina was wearing a dark blue two-piece suit and a contrasting white blouse; her blond hair pulled back and fastened into a small bunch, clipped to the back of her head. She turned, and smiled nervously at Gregory as he sat alongside her in the middle of the large oak table and gave her a reassuring squeeze on her right forearm and wished her *"Happy New Year."*

Francis wore his customary blue pin striped suit and striking red silk tie; secured with a perfect Windsor knot; his orderliness *reminiscent of Christophe Schultz* thought Georgina, for a fleeting moment.

The four Partners sat two either side of Francis; he sat immediately opposite Georgina. He scanned the room and waited for a few moments until Nadia was seated comfortably, pen poised; directly opposite the electronic smart board at the far end of the table.

After taking a final sip of sparkling *Perrier Water* and conscious that her heart rate was far higher than her customary sixty beats per minute; Georgina took a deep breath and momentarily collected her thoughts. The assembled audience sat in silence; awaiting her performance.

The early morning clouds had started to lift and a ray of sunshine grew effortlessly in intensity as it swept across the Boardroom, just as the Grandfather Clock in the hallway chimed nine times.

"A good omen I believe Georgina: the sun shines on the Righteous."

Francis received a muted ripple of approval from around the room as everyone lightly tapped the table in unison. He gestured to Georgina with a warm smile and slight forward tilt of his forehead head; his spectacles balanced perfectly upon his nose.

Georgina looked down the row of expectant Partners' faces from left to right, and back again, before fixing her gaze on Francis; looking just above the rim of his spectacles.

"Good Morning Everyone. *A Very Happy New Year to you all* and Thank You for taking time out of your busy schedules for this meeting."

"I would like to outline the case for Dr Schultz' Appeal."

The clock struck ten o'clock as Georgina began summarising the case; before inviting questions.

"The DNA evidence submitted at the trial of Dr Schultz' could reasonably have been acquired from Dr Schultz apartment:"

"Firstly, the latex gloves which Dr Schultz used during masturbation as a potential source of both semen and finger prints: both items acquired from a black waste disposal bag, taken from the garbage chute which services his apartment block; by person or persons unknown."

"This ties in perfectly with the anonymous 'phone tip off which lead the Police to the Westminster location where a single size 8 right hand surgical glove was discovered in a recycling bin. The caller's identity was never ascertained and the Prosecution alleged that the assailant wore the surgical gloves when he strangled Professor Justin; hence the absence of finger prints on her neck."

"So in practical terms, the murderer penetrated her leaving the bruising around her anal verge. He would have worn his own condom during the act and thereafter used a sample from the stolen surgical glove to insert semen into her rectum and mouth....once she became unresponsive if sedated, (by the unknown drug compound X, exhibit 9166): or immediately after killing her."

"Secondly, the minute saliva traces found in the deceased' rectum during the second post-mortem which could have been extracted from one or many disposable toothbrushes, used by Dr Schultz; sourced from one or more garbage bags from the aforementioned chute.

"We are aware that as a consequence of his longstanding obsessive-compulsive behaviour; Dr Schultz uses a new toothbrush daily and his masturbation ritualistic behaviour whilst more unusual; is commonplace to him."

Martin Fothergill was the first to pose a question. His pointed features and swept back ears had played a part in the origin of his nick-name amongst the Pupils: *the Hawk*. His eye for detail was undisputed; often merciless in his attack on unwitting Defendants in Court. He specialised in Fraud cases, reflecting his early training as an Accountant, prior to reading Law in his early thirties.

He read from his pencilled notes, held within a small leather clad binder; as he spoke.

"Georgina you used the phrase: *"could reasonably have been acquired"*.

"What do you mean by that statement?"

"*Three years ago: in June 2013 to be exact*, one of the residents from the same apartment block as Dr Schultz, was the victim of an identity theft."

Georgina sifted through her A4 file of notes.

"*Mr Colin Ford*, a forty-two year old chef lost over twenty thousand Pounds from a bank account. The two men who were convicted of the Offence had stolen an old Passport from Mr Ford. He had disposed of the Passport in his trash. One of the men convicted admitted that he had taken black bags of garbage from the chute in the basement of the Apartments; from which he had procured forged documents, supplied by the Second Defendant.

"Mr Fothergill, I believe it is perfectly reasonable that a *copycat crime* could have been perpetrated; this time with the intention of acquiring Dr Schultz' DNA. The Case is easily searchable on Lexis-Nexus or WestLaw data bases."

"Was Security improved at the Apartment block after the Court Case disclosed the risk from the waste disposal chutes?"

"Apparently not. The case was also reported on local news channels and was picked up by the Daily Chronicle in Surrey."

"The access to the underground waste disposal was via two routes: an externally locked door, the key to which was held by the Waste Management Company; and a second internal corridor, available only to residents. The underground facility also housed fuse boxes for the Apartment block and the exit route formed a Fire Escape in an Emergency."

"Waste disposal personnel (or of course anyone who picked the external lock): could readily access the residents' trash."

"I accept the possibility of a copy-cat crime, based on the facts and *modus operandi*." Martin Fothergill stroked his pointed chin as he spoke.

"My second question relates to the DNA. You have an independent forensic witness who will attest to the veracity of the humble toothbrush as a source of saliva?"

"Indeed we do. Professor McKinnon' evidence was crucial during Dr Schultz trial and we will produce two additional witnesses. Professor Martin Glover is a forensic pathologist who studied alongside Professor McKinnon; the men have a great deal of respect for one another."

"Secondly Professor Gloria Manning; an expert in DNA extraction and sequencing techniques. She was a pioneer in the elaboration of trace DNA through PCR technology: Polymerase Chain Reaction: essentially amplifying the number of DNA strands extracted from less than a dozen cells derived from the oral mucosa of the donor source."

"She has given evidence in a number of high profile Acquittals."

"I have called '*Gloria* in on a number of cases Martin; she doesn't take any prisoners." Francis responded dryly, casting a look at Martin.

Amanda Devenish Q.C. focused intently on Georgina as she spoke.

"The remaining DNA evidence at the crime scene – the *partial prints* on the bed frame and bedside light, were the result of the legitimate visit which Dr Schultz made to Professor Justin's Apartment on the afternoon of *December 26th 2015*; when he claims they had *consensual vaginal intercourse*."

Georgina nodded.

"Did 'Schultz ever indulge in anal intercourse to our knowledge?"

"He was questioned by the Prosecution at trial and he vehemently denied the allegation of *ever* having performed anal intercourse. We argued that his obsession with cleanliness, his *routine* around toileting for example; was intuitively supportive of his denial."

"At trial of course, we didn't have the evidence from his on-line Counsellor, *Barbara Turner*.

"She is willing to give evidence citing the abuse suffered by Dr Schultz as a teenager and the impact this has had on his behaviour; particularly his O.C.D."

"I am not convinced her evidence will be compelling in that specific aspect of the Appeal Georgina." Amanda Devenish responded.

Francis looked stoic as he intervened and suggested a comfort break.

"Right everyone, let's take ten and then move onto the CCTV evidence."

Chapter 21

10:50 a.m. 2nd January 2017

"Amanda – I presume you have further questions?" asked Francis as the Team took their seats and Georgina refreshed her glass with a new bottle of Welsh Spring Water.

"Yes. Thank you Francis."

"Crucially, the new evidence gleaned from Daniel Ennis, points to remote access to Dr Schultz' Personal Laptop. You are arguing that by remotely accessing his Computer camera, the perpetrator would have been aware of 'Schultz use of latex gloves during household cleaning and most importantly during his sexual activities, and was therefore able to procure one or more pairs of gloves from his refuse chute and leave DNA at the Crime Scene and thereafter deposit a used Surgical Glove in a recycling bin in Westminster: before contacting the Police anonymously."

"Thats' quite a list of suppositions...without any evidence to substantiate the activity. It's all circumstantial evidence..."

"However, Professor Justin's London Address and the six digit security keypad number, used to gain access to the Underground Car Park at her Melway Mews Apartment, were remotely accessed via Dr Schultz' laptop computer, *in his absence.*"

"Furthermore, your independent IT expert Jonathan Clarke has confirmed that the CCTV procured from First Southern Trains as presented by the prosecution at the original trial had been edited:"

"*Based on the Balance of Probability.*"

"I think that's sufficient standard for the Appeal Court." Interjected Francis.

Amanda nodded and continued:

"You cited a train journey undertaken by 'Schultz on the evening of Professor Justin's murder. That was a journey which included a five minute stop at *Clapham Junction*. You cite the "lady in blue" as the enigma which exposed the Fraud."

"Is there any other explanation apart from evidence tampering that would legitimise the CCTV recording?"

"None that we could discover Miss Devenish or Jonathan Clarke could envisage."

"We believe the data and time records were *superimposed* onto the original recording. Jonathan Clarke was able to replicate fraudulent CCTV very easily using a sample of CCTV footage from a recent journey he had me undertake from the very station which Dr Schultz boarded the train in the original recording."

"So we encourage our Pupils to indulge in crime scene reconstruction now Francis?"

Amanda smiled as she turned to Francis for his response.

"Indeed we do Amanda; but only the most promising of candidates!"

Georgina blushed and looked down at her A4 file modestly as the team laughed approvingly.

Francis continued:

"In the corrupted CCTV evidence submitted to the Court, the video footage had been edited to enable the time frame link to the *genuine* CCTV security coverage taken from security cameras at Waterloo station.

This fact is material to the timeline evidence presented by the Prosecution relating to the night of the Murder."

"The individual who was seen crossing Waterloo station is highly likely to be the same individual who undertook the journey between Waterloo station and Professor Justin's apartment; or an accomplice to the crime."

"Equally we know that Christophe Schultz cycled for a mere ten minutes having left the train station at Waterloo; before abandoning his journey. Although his exact route has not been confirmed by CCTV as yet, we fully expect to procure this evidence before we submit our Appeal in the next seven days. Jonathan Clarke is pulling that CCTV together as we speak, given the revised timelines."

"He's called in a few favours from his colleagues at M15."

"Are there any other questions for Georgina?"

"Okay. In which case thank you Georgina, meeting adjourned."

Francis sat cleaning his spectacles as the Partners left the room.

Taking his lead, Nadia, Gregory and Georgina remained seated.

Francis took up the baton again.

"Right Team. Now the work really begins."

PART 5

Chapter 1

22:30 Monday 19th September 2016 Highgate, London

Natalia sat on the edge of the single bed wrapped in the damp nylon stained quilt which was peppered with brown and yellow stains. The top floor gloomy bedsit felt even more humid than usual and she could smell the rank cooking coming from the local Chinese take-away three buildings down the main drag. Sweat trickled down her forehead and she wiped it away with a corner of the quilt before smelling the fabric and turning her nose up in disgust.

She studied the gold Rolex™ watch on her left wrist: a thing of *unbridled beauty*. She released the bracelet lock and clasp, turned the watch face over and read the small inscribed initials *F.M.* just as she'd done a thousand times before, since the moment she'd acquired that which was *rightfully hers. An inheritance of sorts.*

After all, she'd looked after *them* for all those years. She'd wiped their stinking, shitty arses and made them tea and biscuits before dolling out their pills, morning, noon and night time; whatever the *bitch* of a boss had ordered her to do. Yeah it was hers alright; she'd earned something special: *something beautiful.* It brightened up the shit hole she lived in and she could see people look at it when she wore it outside: envious and pious hypocrites: judging her, looking down their snotty noses at her.

HE had numerous expensive watches; she'd seen them when she was there: *his house, with his whore, drooling over his expensive possessions.* Time-pieces squirrelled away in red, black and gold cases. When they were out, she'd sneak a look at them; even showed her half-brothers once, but then they'd snitched on her and he'd beaten her. *BASTARD*: she hated him and his latest *trophy wife.*

That woman was not and never would be her fucking mother. Her fucking mother was dead to her:

SHE had everything and nothing. An empty vessel: devoid of love.

The bleach was growing out of her short blonde hair leaving auburn tinged roots which reminded her of match sticks as she stared into the tiny blue framed plastic mirror which hung above her bed. She couldn't afford to have a hair do'; not until the end of the month.

She lit a roll-up and pulled up the black plastic venetian blinds so she could puff smoke out of the window. The traffic was snarled up again; long snaking lines of tail lights slithering right and headlights jerking left. Night and day, over and over; relentless fucking people in their prized dick-wagons.

Then it would start at 11p.m.; just as she needed to sleep: Police sirens and ambulances wailing. More of them queuing up; *some of them would become hers over the coming weeks and she knew it*. The old ones anyway; the ones who couldn't wipe their own arses or pissed the bed after she'd put on clean sheets, or worst of all, the old pervs' who groped at her tits and fanny. They'd pay, one way or another. Cold hard cash or something she could sell. She'd even give them what they wanted if they could pay. 'Twenty would do it, and for that they could cop a feel.

She blew smoke rings. A group of young lads started calling up to her from a passing car; an old Ford. She birded' them with her right middle finger and went back inside the room. She threw off the quilt and lay back on the green candle-wick bedspread and put her headphones into her ears. *FUCK IT*: they could do without her tonight.

She woke up and needed to pee urgently. She looked at *her* watch: 1:30 a.m.

The floorboards creaked as she sidled down between the cheap chest of draws and the door way. She stubbed her right foot on the metal bed stand.

"FUCK." She plonked down on the bed and felt another spring falter in the mattress; pressing into her ass. It reminded her of those pigs *up' North*; where she'd worked.

Using all of her holes then throwing her a few stinking notes covered in hash and speed'.

Her toe began to bleed where she'd torn the skin; she could feel the warm blood ooze down the side of her foot. She grabbed a handful of tissues and bent over putting pressure over the split skin until it stopped throbbing.

Nat' removed the wooden chair which was wedged under the door knob and unlocked the door with the old brass key left in the lock. As she opened the door the stench was strong: the corridor smelled worse than usual; she was sure someone had puked on the floor somewhere below: probably the druggie from the third floor she thought. What was his name? *Shaun*: that was it. *"Shaun the fucking undead."*

She used her foot to open the door to the communal toilet; *or cess pit as she called it*. Two toilets between ten residents: or double that number when "guests" were entertained. Dirty bitches some of them. 'Could barely piss straight after fucking.

The energy saving bulb came on; well one out of three wasn't bad for this place she scoffed. As usual no one had flushed. She pulled the lever and nothing happened. No toilet paper. She squatted and then finished by pulling her jeans up; no underwear: *"a drip dry."*

As she walked back to her room the *pig* from next door came out; dressed in his grey spunk stained dressing gown.

"Hey sugar, how ya' doin' Nat?"

"How about a blow job; I'll bung you a fiver?"

"FUCK OFF LOSER! No wonder your wife kicked you out with the size of your knob."

She waggled her little finger at him emphasising her derisory put down.

Ken leered at her in the dimly lit corridor as she looked over her left shoulder at him. He turned into the toilet. She locked her bedsit door again and put the chair back under the wobbly wooden knob of the bedroom door.

Two minutes later the door banged loudly as her neighbour kicked it as he returned to his own bedsit paradise.

"You know you'll come running again when *your fuckin' rent's due*: *fuckin' dirty little BITCH!*"

She ignored him and put her Bluetooth headphones into her ears and waited for them to connect. She chose a local station featuring *rock classics* on her mobile and kept beat stamping her feet in time with the beat. She flicked through the entries in her contact list until she found the number.

"I need some more money; I need to get out of this shit-hole soon."

She pressed send and her PAYG [Pay As You Go] balance pinged up as £8.33. The pockets in her jeans were empty. She flicked the bedside lamp on and started searching the drawers for spare cash. She found £2.25 in cash. *Enough for chips* she thought. She put her pumps on and a denim jacket over her white tee-shirt; then thought better of it and threw it back onto the bed.

The music next door got louder and she locked her door before she gave Ken's door a resounding kick and felt it rattle on its hinges. She took the stairs two at a time as she headed down to the ground floor. As she reached the entrance hall she could hear the couple in Room One having another shouting match. Screaming and crying in equal measure as she went past their door. She opened the front door and headed down the short gravel path onto the main road.

The night air was laden with the smell of car fumes and stale tobacco admixed with hash as she sauntered pass rows of bed sits and student digs. Every house had multiple lights on. Plasma screens were the must-haves; unless you were a have-not, like her.

A tall rather stooping older silver haired bloke walking his dog looked at her and smiled as he walked by; showing his tobacco stained teeth. She thought of *HIM* and his teeth whitening kits and dental floss; running from his years as a smoker. *Hiding the truth: living the lie.*

A dog as a babe magnet: *sad fuck*, she mused as she looked over her right shoulder at the guy wandering aimlessly along the road with his 'retriever.

The smell hit her nose before she reached the shop. The pungent aroma of hot oil scythed through darkness like a hot knife through peanut butter: her favourite.

The bright flickering fluorescent lights took her by surprise and she blinked; rubbing the crustiness from her eye lids and the corner of both eyes.

"Large chips mate."

He barely nodded. *"Open?"*

"Yeah, does it look like I want them wrapped for Christmas?"

He shook his head dispassionately and nodded to the salt and pepper on the far end of the counter. She clocked him look at her wrist.

"Help yourself."

She placed two pound coins and a twenty-pence piece on the counter.

"Keep the change."

"Smart-arse' bitch." He muttered under his breath as she left the shop. *"Where'd she get a watch like that?*

She sat on a low partly crumbling brick wall outside the chippy and munched on the hot chips which burned the inside of her mouth; despite being heavily doused in vinegar.

Her phone pinged with a code; she opened the App: a money transfer. Only a few hundred'; but it was enough.

She smiled and munched her way steadily through the pile of soggy chips.

"Blow job" she mused as she thought of sad old Ken laying 'there pulling his hood: *"he can kiss my sweet arse."*

Chapter 2

2 Years earlier....

Wednesday 10 August 2014

"*Your English is good*?" he looked unconvinced.

"I had no complaints working in Bradford for two years: waiting tables."

"Bradford?" He scrunched up his nose; as though she'd answered *Mars.*

"England - the North."

"Hmmmm" he replied looking doubtful and picking at a speck of dust on his black woollen jacket: *feigning disinterest*.

"Casual work mostly…" *Natalia* broke he silence.

She also went by the name Lydia when it suited her. Ever since Bradford.

"*Two years you say…*"

He looked her up and down and there was a note of scepticism in his voice.

(Take it or leave she thought: *fuck him if he wants to play games; she wasn't here to blow him.*)

She shrugged her slim shoulders and ran her fingers through her short blonde hair as she looked apparently disinterestedly over his right shoulder out of the window: consciously mimicking his approach.

She knew his game alright. She could feel his eyes on her and read his body language; he clearly fancied himself.

"…And now?"

(She wanted to say well look at it this way *dick wipe*: if I was working I wouldn't be stood in front of you whilst you eye me up and down like a back street pervert; she settled for a simple reply.)

"*I have not been in Amsterdam long*: I share a flat with my boyfriend in the suburbs."

(That was a lie but he wasn't going to check and it was only cash in hand for a few days..)

"*References*?"

She gave him a look as much as to say..*it's your choice buddy*..she shrugged her shoulders again and put her hands into her skin tight jeans emphasising her slender body and pulling the material tight around her mound. She'd put a tiny red G-string on just in case he needed persuasion....if push came to shove....

She knew he was the type to make decisions with his dick she could read him like so many other arseholes she'd met. He'd be hoping for a free-bee..."

"*Ok it's a three day meeting*: a Conference. "

(*She'd done her research: that's why she was here.*)

"You will serve breakfast, mid-morning coffee, buffet lunch and afternoon tea."

"You start at 6 a.m. sharp and finish at 4:30 p.m."

Between duties, *customer-facing*: you do what you're told: wash-up, keep the kitchen clean and do whatever we ask."

"*Clear*?"

"*Crystal.*" Was her mono-syllabic reply.

"Pay is forty Euros a day, cash: at the end of three days. Tips are yours. Take it or leave it."

"If you leave before three days are up: you get nothing."

She nodded.

Bastard she thought; more money in his back pocket if he touches me up or I piss off early.

She watched him as he picked up the receiver and dialled "5".

"I will send her down. Her name is Natalia."

"Yes just for the conference."

He lowered his voice: *"Zero hours contract: keep it off the books yeah'."*

"Then we'll see…" he raised his head and let his eyes survey her from top to bottom…stroking his coffee brown goatee beard as he did so.

She turned side on and looked at the rota on the wall… to give him the view he needed: the view she *knew he wanted..*

"If she's a good girl..maybe more." He grinned and replaced the receiver.

She'd met his type throughout her life; after all he could get..and take..from the girls.

"Ok take the lift to floor minus one."

"Evie will meet you and show you the ropes."

He grinned.

"Don't fuck up and maybe we'll come to an arrangement..I can be good to you if.. "

"Maybe.." She faked a smile as a loud knock on the door interrupted his chat up line. She knew where he was going and didn't want to give him any excuses to get rid of her until she got what she'd come for.

"Come" he shouted; looking irritated and annoyed by the untimely interruption.

One of the waitresses clad in a customary white blouse and tight black skirt, wearing a little white apron; gave her a dirty look as she waited in the doorway.

"Sorry Claude."

He gave a brief dismissive nod.

"I need a quiet word." She looked down at her feet.

She looked slightly uneasily at Natalia: guilt evident as her chin began to quiver.

With a glance Natalia summed her up in an instant: it was a look she had seen a hundred times on the faces of the girls in Bradford when they'd missed a period.

Claude feigned indifference as he waved her forward and spoke to Natalia without looking at either of them.

"Okay you can go. *Remember what I said..*"

Natalia brushed the girl's shoulder with her own as she left his office and glanced closely at the girl's moistened eyes. Her name badge identified her as *Rosie*: her name matched the colour of her cheeks as she looked again at Natalia.

She closed the door slowly enough to catch Rosie's opening gambit:

"I'm pregnant..." then sobs broke out as Natalia walked away leaving them to it.

"BASTARD she said inside her head....Pigging bastard."

Eight circular tables were positioned in front of the raised rectangular stage at the far end of the hall. Each individual table was surrounded by eight chairs adorned with red fading padded seats which had seen better days. The gold paint on the wooden ornate chairs was peeling in places and added to the facade of a fading dynasty, which doubtless struck discerning visitors to the Hotel.

In its heyday, the *Imperial Tulip* would doubtless have been overbooked and oversubscribed. The advent of online booking and spare rooms to let had changed all of that.

Whilst Amsterdam steadily evolved into a top 5 *must see* European, hip, happening City: Natalia knew that the twenty' and thirty somethings' wanted cool decor and charging ports for their smartphones rather than faded fabric accessories and dark overdressed dining rooms clad in ruby wine coloured cushions.

A musty scent clung to the air and further accentuated the feeling of stepping back in time, *and not in a good way.*

Natalia smiled inwardly as she set about her tasks because it was one of the few places she'd been of late which didn't remind her of boiled cabbage and old men: both were conspicuous by their absence.

(She was twenty' and living with her half brother; even if it was only for a few weeks. How much of a saddo did that make her feel? *A big fuckin' saddo: but it was all for a reason:* and Alexei was right behind her: ready to do whatever it took.)

(In truth, did she but know it; her brother despised them both as much as she did: *even if Papa as he liked to be known; had given Alexei everything he needed*, including a monthly allowance which was enough to make his pad in Amsterdam comfortable and more than a little on the side for his wilder adventures at in the infamous Red Light District....like father, like son.)

Natalia's previous three months at the *Sweet Memories Nursing Home* had taught her one thing if nothing else: older people could be pressurised into eating soft tasteless vegetables boiled to within an inch of their lives, with lots of cabbage for good measure and many had little recollection of the previous day's activities: at odds with the name of the *"home from home"* as the Ad' guys had marketed its charms.

Memories of consuming white cabbage as a child filled her head as she began laying out plates, cutlery, cups and saucers and utensils around the tables, ensuring she used equi-distant place sittings. Appearance was everything.

Natalia started at the tables closest to the stage; which was edged with a starched white cloth carefully pinned in place; to ensure it looked clean and smart: *Hospital-Esque she mused*: *how appropriate*.

Natalia worked swiftly sensing eyes were assessing her progress and the next twenty-four hours was all it would take. She just needed confirmation; she just needed to witness them together for herself: *to be sure*.

As she started work on her third table, she moved swiftly around in her black pumps and out of the corner of her eye she spied *Claude* who had his arm on *Rosie's* shoulder. He looked as if he was pacifying her.

"Poor little kid," she thought, barely nineteen and pregnant with a wanker like that as a father to her unborn kid; it was never gonna see the light of day. He'd see to that: pressurise her until she gave in and made a clinic appointment.

Sure enough Rosie sniffed and wiped her nose as Claude glanced across at Natalia with a smirk on his face: eying her up as his next victim.

Natalia stopped to shine a couple of pieces of cutlery with her apron so she could watch their body language out of the corner of her eye. The girl was pulling away from him and shaking her head. Whatever he was saying to her, he wasn't taking no for an answer. That confirmed her suspicions. She turned her back on them again and could hear snippets as she moved to the adjacent table.

"*But you love me right*?" More sobbing. "So why would I...?"

Fuck me, you can't see the wood for the trees luv' can you? Thought Natalia.

The swing doors clattered behind her as a strawberry blonde haired waitress entered the dining room and with her hostess trolly squeaking as she made progress. She began laying out dishes onto the hot plates on the lines of tables which ran perpendicular to the stage, along the right side of the hall on entry.

"*Remember the food labels Rochelle*" barked Claude towards the waitress, "and change that stained apron before service begins."

"*I'm on it*." Came the reply laced with a heavy French accent.

Claude left the room closely followed by Rosie, sniffling as she stayed close to his heels like a little lost puppy.

Just as Natalia finished the last of the eight tables and stood back to check the layout, the first customer peered around the door and walked swiftly towards the hot platters of food.

"*Breakfast*?" He said rhetorically.

"*Yes Sir*." Nodded Natalia and smiled at him.

"Hot dishes and cold dishes. Coffee and tea bags that end:" she gestured left towards the stage as she spoke.

"*Please help yourself*." He nodded and smiled back and set about the serious business of peering under metal lids using the napkins wrapped around the hot handles whilst trying to read labels.

She watched him as he squinted at the *hot potato* sign and checked his jacket pocket having obviously forgotten his glasses.

"*Can I help you Sir*?" Natalia asked, mindful that a few tips wouldn't go amiss.

He smiled as she walked over and gave him the spiel and the tour.

"Thank you. *Natalia.*" He nodded appreciatively having read her name badge as she headed back to the kitchen as guests began arriving on the stroke of 6:30 a.m.

By the time she returned from the kitchen carrying a large tray of hot freshly baked croissants the room was awash with a throng of conference attendees shifting purposefully between breakfast offerings, shaking hands and renewing friendships.

Some of the guests had purpose made badges strategically clipped to their breast pockets but most used the lanyard which had been supplied by the Conference Organisers. Everyone knew everyone else; or so it seemed to Natalia.

The inviting aroma of crisp bacon and German-style Wurst sausages made her stomach rumble; but she knew she'd be a couple of hours before she could satiate her appetite. What's more she had more important business than food.

She began waiting tables and poured freshly brewed coffee for customers. They were invariably polite and all were either Doctors or Professors indicated by their names badges. Her coffee jug was soon emptied and as she headed for the side door into the kitchen the swing doors opened and there she was; *she knew her in an instant.*

Dressed smartly in a two-piece beige suit with matching Prada shoes and carrying a blush pink handbag she looked immaculate, stylish and supremely confident in her stride.

Natalia felt her heart beat rapidly and she headed straight for the bathroom; leaving the coffee pot on the side table in the kitchen.

Chapter 4

"*Good Morning Ladies and Gentlemen.* A warm welcome and on behalf of the Organising Committee….."

Professor Henderson opened his arms wide as he spoke and smiled with his eyes as much as his facial musculature: highlighted by the lighting which had been activated so that the Speakers, Committee and Chairperson, were preferentially illuminated; leaving the audience in more subdued light.

"I'm *absolutely delighted* to welcome you all to sunny Amsterdam and the *Third European Society of Immunology and Therapeutics Summit.*"

"Its hard for me to believe that two years have passed since our last gathering and I'm sure like me you're all as eager as I am to hear from our eminent speakers from across Europe *and beyond.*"

"Can I remind you to switch your mobile phones to silent and point out the Emergency Exit signs which are both illuminated behind you. I'm assured that we are not expecting any Fire drills today, so if a continuous alarm does sound, we will need to evacuate the building swiftly."

Customary announcements over, he proceeded:

"So without further ado and on behalf of *Professor Edwina Justin and the Committee,*" he gestured left and bowed slightly to Edwina Justin, then right towards the Committee Members…

"It gives me great pleasure to to welcome our first speaker who needs no introduction to any of you; we are indebted to him for taking time to join us…and I hope….. escape from the rather harsh weather conditions you're currently experiencing in Moscow!"

The podium is yours: "*Professor Edgar Radzinsky.*"

A quiet ripple of applause grew into a steady clap as the grey suited silver-haired clinician ascended the steps from the far left of the stage, which was partly cloaked in darkness; and onto the podium.

Natalia could feel her heart pounding in her chest as she watched him stride proudly across the stage behind the seated dignitaries of the Committee, each of whom turned to acknowledge him as he approached. He shook hands with the black-suited Professor Henderson, before bending down momentarily and pecking Professor Justin on her right cheek and placing his black leather case on the chair to her left. She whispered into his right ear as he did so and his smile grew from ear to ear in an instant.

At that very moment, Natalia knew she'd been right all along.

Bitterness filled her mouth and she fought back the revulsion as her stomach churned and she wanted to puke her guts up.

No one noticed the as the young waitress swiftly exited the hall via the kitchen and ran down the corridors before she barricaded herself into the ladies cubicle; bolting the door firmly behind her momentarily before she projected bile effortlessly into the toilet bowl.

She fumbled for the faded worn photograph of the woman and ripped it from her skirt pocket before tearing it into a myriad of pieces and flushing the cistern.

Her heart was galloping as she felt the rage growing inside her like an erupting volcano and she started to tremble with fury and vomited again: a deep guttural vomit which felt like it emanated from the very bowels of the earth itself, spewing her lava everywhere.

Anger surged through her veins like a lightening strike in its ferocity and her eyes widened as she began pummelling the porcelain cistern with her bare fists. She lashed out at the tissue dispenser and ripped it off the wall before hoisting her skirt up above her knees as she began relentlessly kicking at the exposed pipework behind the cistern until the damage to the soft tissues in her left foot propelled sharp jolts of searing pain up her leg.

She tore off her white apron and mopped her soaking brow before throwing it down the toilet and spitting on the wet cloth as it submerged into the green bile stained water. She opened her legs wide and stood astride the toilet bowl before pulling her flimsy red G-string to one side and parting her nether lips as she urinated gratifyingly over the cloth.

She wrenched her skirt back down and jolted back the bolt on the door before thrashing the wooden door back against the metal closet walls sending vibrations through the housing as she exited the cubicle.

Natalia looked briefly at her pale drawn face in the mirror and took a handful of water and splashed it across her lips, swilled her mouth and spat into the basin.

She didn't look back as she exited the revolving doors of the Hotel: her carotid pulse still hammering in her slim neck and oblivious to the blood seeping through the cotton material of her black left pump.

Moments later Alexei read her text and fired up his computer: the time for waiting was over.

His cold blue eyes were unwavering as he navigated swiftly deep down into the murky depths of the Dark Web.

Chapter 5

Monday 19th December 2015: London Highgate

Alexei' had text' Natalia the moment he was certain their target was out and about: information he gleaned from her mobile GPS signal.

He'd been interrogating *"HER"* text messages and emails ever since Natalia had seen *"THEM"* together in Amsterdam. Fortunately *"SHE"* was a creature of habit and had transferred her mobile number across from her old mobile using the PAC Code when she'd purchased her swanky new mobile phone in Knightsbridge; her early Christmas present to herself. He'd seen the electronic bill. He was pretty sure even his *beloved father* wouldn't spend three grand on a mobile.

When ever Alexei and Natalia traded SMS: they always referred to *"HER, HIM or THEM."*

The weather was gloomy and Natalia had nothing else planned for the day, despite it being so close to Christmas. She'd have otherwise been sitting in bed on her phone: watching *YouTube*.

As soon as Alexei' text landed in her inbox, she swiftly donned her denim jeans, black pumps, put on a denim jacket and her favourite red cap; raced down the stairs from her room and hailed a cab on the street outside her bedsit.

The Black Cab drove past her then executed a wide "U-turn and called out to her. *"Where you going mate?"*

"Garroways' Bookshop: Tottenham Court Road."

"Jump in fella out of the cold."

She was used to people mistaking her for a boy and she paid him no heed. He tripped the meter as she clambered into the back seat, grateful to escape the icy cold northerly wind; which nipped at her fingers and chilled her skeletal body to the core. She'd not eaten for nearly twenty-four hours and she felt hollow and needed a fix of hot coffee to pep her up; she had no money for *uppers or cash to score gear to give her a high.*

She'd scored *"H"* three days ago: just the one hit; straight lining always took away her appetite: but she'd escaped her shitty life for the rest of the evening; lost in paradise amidst dreams of island tranquility and technicolour azure clouds melting into blissful serenity. Every time it was different but it didn't last long; it never did. Back to the dump with a bump: back to life and the reality of the daily grind at *Sweet Memories Nursing Home: sweet shit more like it;* most of the time anyway.

Shirley had been her only friend at the N.H.; a tall skinny gangly girl from South London who had a kid to take care off. Her mom did most of the caring; by the time Shirley got off shift she was fit for nothing' always looking for her next *hit of smack.* Shirley had taught her the ropes when they went *on the rob'* together in Central London.

"Studying are you: student? What you reading? Me, I'd read History if I could. Never been to Uni' myself. Enjoy it do you?" Loads of reading I guess. Never was much of a scholar myself."

Natalia just listened and nodded occasionally as he held a one man conversation: not waiting for responses to his questions or statements before he carried on talking.

A One Man Rhetorical Roadshow.

She could visualise the signs outside the theatre.

He didn't stop yak' yakin' about the weather, the fall off in visitors and anything and everything: he was doing her head in' and she couldn't wait to get out of the cab.

Her stomach ached for food and she had a throbbing headache. She scratched at her needle track absentmindedly.

As she left the cab she even gave him a tip rather than wait for the change and listen to more of his clap-trap.

"*Thanks Mate, good talking to you.*" He yelled as he drove off in a cloud of diesel exhaust which made her cough.

As she rushed towards the store to escape the biting cold a tall young well dressed guy with blond hair and blue eyes dressed in a long grey woollen coat held the door for her and smiled broadly. She could smell his expensive aftershave as she brushed past him and she instinctively averted her gaze and headed off in search of her prey. Sex was the last thing on her mind and she knew men were all the same once stripped of their finery.

With a practised eye she perused the rows of bookshelves at the rear of the store and began systematically checking out each of the aisles as though simply searching for a specific section and book title. She worked steadily around on each floor before finally reaching the Fourth Floor where she took a quick diversion to the loo and washed her hands in warm water and used the air dryer to warm her hands up.

Her eyes scanned the coffee shop and she caught her breath suddenly as she spotted *HER* sat on the long rectangular table at the rear of the coffee shop. Wearing a plum coloured three quarter length coat she sat entranced by a travel book on Southern Asia. The high stool gave her a vantage point from which she could survey the whole area as tourists and shoppers mingled and selected seats; armed with hot drinks and plates of assorted pastries.

Natalia's stomach rumbled loudly as she smelled the home cooked scones and she carried on past the entrance to the coffee shop and selected a vantage point with a clear view of her prey.

Carrying a tray with two mugs and two plates with pastries she caught sight of him for a second time: the same sweet-smelling blonde-haired guy who'd held the door open for her at the entrance to Garroways; just ten minutes earlier. She dipped her head and turned away as she sensed him heading directly towards *HER: seated at the High Table like some Priestess watching over her minions.*

She felt anger sear through her veins and her mouth dried as her head began to throb more intensely. She balled her fists inside her denim jacket as she watched him take a seat opposite her, of all people; and serve her with a piece of cake and hand her a mug of hot coffee. She could see the froth on his mug of cappuccino. She could sense their mutual attraction by the way he tended her.

She watched his cheeks begin to glow as they started talking. She could sense his intensity as he hung on her every word: soaking up her rhetoric. She looked away from them both as she moved to the stair case having picked up a flyer on a forthcoming book release. She watched *her* as she sipped her drink; using a white napkin to dab her bright rose red lipstick as she sipped her beverage.

Her eyes never left his whilst they spoke but their body language was friendly, not intimate. Neither leaned in to talk; there was no touching or caressing or grooming of hair. Natalia idly checked her phone messages before she engaged the camera and took covert shots of them both before she set the video to run and capture their conversation. They were too far away for her to hear the conversation but she knew Alexei had the means to enhance the conversation and eves drop.

She walked slowly back downstairs to the third floor and sent the pics and video to Alexei. She pored over books removing several from the shelves as she waited for them to exit the coffee shop.

Chapter 6

Friday 13th January 2017

Louise swiped her identity card vertically down through the sensor and the electronic door release gave an audible click; a moment later she entered the large somewhat imposing north facing Evidence Room.

(It was part of the old section of the Nick and the lofty ceiling reminded Louise of the University Library where she'd studied hour after hour for her degree and subsequent Masters in Forensic Psychology before she'd joined the Police Force.)

Louise headed straight across the Office to the desk at the far end of the room where a squat sturdy W.P.C. with short dark hair stood with her back to anyone entering the room; engrossed in her task of sorting evidence bags.

"Hi Diane: how are you?"

Louise was eager to catch up with her long time friend from the Cadet Cadre at Hendon Police Training College.

"Sorry I'm later than expected but it's been one of those mornings. I'm gasping for a coffee and a gossip."

Louise eyes swiftly scanned the numerous items of clothing and High Street fashion jewellery neatly folded and laid-out across the large shiny metal desk, reminiscent of a customs' inspection area at any modern airport in the World. Diane was preparing Police Evidence bags and documenting the items on a Police Log on the computer terminal.

"Wow: you look as though you've got your hands full with that little lot." exclaimed Louise.

Diane gave Louise a brief smile as she looked over her left shoulder and continued to check items against the manual list she had compiled which was fastened to a clipboard.

"No worries Louise, I was just finalising the inventory on this morning's haul."

"'I take it you've had another trip to Oxford Circus for a shopping extravaganza?"

"You' got it in one: except this young shopping addict didn't plan on paying for anything. Her backpack was loaded and she even had jewellery hidden inside her baseball cap and underwear!"

"Another good reason to have your glamour gloves on!" joked Louise noting that Diane still had her blue latex-free gloves on.

"*This looks expensive.*" Louise picked up a gold framed Rolex watch and viewed it through the newly labelled evidence bag. She looked at the reverse and squinted at the small italic engraving:

"*To FM: with everlasting love CM.*" Louise read aloud.

"Are the initials hers?"

"Nope and what's more *Mohammed* says it's a real Rolex; his dad has one just like it. It retails at over ten grand' apparently. His was a Retirement present from the family when his dad finally handed over their family jewellery business to his brothers."

Louise picked up the worn black backpack turned it over and looked hard at the motif emblazoned on the flap. A hammer and sickle: hand sewn in red. Louise looked intently at the backpack; all thoughts of coffee now far from her mind. She retrieved a red cap which was bagged separately, sitting on top of a pile of white V-necked T-shirts.

"The girl you arrested: was the girl wearing this cap at the time Diane?"

"Yeah, that's how we spotted her near Oxford Circus. She had shown a clean pair of heals when the overweight security guard gave chase and luckily Mo' and I were less than a minute away from the store when we took the call. The dispatcher gave us a very good description. The perp' was doing a good job of blending with the crowd but her back pack gave her away. A minute or two later and she'd have made it to the underground."

"Yes it certainly is distinctive. Do you have a name for the girl?"

"Yeah, she's Russian: *Natalia Yeltsin*."

Diane looked inquiringly at Louise as she spoke. She could sense Louise' interest was more than idle curiosity; apart from which it was ordinarily very difficult to distract her when she had coffee or food on her mind and it was already 1:55 p.m: *way* past their 1p.m. agreement.

"Diane, I'd like to borrow this rucksack and baseball cap. Can you book them out to me please?"

"Sure no probs', but do you want to tell me what all this is about?"

Louise gathered up the two items and was already heading across the tiled office in her white pumps. Her cheeks were flushed with excitement and she spoke quickly.

"Just a hunch right now; thanks Diane I'll catch you later?"

"What about lunch?" called Diane after her friend as Louise pushed the green exit button and was already halfway out of the office.

"I'll catch you later Di', carry on without me today!" Her voice trailed off as the heavy glass panelled door pulled shut behind her and the lock clicked loudly.

Diane rolled her eyes and sighed just as Mo' swiped into the office and joined her to survey their morning haul.

"She stood you up again?" he nodded in the direction of Louise who had brushed shoulders with him as she headed for the stairwell; barely acknowledging him.

"Sadly.... the story of my life Mo'....." Diane replied ruefully. Her brief smile was met by Mo's broad grin as he towered over her.

"Well if you don't mind a quick sandwich in the canteen I'm all yours."

"You certainly know how to woo a girl Mo'."

"*Okay Billie no mates*, you're welcome to go it alone."

"Okay okay keep your jock strap on; I'm all yours in five minutes. I'll just complete this damn inventory; another volume of War And Peace."

"Hey' don't knock it: that's my favourite novel!" Called back over his shoulder as he headed across the echoic room; his deep voice bouncing off the walls.

Mo' logged onto to the Metropolitan Mainframe Computer in the far corner of the rectangular office, looking for previous convictions for *Natalia Yeltsin*." He stroked his short trimmed black beard intermittently as his fingers nimbly darted across the computer keyboard.

"Well Russia's little sprinter has got *'no previous'*."

"I take it you mean *Natalia*?" Diane held the door for Mohammed as he led the way to the canteen.

"The very same: did you notice the track marks on her forearm?"

"Yep, do reckon that's how she feeds her habit?"

"Sure. My best guess is she's been *'on the rob'* for a while, and we just got lucky. So what did Louise want - apart from standing you up for lunch?"

"I'm not sure. She took the backpack and baseball cap and seemed in a hurry to get back upstairs."

"Yeah she barely noticed me as she raced back upstairs. I take it.....this might have something to do with Murder Division?"

"Your guess is as good as mine. Louise does keep things close to her chest where work is concerned."

Chapter 7

Sally Benson was scrutinising the departmental Over-Time Budget report when Louise knocked on her office door. She was sat with one elbow on the desk supporting her chin, running her fingers through her freshly dyed raven hair with her right hand.

(She was wearing her newly acquired green designer framed reading glasses as she surveyed the rows of figures. She figured, if she had to wear blessed glasses to read, the least she could do was make a stab at trendy and these hit the spot beautifully.)

Peering over her glasses, she smiled and gestured to Louise to come in, with a nod of her head.

"Got a minute Boss?" Louise sounded a mixture of breathless and excited, mused Sally as she looked at Louise's neatly tied back blonde hair and earnest features.

"I'd be glad of the interruption to be honest Louise; whichever way I spin these numbers they add up to the usual monthly overspend. I think we need a big Lottery® handout! *What have you got for me*?"

She pulled the laptop lid down and gave Louise her undivided attention.

Louise placed the red baseball cap and black back-pack down on the dark-wood desk without a word.

"What am I looking for Louise?" Sally scrunched up her nose and removed her glasses placing them back into their black hard-case to the right of her computer.

Sally picked up the larger evidence bag and turned the backpack over: revealing the rather striking insignia.

A smile of recognition crossed Sally's face and she widened her eyes and looked at Louise and slowly nodded as the significance of the baseball cap now fell into place.

Louise updated her on the discussion she'd just had with Diane.

Sally stood up, adjusted her skirt and headed for the door.

She spotted Karl at the photocopier, replacing the A4 paper in one of the lower trays. He stooped awkwardly between rows of case files which were accumulating in the crowded corner.

"Karl can you join us for a minute please?"

He closed the compartment door and reset the master control. The copier whirled back into life and he turned to the D.C.I.'s office a moment later.

"Close the door. *Take a look at these two for me.*"

"Whoa, where did these come from?" Karl was wide-eyed and quick to spot the link to the 'Schultz murder investigation.

"A Russian shop lifter has just been brought in downstairs. She was arrested in Oxford Circus by Diane Jones and her partner Mohammed Timms this morning. Louise astutely spotted these two items as Diane was bagging and cataloging evidence."

"You said *she* Boss'?"

He looked quizzical.

"Exactly, we'd always assumed the Visitor to Melway Mews was male based on the footage and the witness testimony from Edwina Justin's neighbour: the Thai housekeeper at number 12. If I recall you took her original statement?"

"Absolutely Boss: *she was adamant on that point.*"

"We need to look at the video-footage from Boxing Day pronto. I'll bring it up right away boss."

"Use my laptop Karl." Sally entered her Username and Password, minimised the overtime schedule and inserted the computer into the docking station.

"Thank God the management Company came up with footage from the Christmas and New Year period." Sally talked as Karl navigated quickly through the team filing system.

"If there hadn't have been a delayed hand-over in the middle of January when the system was updated the tape would have been over-written per the current Company protocol." Sally mused.

Karl quickly located the video-footage from the lift at *Melway Mews* and initiated the recording.

The lift footage was short but clear since forensics had enhanced the imaging. A red baseball cap and as the visitor left the lift, the red hammer and sickle insignia was discernible on the rear of the back-pack.

"She's in the Custody Suite in a cell?"

"Yes Boss." Louise couldn't resist a smile of satisfaction as she answered.

Sally wasted no time in calling *Andrew Smythe*; the Duty Custody Sergeant.

"Thanks Andrew and remember give her a cup of tea *but no one is to interview her before we speak to her."*

She re-cradled the hand-set and gave instructions.

"Right Louise – ask Dianne for the full Itinerary List *Pronto.*"

"Karl – 'call Brian and update him straight away."

"Louise you and I will interview the suspect together once Brian arrives. *Go to it Guys.*"

Neither needed telling twice.

Brian was on his way back from a visit to the Crown Prosecution Service in Birmingham when he took the call from Karl. He called Sally on his hands' free mobile using voice activation immediately after they'd spoken.

"Brian thanks for calling. Karl filled in the detail for you?"

"He did. Are you thinking we have a *new suspect in the 'Justin case*?"

"Either way, it adds credence to Schultz' statement concerning a Visitor on Boxing Day: and we now suspect that the Visitor in the lift is likely to have been a woman".

"Odd you'd think a Doctor could tell the difference." Brian had a note of sarcasm in his voice.

"How far away are you Brian?"

"Should be with you in two hours boss; give or take: the traffic is heavy"

"Okay, I will take Louise in with me once you arrive. I don't want to spook her too early and I want you here to observe."

"Good one. See you soon."

The line went dead.

Chapter 8

Natalia sat back in the custody chair picking at her left forearm; the sleeve of her hoodie pulled up above her elbow. Her hair was short spiky blonde and looked unkempt; her dark red roots were visibly emerging. Grey half - moons were visible beneath her eyes which emphasised her pale complexion and lack of sleep; she looked like a malnourished Panda, *W.P.C. Rita Datta* had observed when she first cast eyes on her.

Natalia bit her red-painted fingernails as she sat waiting in the interview room. *Rita Datta* stood in the corner of the room but Natalia seemed oblivious to her presence; a preoccupied look on her young drawn face.

"How old is she?" Sally asked.

"Twenty-two Boss; but she looks older."

"Narcotics age you."

Sally glanced at Louise's make-up free skin as she made the remark and felt a tinge of jealousy at how fresh Louise looked: thirty three and life-long drug and smoke free she imagined. As far as Sally knew, Louise didn't drink alcohol either.

(When the team went to the Pub to celebrate their small victories in the daily fight against Crime, Louise invariably drank a lime and lemonade with a few chunks of ice; and was teased mercilessly for it by Brian and the team who had taken her to their hearts.)

"Okay Louise, let's kick off and remember, *slowly-slowly*. We don't want to frighten her off."

Brian sat in the adjacent interview room as they entered: watching his remotely connected computer screen as the interview began. He put a blue-tooth receiver in left ear so that he could hear the interview without activating the loud speaker.

Everything was *"need to know"* at this stage. After all, Dr Christophe Schultz had been found guilty of the Murder of a highly eminent Professor of Oncology: the last thing the department needed was some hack getting hold of a sniff of a Miscarriage of Justice.

Sally activated the Police recording monitor, waited a moment for the audible buzz to silence and began introductions.

"Natalia I am Detective Chief Inspector Benson and this is Detective Constable Shepherd. May I remind you that you are still under Police 'Caution for *alleged* Theft of Property and have refused Legal Representation."

"It is 16:55 13th January 2017."

"P.C. Datta will now leave the room."

Sally nodded to the constable who promptly left the room.

"For the benefit of the tape Natalia, could you please introduce yourself with your full name and date of birth please *and country of origin please*?"

Sally wanted belt and braces on this one: no mistakes, no omissions, no C.P.S. or High Court discharges on a technicality; if, they finally had their culprit, *"their man as it were"*: but in this case: *a woman.*

Natalia Yeltsin sat before them on the opposite side of the small metal desk.

"For the benefit of the tape: Miss Yeltsin has given no response."

"Natalia would you like us to arrange a solicitor for you?"

No response.

"For the benefit of the tape: Miss Yeltsin gave no response. We are fully aware that *Miss Yeltsin* understands and speaks excellent English."

Natalia remained silent and stared at her fingernails which were bitten short and covered in poorly applied red nail varnish which was beginning to flake.

"I used to bite my nails as when I was younger." Louise volunteered, by way of an ice-breaker.

"My mother was constantly on my case; said it was my nerves."

No response.

"I blamed my father, always correcting me for some mistake or other." Louise spoke softly and inclined her body gently towards Natalia as she spoke.

"What about you Natalia, do you see much of your parents?

"My father hates me." A statement of fact, no emotion, no eye contact; but a start.

"We all think that about our parents at times; I'm sure it's not true."

"How would *you* know?" Natalia almost spat out the words; her tone suddenly aggressive and her eyes filled with anger as she shot a look at Louise; the angry mantle soon faded and was replaced by a sullen, childish demeanour.

She crossed her arms and hugged her shoulders as if to display what she needed most: human affection. A hug.

"You know nothing about me."

"So tell me, let me help you."

She narrowed her eyes again and furrowed her brow as she glared at Louise.

Louise resisted the temptation to shuffle backwards in her seat, instead concentrating on keeping her voice calm and reassuring. Her lips gently parted; her breathing slow and rhythmical.

"Why would you want to do that?"

Louise could sense the young woman's pain as Natalia began rubbing her upper arms as if trying to warm up.

"I can see the needle-marks on your arm; I'm guessing your skin is itchy and you have tummy cramps?"

"'Been a user have you?" The sullen face returned.

"No: *but we can help you.*"

Silence again as she began to bite the fingernails of her right hand.

"Would you like some tea?"

She nodded affirmatively and resumed scratching the skin of her forearm.

"Have you eaten today?"

She shook her head.

"Okay let's fix you some tea and biscuits before we talk."

"Interview suspended seventeen-ten." Sally waited for Louise to open the door and followed her into the corridor.

"Do you think she's fit for interview Boss?" was Brian's first question as they filed into the small adjacent room, where Brian was watching Natalia on the screen.

He watched as Rita Datta re-entered the room.

"You're right Brian; we might need the FME in before we go much further. I think we have a window but let's give her ten minutes to settle before we resume."

"If she is heading towards *cold turkey* I want to make sure we take good care of her." Sally looked concerned and distracted. The events whilst Christophe Schultz was held in custody were still at the forefront of her mind. Natalia looked tired and vulnerable.

*Could that inner voice that had led her to question 'Schultz' guilt be growing stronge*r? wondered Brian as he studied Sally's expression which he found hard to read.

"Interview resumed 17:25."

Sally repeated the list of attendees for the sake of the tape and reminded Natalia that she remained under 'Caution. Rita Datta dutifully left the room again.

Louise sat quietly whilst Natalia sipped her sweet tea and stared at the table between them.

"Natalia as you know we have a long list of items found in your clothing and recovered from your back-pack when you were arrested this morning. Did you pay for any of the items you had on you when you were arrested?"

Sally paused momentarily to let the words sink in, before she continued her line of questioning.

"You were captured on the closed circuit TV from the store where you stole the clothing and the security guard clearly saw you putting some of the tee-shirts recovered from your backpack under your hoodie. Do you have anything to say?"

"You declined the services of a solicitor earlier, is that still the case?"

Natalia shrugged her shoulders and emptied the tea cup with one noisy gulp.

"What's to say; I needed the money. Charge me and I can go. I don't want 'no brief."

"OK..please inform us if you change your decision at any stage of our interview."

"You said *detectives......*" Natalia made the comment an assertion, rather than a question.

Neither detective commented.

"Tell me about the back-pack." Sally responded.

"What about it?"

"Is it yours?"

"Yeah: so what?"

"Did you steal that too, along with the other gear?"

"No I bought it."

"Where did you buy it?" Sally scrutinised Natalia carefully as she waited for a response.

Natalia sat head down, picking at the nail-varnish on her left forefinger.

"Soho: a second hand shop. Five quid if you must know."

"What was the name of the shop?"

Silence.

"When did you buy it?"

"A year ago, maybe two; I don't know. Why?"

Sally fell silent.

Natalia finally looked up at her without making eye contact.

Louise sensed her opportunity.

"Do you live alone Natalia?"

This time the eye contact was immediate. She looked at Louise and softened her tone a little.

"Yeah: a grotty bed-sit in High Gate."

"Expensive area: even for a grotty bed-sit." Louise responded.

"How do you manage with the rent?"

"I had a job didn't I. Lost it two months ago."

"Does anyone help you with the rent now?"

She started to speak; then hesitated.

"A friend; or maybe someone who stays with you?"

"No one stays over: no friends and no family." She huffed as she answered.

"Tell me about your family?"

"*I don't...click with my father.*" She made clicking sounds with her tongue in the floor of her mouth as if playing a childhood game.

"*What about your mother.*"

They both noticed her response – the change in tone of her voice; the underlying emotion as she caught her breath for a moment before clearing her throat and replying.

"*She's dead.*"

"I'm sorry that can't be easy for you." Louise spoke softly again, leaning in towards Natalia as she did so.

Silence again as she picked at the skin of her right elbow.

"*I need a doctor.*"

"How do you feel?" Louise's question was as a mother to a child though there was barely ten years difference in their age.

"My stomach hurts and I feel dizzy and sick."

Sally was quick to intervene.

"Interview suspended seventeen-forty five."

"Okay let's take you to the medical room." Louise went around the table to join Natalia and waited for her to stand.

Looking pale and beginning to perspire, Natalia left the room and was escorted slowly to the medical room by Louise and W.P.C. Rita Datta who was already waiting outside with Brian.

Rita Datta organised a plate of sandwiches and more tea for Natalia.

Andrew Smythe was busy on the 'phone, contacting the duty Forensic Medical Examiner [FME]: as they left.

"Let's go to my office Brian. I need a coffee." Sally led the way to the canteen.

Ten minutes later they sat on the fading tatty black leather sofa in Sally's office; side by side each sipping a hot Americano from a disposable cup.

"What do you think?" she asked after a long pause.

"Still waters run deep. She's too keen to be charged and let go: 'even refused a brief."

"That could be the opiates talking. She wants to score again."

"No my gut tells me there's more to her than shoplifting, Sally. She's controlled, despite her apparent outbursts. She's not your average thief. You're right to dig and Louise is doing a good job."

"I agree. We need to do our research Brian, the family, her previous work. She would certainly be out of place in Mayfair at Melway Mews; and no mistake."

"See what you can dig up on the internet Brian and run her prints *internationally* as a priority; see if we score any matches."

Chapter 9

19:00 Interview Room

Having eaten sandwiches and consumed several cups of tea, Natalia was keen to press on with the allegations against her and Andrew Smythe judged her fit to resume interview.

Following her introductory Caution Sally resumed the interview with Natalia.

"So tell me about the watch Natalia. Start by telling us where you got it."

"It's mine. *I earned it.*"

"Tell me about the *inscription*. Sally removed an enlarged view of the rear of the watch from a series of photographs.

She read aloud: "*To FM: with everlasting love CM.*"

"Tell us about F.M. Natalia. Those are not your initials are they?"

Silence from across the table. Natalia's face had a fixed expression; her lips were pressed tightly together. She crossed her arms.

Sally persisted.

"It's stolen, *but you know that already don't you*?"

Natalia looked directly at Sally for the first time and for Sally saw it in an instance: pure undiluted *hatred*. She'd witnessed that emotion in the eyes of many defendants and it was unmistakable.

"I told you *BITCH*, I earned it."

She spat the words out.

Sally sat back as Natalia sat forward; spit droplets from the corner of Natalia's mouth had landed on the table in front of her. Sally could detect her rancid breath.

"How *exactly* did you earn it? Tell us."

"By wiping *their SHITTY fucking arses'*: *day in an' day out.*"

She spat out the latter words with disgust and vehemence written across her taught features.

"Who are *they*?"

"You mean the *residents* don't you, at the Care Home where you worked as a *nursing assistant.*

Sally paused for a moment.

"The Manager fired you for theft two months ago."

"They had no proof it was me!"

"Well we do now, don't we." chided Sally.

"FM was Frank Morris and CM, Linda Morris, his late wife." He used her middle name *Caroline* during their decades of marriage.

"You stole the *one truly treasured memento: from an elderly resident.*"

 "What kind of a person does that make you?"

"FUCKING DESPERATE: if you *must* ask - you sanctimonious bitch!"

"Why didn't you sell it: if you needed money *soooo* desperately?"

"Why do you still have the watch...two months after stealing it?"

"Does that give you a feeling of power over the Residents?"

A long painful silence and then without looking up:

"It reminded me of *him* if you must know."

"Your father?" cut in Louise

She nodded slowly and deliberately.

"So he's successful Natalia..... *he* has money: enough to buy a *Rolex®*? Surely he could have helped you?"

She nodded again and tears began to roll down her cheeks; leaving dark marks from her eye-shadow which had begun to run. She looked every inch like a pathetic teenager who'd been caught out. Caught with her hand in the cookie jar......

Louise took a tissue from her jacket pocket and offered it to Natalia.

"When did you last have contact with him: Natalia? "

Silence. She ignored the tissue.

"Do you want to call him and let him know where you are?"

"You can have your 'Phone call later if you like?"

Natalia chewed her bottom lip.

"*Maybe I can call my brother.*"

"And where does he live?"

Louise' tone remained soft, encouraging and non-threatening.

"Russia. I can text him. I don't need to talk. He will help me."

"That's how you survive isn't it Natalia, with your *brother's help*?"

Louise was acting on instinct with every question. Piecing together, step by step; this young woman's life.

More tears and gentle sobbing, she began to rock, holding her body with her arms as she did so.

"*He cares, not like....*" her voice trailed off.

Her lips pursed closed she fell silent again.

"*I want to rest.*"

"You can, soon, but we need to ask you some more questions first." Sally was back in the driving seat.

Good cop, bad cop routine.

"Tell me about your rucksack?"

Natalia looked mystified and rubbed the tip of her nose, yellow snot covered her fingertips.

"What is it with you and my *fucking second hand ruck sack?*

"It ain't no designer luvvy: what about it?"

Her comment was laced with sarcasm and bile and she feigned a RP [Received Pronunciation] accent.

"Do you take it everywhere with you?"

"Yeah: and..?"

"You don't use a handbag?"

"Do I look like I buy *fuckin'* Gucci®?"

"No but maybe you steal it." cut in Sally again.

Natalia ignored the comment.

"When you're out and about visiting friends...you take it then?"

She nodded.

"For the benefit of the tape please Natalia." Sally injected.

"Yes....*for the benefit of the tape*.... When I visit friends, go shopping, to weddings and Christenings."

Her voice was heavy with sarcasm; she hunched her shoulders.

"Do you have any special friends?"

"No."

"In Highgate: where you live?

"Just people: no one special." She shrugged her shoulders.

"What about in Mayfair Natalia. Do you know anyone in Mayfair?"

 Sally looked blankly at Natalia as she posed the question.

"Oh yeah, plenty of posh people: I take tea with on a Tuesday *after I go to get my benefits*."

Her sarcasm was laid on thick as she locked eyes with Sally.

"When did you last visit Mayfair?" Sally probed.

Natalia stared back in silence.

"Never." Came her monosyllabic reply.

"Are you sure?"

Silence and eye contact which now had begun to feel like a contest.

"Have you ever heard of *Melway Mews*?"

For a split second Natalia broke eye contact; both detectives saw it.

Underneath the table, she drew her legs up under her chair.

"No."

"Are you sure?"

A cursory nod was her response as she began to pick at her right forearm again.

"For the benefit of the tape please Natalia."

"I'm sure."

"What about Professor Edwina Justin?"

"What about her?"

"So you know her name?" Sally imparted a note of surprise with her question.

"Sure."

Sally could imagine Brian, staring intently at the screen and saying "Christ, it's like pulling teeth."

"How do you know her?"

"I didn't say like....I *knew* her; I heard the name that's all."

"Where did you hear it?"

"On the TV; she got murdered by some German doctor right?"

"Real charmer: *Dr Death from Stuttgart.*" She ridiculed his name as she spoke.

"How do you know he was from Stuttgart?"

Natalia looked bemused for a moment, a rabbit caught in the headlights; then she quickly recovered her composure.

"Must have been on the news...." Her voice trailed off and she shrugged her shoulders and picked at a scab on the front of her left elbow.

Louise looked across at Sally and caught her slight nod.

"Natalia: how did you *feel* about the death of Professor Justin?"

Louise spoke slowly emphasising her words.

"Why would I feel *anything*?"

"Tell me about your mother?"

A pregnant, pause.

"What about her?"

"You said she died...."

"When was that?"

"What's that got to do with Edwina FUCKING Justin?"

Her eyes were blazing with a sudden ferocity as she stood up glaring at Louise.

"*Sit down*." Sally was firm, her eyes fixed on Natalia, who had her fists clenched and stood rigidly upright; any sign of vulnerability, suddenly absent.

"*Sit down NOW!*" Sally's tone was unconditional.

Slowly she resumed her seat, a new fire burning in her eyes, her lids widened.

"That bitch meant nothing to me."

Sally locked eye contact with Natalia.

"Which *bitch* are we talking about?"

She hurled herself across the table without warning, her fingers flexed like talons into a claw like posture with nails ready to dig into Sally's face. Her small frame belied the ferocity of her attack as she clawed with both hands at Sally's face; her fingers grazing through Sally's hair.

Sally's chair tilted on its rear legs as she pushed back from the table and she instinctively turned her face to the left away from Natalia's groping fingers. Natalia grabbed a handful of Sally's hair as she thrust towards her using all her body weight to propel her.

Louise pounced across and secured Natalia's left elbow jerking her wrist down away from Sally's face. With her right arm she leaned down on Natalia's back forcing her against the table as the door burst open and Brian ran towards the assailant with Rita Datta trailing behind him.

"*You're further Under Arrest for Assaulting a Police Officer.*" He snarled through gritted teeth as he held her pinned to the table with his left arm, applying handcuffs to her right arm as he wrenched it up towards her shoulder before securing her left wrist as Louise leaned on Natalia's body.

"*FUCKING BITCH, I'LL KILL YOU!*"

"*You'll need to get past ME first.*"

Brian's words were delivered directly into Natalia's right ear. He could feel the tension in her stick like body and at the same time the raw power as she thrust her head backwards and tried to head butt him.

"*Suck my dick!*" she spat as she bucked once more.

"Now calm down before I add a further charge Assault and Battery to the list of Charges against you Natalia."

Sally was composed as she matter-of-factly delivered her ultimatum.

Sally nodded to Brian and Louise with a broad smile of appreciation just as reinforcements arrived at the entrance to the room.

"This one can cool down in her cell thanks Sergeant Smythe."

Sally, Louise and Brian stood to one side as Natalia was escorted away. Her eyes never left Sally's as she left the room. Pure hatred, pure bile.

They let the door close before they spoke to one another.

"*Are you okay Boss*?" Louise was first to break the silence.

"Thanks to you *both,* I'm fine thanks.

"Well she's a lively one." Brian laughed but couldn't hide the look of concern as he surveyed Sally's face.

"Coffee and it's *my* round team. I think we'll give that little *madam* some time to cool down."

Dr Catherine Newton had always been a stickler for time: *early is on-time and on-time is late*.

Her father, a bank employee for thirty-two years, twenty as Assistant Branch Manager: had instilled this virtue in all three of his daughters. As the eldest of three, Catherine was expected to *lead by example*. As a Junior Doctor she had excelled in a hospital environment, amidst the orderliness and exacting deadlines imposed by her Consultant mentors. But those days were a distant memory.

(The advent of a series of Politically motivated agendas and an overburdened Healthcare system had all but ended the golden era of adequately funded Patient-Centred Care. Her Partners at the General Practice where she now worked, were faced with a constant uphill battle of increasing workload and financial constraint.)

Catherine's day had been a typical mix of never ending Patient Consultations, home visits and a mountain of paperwork, not to mention Computer Based Patient Audits. Despite her best intentions when she'd started work at 7 a.m. that morning; her desk remained submerged under a growing pile of paperwork and partially completed insurance reports when she left eleven hours later, to start her night shift as FME: *Forensic Medical Examiner* for the local Police Force.

The eight o'clock evening news bulletin did little to lift her mood. There'd been more atrocities in the Middle East, endless Political machinations over "*Brexit*" negotiations with EU ministers and more jitters on the financial markets to add to the list of Londoners' woes. She absent-mindedly looked at the clock for the third time in half an hour: progress was slow in the circuitous line of evening commuters.

Her hands-free mobile phone rang just twice before she said "*Answer*" to the on-board computer voice-activated system.

"Dr Newton?"

"Yes speaking."

"Hello Doctor, I'm Detective Constable Karl Madding from the *Murder Investigation Team*."

"I'm just calling for an update on your progress this evening? As you know we have a prisoner awaiting your attention."

Feeling irritated by the third request for an update she felt tempted to say *"I'd be there quicker if you lot stopped hounding me and let me concentrate on my driving and…. by the way what is so important about a shoplifter?"* However as always, she held her tongue and replied politely:

"Thanks for your call detective. I've just been attending a *rape victim*, so my apologies for the delay."

There was no doubt in her mind that she had triaged the cases appropriately. She used intonation on the words rape and victim to emphasise the importance of her first call of the evening.

"I understand doctor, but the case has become more complicated. Can you give your expected ETA?"

"I would if I had a crystal ball and could foretell the future of the Stock Market; I'd also make a fortune and retire early in the Highlands of Scotland"; thought Catherine. However, she replied:

"Complicated by what factors?"

"The prisoner's mood is *volatile* doctor."

"Has she been given something to eat and drink?"

"Yes Doc'."

"Okay well I'll be with you as soon as I can." She hung up with a swift finger movement on the phone keypad just as a white van cut in front of her; narrowing missing her right wing."

"J-E-S-U-S" she blasphemed then took a deep breath as she felt the pulse of adrenaline kick in and raise her heart rate as if she'd just started Stage 3 on her treadmill workout. She resisted sounding her horn and felt instantly better as she saw the driver place a placatory left hand in front of his rear-view mirror as he realised his manoeuvre had been a hasty decision.

"Okay, okay just calm down." She heard herself saying as she flicked the station on the radio to Smooth FM. The blissful sounds of evening jazz wafted through the car and Catherine took a series of long slow deep breaths. The traffic ahead of her began to accelerate and her satellite navigation instructed her to take the right hand lane in readiness for a turn.

Her mobile phone rang again: *"Your mother calling."* announced the computer; in a familiar hollow metallic monotone.

"Hi Mom: how are you, how's Dad?"

"Oh we're both fine Darling. I'm calling to remind you about the arrangements for our wedding anniversary next month. Have you managed to re-arrange your Duty rota so that you are free for the whole weekend? Daddy is so looking forward to having all three of you girls at home; it's been so long since...."

"Keep right in two hundred yards." 'Came the robotic command again.

"Sorry darling have you go someone in the car with you?"

"No Mom, it's the satellite navigation system. Look sorry, can I call you back?"

"Well be sure you do Darling and..."

White van man stopped suddenly and Catherine felt the ABS engage as she slammed hard on the brake pedal of her Prius Automatic.

His indicator was on and he was still 50 yards from the turning. Traffic ahead was moving but she had nowhere to go as the inside lane was now accelerating past them.

"*What is he doing? That's all I need.*"

"*Catherine is everything okay*?" June Newton sounded concerned.

"It's okay Mom, just a dim-witted driver in front. Mom let me call you later, I'm still working."

"*Okay Catherine, be sure you do.*"

"Bye Mom."

White van man executed a tyre crunching U-turn and Catherine heaved a sigh of relief as she took a right turn into Mortimer Street, only to be greeted by more tailed back traffic.

The dulcet sounds of "*I'll Be There*" sung by Gerry and the Pacemakers' wafted across the airwaves: Catherine felt a sense of calm returning as she hummed along to familiar words.

Chapter 11

20:30 Custody Suite: Medical Examination Room

"She's in here Doc'. For your own protection *W.P.C. Datta* and a male officer *P.C Young* will stay with you at all times. She's a volatile one, not much to look at, but made a lunge for our D.C.I. during interview this evening. The D.C.I. will fill in further background information and the reason for the buccal swab after the Interview Doc': if that works for you?"

"Thank you Sergeant; yes that's fine. I will be as quick as I can and I apologise again for my late arrival."

Sergeant Robins smiled graciously as he opened the door to the examination room using his identity card and ushered Catherine into the now familiar examination room. There was a frosted window at the far end of the room and Natalia Yeltsin sat on a chair in front of it, handcuffed to P.C. Young.

"Hello Natalia, I am Doctor Newton. I am here to check you over medically."

Catherine was greeted by a sullen, pale faced prisoner who was sat with her left arm partially folded across her chest and her eyelids closed. She was wearing small dirty white ankle socks and a white cotton Forensic Jumpsuit.

Catherine was undeterred and had learned to expect all manner of reactions from those held in Custody; particularly if they had a history of drug or alcohol abuse. She'd been spat on, bitten and bruised during her 5 years whilst working for the Police in her so-called spare time as a FME.

"Okay, first of all, I would like to take a mouth swab and then we can give you an examination to make sure.."

"WE ain't doing nothin'. *YOU* ain't taking no samples."

Ignoring the double-negatives in her diction and the hostility in Natalia's voice, Catherine stayed calm and started to complete the label and the request form for the buccal swab. She was sat at the desk just beyond the examination couch which was positioned in the middle of the room.

"Okay Natalia calm down, the Doctor's trying to help you." P.C. Datta stood on Natalia's left side and she looked across at Catherine as she spoke and Catherine reciprocated with a smile.

Having labelled the sample tube for the *buccal swab*, Catherine took off her white linen jacket and placed it on the back of the small black swivel chair. She opened a new box of sterile gloves, size small and stretched a pair over her hands.

"So Natalia it would be helpful if you sat on the edge of the couch here next to me so that I can take a swab of the inside of your mouth."

Silence filled the room.

"Okay, how about you tell me what's wrong?"

Catherine looked at Natalia's short blond spiky hair and wondered how long it had been since it had been washed. The girl looked tired and drawn.

Using her feet to propel the swivel chair, in a practiced movement, Catherine moved closer to the prisoner and her escorts. She stopped about a metre away from them all and sat patiently; her hands resting in her lap.

Catherine readjusted her brown woollen skirt momentarily and noticed dried-blood spatters from an encounter with a lively toddler earlier that day.

("*Timmy*" had needed a routine blood count to enable review his bone marrow function by the Oncologist and Haematologist who took care of the five year old: *he had made a super recovery from his leukaemia.*)

(The family could have gone to the local hospital for the blood test; but Catherine was always keen to offer patient-centred care especially for her younger patients: they were often unnerved by busy outpatient departments.)

As she looked up Natalia was looking straight at her. *Green piercing eyes with pearl white sclera.* Her pupils were not constricted and she looked relaxed with her shoulders down. Her frown had dissipated and she gave Catherine a hint of a smile. It was a start.

Catherine instinctively reached out and touched her left hand lightly, noting the handcuff with extended chain attached to her right wrist. She looked down at the red nail varnish flaking from her nails which were bitten short.

"Have you got kids doctor?"

"Me? No."

Catherine was taken aback by the question. Not the typical opening gambit she'd encountered as an FME, or Doctor; for that matter.

"Not yet anyway...."

"Too busy or not found the right man?"

"*A bit of both I guess.*" Catherine answered sincerely.

"*Why do you ask*?"

"No reason. But I guess you'd treat them right if you did, yeah?"

"Sure. Has someone treated you badly Natalia?" responded Catherine sensing the girl's need to open up.

"What do *you* care?" The blunt unexpected reply hit home like a jackhammer.

Catherine instinctively recoiled in her chair.

"I can see you're angry."

"*No shit Sherlock.*" 'Came the mocking reply.

"That's *ENOUGH*." P.C. Datta had kids of her own and her response was instantaneous and assertive.

Catherine raised her right hand a few centimetres in a placatory fashion and resumed eye contact with Natalia.

"I thought you wanted a swab or something?"

"Yes but we can.."

"...*Talk*? Was that what you were going to say d-o-c-t-o-r?" She enunciated each letter in a monotonous and sarcastic tone: reflected in her smirk.

"Are you joking? What would *you* understand about *my* life?"

Her scorn was spewed out like bile in a cult horror movie.

"You're all the same, you *do-gooders*."

"*Sometimes it can help to talk, even to a stranger*." Catherine continued in a calm and reassuring voice.

Natalia fixed her eyes on Catherine and tilted her head to the left, wrinkling her brow as if contemplating her response....watching Catherine's mannerisms.

Catherine's phone buzzed on the table.

"*It might be important*." Pronounced Natalia: gesturing to the phone with a slight forward head movement. Her tone was composed and cooperative again.

"Right now, *you're* more important to me." Catherine smiled and inclined her forehead to emphasise her empathy.

A brief smile and a softening of the young girls' features convinced Catherine she was taking the right approach. Prisoner or not, she was entitled to Catherine's time and worthy of her efforts.

"Suppose I had done something wrong? Could I tell you, *Privately* I mean?"

"*That would depend...*" Catherine flashed at a look at P.C. Datta.

"So the answer's NO!"

Back to the recalcitrant child, chided by her mother.

"Do you mean you did something wrong in a *criminal way*?"

"*Maybe....maybe not.*" she cocked her head to the left again as she spoke.

Catherine's mobile buzzed again and once more the caller did not leave a message; it stopped after four or five rings.

P.C. Young shuffled from foot to foot and Catherine sensed he was becoming restless. His sigh confirmed her suspicions. She shot him a brief glance and frowned momentarily. He looked across in an unconcerned manner as if to say, "*another day: ...another dollar.*"

"What if something bad and wrong happened to *me*."

"*Well...*" Catherine began choosing her words carefully. "If what's happened affects the charges which the Police have brought against you, then that's probably best discussed with your Lawyer and the Police. If it's more of a *personal matter..*"

"*Like rape you mean*?"

Catherine recoiled for a moment, struck by the directness of the comment.

"*Are we talking about rape*?" Catherine mirrored Natalia's head cocked to one side action.

No response, Natalia broke eye contact then closed her eyes.

"...*Because if we were*...and that was a recent attack; then we should think about taking some further samples and examination and discussion in a Specialist Unit."

"But *you* could do all that right?" Natalia still had her eyes closed and she shook visibly as she spoke.

"*Well..I could....yes of course Natalia.*"

Catherine touched the back of Natalia's hand again; wondering if things were about to get a whole lot more complicated than a simple case of theft.

They collectively looked down at Natalia, who had hunched forward and was doing her best to rock herself whilst still tethered to P.C. Young.

She began to whimper as she rocked gently forward and backward.

Catherine looked up at P.C. Young and made the sign of a key turning in a lock to gesture her willingness to see Natalia's handcuffs removed.

P.C. Datta looked across and hesitated, then slowly nodded. She could only imagine the hell this child must be suffering. Young released the cuff on his left wrist and extricated his hand from his cuff.

Her movements were swiftly and meticulously executed.

She sprang up on to her feet, raised her right arm forcibly and smashed P.C Young directly in the nose with her cuff and chain before leaping forward and encircling Catherine's neck with the chain of the cuffs. She crossed the chain anti-clockwise around Catherine's neck and dragged her backwards on the swivel chair out of the range of W.P.C Datta who had been slow to react. Blood spattered across her face as her colleague's broken nose haemorrhaged blood. He groaned and slid down the wall behind him.

Dragging Catherine back toward the desk Natalia positioned herself on the table with a choke hold on Catherine whose arms were flailing as she struggled to draw breath. Her lips were rapidly turning blue and her face was red and contorted with fear. Her eyes bulged and her pupils dilated rapidly as adrenaline coursed through her veins.

P.C. Datta rushed forward towards the panic button but stopped short as Natalia screamed at her.

"Touch that BITCH and I'll FUCKING kill her!"

Natalia tightened the chain around Catherine's neck and P.C. Datta registered the sheer look of panic on the Doctor's face. Their eyes locked momentarily before P.C. Datta hit the alarm and leapt forward towards Natalia. With her arms outstretched she propelled herself forward and extended her fingers aiming straight for Natalia's face as she forced Natalia's head back against the wall behind the desk. All the while, Catherine was dragged back on the swivel chair as their three bodies collided.

Catherine's hands tore at the chain around her neck and in the instant it loosened momentarily she gasped air and began coughing violently, desperately flinging her arms up to the chain which was looped and crossed around her neck.

P.C Datta heard a crash as the door flew open and shouts as she was pulled backwards. A blur of uniforms and hands ensued as Catherine struggled and kicked. Her legs were immobilised by strong hands and her lungs filled with air as the chain around her neck was removed. Her shoulders were lifted and she found herself on the examination couch with concerned faces looking down at her.

"Catherine it's me – Sally. It's all over, you're safe!"

A mist of tears covered her eyes like a swirling sea cloaked in pervasive fog. Sally's words were barely audible above the sound of the klaxon.

"Someone switch that bloody alarm off and get two Ambulances here stat!" Sally shouted with the bark of a Sergeant Major in the Armed Forces.

There was no way on God's Earth Sally would countenance Catherine Newton travelling in the same Ambulance as Natalia Yeltsin for treatment of their respective injuries. P.C. Young had already been removed from the examination room as Sally gave her instructions.

Chapter 12

20:50 Sally Benson's Office

"So how do you want to handle round two *Boss*?" Louise asked.

"Well, without any knock out blows would be good!" piped up Brian, re-energised by his coffee Americano.

"You'll get no argument from me on that count." Sally confirmed dryly and they laughed in unison.

Much to her personal disappointment in her own willpower, Sally had chain-smoked two cigarettes in the time it took Brian and Louise to nip to the local coffee shop and secure the three steaming cups of coffee which beat the hot black stuff from the 'Nick any day of the week.

"The good cop, bad cop routine has worked well so far; I would vote for more of the same."

Brian gave Louise a playful wink as he made the suggestion.

"Okay, let's take a step back from the Mother angle as she clearly has some unresolved issues on that front. Louise let's get her back on track with her visit to Melway Mews."

"Brian do we have the CCTV footage ready?"

"All sorted boss."

"What does the facial recognition software reveal?"

"We're waiting the forensic view but *Peter Roberts* was hopeful of a positive match, although because of the CCTV angle he couldn't be sure. The backpack is a different matter; *no doubt it's a match*."

"When will he get back to us?"

"'As soon as he's run the computer programme, fully: certainly today."

The Forensic review of the back pack could take a while; lots of trace evidence at first blush of inspection.

"What did the FME say Louise?"

"She's been delayed by a Rape case in Fletcher Street Nick boss, but will be here as soon as she can; within the hour. That update was forty minutes ago."

"Any news from Forensics on finger print matches either inside or outside the apartment?"

"Peter's got that on the list to do."

"Okay, let's hold off for a couple of hours until we've got our ducks in a row. Brian in the meantime let's all review Schultz' statement covering Boxing Day until we get a forensics update."

A knock at the door interrupted their discussion.

Karl popped his head around the door.

"FME is here now and has begun assessing Natalia boss."

"Thanks Karl; ask her to pop up when she's finished to give us the go-ahead for her next interview."

Karl nodded and closed the door just as the phone rang on Sally's desk.

She grabbed it on the second ring.

"What? How the hell did she manage that?"

"We're on our way."

"Christ, let's get to the FMEs office. We've got a potential Hostage situation."

"Natalia and the DOC'?" Brian sprang up as he spoke.

"You've called it."

"Karl, QUICKLY: with us NOW!"

Brian called across the office as they exited en masse.

Chapter 13

"Would one of you two like to explain to me exactly how Natalia Yeltsin managed to virtually choke the FME to death?"

Sally barked loudly as she approached the two P.C.s who had been supposedly present to supervise the FMEs assessment; in light of Natalia's volatile mood.

W.P.C. Rita Datta was first to speak.

"It all happened so quick Ma'am.."

"And don't call me Ma'am again or your future at this nick is over before it's begun W.P.C. Datta!"

"Guv' I take full responsibility for the lapse in concentration.." P.C. Richard Young spoke with marked nasal intonation: he'd had surgical tapes applied across the bridge of his nose, the nasal bones of which had been readily reduced to alignment in the Accident and Emergency Department.

"Lapse in concentration…!!! Is that what you bloody call it, a lapse in concentration Constable?"

Sally glared at P.C. Young who visibly blushed and looked almost intimidated by Sally's uncharacteristic loss of composure.

He was smart enough to keep quiet and he pursed his lips tightly as he stared at his feet.

"We almost lost an FME. On my watch…do you know how ANGRY that makes me feel…"

"Would you like to be the one facing the Doctor's parents explaining how…under our very noses, a twenty-two year old detainee was able to overpower two officers and hold their daughter hostage?"

"What about you W.P.C. Datta: would you like that job?"

"I want you both to go right now and prepare your statements and have them reviewed by the Custody Sergeant before they reach my desk by midnight tonight."

Sally let the instruction sink in before she added:

"Then and only then, P.C. Young: you take seventy-two hours leave and rest your injury."

"There will be an internal inquiry and I find any evidence that either or both of you have neglected their duty: you will rue the day you entered this Nick."

"Clear?"

Two heads nodded in unison.

"Go...out of my sight now: both of you!"

Chapter 14

"D.C.I. Benson?"

"Yes."

"I'm Doctor Mathew Emerson, Accident and Emergency Consultant: I gather you're here enquiring about Catherine Newton?"

"Yes, how is Dr Newton?"

"She's quite shaken up: to state the obvious."

He gave a transient smile as if to reassure Sally; acutely aware she must be feeling responsible for the incident which could so easily have ended in tragedy earlier in the evening.

"She should make a full recovery. She has significant bruising and swelling due to soft tissue injury around her neck but mercifully her hyoid bone is intact and there is no sign of airway compromise."

"I have given her a mild sedative and we'll keep her in our small overnight Ward in A&E for regular observation."

"Next of kin have been informed and her parents are travelling down as we speak."

"Is there anything she needs doctor: *anything at all*?"

He smiled and shook his head.

"Have you also dealt with Natalia Yeltsin?"

"Yes her scalp lacerations were easily closed with simple suturing but given the possibility of a head injury whilst in Custody; we've admitted her to be sure. As you're very aware there was a question surrounding use of narcotics, so we've taken all relevant blood tests.

Your young Detective: *Karl Madding*, I believe…..?

Sally nodded and smiled…

" …..elected to stay with her overnight and she is hand-cuffed to her bed, given her history of violence against You and Doctor Catherine."

The Nursing Staff, sadly, are rather accustomed to violence these days and a female security office has also been requisitioned, so to speak, to ensure the safety of everyone involved with her care. She should be ready for discharge after rounds tomorrow morning.

"Okay Thank You Doctor, you've been most helpful; and you're sure there's nothing I can do?"

*"They will both benefit from rest….*and I would suggest you should do the same Detective Chief Inspector." Mathew Emerson looked at his watch as he spoke.

Sally gave him a weary smile and with a nod left the waiting room just across from the Ward in which Catherine lay bruised and exhausted.

Sally did feel personally responsible for Catherine Newton; Sally's team had let Catherine down and damn nearly cost her everything. *First 'Schultz, now 'Newton*…she felt exhausted but couldn't rest.

Sally had a thousand thoughts buzzing around in her head but couldn't organise them right now into a coherent stream of thought. She needed a coffee and a shower. But at the back of her mind something was bothering her: she had to discern what it was. She knew she wouldn't sleep until she'd nailed it.

It was 3:20 a.m. when her mobile rang, it was Brian.

"Hi Boss, how's the Doc'?"

"She'll be fine; I am just heading back to the office now. What are you doing?"

"'Reviewing the CCTV from the lift and today's interview footage."

"I sent Louise home; she looked knackered."

"OK *good, see you in twenty minutes*." She hung up and headed outside for a cigarette: she settled for two and chastised herself for the second time in twenty-four hours for her lack of willpower.

The moment she stepped into her office her mobile rang.

"Louise, you should be sleeping."

"Chance would be a fine thing Boss."

Louise was snuggled up in bed with the T.V in her bedroom switched to mute. She'd been watching re-runs of 'eighties comedies to help her unwind.

"I was thinking Boss..."

"What if Natalia *didn't* leave Melway Mews on Boxing Day simply because Edwina Justin was entertaining; what if she left because of *Christophe Schultz*. Maybe it was because of him *specifically*."

"I'm listening." Sally sat down feeling weary; she leaned back and kicked off her stilettos; rubbing the soles of her stockinged feet together.

"Well suppose she thought he might recognise her?"

"Where would he know her from... he didn't mention recognising her in any of his statements." Sally looked puzzled.

"I know I've been running over them in my head. He did say the visitor on Boxing Day stood there looking at him for a while. His exact words were: *"frozen to the spot."*

Sally entered her password and opened the file which she'd read a hundred times.

"You're right Louise, those were his exact words." She pondered for a moment.

"What does your instinct tell you?"

"That she had too much to lose to show her hand; so much that she never made contact again."

"As far as we know....." Sally cautioned.

"Are you thinking blackmail as a motive: public figure, too much to lose by the scandal emerging........ *of an illegitimate child*?"

Suddenly it all made sense to Sally; Louise had struck gold...

"It's possible Boss. We know she was hard up and why make contact after all these years unless she had an ulterior motive? Perhaps she figured Schultz might recognise her in the future so she backed off."

"It's a good thought Louise: outside of the box, but a good thought. Whether she recognised him, or he recognised her, the key thing is she walked away."

Sally rubbed her temples with her thumb and middle finger of her right hand as if attempting to unlock her brain block.

"Now get some sleep Louise and we'll talk about later on this morning okay?"

"Goodnight Boss."

The line went dead.

Sally needed another cigarette and a coffee in that order. Her head was buzzing and she had a knotted feeling in the pit of her stomach. Something was eating away at her and she couldn't cast off the feeling that Louise was right; they were missing a trick. *Something didn't fit.*

She put on a pair of flat shoes and headed out of her office.

Brian was re-running the CCTV from the lift at Melway Mews. He looked alert despite the late hour.

"Smoke break?" she spoke over his left shoulder.

"No thanks Boss I'm going to try and get some kip soon. You should do the same."

She nodded wondering whether she would set up her camp bed in the office.

"Goodnight Brian." She called over her shoulder as she headed for the stairs and the smokers' shelter.

She'd only gone down one flight when she stopped abruptly.

"Shit! *Surely not...?"* She heard herself say out loud as she turned and headed back upstairs.

How could they have missed that? She hurried back upstairs determined to catch Brian before he left.

He glanced up from his computer.

"That must have been some sprint back from the shelter?"

Sally wasn't in the mood for jokes.

"The statement from the resident at number 2 on the Ground Floor: the elderly lady who let *Natalia* into the building on Boxing Day?"

"Karl took the statement from her if I recall?" It sounded like a rhetorical question.

Brian got up from his desk and stretched out his arms and arched his back briefly before following Sally into her office.

Sally was already typing on her computer, re-entering her password. The system had shut her out as she'd left her computer unattended for longer than two minutes.

She scanned the pages.

Brian stood over her shoulder.

"Yes here it is. She said *he* in her statement which is why we always assumed that the CCTV footage was of a man or a teenage boy."

"It's something Louise suggested Brian. Suppose Natalia had recognised Christophe when he answered the door, but just like the Thai housekeeper from Apartment 12, he had mistaken her for a boy and therefore failed to recognise her as a consequence in *another context; maybe they had met before*?"

"Natalia didn't speak to him having rung the doorbell, so he'd have seen the baseball cap which largely obscured her face anyway, registered the back pack when she walked away; but otherwise thought no more of it."

To Schultz: *it was a boy who had rung the doorbell.*

The maid at number 12 had likewise been mistaken: the person she mistook for a boy seen exiting the lift: *was in fact a girl; Natalia Yeltsin.*"

"*They were both sure of it and both mistaken.*"

"And I can imagine without make-up, given her short hairstyle that she could easily be mistaken for a boy, even by an experienced Doctor at close quarters."

Chapter 15

"The time is 09:30 on Sunday 15th December 2016."

"Interview recommenced: persons present – the accused Natalia Yeltsin, DCI Sally Benson and DC Louise Shepherd. *W.P.C. Datta in attendance: as an Observer.*"

For the benefit of the record: The accused Natalia Yeltsin is wearing handcuffs having attacked DCI Benson and Dr Catherine Newton, respectively.

"In addition to the existing charge of Theft, Miss Yeltsin has been further charged with one count of Assaulting a Police Officer: and a further account of Assault occasioning Actual Bodily Harm and one charge of Unlawful Imprisonment; the latter two charges relating to Dr Catherine Newton."

"At the time of this recording, a further charge of *Attempted Murder* relating to Dr Catherine Newton is under consideration by the Crown Prosecution Service."

"May I remind you that you are still under Police 'Caution."

"Do you wish to have legal representation by a Solicitor given the gravity of the charges against you Natalia?" I would strongly advise you to take this option."

Natalia Yeltsin watched Sally the whole time she made the recording, her wrists shackled by handcuffs.

"For the benefit of the tape: the Accused has made no response."

"*How are you Natalia?*" asked Louise.

No response.

"*The last few days have not been easy…. for any of us.*"

A smirk crossed Natalia's face as she diverted her eyes from the table top towards Louise.

"Don't you want to know how the FME is today?"

A quizzical look was her response.

"The doctor: who was trying to help you on Friday evening?"

"...The doctor who YOU tried to ...s-t-r-a-n-g-l-e."

Sally shot her a dark look as she spelt out the word syllable by syllable.

"You mean I didn't s-u-c-c-e-e-d?" responded Natalia with a reciprocal intonation, followed by a self-satisfied smile.

"So you think this is a joke?"

Sally asked without a hint of sarcasm in her calm demeanour.

No response.

Just an icy stare: in response to Sally's question.

Piercing green Emerald eyes.

No one spoke until Louise took a different approach.

"Natalia....we are all *genuinely concerned about you."*

"We can feel from your angry outbursts...that you are seriously hurting inside."

"Please...help us....to help you."

"How?" was all she said in her reply.

Not for the first time Brian felt impressed by Louise' ability to touch a nerve; to reach out and make contact.

"Help us try to understand how things have 'gotten this bad."

"You mentioned your brother.....when did you last see him?"

She opened her mouth to respond....then seemed to re-think her response.

"Do you keep in touch on social media?"

Nothing....she stared at the table.

Tears began to well up in her eyes.

"Can we offer you a cup of tea Natalia?"

A slow nod: in the affirmative.

Louise gestured to P.C. Datta with a nod and a smile as Rita left the room.

"For the benefit of the tape: W.P.C. Datta has left the room."

They sat silently but for Natalia's gentle sobbing.

Rita Datta had chosen a cup of tea from the office teapot. Brewed a while ago; she was not about to put a boiling hot brew in the hands of Natalia after the events of the previous day.

Five minutes later Rita Datta returned with a two-thirds cup of tea.

No thanks or acknowledgement for Rita Datta were forthcoming form Natalia as the polystyrene cup was placed in front of her.

She simply sat her eyes transfixed on a spot on the table; her head cocked to the left side.

Louise and Sally watched Natalia very carefully as she gingerly raised the cup to her lips.

They had no intention of removing her handcuffs.

"Interview recommenced: 09:45: same persons present: W.P.C. Datta has re-entered the room with tea for the Accused."

Sally spoke calmly and waited for Louise to interject.

"Natalia...we would like to understand more about your life-style...."

"You told us yesterday you have no real friends in London....where you live in Archway..."

"Nor relatives....certainly none near Melway Mews..."

"I told you I don't know anyone in Mayfair.."

Brian punched the air: "Gotcha!"

"Mayfair......" replied Louise

"But you've been to Mayfair before....walked through it...or"

"Maybe...I don't rem....."

"But you know Melway Mews is in Mayfair..." interrupted Louise.

She narrowed her eyes and darted a look at Louise.

"I never said...."

"Did you ever go into Melway Mews....for a look around?"

Silence.

"What I don't understand Natalia...is we have a witness who saw..."

"What witness..who saw me.." Natalia's interjection swift and implicit to her presence at the 'Mews.

Silence and she visibly bit her lip.

"You were going to say...who saw me in Melway Mews, weren't you Natalia?"

Sally leaned forward slightly as she spoke: fixing Natalia's gaze.

"So what if I did BITCH..you got nothin' on me!"

Sally sat back.

"You fucking pigs got nothin' on me."

"Big fat nothin'!!"

She started to laugh out loud, arching her neck back and laughing and suddenly began talking in Russian.......faster and faster...then a howl....as she started to laugh and cry...

"Interview suspended at 10:05."

Sally pressed the stop button on the device and Brian entered the room accompanied by two male large male officers whose shift had started an hour previously.

"Thank you. Back to the cells please."

They stood as Natalia was half escorted half frog-marched back to her cell.

"My office: now please both." Quietly pragmatic and deep in thought.

Sally led Louise and Brian up the stairwell.

None of them spoke.

Chapter 16

Sally updated the A.C.C. as soon as she arrived back at her office.

He listened intently and didn't hesitate to support her proposals for next steps.

Five minutes later she called Brian and Louise into the office for an update.

"Okay I've just updated the A.C.C.

"*I believe Natalia Yeltsin was involved in Edwina Justin's Murder.*

Brian and Louise nodded affirmatively.

However, after yesterday's events and her labile mood today: she needs a full Forensic Psychiatric Assessment."

"I will be making arrangements with a Home Office approved centre: location yet to be determined."

"The A.C.C. wishes to discuss the matter with the Home Office personally, given Professor Justin's profile and the facts surrounding Dr Schultz."

"'Understood Boss." Brian responded.

Shall I rally the troops later today or tomorrow morning Boss?

"*Midday tomorrow please Brian*: I need time to review the Witness Statements from Melway Mews and I want to take a look at the Court transcripts today."

"Louise you can take a lead on the lines of questioning we pursued...give an overview of Natalia's mood please Louise. Take a break from the office environment but come prepared tomorrow after a good nights sleep."

"Your background in Psychology is hugely valuable: as has been your approach to her interviews."

"Good job!"

Louise blushed and merely thanked Sally with a broad smile.

"*Great teamwork*!... *both of you*." Brian added as they left Sally's office.

For the first time in the last few weeks, Sally smiled inwardly. She needed a few hours at home. A long soak in the bath and then time to study.

Chapter 17

12:15 Monday 16th January 2017

For the first time in several days, the entire team was gathered in the briefing room.

Sally clapped her hands briefly.

"OK Team: eyes front. Let's crack on."

Brian and Louise were on their feet too: the rest of the team took their seats, and looked directly at the large white board as Sally gave an overview of recent events.

"You've all heard the recordings of our interviews with Natalia Yeltsin."

"She's our front runner now as the most likely suspect involved in, or fully responsible for, the Murder of Professor Edwina Justin."

Christophe Schultz' Legal Team and the Home Office have been updated in respect of the *New Evidence* which has come to light since Natalia's Arrest: I took full responsibility for enabling this process, yesterday afternoon; after reviewing the entirety of the evidence presented at the Trial of Doctor Schultz.

(The "penny dropped" and Brian and Louise exchanged glances as they fully comprehended why Sally had elected to take time out of the Office on the previous afternoon.)

 "Natalia has clearly got a hell of a temper and knows how to inflict harm.....her moves are swift and effective."

"She has no compunction in attacking Senior Police and Medical personnel alike.."

"But what's her *motive* in killing Professor Justin?"

"Bang on: Karl. "That's exactly what we need to establish." Sally paused for a moment.

"It seems *absurd that she would have conspired* with Christophe Schultz to commit murder and we have no reason to assume they had ever met before, or after, December 26th 2015.

"We were under the misapprehension that the visitor to Edwina Justin's apartment at Melway Mews *that Boxing Day afternoon*; had been a young man, sporting the rucksack and baseball cap which is now familiar evidence to all."

In any event, today *Natalia Yeltsin* will begin her formal evaluation at a Secure Psychiatric Unit."

That news was greeted with quiet nods of approval from around the room.

Given the scrutiny which Natalia will be under at the *Tempest Institute* in Hampshire, during the next couple of weeks or so, we should thereafter be in a far better position to continue our interrogation and thereafter press charges after the C.P.S. review of all the evidence and crucially, Judge her Mental Capacity to plead in light of her crimes to date."

"Her mood is labile and judging from her behaviour whilst in custody...*she may well be Psychopathic*."

"Louise will give you her own *Psychological Profile of Natalia*, based on what we have gleaned to date."

"Brian will brief you on the circumstances of her arrest and the findings from her mobile phone."

"Karl I want you and Tom to accompany Brian and Louise on a search of her flat soonest."

"*No stone unturned...understood?*" Remember to lift the floorboards!"

"*We reconvene at 4 p.m. sharp.*"

As planned Sally left the briefing and headed off to her meeting with the A.C.C.

At 12:30 precisely her mobile rang and she picked up on the third ding.

"D.C.I. Benson?"

A familiar voice but on a withheld number.

"Speaking."

"*This is Georgina Townsend*. I wanted you to hear this from me before the News is made Public."

"Doctor Christophe Schultz has been exonerated by the Court of Appeal this morning: he has been released from Prison and his the Conviction for the Murder of Professor Edwina Justin has been overturned."

"*He is a free man.*"

Silence. No recrimination. No cynicism or one-upmanship.

Georgina had spoken plainly and clearly.

"*Thank you for calling me directly Miss Townsend.*" replied Sally.

"*Thank you*: Detective Chief Inspector."

The phone line went dead as the colour drained from Sally's sallow complexion. Somewhere buried deep inside her Psyche, this entire disclosure came as no surprise to Sally: it was almost a relief to know that her instincts had been correct all along. She stood quietly for a moment and gathered her thoughts, before retracing her steps.

Brian had already started bringing the team up to speed as Sally returned to the Briefing Room, five minutes later.

"*Brian - excuse me interrupting*: I need to update you all....there's been an important development in the case of the Murder of Professor Edwina Justin...."

Chapter 18

13:30 A.C.C. Office, London

"Sally I have no doubt that you've done everything by the Book."

"But the key issue is how the FME was injured with *two Officers* in attendance, in a Police Forensic Examination Room?

"But for *your* rapid intervention she would have been strangled as I understand it?"

"I can see the Headlines now: 'A *dead General Practitioner* to add to our list of fatalities."

"I'm sure I don't need to impress upon you that the Home Office wants answers and a Conviction, *especially given the 'Schultz Appeal was successful!*"

He never broke eye contact with Sally for a moment: despite his insistence on the Charges having been brought against Dr Schultz in the first instance; despite Sally's misgivings.

"I understand that the recommendation of the Home Office after discussion with Forensic Psychiatrists; is that an Assessment Period of at least *fourteen days* will be required to determine the fitness of Natalia Yeltsin to undergo further questioning."

"During that time I want *all* loose ends tied up and the Charges agreed up front with the C.P.S., so it's full steam ahead once she's returned to our Investigation."

"Do I make myself clear?"

"Yes Sir: abundantly clear."

"Is there anything else I need be made aware of?"

"No Sir."

"Then that will be all."

His tone had turned dismissive and he waved a hand towards Sally as he dismissed her; only then did he break eye contact.

For her part, she nodded transiently and left without looking back.

Part 6

Chapter 1

Friday 20th January 2017 Clapham Common

Unsure whether she was still dreaming, *Sally Benson* stretched out her left arm and fumbled for her mobile phone which was buzzing repeatedly on the bedside table. Scant light from the illuminated screen display, cast unworldly patterns on her bedroom ceiling.

The green luminescent hands on her bedside clock displayed 5.15 a.m.

It was barely two hours since Sally's eyelids had finally closed over her bleary eyes. After tossing and turning for what felt like an eternity she had descended into a disturbed world of violence interwoven with distorted fantasy; where everything had seemed tangible and believable. Her brow was hot and she'd been perspiring heavily in her sleep.

A thick Scottish accent at the end of the 'phone, brought her back down to earth in an instant.

"D.C.I. Benson?"

"Yes speaking." Sally rubbed her eyes which felt gritty and sore from too much reading and weeks of sleep deprivation.

Fatigue was audible in Sally's voice to her dawn caller who was accustomed to working throughout the night and delivering unexpected news.

"I'm sorry to disturb you at this early hour." His voice was calm and sincere and dispassionate in equal measure.

"My name is Professor Alan McBurney. I'm calling from the *Tempest* Institute."

His tone was unhurried and precise, no hyperbole. He underscored the word "Tempest" with deliberate intonation.

Sally sat bolt upright in bed and clicked on the silver framed spotlight above her head which illuminated only the area immediately around her pillow; she'd chosen it as an ideal light to read by on those long and sometimes lonely nights, when sleep frequently evaded her.

"Yes, I know your name of course Professor McBurney; how can I help?"

Professor McBurney was well known in Judicial circles for his huge contribution to Forensic Psychiatry: he was often called as an expert witness in court and seemed to show no leaning to either defence or prosecution. He did his job with the utmost professionalism. Sally had been expecting an update from the Tempest Institute at some stage; *but at this hour of the morning*?

Sally held her breath for a moment sensing bad news; she felt her heart skip a beat; a sure sign of her customary excessive caffeine intake and physical exhaustion which was integral to the job these days. She reflexively flashed a look at the black plastic strapped monitor on her left wrist. Her pulse rate was 111 beats per minute.

"I am calling with an update on *Natalia Yeltsin*."

Sally braced herself for the impending bad news. It was never good news at 5' in the morning.

"Regrettably, Miss Yeltsin was pronounced dead at 4:55 a.m. this morning."

"*Jesus*', twenty minutes ago." thought Sally; as she raised her right hand, rubbed her aching eyes again and scratched her perspiring hair-line, absent-mindedly.

"How did she die Professor?"

Alan McBurney noticed that her voice was subdued: concern, disappointment maybe, but not the stunned grief reaction he so often encountered in his job when dealing with relatives. For that at least, he was grateful tonight.

(The evening and early morning hours had been busy with new admissions to the General Psychiatric Wards. He'd been on-call, so had kept himself abreast of all admissions and working diagnoses, for which he'd carried ultimate responsibility that night.)

"*At this stage it would appear to be a suicide*; a sharp modified razor device was found by the nursing staff, near the deceased' body. The Forensic team has just arrived at the scene."

Alan McBurney knew better than to jump to conclusions after twenty-five years as a psychiatrist, eighteen of which he'd spent mastering forensic psychiatry. He stroked his chin and his forty-eight hour prickly stubble which was at odds with his usual closely shaven face. It had been a busy week at the Institute.

"I should be able to update you in a couple of hours time Detective Chief Inspector."

Sally considered his proposal for a moment, mindful that Hampshire C.I.D. would have immediate jurisdiction over the scene of an unexpected death of a potentially violent patient; particularly in a secure psychiatric wing and so soon after her arrest.

Alan McBurney sensed her hesitation; he added:

"I will ensure that *your* team have unrestricted access to the room where Natalia died."

There it was again - that subtle intonation - this time for the possessive pronoun: *your* team.

"Thank you Professor McBurney. I appreciate your prompt call and consideration. Please call me on this number in the first instance with any updates, *no matter how small.*"

She knew a man of his gravitas would only call her with salient or unexpected forensic findings.

"Of course: Goodbye." His manner was polite and pragmatic.

Sally's head began to pound; she could feel the investigation slipping away from her grasp *again*. A key witness: dead within a week of her arrival at the Tempest Institute.

"Shit, shit, shit.." she muttered to herself; swinging her legs out of bed onto the hard wood floor which felt cold beneath her bare feet.

(She'd hired a sanding machine a year ago and after applying the dark stain she'd bought at the local DIY store and was delighted by the results of her own handy-work but first thing in the morning; missed her old white woollen carpet that she'd inherited with the house when she'd bought it five years previously with her ex-husband. By contrast he was either incapable or unwilling, mostly the latter; to sully his hands with D.I.Y.)

Sally wondered whether Natalia's fierce temper had contributed in any way to her death; maybe she'd angered another patient who had enacted revenge? She tried to dismiss the thought from her head as she changed out of her silk white pyjamas and into black linen trousers and a white blouse, having sprayed herself liberally with antiperspirant spray. She'd forego an early shower in favour of a long soak in the bath later that evening. She packed a change of clothes and essential toiletries in a small soft black leather holdall and headed straight to the car where she opted for the speed dial on her phone.

Chapter 2

5:25 a.m. Friday 20th January 2017 Clapham

Brian answered his phone on the second ring; spilling black coffee on his faded denim jeans as he did so.

"Hi Boss. Can't you sleep either?" He didn't expect a reply as he knew they *"were birds of a feather".*

"Natalia Yeltsin has been found dead Brian. I will explain at the office. Can you call Louise?"

Silence greeted her request.

Brian stood fixed to the spot for a moment, his expression frozen.

"Brian?"

"Yes Boss, sorry, of course. See you in thirty'."

He hung up.

"Geez' this case gets better and better..." he muttered to himself; shaking his head disbelievingly.

"And what are you after?" His tabby cat looked up at him wide-eyed and expectantly and rubbed his wet hair against Brian's legs, shedding long brindled hairs on his jeans.

Moments before his call from the Boss, *"Wilson"*, his four year-old feline house mate, had come into the kitchen through the cat-flap and deposited a dead field mouse at Brian's feet: a familiar morning greeting. He was now pining for his reward for the night's killing spree.

"Come on then *trouble*." Brian poured his freshly brewed coffee down the sink and opened a large tin filled with Sainsbury's pilchards in tomato sauce onto a saucer. Wilson emptied the plate voraciously as Brian smoothed the fur on Wilson's back before retrieving the mouse, carefully wrapping it up in an old evening newspaper and depositing it in the stainless steel waste bin. As the swing lid clattered *Wilson* looked up expectantly; hoping for more pescatarian delights.

"Later, later, get some sleep Wills'."

Brian vigorously rubbed Wilson's damp fur as his beloved housemate purred loudly in appreciation of the impromptu attention.

Brian grabbed his mobile from the breakfast bar of his galley kitchen.

"Louise? Hi sorry to wake you. Boss wants us at the Nick pronto. *Natalia is DEAD."*

"S-H-I-T." Was all she uttered as they stood silently in mutual disbelief.

Louise' favourite word at times of crisis thought Brian.

"You read my mind. I don't know anything more at the moment. The D.C.I. will update us when we get there."

"Okay, I'm on my way Brian." The phone went dead.

Brian was in and out of his walk-in shower, dressed in a fresh pair of black denims with a matching blue shirt and ready to leave within ten minutes.

Wilson was already curled up in a ball sleeping on his oversized brown pillow near the breakfast bar by the time Brian checked the back door leading into the garden was locked. He replenished the water bowl and smiled down at *Wills*; his ex-wife's shortened version of *Wilson*.

(Shortening names: It was a habit his ex- never grew out of and one which only rankled with him when she referred to him as *"Bri'" in front of friends and family*. When their marriage hit stony ground, she did it all the more to irritate and then finally to *enrage him*. He only lost it' the one time with her, but suffice to say her bags were packed within an hour and the locks changed a day later. He had put every penny of his hard earned cash into the 1930's semi- in Battersea and all she knew was how to *spend, spend, spend*!)

He locked the front door and headed for the car. He gazed up at the dreary grey sky. The early morning rain looked in for the day and it was still only 5:40 a.m.

Thankful for the quiet roads, Brian arrived in the office twenty minutes later. Sally was already talking on her mobile phone, pacing up and down in her glass-clad, fish-bowl style office: irritation etched all over her face.

The dark skies and dreary start to the day reflected the *Assistant Chief Commissioner's* mood on hearing of the untimely death of their chief subject in a murder investigation. Sally had rung the A.C.C. as soon as she'd arrived at the office ten minutes previously and his attitude had been borderline aggressive as he took in the news: as though Sally herself had in some way been responsible for Natalia's untimely death.

Sally listened to his diatribe, nodding on the end of the phone, occasionally rolling her eyes heavenward. *Why did he always see fit to lecture her on procedure at times like this*: she'd been doing the job for fifteen years; ten in the murder squad?

Brian fired up his laptop, half an eye on Sally as Louise arrived wearing a long black trench coat: carrying a cardboard tray of large coffee cups which had been swiftly prepared by her favourite barista: two minutes from the Police Headquarters in which they worked on the South side of the River Thames in London.

Louise' flat was a mere ten minute walk from the office; five minutes on days she ran to work. Today was no day for a refreshing run.

"Glad to see someone's got time for coffee."

Brian teased with a glint in his eyes. He had learned through bitter experience that when the going gets tough, it is was vital to maintain a good sense of humour and in any case a smile used fewer facial muscles than a frown and for the MIT, banter was second nature when the pressure was on; rather akin to doctors who used *gallows humour* at times of stress.

Louise headed straight for her desk and took off her coat which she draped over the back of her chair, removed a paper bag from her pocket then engaged his banter:

"Well that would include YOU then: *or so it would appear*?"

She carefully placed a large cup of *Americano coffee* and accompanying plastic lid on the edge of his over-stacked desk.

"And would *your Lordship* like a Danish pastry too?" She did a mock curtsey and handed him a fresh Danish pastry wrapped in a large white serviette.

Brian bowed graciously in his seat and eagerly took a large mouthful of moist, freshly baked pastry.

"*Touché!*" He mumbled through a mouthful of food and broad grin. He engaged eye to eye contact with Louise and held her gaze lifting his eyebrows flirtatiously.

"I'm finally beginning to think my decision to purloin you from uniform *WAS the correct one after all.*" He laughed mid-bite.

Louise shook her head and raised her eyebrows momentarily as if dealing with a naughty schoolchild.

"Oh it was *your* decision was it?"

She took a slurp from her steaming coffee and glanced at Brian's computer screen.

"*So what's the story with Natalia*?"

"I think the Boss will need her coffee this morning." Brian nodded towards the corner office where Sally was still extricating herself from the challenging phone conversation with the A.C.C.

Chapter 3

6:15 a.m.

"Brian, Louise: my office, now." Sally's tone was no-nonsense and unusually terse; notwithstanding the early hour and her lack of sleep.

The A.C.C. must have raised her hackles thought Brian. Louise had the same thought as she gave Sally a brief sheepish smile heading into her office.

Sally looked flushed as she sat down and waited for Brian to close the office door before she un-muted the land-line. Brian simply nodded at Sally as he took his seat. They'd worked as a team for over five years and he knew when to keep quiet.

Louise ran her fingers through her shoulder length blonde hair as she sat opposite the Boss. She exchanged a brief look with Brian who had his notebook ready and poised on his knee.

Sally laid her mobile on her desk between them and unmated the speakerphone.

"Professor McBurney my colleagues have joined us: D.S. Brian Mann and D.C. Louise Shepherd."

"Please continue."

"Thank you D.C.I. Benson." His calm demeanour: unhurried and precise.

"For the benefit of your colleagues: I am *Alan McBurney*: Director of the Tempest Institute and Senior Forensic Psychiatrist."

"As I was saying, our brief as you know, was to assess Natalia Yeltsin's mental state under secure hospital conditions, given her history of violence whilst held in police custody and to explore a possible history of drug misuse."

"Sadly, Miss Yeltsin was pronounced dead at 4:55 a.m. this morning and it is likely that she took her own life: severing arteries in her arms with a section of razor blade."

Professor McBurney spoke with a strong Glaswegian accent and his pragmatic narrative was honed by experience.

(His role involved daily networking with Health Care Professionals, the Police and the Judiciary. Much of the news he imparted, was not for the faint hearted. He had assessed some of the most dangerous psychopaths in the UK over twenty-five years of Medical Practice: many of whom had been charged with Murder and serious Assault and Battery as well as the most disturbing crimes of ritual killing, torture and imprisonment, kidnapping and rape.)

He continued with more compassion in his voice...softening his manner.

"Natalia was socially withdrawn for the first seventy-two hours of her admission and did not willingly interact with other patients or staff members. She consented to both physical examination and blood tests on the morning after admission and we found no evidence of abuse of narcotics or illegal drugs. Her urine revealed small traces of cannabis metabolites, but nothing more. As you're aware, some cannabis metabolites - *cannabinoids - can* persist in urine for up to a month after smoking cannabis, or even longer for heavy and persistent users."

That subtle emphasis again observed Sally. She knew more typically it was a fourteen day window but highly sensitive Gas Liquid Chromatography techniques brought highly sensitive results.

"*I met Natalia on three occasions all told*, immediately after her detainment, whereupon I countersigned and completed *Section 2* of the Mental Health Act, thereby authorising her detention; and thereafter within one and three days later, respectively."

"On day six of her detention, this morning around 3:40 a.m., she was found in the bathroom. The appearances were consistent with her having taken her own life."

He paused momentarily but no one interrupted his chain of thought.

"A section of razor blade was found near her body. The injuries to her arms included deep lacerations which 'likely severed the *brachial arteries in one or both of her forearms* according to *Professor Atkins*, the forensic pathologist who attended the scene at around 5:30 a.m. this morning."

"At this time we have no reason to assume anyone else is implicated in the death. Nonetheless, there will need to be a full review of ward procedures as this is a serious breach of our Standard Of Care. We are currently on *full lockdown* until the forensic scientists have completed their duties."

"Of course, thank you Professor and we appreciate that this must be a hard time for you and your staff." Sally expressed genuine concern by her tone as she spoke.

"I understand her post-mortem will be undertaken by *Ted Atkins* this morning." Professor McBurney added.

"Professor, Louise speaking: 'were the paramedics called to the scene?"

"Yes and she had essentially bled out by the time they arrived. Death was confirmed by one of our resident Psychiatrists."

"Ordinarily we are bound by patient strict patient confidentiality, but on this occasion, I will take you through her history later this morning. I believe the details are extremely pertinent to your ongoing enquiries."

He hesitated for a moment, cleared his throat and continued in a compassionate tone:

"Her third consultation with me was I believe; her *final confession*."

Chapter 4

10:30 a.m. Friday 20th January: Hampshire

Standing five feet nine inches tall with a long distance runners' physique and an oval face adorned with large dark brown eyes; *Detective Inspector Ross Linden* was destined to turn heads from the moment she joined the police force in 2005. She combined a razor sharp nose for criminal intent with a First Class Honours degree in Law, awarded by the University of Oxford.

She took a few steps forward and greeted Sally with a broad smile and enthusiastic handshake as the three detectives arrived at the entrance to Harvey Ward.

D.I. Linden wore a two-piece black suit and mauve blouse. Her identity badge hung around her neck displayed within a Hampshire Police lanyard.

"Hi Sally: or should I say 'Guv'? Good to see you again. How long's it been?"

"Must be five years... Congratulations on your promotion Ross: richly deserved I hear."

She continued quietly:

"Thanks for the heads' up that you'd taken the case before our arrival: I know I can count on your discretion especially in the light of Dr Schultz' acquittal on all charges...."

As an afterthought, she added:

"Sally is fine when we're off duty." She winked at Ross.

(Ross didn't even blink at the playful admonition: she understood exactly how much pressure her former boss must be under with the death of her key suspect in a high profile murder case. She would do everything she could to assist D.C.I. Benson.)

Sally introduced her two colleagues:

"*This is Brian Mann my D.S. and D. C. Louise Shepherd; she joined us recently.*" Sally gesticulated towards Louise as she spoke.

"D.I. Linden was my D.S. back in the days when I worked *North' of the River* [Thames, London]."

Ross shook hands with them both and gestured to a side room which was sign-posted: "VISITORS."

"*So what's the latest Ross*: we had an update from Professor McBurney four hours ago?"

Ross handed Sally a brown vanilla envelope with a series of crime scene photos, enlarged to A4 dimensions.

Sally spread them on the small rectangular aged wooden table; ordinarily reserved for visitors' magazines and personal effects. The regular circular outlines of hot coffee cups could be seen indelibly burnt into the wood varnish.

"Professor Atkins was the attending pathologist: he's appointed by the Home Office for cases at The Institute."

"Here are the key photos from the scene before Natalia's body was removed under Prof. Atkins' close supervision."

Ross referred to her pocket book of notes as she relayed the events of the death and duly cross referenced the appropriate photographs using her pen to gesticulate. Brian reflected her activity with his own notebook perched on his knee.

"Natalia Yeltsin was found by *Sister Doreen Birch* who was on night duty last night: she was Natalia's *key worker* as well as being the Senior Psychiatric Nurse. She came on shift at 8pm and supervised the hand-over from day to night staff and stayed late to do vice-versa this morning: once lock-down was lifted."

"Natalia had asked Sister Birch if she could use the shower/bathroom at around 3:20 a.m. this morning. When *Sister Doreen*, as she likes to be addressed; enquired why she needed to shower so early in the morning, Natalia said she had started her menses unexpectedly and needed to clean herself up."

"Doreen checked the cubicle: it had soap and shampoo, but was otherwise empty, before leaving Natalia. The bathroom door was not locked when she left her: per ward protocol. She checked her bed and found blood staining on the sheets and Natalia's ward issue night clothing; consistent with her claim to have started her menses."

"Her bedroom has been secured?" checked Sally.

"Yes Guv'...forensics were hard at work when I came down to greet you. Everything should be ready for you and your team to take a look in the next half an hour or so....after which Professor McBurney will update you himself."

Sally nodded and gave a fleeting smile.

"So...about five minutes later, Sister Doreen was about to go back to check on Natalia and give her some sanitary ware - that's around 3:25 a.m. - but she was called to see another patient who we know to be called *"Monica"*. The patient was very distressed and becoming increasingly disruptive."

"Once she had calmed the patient down sufficiently, Sister Doreen went back to the bath room at 3:40 a.m. when she found Natalia; slumped in the shower cubicle."

"Have we any reason to assume that this was *an engineered diversion*: had there been any particular contact between Natalia and Monica, or any other inpatients?"

"Not that we know of Guv'. I asked the same question and similarly, Sister Doreen was unaware that any of the other patients had got to know Natalia: by all accounts she was simply too withdrawn, or unwilling, to bother making friends or hold conversations."

"*Monica in particular*, was avoiding all the other patients; as she believed them to be aliens!"

"'Fair comment Ross." Sally responded and frowned empathetically at the mention of Monica's aliens.

"What about any of the other *staff members*? Anyone she took a shine to or had a particular disagreement with?" pressed Sally.

"Again, not that we're aware of Guv' – again Sister Doreen had not witnessed any obvious contact; she'd have known given she was her key worker."

"When she got back to the bathroom, and found Natalia: Sister Doreen described Natalia's naked body as:

"*Slumped with her head bent against her chest and her knees flexed towards her torso.*"

Ross read from her notes as she used the exact wording of her interview with Sister Birch.

"Sister Doreen pressed the emergency button on the wall and immediately pulled Natalia from the shower unit onto the tiled floor. She listened over her mouth and confirmed that Natalia had stopped breathing and was completely unresponsive to knuckle pressure over her sternum; her *breastbone.* " she added for clarity.

"Sister Doreen started CPR as soon as *Staff Nurse Terrance McIntyre* arrived to help her. The paramedics and resident doctor on-call arrived to assist around twenty minutes later, but to no avail."

"*Time of death was confirmed as 4:55 a.m.*"

"The blood stains on the edge of the shower unit and the floor of the bathroom are consistent with her having been dragged out of the shower as Sister Doreen described."

She pointed to the photographs of the shower room.

"As you can see, Natalia suffered massive blood loss with the spatter pattern on the walls of the shower literally covered in blood."

"The close-ups post-mortem, show the large deep lacerations on her *ante-cubital fossa on each side*: that's these areas in front of the elbow joints and small abrasions and early bruising, probably caused by her fall; around her wrists."

Sally picked up the A4 image and studied it closely and could see no sign of finger marks or digs consistent with her having been held or restrained in any way.

"Half a razor blade, that's image *SDA 08*; was recovered from the floor of the shower cubicle."

The team sat and studied the photographs silently for a few minutes and Brian was first to comment.

Gesturing to images SDA 08:

"A disposable razor with one of the blades removed, inserted into wood?"

"'*Looks that way Brian.*" Nodded Ross approvingly; looking him directly in the eye as she spoke.

"The pattern of blood spatter inside the shower is consistent with Natalia having remained in the shower as she cut herself?"

"*Yes Guv'.*" retorted Ross.

"According to forensics, the pattern of blood spatter appeared consistent with her having turned the shower to *off* part way through her ordeal: hence a considerable amount of blood remained within the shower cubicle and pooled around her feet."

"*The shoe prints*: are they all accounted for on the floor of the bath-room?"

"The Forensics team have already taken images of the footwear of all attendees and will be able to answer that question over the next few days Brian. In total seven people entered the bathroom, including the paramedics and duty doctor: Dr Bashir. He confirmed death."

"So the nursing staff, Dr Bashir, two paramedics...."

"...And Professors McBurney and Atkin." Ross confirmed as she checked her notes.

"So what about...*Terrance McIntyre*...." asked Louise

"What was he doing at the time of Natalia's shower...or just before she entered the shower...."

"Could he have supplied the blade you mean?" commented Sally

"Sure *he could have*...she had to have got it from someone..." Ross responded.

"*Let's all keep an open mind at this stage.*" Sally stated categorically.

Ross looked thoughtful for a moment and returned to her notes from his interview.

"*Terrance McIntyre* - likeable chap"...continued Ross: "....he *followed*..... '*so to speak*...Professor McBurney from a previous post in Glasgow; where they'd got to know one another."

"Ten years plus working in secure units...standing about six foot three, I think he's there to bring authority when things kick off. He works a lot of night shifts to support his estranged wife and family who remain in Glasgow."

Louise nodded and continued to look through the gruesome images as Sally handed them to her one by one and she shared them with Brian. They sat side by side on a large black leather sofa whilst Ross sat opposite them on a wooden chair with matching black upholstery. The colour was apt for the subject matter as they studied the final pictures of another young life cut short by crime.

"*God only knows how lonely she must have felt*...." Louise looked distant for a moment.....

"*Leaving a lot of questions unanswered.*" Sally responded with an edge of irritation in her voice as she shook her head from side to side.

"*One less murderer on the streets....*" Replied Ross dryly.

"*Alleged murderer..*" *Corrected Sally* sounding and feeling, terse.

"Innocent until proven otherwise." Sally concluded.

Ross blushed, realising she had taken a step too far.

Chapter 5

12:15 Friday 20th January 2017

Professor Alan McBurney stridently led the team into his fourth floor office where Louise was immediately struck by the uncluttered nature of the white walls of his office. Instead of the usual certificates of merit and academic achievement, simple reproduction prints of highland views adorned the north, east and west walls of the room. The south facing windows were gifted with their own natural real-life vista.

Ordinarily, the office would have bathed in the late-morning sun. Today dark threatening clouds loomed overhead and cast their dispiriting shadow over the imposing white-washed Institute.

"Well this is a jolly good tonic for Seasonal Affective Disorder." Louise sighed with an appreciative smile, breaking the silence as she stood in the middle of the small modern, minimalistic office. She gestured towards the floor to ceiling windows; which afforded an unobstructed view across open fields: dotted with cows which peppered the landscape which stretched as far as the eye could see, towards the distant forested area of South Hampshire.

Alan McBurney smiled warmly back at Louise, as he gestured to the three of them to sit down in the white leather clad modern tubular chairs arranged neatly in a semi-circle, to the left of his desk: quite a contrast from the black leather and morbid feel of the visitors' room they'd left an hour previously.

Ross had taken them as far as the secure unit bathroom where Natalia had last drawn breath before bleeding out.

With white head to toe forensic suits and shoe over-covers courtesy of *Colin Chambers* one of the juniors from the forensics team of the South Hampshire Force; they had been led as a group to inspect the blood spattered shower facility where forensics' colleagues were finishing their inventory: before inspecting room 208, where Natalia had slept for the entirety of her six day detainment on the secure ward; known to everyone simply as *"Harvey"*.

After barely an hour at the scene, they'd been collected by *Aileen Turner*, a fifty-something secretary who had taken the three of them as far as the fourth floor, whereupon Professor McBurney met them as they exited the lift.

The sickly sweet metallic odour of the blood-spattered scene of Natalia's death still clung to Sally's nostrils. The more crime scenes she visited, the more intense the after-taste seemed to register in her brain. The equivalent to *muscle memory...*she supposed. For a moment she was transported back thirty-two years in time: to the day she had discovered the body of her late father who had slit his wrists with gardening shears in his potting shed. Her mother had never really spoken after that day; at least, not to say anything meaningful.

"My life has stopped Sally." she would say: *"like an old grandfather clock."*

"I no longer serve any purpose."

When she too had been laid to rest, eight years ago: Sally had thrown herself into her job and tried not to look back. On days like today, her memories were a heavy burden.

She focused back on Professor McBurney who sensed the need to lighten the mood.

"On most days you'd be right Louise, at least from early Spring until Autumn. It's my *antidote* to the rigour of our daily Psychiatric workload."

His thick Glaswegian accent was far more apparent in a face-to-face consultation than it had been over the 'phone six hours earlier and his demeanour struck an instant rapport with Louise. She wondered whether he'd once played rugby as she looked at short-sleeved pale blue shirt which barely disguised his broad muscular physique.

His hair was a military style short back and sides which added to his imposing presence as he sat back in his brown leather upholstered chair.

His dark brown hair was peppered with flecks of grey in places, giving him a distinguished appearance. Most clients judged his age to be five or six years younger than his fifty-five years.

"Some of my colleagues self-prescribe Prozac or whiskey: I take brisk lunch-time walks and make do with the view on busier days; and the *occasional* Single Malt of course."

"That's a great philosophy in life...make the most of the outdoors....and a Single Malt provides an excellent panacea when all else fails!" agreed Brian; with a throaty chortle.

Brian was quietly impressed: this guy was a breath of fresh air compared to some of the pompous asses or stuffy sorts he sometimes encountered when dealing with forensic *experts* and senior doctors alike.

"I guess the weather today is reminiscent of Scotland?"

It was Alan McBurney's chance to further lighten the mood with a belly laugh.

"Aye; but not nearly cold enough!" he engaged his natural broad Glaswegian accent to maximal effect as he spoke.

"Professor McBurney: thank you for your time and cooperation." Sally was eager to press on.

Her pragmatic approach was not lost on Alan McBurney.

"Of course Detective Chief Inspector, *I fully understand your sense of urgency and please call me Alan."*

Alan McBurney sensed Sally's mood was brooding and wondered whether it was just the case, or something deeper.

(*"Repressed emotions seek expression."* Played silently through his frontal cortex.)

(The Freudian idiom, known to every junior doctor and psychology student: floated to the top of his personal arsenal filled with psychological tools as he donned his psychiatrist's mantle.)

He interlaced his tented fingers in front of him and sat with them in his lap as he spoke, occasioning each of them eye contact as if assessing their engagement subconsciously; much as he would do when mentoring trainee specialists in Psychiatry: *teaching - the greatest passion of his life.*

Chapter 6

Born in a tenement building in the dockland area of Glasgow, Alan McBurney had been the eldest of the five sons his mother called *her brood*. She guarded them with the jealousy of a lioness and had a big heart to match her roar when anyone or anything; threatened their collective wellbeing as a family.

A tough but robust family life had been his greatest asset and the best God-given gift for a budding forensic psychiatrist who'd witnessed his fair share of Psychopaths by the time he was barely thirty years of age...experienced gained initially as a teenager on the streets and thereafter professionally as a young Psychiatrist in a succession of training posts, often referred to as a *"rotation"*.

Alan McBurney wore no rings and rarely even a wrist watch whilst at work. His trousers were simple dark blue linen and he wore soft leather Italian hand-made shoes: his one submission to luxury. In short, he displayed none of the trappings of success: enabling smooth rapport and facilitating rapid psychological engagement with his clients, or as he still preferred to call them: *patients*.

Many of his patients had little in the way of material wealth and portraying outward signs of success was only likely to alienate many of his patients with whom he used empathy and body mirroring as a powerful tool to diffuse angry or hostile individuals.

"Envy is a powerful motivation for crime... and revenge often speaks to the very heart of murder.."

This was to be the opening line to his presentation entitled: *"Motive: Man and his Possessions"*: a speech he had been invited to deliver in just under a weeks' time at the Royal College of Psychiatrists, in Edinburgh.

"When we spoke on the telephone you spoke of Natalia's final *confession*?"

Professor McBurney nodded sagely before he answered Sally's opening question.

Sensing the need to share.....he began gently....capturing their attention.

"In many ways that's how it *felt*."

"My father was a Roman Catholic Priest and as children he beguiled us with stories founded loosely on his experience within the confessional."

He looked directly at Sally as he spoke; then held her gaze momentarily.

He detected emotional pain, of that he had no doubt.

(Sally's feelings were almost palpable and mirrored by a deep sadness: *a "tristesse" he surmised*: an intense grief and melancholy often experienced after the loss of a loved one. Her eyes held a deep well of feelings and her tense shoulder posture and tightly opposed lips served to highlight the numerous deeply engrained worry lines on her forehead: yet further visible evidence of the strain she must be under and the personal baggage which all of us carry in our daily lives.)

Sally didn't wear a wedding ring or any other jewellery or adornments and Alan McBurney wondered whether this was her own levelling technique mirroring his own style; either that or she simply lacked the vanity he considered so common in modern society.

Sally had felt it too: *a connection*, something personal in his approach. She leaned back further in her chair in an effort to avoid his attention.

"I very much hope that what I am about to tell you will put the pieces of a larger jigsaw together for you Detective Chief Inspector."

He gently inclined his head toward Sally as he spoke, deferring to and not wanting to appear in any way controlling, of a process he expected to be a two-way exchange of information; rather than the didactic presentation of a detailed report to his attentive detectives.

(From his perspective, this was a collaborative process; especially given the outcome of his own assessment of Natalia which had been cut so short by her untimely demise.)

"My third and as it transpired *final consultation*... with Natalia lasted almost two hours."

"When she was first admitted to the ward Natalia's mood appeared flat and apathetic. She displayed a poverty of speech and her body language was closed. She sat hugging and rocking herself for hours at a time, rather like a child. When I spoke with her she wouldn't make eye contact and occasionally shook or nodded her head in response to direct questions: confirming her name and date of birth for example: she avoided all more searching questions about her mood and feelings."

"At meal times on the ward, she picked at her food in a disinterested fashion and was markedly restless in her sleep pattern as well as displaying difficulty in falling off to sleep and a pattern of early morning waking. She slept barely two to three hours on any given night during her admission."

"It was clear she could not derive solace from human interaction. In short, all clinical indicators were entirely consistent with a severely depressed and/or withdrawn state."

"We kept her under close scrutiny for the first seventy-two hours. She had a discrete nurse escort much of the time and her single room was closely monitored by staff; half-hourly throughout the night."

"*Suicide watch you mean*?" Sally sought confirmation.

He nodded slowly.

(Alan McBurney was acutely aware that as a specialised Institute they'd not done enough: *not nearly enough* as it transpired after the morning's events, to prevent the tragedy of Natalia's suicide.)

(Some clinicians and politicians alike; still waxed lyrically about the inescapability of the final outcome of an individual's life style choices:

[arguing for self empowerment and accountability and not the provision of a "*nanny state*"])

(But to those cynics his response was perennially unwavering: we need to help these kids, teenagers and adults, to unravel the impact of powerful childhood experiences in shaping pervasive traits in an individual's Psyche and behavioural patterns through life.)

(We have to do more to understand the origins and impact of *neglect*; both emotional and physical, alongside sexual abuse and social isolation: thereby recognising the likely outcomes of such serious and indelible life events. Only then will we be able to successfully intervene with effective Patient-Centred Counselling and influence, through Cognitive Behavioural Therapy [CBT]; the patient's future behavioural patterns and emotional landscape.)

(*Then and only then, will we truly impact the scourge of suicide in today's modern, must-have, when many have not: society*.)

Alan McBurney felt passionately, down to the very roots of his being, that every suicide was nothing short of a cataclysm: a reflection of Society's inability, unwillingness or sheer impotence in confronting this scourge of modern day inequality and disregard for one's fellow man.

After the tragic and heart wrenching suicide of a neighbour's son at the age of just twelve, Alan McBurney's father had oft quoted the scriptures to his assembled family over dinner: further embedding a social conscience in his offspring.

"*Sister Doreen Birch* is a very experienced member of the team; she sat in on all three consultations with Natalia. We were both struck by Natalia's unusually labile mood as our discussion progressed in the final consultation."

"A *mixed affective disorder*?" queried Louise.

"*We had no verifiable history of psychiatric disorder* and no medical records; but that was our *working hypothesis*. She may have been displaying symptoms of a *bi-polar disorder*: with *rapidly cycling* mood but as you know that diagnosis would typically require documentation of at least a week long period of either hypomania or two weeks of mania or at minimum a period of hospitalisation whilst manifesting typical symptoms."

"Patients may display social and emotional withdrawal alternating with periods of increased motor activity accompanied by mood elevation or extreme irritability, particularly after incarceration."

"What we previously called manic-depression Professor...?"

"That's right Brian. As many as one percent of the population may display symptoms suggestive of such a diagnosis....but it's often only the clinical picture of alternating or swinging mood states that seals the diagnosis. In reality that definitive diagnosis may take seven or eight years to confirm in many cases."

"And did you start any treatment for Natalia during her incarceration?" asked Louise.

"No... we elected to avoid medicating Natalia in the absence of a definitive diagnosis, and none of her behaviour merited immediate intervention."

"Your final consultation took place when?" interjected Sally.

"On Wednesday 18th January, mid-morning: just forty-eight hours ago at ten a.m."

Alan McBurney looked lost in thought for a moment and the room fell silent apart from the audible tick of the second hand of the wall-mounted 12-inch brass rimmed clock on the wall opposite his desk. No external noises intruded upon the tranquillity of the office, adding to the feeling of sanctuary which was evidently part of Alan McBurney's intention.

(No patients ever entered this part of his domain. It was free of the usual security of the building and afforded a quiet moment for reflection betwixt the external demands of the *madding crowd*.)

"Let me start by giving you some background information: please do interject if you can fill in some of the gaps in *our collective knowledge*."

"So we leveraged some information from computerised archives available to us via a former colleague who now works in Russia; in addition to our face to face discussion with Natalia this week."

Brian began taking notes as did Louise.

"Natalia's birth certificate revealed she was born *illegitimately* in Moscow: parents not disclosed, at least as far as her birth certificate was concerned."

"She took her Surname from a young childless couple living in a small village on the outskirts of Russia who adopted her when she was only four weeks old: she stayed with them until she was nine years of age. *A family crisis*, as yet undefined, resulted in her leaving Russia and we know nothing further except she turned up six years later in the UK; in Bradford."

"Social service records detail a series of interviews held with her in the presence of an "appropriate adult"; given she was only fifteen years old."

Alan opened a grey file for the first time and referred to his notes.

"A *Mrs Maggie James* - had taken her in from the streets and was a surrogate carer, if you will. I have made copies of Social Services' interviews and notes for your reference; including Natalia's Birth Certificate and details of her adoptive parents translated into English."

He handed the notes in an A4 envelope to Louise who sat closest to him.

"Natalia *"was off the radar,"* so to speak, before she came to the notice of Social Services at the age of fifteen."

"At that stage she had been working as a child prostitute in Bradford for several years."

Louise sat forward in her seat and listened intently. *Little wonder she was so angry at life,* thought Louise.

"Natalia recalled little of the details, or simply wasn't ready to talk about her experiences and when asked to recall her memories prior to leaving Russia we provoked a mixture of emotions with some hostility. It was at this point that she became agitated and swore at us in both English....and I believe in *Russian*. Her speech became rapid and it was hard to follow her thinking at times as she became unable to focus and increasingly distracted."

Louise cocked her head to one side and Alan sensed she was about to comment...

He smiled encouragingly at Louise.

"I guess her hostility is not unusual given the impact of *moving away from her adoptive parents* at the age of nine and her sense of abandonment...added to the fact she was then to be immersed in a world of men with no thought for the fact that were abusing a *child*: technically raped every time she was involved in a sexual act..."

Louise' voice trailed off as she took in the enormity of Natalia's early life.

"*I entirely agree Louise.* Repressed anger may have been enough to suggest psychopathy or mimic a bipolar illness: we were pressing powerful emotional triggers in encouraging her to tell her story...."

"She was reluctant to open up at that point in our consultation, even with gentle encouragement from *Sister Doreen* who has a lot of experience with kids who have been raised with foster families and abused inside and outside the sanctity of the family unit."

"*Sister Doreen* fostered children herself and later worked within social services, before entering Psychiatry as a specialty, directly from General Nursing."

Louise nodded her appreciation for the extra detail. It was self evident how much Professor McBurney valued Sister Doreen's input to their work.

"*We do know that Natalia was quite resourceful*. At the age of sixteen she went off the radar again and spent time in mainland Europe where by her own account she'd been waitressing and generally taking cash in hand work in bars and the like."

"We gleaned this information in the first part of the consultation, before digging deeper into her early teenage years...so have a little more detail."

"She returned to the UK at the age of *eighteen* and found a part-time job in London waiting tables and hooked up with a group of teenagers who shared a squat for a year in North London. During that time which appeared to be a more stable period in her life; she initiated contact with social services who were *unable* or possibly *unwilling*, to provide her with any details of her biological parents or her adoptive family in Russia."

"*Sister Doreen and I had the feeling she wanted to re-build bridges*."

"*Unwilling?*" Sorry Professor, you said: "Social Services may have been *unwilling to provide details*: I might interpret that as you felt they might be deliberately obstructive?" interrupted Sally.

"Sure, as you know it's not unusual for biological parents to absolve themselves of all liability or further contract after making a decision to have their child adopted. I guess they feel it's better to have a clean break. But.."

"*Rarely better for the child*." observed Louise.

"I would agree with you in the majority of cases...."

"And in Natalia's case...specifically..you were about to add something?" asked Sally

"Yes..Natalia clearly wanted answers....especially when she'd become aware of her *brother*...."

"We do know from her interview with us that she'd been in contact with her *brother*, in Russia." Brian chipped in.

"This is where the story starts to get interesting Brian. You're correct: she mentioned a *step-brother* called *Alexei*. They shared the same biological father, a Russian diplomat or official; evidently well connected at the Kremlin."

"Natalia hadn't seen Alexei for several years, but they regularly connected on social media and also via email while she was in Europe."

"So had she spent time in Russia with her family or step-brother?" Louise looked quizzical as she posed the question.

"Yes around four weeks when she was nineteen years of age: before heading back to mainland Europe for a while longer.

"Your next question is how did she make contact with Alexei?"

"This is where Natalia was *intentionally* vague. She had traced him when she was sixteen years of age and that appears to have been the first contact. Thereafter, one of the squatters she'd got to know was a *computer hacker*, probably some form of political activist from the little she revealed. He got access to her on-line *obstetric* medical records: something that as yet, we have failed to achieve."

Alan sat back and looked each of the detectives briefly in the eye before continuing.

"These records confirmed that her biological mother was just a student when she met with the young Russian: *Demetriov Radzinsky*."

"They apparently spent a few weeks together and it was during that time that she evidently conceived Natalia."

"They broke up when she discovered that Demetriov was already married."

"Young love...." mused Louise out loud and blushed as she saw Alan McBurney look directly at her.

"She stayed in Moscow as she had an agreed one year placement before returning to the UK to complete her studies."

Sally sat forward on her chair and was the first to lock eyes with Alan.

"What was she studying?"

"You've got to be kidding me." Brian's eyes widened and he too sat forward as he posed the next question which was now on everyone's lips...

Chapter 7

"Medicine"

"The young student's name was..."

"Edwina Justin!" Sally spoke the words before Alan McBurney could fill the void.

He nodded slowly, surveying the reactions of Sally, Brian and Louise in turn.

"Had Natalia ever met Professor Justin?" Sally fired the question at Alan McBurney.

"No. Not as far as we know."

"Had she attempted contact?"

"Not before Boxing Day 2015." He confirmed.

"So she *did* go to Professor Justin's apartment?" Brian said with a knowing smile.

The CCTV footage from the lift had not been definitive, but the rucksack and baseball cap were highly distinctive and now they had independent corroboration.

"Yes, but it was *Dr Christophe Schultz* who came to the door." Alan McBurney stated.

"Well that would explain a lot.....what happened exactly?" Brian leaned forward intently; mirroring Louise' body language as his eagerness grew.

"Initially when she rang the doorbell there was no reply. She was about to leave when Dr Schultz came to the door wearing a bath robe."

"She left without speaking to him."

"And that's it?" Brian looked bemused.

"She simply hadn't expected Professor Justin to have a guest. She shrugged her shoulders as she recounted the story. I had no reason to disbelieve her account."

"It was Boxing Day and most people would be with friends and family." Sally observed making the point.

"And I think that's what she was attempting to do. *Be with her family*. 'Schultz would have been an outsider and an unwelcome intruder into what would have been a defining moment for Natalia: *meeting her biological mother for the first time: and of course, it was her mother's birthday*."

"Imagine how devastated she must have felt...her expectation and hopes, very high, whether that's reasonable to us with "normal lives" and families is not the question in point. It's the perception of a young...and psychologically traumatised woman...that's the case in point." His tone was filled with genuine concern for Natalia.

Sally nodded.

Alan McBurney continued:

"Natalia had done her homework. She knew Professor Justin had no family in Europe; only distant relatives in China."

"The good old internet search engine?" Brian had long felt that too much personal information could be gleaned from the web. His comment certainly came over as somewhat cynical.

"*Yes and what's more Alexei proved invaluable once more*. He helped her to fact check; he may even have hacked Edwina Justin's email account and confirmed she'd not made plans for Boxing Day."

"'*Christ!*" exclaimed Brian. *It's a brave new world and that's for sure*!

"So did Natalia attempt to or make further contact with Edwina Justin, after her failed encounter?" Sally now looked perplexed.

"*Apparently not*, she didn't write or even attempt to visit her again. On this point she was adamant."

"And did you believe her Professor...*Alan*?" asked Louise coyly, conscious of using his first name.

"*I'm not sure Louise*. That question has been bugging me given Professor Justin's murder....."

Louise blushed visibly as Alan held her gaze for a moment too long.

She subconsciously crossed and uncrossed her legs, but Alan's eye did not stray from her face.

"What do *you* think?" he added.

"She must have felt disappointed, deflated, let down....to have got so close and then...." Louise trailed off deep in thought and wondering whether she was actually flirting a little with Alan McBurney.

"*So where do you think all the anger came from*?" Sally interjected.

"*From' a single failed encounter*?" Sally looked and sounded dubious.

"*Is that truly enough of a trigger for murder*?" Sally looked entirely unconvinced. She could hear the A.C.C. voice resounding inside her head:

("*I want a definitive result on this case Sally*: even in the absence of your prime suspect. No room for reasonable doubt. Just get it done.")

"*I think this is where we get to the confession Sally*." Alan McBurney continued.

"*She never expressly said so*, but I believe she was subject to abuse as a child, likely to have been sexual."

"Perpetrated by whom?" asked Brian.

"A member of the family... or their friends' circle; I can't say: but before she left Russia at the age of nine."

"What lead you to your conclusion Alan?" Sally interjected.

"*A history of drug abuse: her adoptive father in Russia.*"

Alan McBurney stroked his chin thoughtfully.

"Natalia hinted at it when I asked her about her relationship with individual members of the family who adopted her. She declined to discuss anyone beyond her foster mother and half-brother: that's to say *Alexei.*"

"When I asked her about her step-father or relatives she clammed up, was defensive and grew irritable again."

Alan McBurney re-read a section of his notes again before continuing:

"She replied: *some things are best kept within families.*"

"Natalia used those *precise words*?"

"And very noticeably her body language became closed: she began rocking backwards and forwards with her arms folded around her chest. She avoided eye contact....with either of us....and fell silent for around ten minutes. Literally: locked into her thoughts and comforting herself."

He fell silent for a moment and chewed his lip; as if in personal commemoration of Natalia's suffering: his first physical external sign of his inward struggle to deal with the Institute's failure.

"At that juncture we offered her counselling with our sexual health specialist. Her reply was stark:"

"*What's done is done; I cannot undo all that shit.*"

Alan stroked his chin again and frowned, suddenly looking older and wiser than his years.

"I believe this was the first time she'd discussed the abuse with anyone and that alone may well have fuelled her repressed anger: re-ignited the flame, so to speak and maybe culminated in her suicide."

At that point in the consultation, she pulled away from us emotionally.

"*She retreated back into her shell.....*" to quote Sister Doreen.

"We decided that there was little to be lost by some more direct questions once we'd given her a break and a cup of tea."

But thereafter we gleaned no useful information."

"She refused to discuss the theft of the watch or her ongoing pilfering?" clarified Sally.

"That's correct."

"On a positive note, Natalia seemed relieved after our consultation; the staff noted her change in mood. She was more interactive yesterday, with staff and a few of the other patients."

"*Sadly however, we didn't foresee her suicide.* It's not unusual of course, having unlocked a Pandora's Box of past painful memories, to find the confrontation of that repressed emotion provoking feelings that Natalia felt ill-equipped to deal with."

With a note of self recrimination he added:

"In retrospect I should have reinstated her suicide watch and not have allowed the nursing staff to leave her unattended in the bathroom. I intend to make this clear at our internal inquiry. It's important we all learn from these painful outcomes in patient care."

Alan McBurney looked deep in thought.

Louise had an overwhelming desire to offer him words of comfort; but

felt that would be trite. She sensed that he took Natalia's suicide as a

failing on his part: more than a failing in his "*duty of care*"....more of a personal failure to provide Natalia with the support she'd needed, when she'd needed it most.

Sally's phone rang, breaking the tension and she swiftly retrieved it from her jacket pocket.

The A.C.C. was a chasing progress for the second time that morning.

"I will need to take this call Alan. Please excuse me."

"Of course the office next door is free, turn right as you exit my office."

"Good morning Sir, yes if you give me a moment I am just changing offices as we speak.."

They individually sat deep in thought until Sally rejoined them several minutes later.

She exchanged a cursory nod with Alan as if to say *please continue*.

"Alan, did you elicit *any historical evidence* of psychosis or symptoms suggestive of a bipolar mood disorder beyond the signs of depression and irritability, during your final consultation with Natalia?"

"That's a good question Louise and the simple answer is no."

"That's one of the key reasons why we didn't initiate any form of medication."

"As you're well aware cannabis has been linked as a trigger factor with both *schizophrenia* and exacerbations of both *unipolar* and *bipolar* depression."

Louise nodded affirmatively as Alan McBurney entered tutoring mode once again.

"Paranoid behaviour is more common with the stronger forms of cannabis now available to users and of course we detected trace amounts of cannabis in Natalia's urine. Her blood tests revealed no evidence of opiates."

"What was your opinion on the needles mark scars on her left forearm?" Sally asked.

"We fully documented those of course and the skin appearances were consistent with historical use of her ante-cubital veins for injection and I suspect she habitually scratched the area until it excoriated and the skin breached. It may have been a manifestation of stress: her inner turmoil."

Dermatologists call it *dermatitis artefacta*.

"That would fit with her behaviour during interview." Louise confirmed to the obvious agreement of Alan McBurney.

"Do you think she showed psychopathic tendencies?" asked Brian.

"That's a challenging question to answer Brian."

Alan McBurney pondered and scratched his chin whilst pursing his lips as if about to whistle.

"On balance I would say her labile mood reflected a deeply troubled girl who had anger management issues and she was coming to terms with the death, indeed the *murder* of her mother, *to which she may or may not have been complicit.*"

"The spate of theft she'd been arrested for was possibly a sign of her disturbed mood. More worrying is the theft of the high value watch from the patient in the Nursing Home whom she'd nursed during his final illness....although of course she would not discuss the issue with us during her short stay."

"Why is that *more* worrying? asked Brian.

"It was personal to one of the clients' she nursed: a dying man, no less. It was distasteful at best, *cold-hearted by most peoples' standards.*"

"But in the context of a young girl with her background...?" Sally interjected.

"Quite so..." Alan McBurney seemed to hesitate momentarily.

"She kept the watch and didn't sell or dispose of it; despite the fact she might have pawned it for a few thousand pounds...it was as if...to my humble mind...that she felt somehow entitled to it or it reminded her of her roots perhaps...a well connected and by all accounts wealthy *biological father..*"

"*And a mother who she might have regarded in a similar way… ….*" added Sally.

Alan McBurney looked up at the clock for the first time since they had started their conversation. The three detectives all noted the action.

"*I believe that's all I have to share with you this morning.*" He stated pragmatically.

"Professor McBurney: *Alan* - we are all indebted to you for taking us through your detailed *verbal* report on Natalia. Will you be able to provide a written report soon?" Sally dipped her head respectfully to him, realising the death of Natalia must have triggered a mountainous extra workload for him and his team.

"Yes, I will address these issues in readiness for the Coroner and make sure they are sent to you as a priority Detective Chief Inspector Benson. Give me forty-eight hours."

He bade them farewell with a simple expression from his youth:

"God Bless and take care."

Chapter 8

6 days earlier...

23:30 Sunday 15th January 2017 Harvey Ward: Maximum Security

There they were, seated the three of them; in a row, ahead of her.....

Her inquisitors, her Judge and Jury: *her captors.*

She surveyed their badges as they spoke, keeping her head bowed and not meeting their eyes.

He spoke first: *the dishy one.* Quite a catch and no mistake. She'd give him a freebie any day of the week.

"Welcome to the Tempest Institute Natalia. This is Harvey Ward."

"I am Professor McBurney and these are my Colleagues....." he gestured to his right as he introduced the Nursing Staff:

"Sister Birch: she is known as *Sister Doreen* to most of our clients; she is responsible for the smooth running of this ward."

(*Birch by name and birch me later*, she thought: the moment I step out of line...)

He gestured left to the bespectacled male nurse:

"This is Staff Nurse *"Wyn Parry"*; he works alongside the nursing team on the ward and also runs Occupational Therapy art lessons which we would encourage you to attend."

(*Dim fuckin' Wyn! He'll need to pay and no mistake: I'll charge him double for a BJ and triple if he wants Birchy baby to watch...*)

"I realise you came in from Police Custody, in handcuffs. This ward, is not a Prison. It is locked for the safety of both patients and staff."

"We don't tolerate violence..."

(*"Fuckin' right."* She thought...*"but don't worry sweetheart...I'll be good for you..."*. She shot a look at his inviting crotch and the bulge which looked very tempting: she'd not eaten for a while...)

"Towards staff or other clients.."

"You're here for an assessment at the request of the Police who are investigating a number of *alleged crimes.*"

"We..are not here to establish your guilt or otherwise, only to assess how you are psychologically: your mental well-being given the events over the last twenty-four hours or so, whilst you've been in Police custody."

Professor McBurney watched her closely as he spoke: looking specifically at her appearance and behaviour.

Natalia's hands were ingrained with dirt, short bitten nails with remnant flakes of nail red varnish. Hair short blond spikes, with dark red roots belying her normal hair colour; it looked unkempt and he noted the external evidence of her scalp laceration which had been covered with a sterile dressing after her suturing at the hospital; prior to her arrival at the Institute.

Natalia wore a white Police Forensic jump suit which swallowed up her slender body. She wore white plimsoles without laces which looked cheap and she had traces of black mascara on her face.

Natalia avoided his gaze as he spoke. She held her arms across her chest in a self-hugging, self-comforting pose. She showed little spontaneous facial expression and appeared calm albeit somewhat quiet and withdrawn.

"Having admitted you so late this evening Natalia, we'll have our first proper meeting tomorrow, when Sister Doreen, you and I, can get to know each other better and help us to provide whatever guidance or practical assistance you need."

Mmmmmmm, not slow to offer a threesome..she mused.

He paused.

"Do you have any questions to ask any of us?"

Natalia slowly shook her head.

"OK, in which case sister Doreen will show you to your room and give you something to eat and drink."

Professor McBurney rose from his seat, turned to Sister Doreen and momentarily smiled before he left the small interview room, closing the door behind him.

Mathew Flack, didn't say anything or move. He stood in the corner of the room as he had since Natalia's arrival at the electronically controlled double entrance to the ward.

Standing at six feet five inches, his role was to observe and shadow high risk patients when they first arrived on the ward and discontinue shadowing once staff were satisfied that a new *patient* did not pose a major risk to ward staff and other patients.

"Right Natalia let's get you some clean clothes and something hot to eat and drink before we show you to your room. Doreen led the way followed by Natalia and thereafter Wyn; as Mathew held the door open for them without saying a word.

His eyes never strayed from Natalia and his were the skills they collectively hoped would not be deployed.

Chapter 9

7 a.m. Monday 16th January: Harvey Ward

Doreen put her head around the door; she suppressed the urge to yawn and took a moment to rub her tired eyes. The night shift had been a busy one, with three admissions after midnight. Natalia had been only the first of four to arrive late to the ward.

Natalia was gently snoring with only the crown of her stitched head visible. The starched white sheet barely ruffled since the bed had been made in readiness for her admission. The clothes Sister Doreen had given her were piled on the chair alongside the bed. Otherwise, the room was simple; devoid of furniture or fineries: window-less with bare white-washed walls.

(This was standard practice at the Tempest Institute for all new admissions. The chair was constructed of light simple white moulted plastic; not suitable for self-harm and with limited utility if brandished as a weapon by aggressive, distressed or psychotic clients.)

Doreen hesitated for only a moment, before quietly closing the door behind her. Another ten minutes wouldn't make any difference; she'd wake her on her return trip from the ladies corridor. *Gladys Brooks* always took some rousing so it would be at least ten minutes before she'd be back. Natalia had been too restless to sleep until at least 4 a.m. and had declined Sally's offer of a 2mg dose of diazepam to help her relax.

The emergency klaxon sounded just as Sally reached the end of the ten bed corridor. *Gladys would have to wait.*

She turned swiftly on her heels and hurried up the corridor as weary residents began emerging from slumber and putting their heads around doorways to see what all the commotion was about.

Wyn stood near the entrance to B wing where he waited for her to arrive before he held the heavy door open; giving her a quick update as they made haste.

"It's *Monica Brewer*: she's acting out in the day room."

Wyn was breathless and had removed his spectacles as he'd hurried off in a bid to find Doreen. Though twenty years his senior, she was nimble on her feet.

"FUCK OFF! FUCK OFF! FUCK OFF! *BASTARDS GO AWAY!*"

They could hear her cries long before they reached the scene.

A small crowd of the early risers amongst the male residents of the ward were stood on the corridor cheering and egging Monica on, as three members of staff were doing their best to keep them back from the entrance to the day room and calm them down.

"*Wyn please de-activate the alarm.*" said Doreen as she arrived to survey the scene; calm and assertive in equal measure.

"Right you lot, back to your rooms, shower and prepare for breakfast. *Show's over!*"

Her tone was firm but friendly. *She was the Boss and they all knew it.*

Staff Nurse Felicity Marsh stood in the middle of the day room trying to coax *Monica Brewer* down off the circular wooden dining table in the left hand corner of the room.

"*Is she hallucinating again*?" Doreen asked as she stood next to Felicity; just as Monica began jumping up and down in an attempt to hit two of the sunken spot-lights that she figured were within range of her long-handled hairbrush.

"Yes unfortunately Dudley told her the spotlights are lasers; so now she's trying to destroy them."

"Okay we'd better get her down before she injures herself."

Wyn returned and closed the doors to the day room behind him. Mercifully the alarm had been silenced.

Monica began resuming her tirade at the top of her voice.

"FUCK OFF, FUCK OFF, *FUCK OFF...LEAVE ME ALONE*..."

They stood for a moment watching Monica: assessing her behaviour and in particular her risk of self harm from a fall. Despite her colourful language and psychotic behaviour: the vast majority of schizophrenic patients like Monica were rarely a risk to others.

"Wyn - would you fetch me the fire warden's jacket please?"

Wyn shot Doreen a quizzical look but knew better than to question Doreen's request.

Doreen moved forward towards the table and spoke sternly but calmly to Monica.

"Monica: *you need to calm down now*. You are safe with us. We're here to help you."

"Let's take you out of here and find you somewhere quieter."

Monica was clad from head to toe in black, just as she had been during her admission at 2.30 a.m. forty-eight hours prior to this outburst. She was twenty years old and pipe-cleaner thin, wearing a long black woollen dress which had seen better days and a white bandana with a bright red star sewn into the material at the front. She was bare-foot and had black painted toe nails to match her false finger nails.

This was her third admission in the past thirteen months, although on this occasion she had not threatened her mother whom she blamed for most of her ills. She'd been detained by the Police in a local supermarket after removing a plastic children's water pistol form the shelves and randomly "shooting" customers with fizzy water from one of the aisles: accusing regulars at the Co-op of being invaders from Mars; hidden in plain clothing and posing as *real people*.

Wyn arrived carrying the fire-wardens high visibility jacket and handed it to Doreen. She walked directly up to the edge of the wooden table which stood three feet from the ground.

"Monica, you need to come with me now. I can help you put your armour back on; you'll be protected again. Here we are. This is your *armour*."

The shouting stopped as she looked down at Doreen.

"*Did they tell you to give it to me*?" She screamed like a banshee, which fitted with her overall appearance. Her long dark hair was dishevelled and matted in parts, stuck together with hair gel.

In Medieval times gone by, she'd have been tortured, ducked or burned at the stake: branded a witch for her ramblings and obscene outbursts.

"I can hear them talking about me now." She whispered out loud in a conspiratorial tone as Doreen drew closer.

She looked skyward again and began raising her hairbrush to her imaginary abductors, becoming ever more distressed in her cries:

"BASTARDS, FUCK OFF YOU BASTARDS. YOU'RE NOT TAKING ME. *I DON'T WANT YOUR FUCKING MUTANT BABIES!*"

She gathered the material of her dress and her hand in a protective clutch over her vulva as she shouted. Urine trickled down her legs and began dripping onto the floor of the dayroom with a gentle pitter-patter.

Doreen adopted an assertive tone but smiled as she delivered her words: constantly coaxing and encouraging the distressed girl.

"*Monica, we are here to help you: and this will protect you against them: trust me. You know me. I'm Sister Doreen.*" These are my friends, they will help you too."

Felicity bit her bottom lip as she watched the scene unfold. She'd been on the ward for barely two months and found the behaviour of psychotic patients a challenge. She knew that schizophrenic patients were more at risk of harming themselves than others, but couldn't shake off her anxiety, particularly on a night shift; particularly when patients' delusions were so bizarre.

Monica continued to battle her unseen demons, waving her hairbrush around her head like a helicopter about to lift off but leaking fuel. In this case, the fuel smelled distinctly of concentrated urine.

"Unfortunately Monica's symptoms are yet to be controlled with her anti-psychotic medication." counselled Wyn as he stood alongside Felicity; sensing her anxiety. He could see her hands were trembling and she bit her bottom lip nervously. He placed a reassuring hand on her upper arm.

"What's more there's been a manufacturing issue with her usual depot treatment which is administered monthly by injection: so Professor McBurney has decided to switch to the latest anti-psychotic currently going through Phase IIIb clinical trials. The results look promising in younger patients with poorly controlled *positive* symptoms: hallucinations and delusions."

Felicity nodded, only half-listening to Wyn and without taking her eyes off of Monica. She couldn't help thinking how tough it must be for her family watching their daughter so distressed. Her own daughters were only seven and nine years of age and she knew the life-time risk of mental illness was as high as one in four: a daunting prospect for any parent.

"Monica, we need you to come down *NOW!* Come on let me help you put this jacket on."

Doreen stood with the overall stretched out with the lining facing her young ward; so that Monica had only to put her arms in.

"Let me take the hairbrush from you first and that will make it easier."

She held her outstretched arm up towards Monica.

Monica's father, a devoted Roman Catholic with an unwavering faith, had told his wife and the Psychiatric team that this was "*God's test*" and failed to accept the guidance that his daughter should be administered an anti-psychotic medication a year previously.

Thankfully, all that changed when prior to her second exacerbation; Monica had been ready to leap from the top of a local multi-storey car park in order to escape from a "group of aliens" who she was convinced would abduct her and mutilate her genitalia. The actions of the local fire brigade had saved her life.

Monica's mother was less pious and far more pragmatic in her approach: she blamed her daughter's illness on her child's fondness for cannabis and "legal highs"; a habit she'd perfected at an all girls' school. As a consequence, she had home schooled her daughter for the final two years of her education before she reached eighteen.

Monica looked down at Doreen with a sudden look of concern on her face.

"Who are those others behind you? What do they want?"

She gestured towards Wyn and Felicity with the hairbrush.

"They want to cut me up like them. BASTARDS, FUCK OFF, LEAVE ME ALONE!"

"Okay, Monica, calm down, don't let them scare you. I'm here to take care of you."

"Now let's put your jacket on now and take some rest."

"*DO IT NOW: please!*" Her instruction was measured but very forceful. She didn't want to involve security and wanted to maintain Monica's trust at all costs, even while she was psychotic: *out of touch with reality.*

Doreen stood back a little, to ensure she was out of range of the edge of the table as Monica inched forward. She didn't want her patient to lash out at her at the last moment; given her labile mood.

Without warning, Monica sat down abruptly, splashing into the small pool of accumulated stale urine and Doreen seized her chance and moved forward with the jacket, wrapping it around the girl's skinny shoulders. She could feel her shivering with fear and exhaustion. She'd barely eaten since her admission: fearing that her food was being poisoned by intruders.

"*Now that's much better Monica*, we can help you down now and find you something to eat and drink."

"You must be starving after all that activity. Let's get you out of these cold wet clothes and find you something more comfortable."

Doreen transformed instantly into a surrogate mother to her young ward: with all the gentleness she bestowed on her own family.

Monica began to sob, her body moving rocking involuntarily. Her black mascara was already ingrained into her cheeks and tears fell uncontrollably like large raindrops as they led her slowly away from the table which had been her temporary fortress.

Doreen put her left arm around her and gently reassured her.

"Okay, you'll be safe now. I'm here: I won't leave you."

"*We're all here to help you Monica.*"

Chapter 10

10:30 a.m. Tuesday 17th January 2017: Harvey Ward

Monica Brewer wore a long red dress (which was decorated with multiple tea coffee and soft drink stains accumulated during her time on the ward) and a matching cotton bandana: her attire was finished off with red flashed white pumps. She sat experimenting with an array of garish colours.

She was recreating her very own *Aurora Borealis*: having been inspired by a TV programme she'd part watched the night before on one of the communal ward televisions in the day room. Whilst the science flew over her head quicker than a nuclear powered rocket, the vivid colours jelled with her new found spirit of creative undertaking.

Monica sat for a few minutes at a time before uprooting herself and her painting paraphernalia in order to occupy a different part of the long lightweight newly installed art table.

The purpose built Occupational Therapy Unit [O.T.U.] was supervised by *Wyn Parry;* the O.T. Team Leader on Harvey Ward. He watched Monica's movements carefully from across the room.

Monica was using water based paints and despite being in a clinically elevated mood state; she had stopped fighting her would-be Martian abductors and was more content with the table as a place of recreation; (rather than a a vantage point for defending herself from alien attack.)

Staff Nurse Felicity Marsh sat alongside Monica as she painted in long flowing strokes and narrated every colour change and modification to her painting as she progressed her creation. Her attention span was short but intense.

Felicity was shadowing Monica for the duration of her eight hour nursing shift; an arrangement which Monica found highly agreeable as she maintained a constant flow of chatter and was oblivious to replies or silence in equal measure.

It was looking increasingly likely that Monica was starting to display symptoms and signs of hypomania. She displayed episodes of elevated mood: with increased energy, motor activity, pressure of speech and disinhibited behaviour. Put simply, she was highly excitable and easily distractible, couldn't stop talking and rushing around; and worryingly, had started flashing her private parts on the ward to all and sundry.

Sister Doreen had taken the decision to *"special Monica"*: a member of staff would constantly escort her during her waking hours to ensure her safety and that of others.

(Doreen Birch would de-brief with Felicity later in the day which would provide her with an ideal on the job training opportunity for her Continuing Medical Education [CME] Module which would need completion within her first year in Post.)

The creative side of O.T. activities helped those patients who were more withdrawn by virtue of symptoms of depression; contributing to a lifting of their spirits and equally gave vent to the creative talents of all the patients and in particular those with an artistic flair, by nature or nurture; or by virtue of elevated mood.

Wyn Parry was an experienced Artist in his own right; having studied Art prior to having pursued Psychiatric Nursing as a vocation. Wyn had successfully sold several of his more abstract pieces to collectors; having held his first and only gallery exhibition with the sole purpose of financing his Nursing Studies.

Although the unit was within the confines of the secure ward, Wyn always had at least one assistant instructor or colleague to ensure his personal wellbeing and that of other patients.

That morning after medication, breakfast and a short period of respite, a grand total of three patients had volunteered to join Wyn's class.

Natalia sat quietly with a set of coloured pencils and diligently spent time doodling and re-creating Russian tags which she recalled from childhood and more recently from internet surfing. Outwardly she appeared withdrawn and non-communicative. Inwardly she felt alert sharp and watched everything around her despite her apparent absorption in her morning activity.

Wyn was instructing Maureen Moon on the construction of a twenty-four segment twelve inch square jigsaw, depicting a meadow scene.

Natalia yawned and stretched backwards on her chair then strolled across to the school-like desk and took a look at some of Wyn's fine artwork. She picked up the wooden pencil case and took the opportunity to slowly sharpen each of the pencils in the desk mounted unit. Wyn glanced at her repeatedly as she went about her task.

Meanwhile, Monica was beginning to act up and getting frustrated at her inability to find a selection of green colours to complement her rainbow of Aurora shapes.

"NO ..... F-E-L-I-C-I-T-Y....I don't need help..I need green...not blue and yellow.... NO....NO...NO..."

Wyn watched Monica's movements carefully from across the room.

Felicity was beginning to look a bit flustered as Wyn kept a watching brief: conscious of Monica's elevated mood which could easily turn from simple frustration to full blown agitation...

Maureen Moon was getting no where fast with her jigsaw and Wyn stood up and with a side glance at Natalia, he headed over to give Felicity moral support with Monica.

Natalia seized her chance.

"But I'm not finished: my *"Borora"* needs green..." protested Monica pulling off her bandana in irritation and tossing it onto the floor as she stood up and crossed her arms across her flat chest.

"*'It's pronounced Aurora"* corrected Felicity for the third time as Wyn approached them both and shook his head subtly at Felicity and nodded towards the door as he walked towards them across the classroom.

"OK Monica: great job: *Hey* I love your '*Borealis"*.....

He let out a long approving whistle as the three stood shoulder to shoulder momentarily and admired Monica's efforts.

Neither of staff noticed Natalia reach high up onto the staff shelving unit for the small item which she grabbed and deftly placed into the side pocket of her jeans.

Wyn called time on the Art session and the five of them headed back onto the Ward via the short corridor. Wyn was last to leave and secured the door with a key in addition to the existing security door which needed identity card entry to enter the O.T.U.

Chapter 11

Apartment 12a Hope Apartments

As Christophe waited on the end of the phone he could feel his heart beating like an iron fist inside his boney rib cage. In prison he'd lost his appetite: part fear, part depression, part desperation.

His mind was racing. He couldn't eat, sleep or rest; he had to know.

Above all, he needed to speak to his former mentor, to get to the truth; but fear now gripped him like a vice, squeezing his intestines like a giant fist.

If there was a connection between recent events and a former patient, he was the only one who could establish the link.

In spite of his acquittal for murder; he felt dirty, sullied and shamed.

His career lay in ruins. Mud sticks. No smoke without fire.

The Appeal in may ways had felt worse thank the original trial: his personal life laid bare for all to scrutinise and judge.

He felt like a microbe under examination in a laboratory; studied and defiled: no part of him was private.

Suddenly, a familiar voice responded at the end of the phone with a simple *"Hello"*.

"Good morning Professor Ennis – thank you very much for taking my call."

He virtually blurted out the greeting he had mentally rehearsed over and over, before placing the call ten minutes earlier.

He was trying desperately to sound relaxed; trying to sound *normal: whatever normal was*. He could barely remember his former life before it transformed into one long nightmare of Police investigations, forensic scrutiny and lawyers.

Thank God for Georgina: at least she had represented him with the human face of the Justice system.

Now his lawyers had began talking of Compensation for his wrongful imprisonment; but nothing could have been further from his mind. He just needed answers.

Christophe was conscious he was hyperventilating as he spoke; he could feel pins and needles in his finger tips and around his mouth. He consciously slowed his breathing and tried to visualise the word *"relax"*; as the hammering of his heart rose up into his throat.

"Good morning Dr Schultz: *Christophe* it's so good to hear your voice again after so many years. How are you? I am conscious you've had a *dreadful* year."

And there it was in an instant: the human qualities he'd prayed for but had no right to expect, the humility, the empathy, the compassion that characterised and was unique to Professor Ennis *MBE*.

"*Much better now, thank you Professor.*" replied Christophe trying to sound upbeat.

The reality was, he felt intensely nauseated and his head was spinning.

He took a deep breath before continuing.

"*Take your time Christophe.*" replied the kindly voice; sensing his discomfort and sounding concerned.

"To be direct Professor: I need to speak to you face to face, as a matter of urgency."

"My door has always been open to you Christophe; more especially now. Can you drive over to my office on Friday morning, *are you fit enough to drive?*"

"Yes, of course."

(The very idea of taking a train filled him with dread after the events around *'First Southern..he rather doubted he'd ever use a train again...*)

"Shall we say ten o'clock?" suggested Professor Ennis.

"Okay I'll be there; thank you." Christophe confirmed gratefully.

"Reception will direct you; we've had a few changes since you last worked here."

"I'm sure I'll be okay." Christophe responded; with a certainty he did not feel.

"Excellent. Until Friday then. Good bye Christophe."

Christophe heaved a huge sigh of relief and sat back down on the leather sofa, exhausted by the effort of making the short phone call; his heart still racing. Poignant memories came flooding back. Busy days on the wards, exhausting nights; but above all: a feeling of family, of *belonging*. He looked around his apartment, so barren, cold and isolated; just the way he felt.

Tears began to flow down his cheeks as he sobbed quietly, shivering and crossing his arms as he held his body and gently rocked backwards and forwards. His shoulders and neck ached and he felt empty and alone. A sudden rush of grief claimed his body; feelings so intense he could not hold back. Weeks, months and years of repressed feeling erupted into a deluge and he shook violently, uncontrollably. His mouth filled with bile and he gulped trying hard not to vomit. He lay back shivering uncontrollably and started to breath; slowly, deliberately; steadily in and out. He covered himself in his duvet. Finally, mentally and physically exhausted; he slept.

A distant car alarm woke him. It was one o'clock in the morning. His mouth was dry and his head ached: but he felt more peaceful. Taking a bottle of chilled water from the fridge, he drank it with handful of blueberries. He climbed under his duvet and slept.

Chapter 12

6 a.m. Thursday 19th January 2017

St Agnes-on-the-Hill, Surrey, UK

The chilled early morning fog lingered eerily like dense grey hovering mushrooms, which the dawn light barely penetrated, as *Christophe* began the slippery steep grassy descent towards a distant hedgerow which was hidden from view at this early hour.

Dog walkers had been donning gum boots and bikers drinking hot coffee culled from coloured flasks as Christophe had backed his car into the parking spot near the end of a long row; at Westbrook Corner, just a few miles outside of Guildford. It was a walk he'd enjoyed many times before his job had all but consumed his spare time.

Since his acquittal, Christophe had decided that early morning walks through the Surrey countryside would be his new fix for all ills: and solitude this morning, was his companion of choice. He needed to clear his head.

He'd slept soundly after his telephone call to Professor Ennis and the emotional turmoil which had penetrated the very core of his being. His catharsis had been physical as much as emotional and he had only twenty-four hours to endure before he might glean answers to some of his burning questions concerning the reasons he'd been framed for the murder of Edwina Justin.

Dear sweet Edwina...he'd tried hard to bury the images which were burned indelibly into his visual cortex and replace them with positive affirmations which might help him learn to live with the knowledge of her murder and the hideous manner of her death.

Answers to some of his questions might be one way of his developing his coping strategy as he moved forward with his life. Whilst he would never see Edwina Justin again, he more than many, now understood the true value of freedom and choice as to how he lived his life moving forward.

The grass was like a slippery ice rink prior to re-surfacing; and the ground boggy, from recent rainfall. At times his footing felt precarious as Christophe descended the two hundred metres on the steep incline down to the hedgerow which marked the gateway to more level terrain.

Thank God for cross-trainers he smiled to himself; even layered in mud they appeared almost trendy and did the job with a fraction of the weight of his ageing brown leather German hiking boots which were relegated to the back of his store cupboard.

He picked his way carefully past the calling cards of dog excrement and walked on into the covered woodlands, thereafter meandering slowly up-hill towards his goal. When his path intersected with road he took the narrow hedgerows in preference to the circuitous roadway; even though he was regularly entwined in faded blackberry bushes laden with early morning dew which spilled into his collar as he bristled past them.

Cows created eerie shadowy and at times, foreboding figures; as they turned to watch his steady progress alongside the perimeter of farmland and grazing pastures.

Christophe's breathing grew heavier as he started to ascend the final sandy ridges which led to the rusting gate of the small graveyard, perched 500m above sea level. Atop St Agnes Hill for a millennium Christians had gathered to worship their saviour; whilst in modern time walkers, runners and devotees of the North Downs had come to marvel at the spectacular views afforded by the idyllic little church on the Pilgrim's Way betwixt Canterbury and Winchester.

Christophe perched on one of the damp aged wooden benches with splintered edges burnished by the four seasons; his back to the cold stone wall of the Church which bore witness to the impact of centuries of storms, snow and hail.

The view this morning was limited by the early morning mist, but he knew the vista well and he slowly surveyed Chilworth and Tyting, hiding somewhere in the distance; whilst taking in the unsullied air and tranquillity.

No cars, no people; just the sound of his laboured breathing as he relaxed his shoulders against the cold custodian wall of the Chapel.

A ping in his right hand breast pocket momentarily interrupted his long overdue moment of serenity.

Christophe opened his personal emails scanning down his three unopened messages: one name immediately caught his attention – *Dan Ennis*! A fond memory of a holiday in Italy stirred as he opened the text of the email.

Hi CT been a while. How are you after your ordeal? Rough Justice mate!

I'm back from Central Europe.

Archie and I broke up, long story; will fill you in when we talk.

Couldn't reach your mobile – guess you've switched, or just back on line?

Need to chat. Serious shit at my end; need your help.

Don't email back: am using an internet cafe.

PLEASE call me. NEW number: 07779 515090.

N.B. Use a PAYG.

Ring me!

Dan xx

Christophe re-read the message several times, distilling the information and analysing his options. "*Serious shit*?"

He was fully aware that Dan's meeting with Sergei in Amsterdam had given the Russian access to his computer but had assumed that was the limit to his involvement in the sworded chain of events.

Why was Dan using an internet cafe to send an email and insisting he use a "Pay As You Go" phone to call him?

Could it be a hoax email, or a scam?

No, few people called him CT, which was a joke from his medical student days; and even fewer would have known the real nature of Dan's relationship with Archie: to most of the world they were just friends.

A practical joke; maybe?

No, that wasn't Dan's style; he was the sensible one: politically astute, a true polyglot - proficient in seven languages, always travelling; with a big network of friends. Besides which, he wouldn't waste Christophe's time with a ruse like this, especially given recent events; Dan would have some insight into the pressure which Christophe had been under and clearly knew he'd been released following his Appeal.

Uppermost in Christophe's mind, however, was why Dan would need to use an *internet cafe* to message him? Dan was always IT savvy.

He needed time to think and not react instantly. That much he'd learned from his experience with the Law and use of technology.

Christophe removed the stainless steel cup from his pocket flask and after carefully opening a refreshing hand towel from its packaging; he cleaned the inside and outside of the small cold vessel. Removing the stopper from the flask he decanted freshly brewed decaffeinated coffee into the cup and slowly sipped the refreshing brew.

The rich smell of coffee transported him instantly back to Rome and his glorious holiday with Dan. God how they'd laughed together. Long days of sightseeing - the glorious walks around the Vatican, the Coliseum, the galleries and the refuelling: with pasta and wine - especially the wine. Then there were the long hot, humid nights enriched by stories narrated so eloquently by local people; old and young.

Dan and Christophe had seen each other off and on in the years following Dan's graduation. Two long weekends in Stratford for Shakespeare's "King Lear" and "Much Ado About' Nothing"; a night in

London at the Globe for "Romeo and Juliet"; but it must have been two years since they last met up face-to-face. Emails had been their optimal way of staying in touch.

Christophe finished his coffee and made his way towards the graveyard gate, turning one last time to admire the view before he began his descent.

He resolved to contact his old friend later that day.

Chapter 13

Friday 20th January 2017

United Hospital, Cardiff

As he drove into the multi-story car park Christophe looked at his watch: 09:45. He parked up and headed for the Main Entrance to the Hospital. As he walked briskly up the familiar sweeping drive bordered by ornate hedges and evergreens; he avoided eye contact with the hordes of early morning visitors and patients filing in and out of Reception.

Professor Ennis was sat behind his familiar large redwood desk [which he'd had shipped in from Scandinavia]; and he rose to greet Christophe as he entered the room. His firm handshake was as welcoming as his broad smile. Christophe sat opposite his former Boss but couldn't bring himself to make eye contact with his former mentor.

"It's good to see you again my boy!"

Roger Ennis spoke without a hint of patronisation.

Christophe finally made eye contact and sensed no hostility or judgment. He felt relief and anxiety flow through his being. The recent media furore had left him feeling petulant, naked and exposed.

Roger Ennis spoke slowly and deliberately.

"We followed your case via the media, and we were all frankly mortified by the outcome; by your sentence."

He looked at Christophe and hesitated. Christophe looked down at the files on the desk and then looked back at the Professor, avoiding direct eye contact again.

Never one to avoid speaking candidly, Roger Ennis continued:

"Well, it's good to see that common sense has finally prevailed and you are a free man again following your successful Appeal."

Pressing on, he added:

"I presume your visit is linked in some way to evidence arising from your Sentence or Court Appeal?"

Incisive as ever: Professor Ennis had not changed a jot since they'd last met; and the years had been kind to him observed Christophe.

"Yes indeed." confirmed Christophe succinctly; knowing that brevity was important as time would be limited and sensing Roger Ennis' encouragement; he carried on.

"Professor I need to ask you about a patient under your care in 2002, a patient by the name of *Robbie De Sanchez*. From memory, he was a teenager who had flown in from Cyprus with a fever and cough. He subsequently suffered a cardiac arrest and despite our best efforts, he died on I.C.U. His post-mortem suggested a possible viral infection of his heart."

"I am relieved to see that prison life has done nothing to blunt your razor sharp memory Christophe!"

Roger Ennis was relieved to finally see a spark in the eyes of his former protégée whose memory was a well honed tool he'd deployed smartly as a young clinician.

(Memorably from Roger Ennis' viewpoint; Christophe barely referred to a patient's notes once said patient had been admitted and he had duly compiled the case notes. When presenting during ward rounds, Christophe invariably gave colleagues a succinct clinical overview, purely from memory. He displayed passion and commitment for his vocation in equal measure.)

Roger Ennis raised the telephone to his right ear.

"Sharon, could you hunt down a set of notes for me *urgently* please?"

"The patient's name was *Robbie De Sanchez*. He was around eighteen years of age and admitted under my care in the latter half of 2002; post the August intake of new Junior doctors."

Roger Ennis added; thinking aloud as he spoke:

"He unfortunately died and there will therefore be a full Post Mortem report appended."

"Thank you." he listened momentarily, then replied: "yes: *right now would be excellent*."

He replaced the headset in its cradle.

"We recently undertook an audit of our hospital Mortality figures covering the past twenty years, examining five-yearly mortality trends; all part of improving standards of care, as you're doubtless aware."

He opened a file on his desk and shared the top-line data and graphical representations with Christophe who listened silently as Roger Ennis guided him through the data with consummate ease.

When they'd finished their discussion, Roger Ennis sat quietly, like a priest in contemplation; his head bowed and his fingers tented; thumbs opposed.

Christophe scrutinised Roger Ennis' smooth scalp, which had barely any sun damage despite his advancing years. Roger Ennis preferred hiking in Scotland and sun kissed mountains as opposed to relaxing on sun drenched beaches.

Sensing the need for lighter conversation, Roger Ennis looked Christophe directly in the eye and enquired concerning his son.

"*So how long is it since you've seen my wayward son Christophe*?"

Christophe was wrong - footed by the question and tried not to appear anxious.

"It's been a while Professor, we caught up by 'phone recently and I know he's been travelling a lot".

(He was mindful that his answer fell someway short of the truth. Alarm bells began to ring inside his brain again: his conversation with Dan the previous day, still fresh in his mind.)

"*Tell me something I don't know*! Responded Roger Ennis. He chuckled softly as he spoke and looked distant for a moment.

"I had always hoped *Daniel* would put his language skills to good use, working with the *United Nations* or at the very least a respectable Charity; '*God knows there are so many deserving causes*."

"Instead, well as you know, he does like to travel and explore new business ventures, particularly with his friend what's his name…?"

"*Archie*?" Responded Christophe, ever more conscious of their recent split.

"Yes that's the chap…"

He raised his eyebrows and looked lost in thought again; then continued:

"*Ask him to call me when you next speak: we haven't caught up for quite a while*."

Christophe was grateful for a tap at the door which interrupted their conversation. He simply nodded his confirmation.

"*Come in*."

Sharon bustled hurriedly through the door, breathing heavily and carrying two volumes of notes; each pack secured with large red elastic bands and wrapped in a red sheet of A3 paper; indicating that the patient was deceased.

"*Gracious that was quick Sharon*!"

"*How on earth did you track these down so quickly*?"

Sharon blushed; looking delighted with the spontaneous praise and replied modestly:

"Thank you Professor, I have a good friend in records department. One telephone call and two flights of stairs later, and here we are!"

She left closing the door quietly behind her, but not without first glancing over her right shoulder at the handsome young man sat opposite her Boss. She seemingly recognised his face from somewhere, but where?

(She'd already checked the entry in Professor Ennis' Outlook electronic diary which simply read: *Private Meeting*.)

Roger Ennis checked the deceased patient's summary page and admission dates before slowly sifting through pages to examine handwritten entries.

Christophe waited patiently.

 (He was relieved to have moved on from the conversation concerning *Daniel*; only his devoted father ever used Dan's full christian name.)

Christophe knew he needed to focus all of his attention on the task ahead. His headache re-emerged as a dull ache across the front of his forehead; he massaged his temples with slow rhythmic circular movements of the first two fingers and thumb of his right hand while Roger Ennis studied the notes in front of him.

"As you say, Mr De Sanchez was admitted by your colleague, *Dr David Winters, (a Registrar at the time)*: with a fever and cough. The morning after admission, he suffered a cardiac arrest on G4 Ward and after successful resuscitation was admitted to the Intensive Care Unit."

"The working diagnosis was viral pneumonia based on serial x-rays and negative blood cultures. Despite intravenous antibiotics, antiviral agents and supportive therapy he re-arrested several times and died four days later. The Post-Mortem confirmed pneumonic consolidation of his lungs and histology was consistent with *viral myocarditis*."

We continue to see a steady stream of deaths caused by presumptive viral infections, damaging the heart muscle and contributing to cardiac failure."

"Professor Ennis I don't recall meeting any direct relatives of the patient, only a friend who declared himself *"next-of-kin."*

Roger Ennis looked mystified by the question. He furrowed his brow and momentarily looked over his silver framed spectacles at Christophe, before returning to the notes; sifting through the ICU record.

"*Yes, here we are*: twenty-four hours *after* Mr De Sanchez' admission, a young man who simply called himself *Anton* came to the ICU."

"The nursing staff spoke with him, as did the duty doctor on call that evening. Dr Hughes' written record of their discussion is cursory but he did note that the two young men had flown in from Cyprus *together*; just as you correctly recalled Christophe."

"The patient had of course been brought by Ambulance directly from Rhoose Airport [Cardiff]; and Anton must have travelled independently after picking up luggage and such like."

Roger Ennis looked across at Christophe, noting the dark rings under his eyes and wondering how he must be bearing up under the strain of his recent Court ordeal, incarceration and release on Appeal.

"*Unusually Anton could not give the deceased' contact details to enable us to contact his relatives.*" Roger Ennis, looking baffled as he read the details entered on the nurses' report.

"Let's take a look at my entry *after* the demise of the patient."

"Yes now I review the notes, *I do recall this case was unusual Christophe:* I was called to the ICU *personally* after the death of the patient to speak to next-of-kin."

He glanced up at Christophe, reverting to mentor mode.

"*Grief takes many forms as you are well aware.*"

As he spoke, Roger Ennis reflected on his words; thinking of the Doctor sat opposite him. The anger, resentment and depression that Christophe must have experienced; to say nothing of the lost opportunities he now faced having spent time in Prison. It would clearly take time for him to be reinstated on the Medical Register after his conviction for murder.

"I broke the news of Mr De Sanchez' sad demise to the young Anton personally. He said *absolutely nothing*: when I shared the tragic news of his friend's death. He just sat there and stared at me."

"*Sister Taylor* sat with us and she wrote your name and bleep [pager] number; on the top of the discharge summary which she handed to Anton. We hoped that a family member would contact you at a later date to request further information about their son's final illness: giving us an opportunity to reach out to them in their hour of need."

"Family liaison services were informed but in the absence of N.O.K. information in his passport or any family identifiers; they had no ways of contacting Mr De Sanchez' relatives."

Roger Ennis looked thoughtful for a moment as he returned to the summary pages and the family liaison entries.

"In retrospect, we should have documented contact with the Police *Internationally* to ensure contact with his family. *I will mention this to family liaison and ensure the information did eventually get through as there's no mention of this follow up on the summary pages.*"

Roger Ennis popped a yellow advice sticker on the front of the notes as an aide memoire to ensure all details were reconciled.

"Sister Taylor handed Anton the notification of death in the absence of any other obvious recipient."

Roger Ennis concluded.

They sat in silence whilst Christophe digested the details.

"From your encounter Professor, what can you recall about the friend: about *Anton*?"

"I do remember that even whilst seated he was an imposing character. He had blonde hair and piercing blue eyes; unless I am greatly mistaken".

Christophe was now edging forward on his leather clad seat: listening intently, his pulse racing.

"It was all rather odd really. We knew Anton spoke English but the three of us just sat in a small circle and he simply fixed his gaze firmly on my eyes before he stood up and turned to leave the department. Before leaving ICU he scrutinised the staff identity board on the wall of the department. I remember feeling uncomfortable with how we'd left things and I followed him into the corridor, worried he might, become *agitated or angry*; a gut instinct I suppose."

Roger Ennis raised his eyebrows as he spoke:

"I recall he rather reminded me of a villain from a spy novel set in the Cold War Era."

Despite the apparent light-hearted remark, Roger Ennis didn't smile as he recalled those details; rather he looked perturbed by the recollection."

"I entered the lift to the ground floor along-side him. He didn't acknowledge me or other visitors in the lift but he did mutter to himself as he left; his mother tongue I suppose."

"And do you recall anything of what he said in the lift?"

"Only that he spoke with a Russian accent".

As Christophe entered the car park he crouched behind a large pillar and vomited repeatedly.

He sensed a glimmer of light shining into a dark disturbing void: maybe now he'd uncovered a motive for the attempt to incarcerate him. The concept of such deep seated hatred and revenge was beyond his comprehension.

Feelings of loneliness washed over him again as he stepped into his Boxster and the engine growled into life.

The gathering storm clouds overhead did little to improve Christophe's mood as he drove East following the A48 Motorway signs to London. The revelation concerning the Russian had left him with a sense of foreboding that he could not shake. A voice deep within him told him that *Anton could well be Sergei and that Dan's life was now in real danger.*

At the next large blue sign for motorway services Christophe exited via the slip road and parked up in a quiet spot. He retrieved his PAYG phone from the side pocket in the door of his car and rang Dan's number.

"Hello..." responded an unfamiliar monosyllabic voice; sounding hesitant.

"It's CT:" replied Christophe, matching the recipient's caution.

"Good to hear from you, it's Dan."

He sounded ambivalent; despite the apparent warmth of his greeting.

It was the first time Christophe could recall hearing Dan out of his comfort zone; genuinely worried: so much so he'd disguised his voice when he'd answered the phone.

"Productive meeting: a possible match for our *mutual friend.*"

Dan was silent as a cold shiver racked his body. He let out a long sigh; then responded:

"Shit, not good news for me?"

"No..." Trying to sound more positive he said: *"But a lead none-the-less...."*

Dan was silent again. uncharacteristically, he hadn't slept much and the news was unnerving.

"Sit tight; my friends will get on the case right away."

Dan was none the wiser; he had no idea which friends Christophe was referring to or how they could possibly help and why his life was threatened?

There was an uneasy silence between them on the phone. Things left unsaid; just as there had been with Christophe's abrupt departure from Roger Ennis' office. His thoughts turned momentarily to his mentor's ignorance of the possible danger his son faced.

Christophe had held so much back during their conversation an hour earlier; he felt deeply guilty to add to his shame over his recent trial and more recently his need to divulge so much about his private life to his lawyers who despite the best of intentions, were none the less now party to personal details he'd never expected to share with anyone except in part; with Barbara Turner as his trusted counsellor.

This self-confessed betrayal of his inner feelings perseverated in his brain, penetrating every waking moment.

"Where do we go from here? I don't understand any of this."

"Stay where you are and let's catch up in a day or two".

"Okay" responded Dan; sounding unconvinced but without other sensible choices.

"I will call you; take care." Said Christophe finally and ended the call.

Dan had to relinquish the whip hand to Christophe: he found this difficult, not because he didn't trust his friend, but more the fact that Archie's betrayal and his experience at the hands of Sergei had left him feeling vulnerable in a way he'd never experienced historically.

As an only child of devoted parents, Dan had wanted for nothing: his parents had indulged him and he had been fortunate to be free of the financial constraints of his peers and friends circle.

His life had been full of certainty and he'd felt safe and secure but all that had changed in a stroke: that security, that sense of self-worth and inner strength had been severely eroded in the space of just twenty-four hours; by his experiences in Amsterdam at the hands of Sergei, just hours after his breakup with Archie.

So much left unsaid; so many emotions without closure. It was as though his life had been encapsulated and suspended in a bubble and only Christophe had the pin to return him to normality.

Christophe for his part wondered whether he should have said more to his friend. He knew Dan must be finding it hellish to be holed up in a small bedsit, waiting for the phone to ring; keeping his head down.

Christophe could see no alternative: until they could put more pieces of the jig-saw together he knew he must help keep his friend safe. The less he knew the better.

Chapter 14

08:55 Monday January 23rd 2017

Jonathan and Francis shared a mutual friend, *Bradley Walker.* The three
of them had crystallised their friendship at University and each followed
the progress of the other; though only Francis' career evolved in the
glare of the public spotlight. By contrast Bradley honed his skills covertly,
with roles in Military Intelligence having seen active service in Eastern
Europe and the Middle East.

Bradley's specialty was finding missing persons. His full *Curriculum Vitae*
was known to few people; his testimonials were passed by word of
mouth to clients who needed a job done: efficiently, discretely and
without collateral damage.

The London Underground was rammed on Monday morning as Bradley
made his way to the nominated coffee shop *Anastasia's*; a five-minute
walk from the Oxford Circus underground tube exit in Central London.

The rain pelted the pavements like a storm of tiny asteroids as water
transformed into ice and hailstones battered the wind-swept swathe of
forlorn commuters.

Bradley weaved his way between dripping umbrellas and watched as a
tide of despondent faces trudged past him, using their umbrellas like
battering rams in a medieval joust. No doubt the tourists were still
languishing in their hotel rooms or tucking into hearty breakfasts; he felt
an instant pang of hunger as he thought of the Officers' Mess at
Sandhurst Royal Military Academy: and the silver cutlery to accompany
the veritable bounty of chef's freshly cooked food in his former
Regiment in Colchester: his inaugural Infantry posting in the UK.

The coffee shop was half full when Bradley arrived; he ordered an
espresso and headed towards a small uncluttered round table at the far
end of the premises. The corner seat gave him a good view of the whole
shop and *eyes on* the entrance.

Most of the customers had stopped off for a take-away refuel before heading into the office for their morning stint.

Bradley watched as a young Asian couple balanced fresh croissants and over-large coffee cups on small trays and negotiated their way gingerly to a large table, decorated with a floral arrangement: a throwback to the previous evening' service.

He wondered how many of the morning customers were aware that in the evening *Anastasia's coffee shop* transformed into a haven for Asian Fusion food, whereupon seats were occupied by an eclectic and discriminating clientele who valued excellent food prepared by a close knit team of Thai and Chinese chefs, with front of house service provided by an equally varied mix of staff from disparate parts of the Middle East and Asia, whose focus was on prompt service and customer-focused attention more akin to a five-star hotel than a modern coffee shop.

By contrast on this busy morning shift the young sales assistant had paid him scant attention to him and failed to make eye contact as he paid for his coffee. The anonymity suited his purpose.

As training which was now second nature dictated: Bradley expertly scanned the faces of those around him, as he fired up his laptop.

He draped his soaking wet raincoat over the chair to his left and pushed it under the table, and drew a second wicker chair from the adjacent table towards his own.

Ten minutes later a familiar face walked in through the glass door, as Jonathan Clarke joined the end of the four person queue and ordered his coffee. He removed his horn-rimmed glasses and dried them in a serviette as he waited for his coffee.

He headed toward Bradley with a beaming smile; his customary black worn oversized computer bag strapped across his body. Bradley stood up and with outstretched arms they greeted one another with firm handshakes.

"*Glad to see you brought the weather mate.*" teased Bradley.

"Not the sunshine you've got used to Bradley; but at least the coffee is good here." responded Jonathan; with a wink. *Glad to see the holiday in Barbados went well; how is Jenny?*"

(Jonathan was aware that Bradley travelled extensively in the Middle East and always sported a heavy suntan. With his dark wavy swept back hair and beard, he was more able to blend into crowds and go about his business without marking himself out as a Westerner. He invariably grew his sideburns long to seamlessly join to his beard. In consequence his prominent cheekbones were highlighted by his deep suntan which was evident above his collar and extended throughout his upper torso.)

(Bradley's mother had been born in Algeria and his father was Spanish, so his eclectic mix of language skills marked him out at an early stage when he was headhunted by the British Security Services whilst studying at Oxford University. He studied Russian and German as an undergraduate, then *Advanced* Arabic whilst he undertook Officer training at *Sandhurst Military Academy*.)

("*Jenny*" and his fictitious holiday home in Barbados was the cover story used to stifle the curiosity of casual acquaintances and it was a construct which Jonathan always liked to refer to in public places.)

Jonathan looked tired thought Bradley as he watched his friend remove his laptop bag and take the seat alongside him. He ran his fingers through his swept back hair and cleared straggling hairs back over his ears.

"*Sorry I'm a bit late; taxi journey was hellish* in the heavy traffic and since my diagnosis of Diabetes', Lucy always insists I have breakfast before heading out. *Best meal of the day*. She reminds me of that idiom with almost monotonous regularity."

"*How is the lovely Lucy*?" asked Bradley with genuine affection unmistakable in his voice. The two of them had hit it off from the second they met when Bradley had stepped up as Jonathan's *Best Man* at his wedding; a decade ago.

(Lucy had quickly come to realise that the two of them must once have been inseparable; sharing a similar sense of humour and an eclectic mix of interests in computing, ancient history and travel. She knew little of Jonathan's time spent working with the Civil Service; long hours networking with IT experts who shared a similar passion for computer protocols, mathematical algorithms and National Security.)

"*She's great*; constantly nagging me about my drinking and eating, but she keeps me sane in this mad old world! Now enough about my little troubles;" Jonathan patted her enlarging waste-line as he spoke: "*How about you*?"

"*You're a lucky man*" said Bradley with feeling. "Wish someone cared about my well being. I can't complain because no bugger listens when I do!" He rolled his eyes.

(Bradley's own marriage had lasted just three years before his endless nights away from Fiona had culminated in her departure for sunnier climes and the welcoming arms of a shady Italian businessman.)

They laughed heartily as Jonathan put on his best West Country accent and impersonated Bradley: repeating his line back to him:

"I can't complain 'cause no *buggerrr* listens when I do!" Rolling his "R" repeatedly until Bradley gave him a swift jab in his ribs.

(Neither of them were quite sure where the Cornish mock accent had originated but it was a ditty they had defaulted to when having a moan about life in general. Devon and Cornwall had always been a go-to destination for them both when they needed to wind down.)

(Jonathan, Bradley and Lucy met up whenever they could; which was ordinarily twice or thrice a year; whenever Bradley had finished a long stint overseas and needed some good home cooked food and *R & R*. The boys referred to it *Army style* as rest and recuperation; Lucy called it: *red wine and ruination*. The latter was much more appropriate to their behaviour when the three of them met up.)

(Bradley always assumed the "ruination" was a thinly veiled reference to his liver. In Jonathan's case it was a reference to his waist-line and lack of exercise. Long walks were Lucy's answer; so they would head for the countryside and negotiate muddy fields, turnstiles and gorge on fresh air.)

Bradley continued to scan the restaurant as they chatted and when he was satisfied that no one was taking an interest in their conversation, he lowered his voice and got down to business.

"Since your call I have read the court transcripts of the case you sent over."

"*Excellent, here are the bits and pieces you need.*" Jonathan handed Bradley a password protected encrypted memory stick enclosed within a small hard black plastic case.

"There's an executive summary of the Appeal with new evidence gathered from the defendant's laptop and the email links we discussed. I have added the prosecution evidence and disclosure from the trial which includes CCTV footage, forensic reports, timelines and key transcripts."

"And photographs?" asked Bradley.

"Absolutely: multiple digital images; the filing is self-explanatory."

"The stick has the usual level of security encryption and the six digit numeric password we have used historically. Here is the ten digit alpha-numeric code for the second level of encryption. "

Bradley nodded and placed the small sealed envelope directly into the inner pocket of his dark green Barbour jacket and zipped it closed. He placed the small black case inside the opposite jacket pocket then gave Jonathan his full attention once more.

(Jonathan had filed photographs of *Christophe* and *Dan Ennis* taken in a variety of locations, and included excerpts from the First Southern Trains CCTV footage. Dan had furnished his most recent copies of digital photographs of *Archie*; taken prior to their break up.)

Bradley listened carefully for the next two hours as Jonathan took him step by step through the relevant trial evidence, the details of the successful Appeal and the recent meeting in Wales between Professor Ennis and his former protege: Dr Christophe Schultz.

As Jonathan talked Bradley listened intently; clarifying points of particular concern. Bradley kept eye contact throughout but whenever Jonathan hesitated or gathered his thoughts, he continued to scan the restaurant to ensure their discussion remained private.

It was 11:30 a.m. when Jonathan finished the briefing and sat back in his chair, hands on his belly.

"So, another coffee? No pastries, I promised Lucy!"

"*My shout*." retorted Bradley and promptly cleared the table and returned with two fresh steaming drinks.

They sat in silence for a few minutes, each pondering different aspects of the case.

"*Okay, that's Ace Jon'*; the picture is clear. Our boy could be in a lot of danger; his friend Dan likewise. Shame the original tablet was destroyed, that would have been very helpful, although given the nature of the images; it's not really surprising he decided to burn it."

"I have a number of questions buzzing around in my head and will have to move fast; but first I need to digest what you've given me here and make some calls. Any way we can get any images of our long lost friend in Amsterdam?"

Realising Bradley meant the Russian known only as *Sergei*, he responded: "I am assuming the hotel will be your first port of call; though it's a bit late for CCTV I guess".

"My thoughts exactly."

"I will need to speak to our friend about his visit to Amsterdam in more detail; you've included the PAYG number of course."

"Yes, for obvious reasons he'll be keeping email silence at present". He's holed up.

"Okay, need to know basis for his address." Instructed Bradley; firmly in the driver's seat here on in.

"And a default contact number?" He added.

"Yep; I have already taken care of that Bradley. I have given him a good old fashioned pager which is tracked; though he doesn't know that. *Likewise: for our client*. They've been instructed to ring my mobile number if paged.

(*Our client* was no other than Francis Ledbetter to whom Jonathan had spoken as soon as he'd received Dan's message concerning the anonymous threatening calls he had started to receive from the moment of Christophe's release on 16th January. He'd made a log of the calls for Jonathan as their content became more unpleasant, more homophobic and increasingly threatening.)

(Dan' shared the details of the calls directly with Christophe following his visit to St. Martha's on 19th January whereafter Christophe immediately contacted Francis: so completing the loop.)

(Given the lengths which Sergei had gone to in contributing to Christophe's indictment and conviction for murder: he was clearly an adversary to be taken seriously and Bradley was taking no chances.)

"*Great.*" Declared Bradley; draining the remains of his coffee cup.

"I have everything I need; I am going to back to my hotel and get reading. I will be in touch in the next forty-eight hours."

They parted with a firm hand-shake.

As he re-entered the street Bradley paused for a moment and walked across the road to look at the window display in the antique shop opposite the coffee bar. The morning rain had cleared and he studied the fine detail of the silver jewellery on display. As he did so he watched his own reflection in the glass and looked surreptitiously left and right.

He then swivelled left and headed towards the corner of the short row of shops where he turned right and right again, encircling the block; pausing momentarily to look behind him. Satisfied he was not being followed, he rejoined the crowds on Oxford Street.

Bradley walked steadily towards the far end of Oxford Street before heading across the busy road towards Tottenham Court tube station where he paused to look at the underground map, scanning those around him. As he did so, his side profile was captured on a Nikon digital camera. The tourist was wearing a beige beanie hat pulled down over his ears to keep out the cold. He lingered outside a camera shop on the opposite side of Oxford Street, apparently moving from foot to foot to keep warm, while studying his folded map of London.

As Bradley disappeared from view into the entrance to the underground station, the man moved swiftly and adeptly between the slow moving traffic and walked purposefully down into the tube station.

Chapter 15

18:00 23rd January 2017

Hotel Majestic, Marylebone, London

Bradley had worked solidly throughout the day on the brief which he had received from Jonathan and made three calls on his secure line; one to Interpol; the second to a trusted colleague in Moscow and the third to *George* from the Intelligence Services at MI5.

Bradley re-arranged three pillows behind his upper back and reclined on the bed listening to the BBC Six O' Clock News.

The hotel Majestic was his regular bolthole when staying in London. He liked the comfortable rooms and the attentive unobtrusive staff. But more than anything, he prized the range of sumptuous pillows which the Hotel provided; sleep didn't always come easy to him in the dead of night. Old friends and foes resurfaced with monotonous regularity in his dreams.

When push came to shove he had two concrete leads, the Russian known as *Sergei* and the computer server in a run-down suburb of Moscow. The description of the Russian and the date of his encounter with *Dan Ennis* would give his colleagues at Interpol a starting point from which to search for him. However given the near absence of border checks in Europe since the introduction of the "Schengen Agreement"; Bradley was conscious this might be search akin to finding the proverbial needle in a haystack.

Jonathan's work in tracing the email sent from Dan's electronic tablet had been inspired. Furthermore he had narrowed down the server location; this would sign post the Russian part of the search. His man in Moscow had close ties to a team of former FSB [Federal Security Service] operatives and they would move in the next few hours to secure the location and collect relevant IT information.

Bradley checked his watch: 18:30. He decided it was time to take a stroll down to the bar.

By passing the lift Bradley headed for the stairs and took two at a time as he headed down to the ground floor. Leaving the exit door he turned sharp left then right and headed for the door marked *Reception*.

The Reception and Foyer area was packed with a mixture of early evening travellers booking in for the night, intermingling with a party of thirty-something revellers who were already creating a lively diversion from the ambient music which was piped throughout the public areas of the hotel. Huddled in groups of three or four they were dressed either in tuxedos or the obligatory "little black numbers" as Lucy would have called them. He smiled as he remembered their last weekend together; the three of them chilling over a few bottles of Merlot in front of the warm stove; the smell of fresh stew permeating all but the stone walls of the two-up, two-down cottage in Highgate, North London: which had morphed into their forever home.

Limo' drivers were arriving and groups decanting through Reception to their awaiting taxis.

The air was full of lively banter, fuelled by early evening cocktails and aromatic canapés.

Next to the revolving door entrance to the Majestic' was a collection of leather sofas and chairs tastefully arranged around ornamental tables alongside vases containing a variety of exotic plants; *the Manager's passion.*

(Born in Algiers, *Samir* was an immaculately dressed, lightly built, well mannered man who understood the supreme importance of customer satisfaction and even more importantly: the value of a comfortable room for weary travellers. The service delivered by his staff was matched by a loyal clientele: each of whom was rewarded for their patronage by an orchid on arrival: a subtle touch for the Patrons of many a romantic weekend.)

Glancing through the revolving glass doors to the entrance as the throng dispersed, Bradley could see the rain had settled and the street outside was already bustling with commuters and tourists.

He stopped for a moment as he passed by the seating area to his immediate right and feigned interest in the menu for evening dinner. *Something was out of place and he couldn't put his finger on what it was.*

He held back and nodded as a couple held open the double doors to the restaurant and politely responded:

"Thank you – but I've misplaced my wallet!" He announced audibly.

As he turned he proceeded to pat the pockets of his jacket theatrically and check his trouser pockets; all the time conscious that whoever was watching him would be studying his every move. *His instincts had not let him down over the years and he wasn't about to ignore that feeling as the hairs on the back of his neck stood on end.*

Bradley walked leisurely towards the lifts; all the time watching Reception. As he reached the lifts an American couple who had chatting loudly to the receptionist whilst their suitcases were collected; held the lift doors open for him and he stepped gratefully inside. The bell boy pressed the button and illuminated floor five. Bradley waited until the lift had passed level two then quickly pressed three. Leaving the lift he took a sharp right towards the exit stairway and waited; his ear pressed against the glass of the nearside Fire door.

Within moments he could hear the sound of rapid footsteps turning around the balustrade in the stair-well and continuing their ascent. When he was sure the coast was clear he took the stairs back to the ground floor, continuing through Reception out of the hotel via the single glass manual door.

Once outside and without giving way to traffic, Bradley headed swiftly across the road to the evident annoyance of two irate motorists who sounded their horns at him just as he finally leapt out of the road and into a covered bus shelter. He turned the collars of his overcoat up and ensured that he was out of view of the main hotel entrance; then waited.

At 19:15 Bradley's patience was rewarded as he watched a tall figure emerge from the hotel. The man was dressed in a long dark trench-coat. He marked himself out by his physique and body language: alert and actively scanning his surroundings. The stranger took one last look up and down the High Street. He checked his watch then reached into his pocket and put on a beige beanie hat covering his short blonde hair. He hailed a black cab and was driven off.

Bradley pulled out his phone and relayed the cab's registration details to George who was sat in front of his computer in a small communal office at M15 comms' division.

Five minutes later he strolled back across the road and into the hotel through the revolving doors where he stopped off at Reception. Ten minutes later he was sat in the Samir's office watching the CCTV footage of Reception and the tall man with distinctive short blond hair.

20:00 Room 512 Hotel Majestic

"Hi Jon', Bradley; calling ahead of time. Just listen please."

"Roger that." responded Jonathan pragmatically.

"I have company; he *may* be aware of our 1:1. We must assume you're also compromised."

"Roger that. Anything else you need?"

"No; sit tight. Speak soon."

Bradley ended the call abruptly.

He emailed two clear images of "Blondie" to his Russian contact.

Chapter 16

Tuesday 24th January 2017

"Hi Vladimir – thank you for calling; how did your visit go?"

"Hello Mr Jones: sorry it's late. Our visit go well: we have two young friends helping us. They bring along their computer for us to watch movies together!"

He laughed out loud at his joke; Bradley joined him, rubbing his eyes. He glanced at his watch: 3:35 a.m.

Vladimir's heavy Russian accent, broken English and sense of humour were both familiar and a breath of fresh air to Bradley's ears; immediately evoking strong memories.

"Any sign of our mutual friend?"

"Ah you mean Mr Blonde; I presume?" replied Vladimir; with a thinly veiled reference to a well known fictional character from the British Secret Service. "He was not in our movies."

"Well I think he may be coming to *my party*" responded Bradley cryptically. Vladimir was quick to catch his drift and instantly replied.

"Well be sure to invite me if you want him to...*sing for you* and your friends at British Intelligence!"

Cue further laughter at the end of the phone. Bradley laughed out loud and raised his eyebrows: visualising the drama that such a Russian-European cooperation might create in the corridors of power at Whitehall.

"An interesting offer, thank you my friend." mused Bradley; "Do you have recent photographs your new friends you can send me; in case any of them turn up *early* at my party?"

"I will send you shots as soon as we have finished 'album and put 'family tree together. Maybe we take a day or two: my friends have 'memory problems."

Bradley nodded to himself; confident that such memory problems would be short lived in Vladimir's capable hands.

"Thank you Vladimir; how is *Olga*?"

"She is a fine woman; *thanks to you Mr Jones*!" pride audible in his voice.

"Thank you old friend; let's speak soon".

"*Not so much of the old,* or we might not *stay* friends!" raucous laughter and the line went dead.

Bradley lay back in bed and smiled at fond memories of Vodka-fuelled sleep-deprived nights in Helsinki.

As he relaxed and drifted back to sleep he visualised Vladimir, his three strapping sons, and Olga; his only daughter. Vladimir had always doted on her. Having been born prematurely at thirty weeks and perhaps somehow having sensed her own frailty; she had cried incessantly during her first year of life. Vladimir had hugged and soothed her to sleep, needing no encouragement: a huge bear of a man, protecting his vulnerable cub.

An organised crime syndicate had kidnapped Olga when she was barely eight years old. The three men held for her for three days, demanding a ransom they never expected to be paid; inflicting suffering they never expected to be revealed.

Bradley, George and a small team had found her. The three thugs were promptly handed over to Vladimir.

After confessing their sins, their punishment was swift and unequivocal.

Every finger which touched Olga was severed. Every organ which penetrated her was excised. Every eye laid upon her was gouged out.

The wild dogs in the ice cold woodland outside of Moscow feasted well that night.

Vladimir rarely slept soundly after Olga's release. He repaid his debt to Bradley many times over: *only death would sever their friendship and end a father's rage.*

Chapter 17

Wednesday 25th January 2017

Bradley woke to the alarm at 06:45.

He checked his mobile for messages and fired up his laptop whilst he put the kettle on for a brew.

Two emails from Vladimir; the first was a name, the second contained a digital picture attachment:

Alexei BABICHEV date of birth: April 10th 1970: a.k.a. Sergei.

The image was a dead ringer for the hotel CCTV images and he needed only a beanie hat to complete the ensemble.

Bradley wasted no time in forwarding the details to *Philippe* at Interpol.

He then emailed a copy to Jonathan entitled a *mutual friend*; without any further explanation.

Retrieving his phone from the bedside cabinet Bradley sent a brief text to Jonathan:

"Mutual friend sent to your email: *your eyes only*."

He made two further phone calls and then sat back and drank his coffee and while he planned his day.

Chapter 18

Wednesday 25th January 2017

12A Hope Apartments, Surrey

Shards of amber light cascaded across the immaculately white tiled bathroom as Dr Christophe Schultz stood naked and opened the pristine white venetian blinds to his en-suite. Dawn had always held a magical quality for him: *sleep is for the dead* me mused, more especially since his incarceration had come to an end.

He held a stainless steel scalpel in his left hand: the razor sharp edge glinting in the exquisite hue of the rising sun.

Knife to skin felt good. As Christophe's blood oozed from the delicate skin of his right forearm he gently sighed; embracing the warm release he felt. He closed his eyelids lightly together and relaxed his breathing, gently and rhythmically inhaling and exhaling; welcoming the temporary escape from reality.

Opening a fresh tube of toothpaste Christophe methodically brushed his pearl white teeth before diligently flossing each crevice; a practice he knew was likely to improve his long-term cardiovascular risk profile. He discarded both brush and paste in the stainless lined steel pedal bin before vigorously showering in the second of his daily rituals; a waterproof plaster covering his newly incised forearm.

Toccata and Fugue in D minor played soothingly in the background as Christophe repeatedly re-tied his purple woven wool tie until he achieved a flawless Windsor knot; before donning his favourite dark blue silk jacket.

He took a long look and critical self-appraisal of his suit in the full length mirror to ensure his appearance was immaculate. Today would mark the zenith of seven years of passion, persistence and disingenuous politics in his role as UK Medical Director with Utopia Pharmaceutical Company.

He would be returning to the Company as a free man, exonerated of the charge of Murder laid against him and would endeavour to hold his head high. But in truth, he had no idea what lay ahead of him. He did his best to suppress his misgivings.

George Latimer had insisted they mark his return to the Company with a one-to-one meeting before he met with the new Managing Partner of HR and thereafter; the entire Senior Management Team. Christophe was fully aware they were preparing a Champagne Welcome breakfast for him: he'd had the heads up' from George's secretary Annalisa; along with the email invitation.

It had been only ten days since his release from Prison, but Christophe had quickly realised that only by returning to some semblance of normality and adopting a daily routine, could he hope to move on swiftly from his ordeal and draw a line under the whole debacle.

In any event, he had nothing to berate himself for: he had shown complete loyalty to the Company who by the same token, had paid for his defence team and all accompanying costs for his Barrister and Appeal: *quid pro quo.*

Christophe exited his apartment building and operated the electrically powered rollover garage door with a single nudge of the power fob on his key-ring. The rear-end of his beloved offspring from *Zuffenhausen*; steadily emerged before his eyes. He longed to hear his twin exhausts burst into action again. During his time in Prison he had missed his beloved convertible more than any of his banal possessions.

Not for him a modern replica of German engineering, with parts sourced from other Companies or even Countries; he remained true to the design specifications of his aged Porsche. It mattered little to him that nay-slayers derided his vehicle as a *"hair-dressers car"*, whilst they drove their gigantic monstrosities.

With a flick of his right wrist, the low rumble of the engine stirred into life and pulled down the hood lock and depressed the switch while he waited the twelve seconds until the hood completely retracted.

The cold January air immediately heightened his senses as he reversed into the communal turning area before exiting the drive onto the deserted road towards London.

The early morning grit scattered wildly as Christophe gathered speed passing local villages and the throaty roar of the engine became more intense as he approached Sunny Oak Village level crossing and slowed in readiness for the clearly marked speed camera; the yellow casing already visible in his left peripheral vision.

The road ahead was narrowed due to road works and seeing the temporary lights at red he slowed and waited; suddenly acutely aware of the cold morning air gently burning the back of his throat. A lone worker in a fluorescent jacket stepped forward towards the right side of the car and gestured to speak.

"Need to close the road temporarily mate; can you detour via Archway Road?"

With only a cursory nod, Christophe made a swift tyre scrunching U-turn and took an immediate ninety degree right turn before picking up speed and following the curve of the bend. With traction control set to off he felt the rear wheels slip momentarily as he took the second right turn towards the arch of the bridge in the road.

Unexpectedly a low-loader sat ahead of him, straddling both lanes of his exit; hazard lights flashing like hypnotic strobes in the early morning light. Without hesitation Christophe depressed the heavy clutch pedal and selected reverse gear, only to find another vehicle behind him; lights on full beam. Dazzled and irritated, Christophe leaned down and forward to disengage reverse gear and switch on his hazard lights. As he did so he felt a sudden pressure and searing pain in the right side of his neck. He lifted his right arm in protest, opened his mouth wide but only a silent scream passed his lips.

A strong hand covered his mouth; the distinct smell of leather and the metallic tangy taste of blood. His vision dimmed and the dashboard became a swirling frenetic firework display of neon lights as deafening drums began to hammer in his ears; he heard distant voices and then, there was only darkness.

Minutes later Christophe's car was fastened securely on the low-loader and driven away.

Chapter 19

11:45 Wednesday 25th January 2017

Location unknown

An excruciating pain in his forehead awoke Christophe with a sudden
jolt. Drowsiness hung over him like a dark drunken cloud and as he
raised his head his eyes focused uneasily on the imposing dark figure
stood directly in front of him. His body refused to obey his commands:
his wrists and ankles were tethered.

Unable to shield his eyes, he squinted and twisted his head away from
the blinding white light piercing his eyes.

 "So finally I have your undivided attention Dr Schultz."

Alexei Babichev's deep voice dominated the room.

Christophe tried to remonstrate but his lips were fastened with duct
tape.

"Don't waste your energy with futile gestures." His tone was scornful.

Alexei approached his prey carrying a syringe. He stood to the right of
Christophe and inserted a needle into the back of his hand. The
intravenous rush was immediate. A thousand firecrackers detonated
deep inside Christophe's psyche releasing a volley of white sparks which
merged into a myriad of tangled florescent webs in front of his eyes. He
felt his body sink deeper and deeper, undulating out of control.

*Alexei yanked Christophe's head up with his left hand and inserted the
scalpel blade deep into the skin of his forehead above the left eye;
pushing vertically until he felt bone. He dragged the knife horizontally
towards his right eyebrow then vertically down from the top towards the
right nostril of his nose. He completed the incision with a horizontal
sweep across his right cheek.*

Alexei cut the ties from Christophe's wrists and ankles and then tore the duct tape from his mouth.

"Focus on the light: open your eyes." The powerful ethereal voice commanded.

Christophe was drawn inexorably towards the dark silhouette in the far corner of the otherwise bare room. There were no windows to shed light on his path, but a white glow shone with such intensity that Christophe felt it begin to scald his eyelids; blurring his vision.

The room was silent and he was suddenly aware of his laboured breathing. He raised his right hand to his mouth, a familiar smell of leather filled his nose; forcing him to retch and choke.

Blood covered the back of his right hand and he began wiping it frantically against his thigh. He grew irritated, wiped harder and rubbed his hands relentlessly against his body and then his face.

"Don't fight it Christophe; come to the light."

As he trudged arduously forward; his legs felt progressively heavy with each step.

A silver scalpel blade partially incised Christophe's right Achilles tendon.

Searing pain ripped through his body. His right leg started to drag as he coughed and retch repeatedly as the acrid leather smell and the taste of blood intensified. Christophe lurched and reeled forwards crashing into a wall. Blood poured from his scalp and as the blood mushroomed and sprayed the walls, it appeared to him like the swell of a storm and the waves breaking on a distant frigid headland.

The second ritual incision was performed from right temple vertically down his forehead, scything the tissue horizontally underneath his right eye, across the apex of the nose, and completed with a final flourish; a vertical sweep down his left cheek.

He felt blinded as blood poured into his eyes. The pain in his right leg intensified with every footstep.

His life force was ebbing away as he dragged his legs forwards, towards the object which was now larger and darker. Suddenly his body fell forwards, his arms flailing as his left leg caught something heavy and he fell; his movements sluggish and uncoordinated; as time itself began to slow down.

Christophe could sense the dark heavy object draining his will to survive.

Alexei injected a further vial of liquid into Christophe's right arm.

Two unseen figures lifted Christophe and lowered him into the rectangular metal box.

Christophe felt weightless, his body racked with pain but he could not move. The black box beneath him felt familiar yet obscure; gravely sinister.

His skin pricked and he felt icy cold. Yellow pustular fluid exuded from large blisters erupting on the back of his hands. He slowly lowered his heavy jaw and opened his mouth, swinging his head from side to side as thick fluid started to drip from the corner of his mouth and the light began to shimmer.

His body was moving with a will beyond his control. He watched as his right hand reached down and he felt cold metal as his fingers burned. He could smell his flesh searing in the depths of the box.

His body began to jerk left then right, then spinning over and over. He screamed and screamed and heard only choking and wheezing; as fluid started to fill his burning lungs and exude from his nostrils. His skin was scorching as his ears began to ache with excruciating intensity. His arms tensed involuntarily and he was drawn into dark box as his body was pulled deeper and deeper into the depths; resistance futile. His vision was clouded by pain as his ears begin to ring with the ferocity of a raging siren.

Suddenly dragged down by his feet, he was wrenched backwards and down into a deep abyss and he felt nothing but the pain searing his skin and the light above him began to fade, as his limbs grew heavier and the ringing in his ears became more distant.

Christophe's head felt heavy and unwieldy as his neck was extended and his body merely hung as if from the gallows. He closed his eyes, drained of all capacity to resist. The pain which had racked his body began to fade and the light was eclipsed as all around him darkness enveloped. Darkness, cold and silence reined; then peacefulness and perfect solitude enveloped him.

Chapter 20

05:30 Thursday 26th January 2017

Bradley hadn't ordered a newspaper. As he retrieved the daily from underneath his bedroom door, a large brown manila envelope, barely disguised within the folded *Financial Times* dropped to the floor. He instinctively retrieved a pair of large latex gloves from the zipped pocket of his business case.

Bradley checked the seals on the envelope and could feel no wires. The contents were flimsy and there was no odour detectable from the sealed flaps. He withdraw one of the blades from his trusty Leatherman knife and carefully opened one corner before slicing open the envelope across the envelope flap: allowing the contents to fall onto a sterile sheet of paper unfolded on the leather surface of the desk.

Two hours later, Bradley took a last look at the type written note with instructions for the meeting. He had bagged the item and envelope as he would any piece of evidence; sure that there would be no fingerprints but none the less, preserving the trail of evidence for Forensic scrutiny.

George would be picking it up from reception in thirty minutes time at 8 a.m.

He would collect it directly from the Hotel Manager.

Bradley opened *Google maps* and began refreshing his local knowledge of the area in question. Though familiar to him; he would leave no stone unturned in preparation for the meeting. He double checked the Underground routes and local bus services. He searched taxi ranks and noted pedestrianised areas. Finally he looked at recent satellite photographs of the specific building of interest.

He updated George on coordinates via his mobile, ensuring he used his encrypted App on his modified tablet.

The lift was packed as Bradley descended to reception and he took his time putting on his overcoat, before leaving through the revolving doors. The early morning air was crisp and plumes of moisture rose as he took several long deep breaths and looked up at the bright blue sky.

The concierge smiled broadly and politely asked him if he wanted a *Black Cab.*

Bradley reciprocated the smile:

"I think I'll take a walk, thanks all the same mate."

Bradley walked briskly up the High Street and crossed to the opposite side of the road as soon as he saw the sign for the jeweller's shop.

A young couple stood next to him arm-in-arm looking at engagement rings together. If they were working undercover with Blondie, they sure *looked convincing*, thought Bradley as he headed up the High Street until he reached Bobby's, the delicatessen. He looked at his watch; it was 9:45 a.m. as went inside.

Having selected a large cappuccino and a pastry, Bradley selected a window seat and began reading a copy of a London freebie newspaper which had been discarded the night before.

He was confident that he now had the undivided attention of anyone taking more than a cursory interest in his activity.

Casually scanning the street outside Bradley saw nothing untoward and slowly sipped his coffee, catching up on the latest soaring house price valuations. His mobile buzzed; Jonathan had acknowledged his text regarding Alexei: a.k.a. Sergei.

Half an hour later he took a right turn out of the delicatessen and after a couple of road intersections walked briskly towards Marylebone Underground Station which stood directly opposite the Landmark Hotel.

Just inside the station hall, a small choir of eight choristers had assembled in front of the cash dispensers near the electronic departures board and Bradley stood and listened to the impromptu rendition of several rock ballads from the 'seventies and 'eighties. Commuters and travellers weaved their way through the station; topping up *Oyster Travel Cards* and checking the departure boards; most oblivious to the musical gems of a by-gone era or too tied up with their own activities to take a few precious moments of time out from their busy schedules.

Bradley surveyed those coming and going from the hall and could see no signs he was being followed.

He took the long escalator down to the underground platforms themselves; standing on the right to allow those in a hurry to rush past him in a bid to save a few seconds of time.

He stopped at the bottom of the escalator where a busker looked forlorn with his empty weatherbeaten bowler hat laid out in front of his accordion. Bradley popped a pound coin into the musician's hat before taking a sharp left hand turn through a short tunnel and proceeding down onto the *Southbound Bakerloo Line*.

The platform was lined three deep with passengers edging towards the bold white line, as the display signalled the train approaching.

The rugby scrum began as bodies pushed and jostled to get aboard the train as though it were the last train to Tulsa, Oklahoma; and they were Art Deco die hards. Bradley could hear the lyrics to *Neil Young's* classic song reverberating through his auditory cortex as he distracted himself from the cacophony of sounds around him: vacuous chatter and the clang of steel against steel as trains arrived and departed on the adjacent platform.

Bradley continued to make his way steadily towards the far end of the platform where the crowd was thinning rapidly. The next train was due in a mere three minutes so he waited patiently, his back against the cold whitewashed station wall.

He glanced down the line of commuters as once again their numbers began to swell. Faces turned towards him, peering up at the arrivals board and Bradley felt a sudden rush of air as the next train was fast approaching the station. No one stood out amongst the crowd. No one gave him more than a passing glance. As the final passengers left the end carriage, he stepped on board with a last look to his right.

The carriage was already heaving and the final few last minute passengers boarded and pressed in behind him just as the doors closed momentarily; then opened again. The guard made a second announcement requesting passengers not block the doors and the train pulled swiftly away with a deep guttural rumble.

Bradley scanned faces. No one caught his eye, most passengers in a world of their own; reading texts or playing games on their smart phones. Passengers swiftly overheated in their heavy winter coats, adorned with scarves and gloves. The humid air was heavy with thinly disguised odorous perspiration inside the cramped carriage which was overdue an upgrade.

Bradley breathed a sigh of relief as he began walking up the mechanised escalator. He exited the train at *Leicester Square* tube station. As he walked toward the first check point he glanced at his watch: 10:52 a.m.

As instructed, he waited outside the flag-ship cinema on Leicester Square, scanning the crowds of buoyant children and tourists wielding digital cameras in every direction; indulgent "selfies" were clearly the order of the day.

Bradley fixed his eyes on the far corner of the quadrangle and then at 11 a.m. precisely as instructed, he strolled down past coffee shops and restaurants towards the unobtrusive building covered in scaffolding. He checked his phone: no messages. He switched audio settings to mute. He lingered for a moment apparently admiring local architecture as he took a final three hundred and sixty degree view of his sun-lit surroundings before stepping under the scaffolding. The red painted front door to the building had been removed and lay to the left of entrance, covered in thick dusty heavy-duty clear plastic.

He stood inside the entrance hall for a moment and let his eyes adjust to the light as he looked to the rear of the building, down the straight dim corridor. He could see through to a back room which had a long industrial sized stainless steel sink along the far wall. A staircase to the right of the entrance hall, headed straight upstairs to the landing. The sign for the toilets was still fixed to the wall; along with a qualifying statement beneath it: "customers only".

"Welcome to Central London!" thought Bradley.

He turned sharply left into what was formerly the main seating area of the disused restaurant. The air was full of dust which clung to Bradley's throat as he moved through the intervening door into the rear service area of the building and on into the abandoned kitchen. His footsteps echoed as he moved through the empty building; leather soles falling on concrete and dust.

The double doors at the rear of the premises were secured with a series of bolts and heavy duty padlocks. He tried the locks; the exit was solid. Barring a pick axe or heavy duty crowbar, the only way in and out would be through the front entrance. Turning back through into the main corridor from the kitchen, Bradley stopped and listened. No noise upstairs. A steady stream of people passed outside, none showing any interest in the gutted building.

He guessed it would be different at night when the local shelters for the homeless were full.

Bradley turned and climbed the wooden stairs cautiously; listening for anything untoward. The three upper rooms and bathroom were empty. The toilet had certainly seen better days; the cistern looking precariously close to losing its attachment to the concrete wall.

11:10 a.m. No messages on his phone; he turned the ringer back on. Bradley walked back down the stairs and out into the crisp morning air; the spicy aroma of Chinese cooking wafted his way momentarily, reminding him of his proximity to China Town. He stood outside and waited. 11:15 a.m. *the rendezvous slot: came and went*. He checked his mobile every ten minutes: nothing. By mid-day he decided to take one final look around Leicester Square. The building remained empty at 12:15.

So what game was Blondie playing?

Chapter 21

Thursday 26th January 2017

10:55 a.m. Highgate Village, North London

Lucy was busily chopping vegetables for a healthy thick soup: a warm welcome home for Jonathan. She had to persuade him to consume his five portions of fruit and vegetables somehow and she loved cooking soups as much as he enjoyed devouring them after a long day in front of his beloved computer.

Radio 4 kept her company on days like this. She sometimes got lonely in the house all day alone. Her family lived two hours away in Leicester and her neighbours were mostly working mums whose income assured their monthly mortgage repayments.

Unusually for him, Jonathan had surprised her with the news that he would be home early for a change and would not be tethered to his laptop all evening.

So Lucy had the evening mapped out: they would share her hearty soup with fresh crusty warm rolls, washed down with a glass of Merlot which was warming gently in front of the fire in the snug.

With the fire roaring they would snuggle up for a romantic night in and a retro romantic movie. *Paradise she smiled to herself*.

Lucy sighed as the clock chimed 11 o'clock in the hallway. She headed to the over-sized fridge and collected butter and assembled the ingredients for a vanilla sponge cake, Jonathan's favourite; a sort of late anniversary present made with a low fat recipe to help him in his battle with his enlarging waistline.

She'd been thrilled when Jonathan had surprised her with a last minute gift the previous evening and she wore the green butterfly broach proudly on her purple woollen jumper.

She set the oven to one hundred and seventy-five degrees Centigrade to pre-warm.

The mixer blades began to clang as they rattled against the sides of the large beige plastic mixing bowl. The door bell rang twice.

"Typical, just as I'm mixing." She hurriedly scraped the pastry mixture from her hands and turned off the machine. *Ginger*, their black and white cat squealed and hissed as she trod on his tail in her enthusiasm to get to the front door. She called after him as he turned and took fright; scuttling off into the snug opposite the kitchen.

She lifted the latch, twisted the handle and pulled open the heavy oak front door and was surprised to see no one waiting. The postman had delivered the mail which hung inside the wire basket on the inside aspect of the door.

Damn she thought, he must have tried to deliver our Amazon package they'd waiting for; more kit for their forthcoming skiing trip. Irritated, she consoled herself that he'd probably try again later or at the very latest, Friday morning. She headed back to her mixer.

The jarring clang created by the mixing blades put her teeth on edge as she turned up the speed on the mixer. She hummed to the music on the radio which was barely audible over the noise of the mixer as she watched the mixture evolve into silky smooth consistency; ready to decant into the pre-lined pastry tins.

The oven was still coming up to temperature so she decided to go and find *Ginger* and smooth his ruffled pride before turning out the cake mix. *Ginger* was coming up to his fifth birthday and she made a mental note to buy him a new blanket so he could snuggle up with them on winter nights without covering the sofa with his long hairs.

"No doubt he'll be nestled into our duvet." Lucy said out loud, smiling inwardly to herself, given that he was conspicuously absent from the snug; where the fire was crackling away and giving off a lovely sunset glow. She toasted her hands, rubbing them eagerly together before going in search her beloved moggy.

Ever since Jonathan had surprised her with Ginger, he'd been her constant companion during the long winter nights when Jonathan worked on his computer. She now longed for summer, the long relaxing evening strolls and the sun on her pale skin.

The nineteenth Century wooden stairs creaked noisily as Lucy headed to the master bedroom; her first port of call. As she reached the top of the stairs she could hear Ginger yowling. "*Oh Ginger you silly old sausage...*" she called to him as she entered the bedroom.

Lucy was rendered powerless as a strong hand grabbed her left shoulder and wrenched her right arm painfully up behind her back. She was forced down onto the double bed; her face pushed mercilessly down onto the duvet just as her left arm was forcibly trapped beneath her body. Panic gripped her as she frantically twisted her head to the right, then left and tried to scream, but she was winded and gasped for breath; just as something wet was smothering her mouth and nose.

She bucked her body as hard as she could to and fro' away from the weight on top of her; suffocating her. She summoned all her strength and kicked back hard with her left leg. She felt her left knee forced painfully into the duvet and the weight on her right knee sent pain up into her buttock.

Moments later she could feel her resistance ebb away; the weight on top of her sapping her strength. She felt sure she would die and could not picture Jonathan as the pink duvet swirled in front of her eyes. All she could hear was her own heavy breathing; ink black darkness reigned supreme.

Chapter 22

16:30 Thursday 26th January

Majestic Hotel

"*He was a no show Jon'.*" said Bradley as Jonathan answered his phone on the second ring; without the need for further introductions.

"Damn. Okay well I'm heading off home now. It's only 4:30 p.m. but I'm done for today. *'Promised Lucy an early finish and an evening in front of the fire; just the two of us and a bottle of red'.*"

"*Sounds perfect mate*; 'nothing we can do until he makes contact again. *Love to Lucy.*"

"Roger that!"

"*Lucky sod*" thought Bradley as the phone went dead and he was left considering his own culinary options. Dinner for one and a glass or two of red; sounded like a plan he could live with. He wasn't much in the mood for socialising anyway. There were too many loose ends for him to tie up.

The letter and envelope had been analysed by forensics. A text message confirmed the envelope was clean; no finger prints. No DNA under the seals either; no surprise there then, thought Bradley as he read the consecutive text messages: relayed via *George*.

No further word from Russia meant *Vladimir* had no new leads as yet.

Bradley took an antacid; Chinese food always did give him indigestion.

"*Why do you always choose the sweet and sour when you know it upset you?*"

His ex-wife's favourite phrase designed to needle him when he least needed aggravation and would have preferred home cooking to take-away, any day.

He smiled thinking about what a lucky chap Jonathan was with a home-maker like Lucy: *every man's dream.*

Kicking back he chose a movie from the drama selection on the Hotel network and settled back against two pillows; edging towards a nap. He'd seen the film before, but familiarity was often comforting during these lonely days and nights whilst working.

His phone rang and he came back to earth with a bump; the film was already working towards the action packed climax. Jonathan was calling.

"Hi Jon' you home yet?"

"YES AND LUCY'S NOT HERE: SHE'S GONE!"

Jonathan's voice trembled with panic. Bradley stood up and focused his attention. He grabbed the remote and switched off the TV.

"Gone, what do you mean?" responded Bradley as calmly as he could; his heart already pounding.

"She was half way through preparing me a FUCKING cake! The oven is STILL ON. The back door was wide open when I got back. Something's happened in the bedroom; there's blood on the duvet cover."

"It's okay mate; she'll be fine." said Bradley pragmatically; his training kicking in.

"Don't touch anything; I'll get a team in STAT. I'll be with you ASAP."

Bradley hung up before Bradley could argue.

He speed dialled George and a team was dispatched to Jonathan's house directly from M15 Vauxhall; they would be at the house way before him in the evening traffic. Ten minutes later a car was waiting for him outside the hotel entrance; *George was driving.*

On route he rang Jonathan again; the line was engaged. He's ringing around friends and hospitals thought Bradley. Fair play, I would do the same.

One question echoed constantly through his mind, turning his blood cold; as they sped towards Highgate:

"What had that beanie headed bastard done with Lucy?"

Chapter 23

18:20 Thursday 26th January

Highgate Village, North London

The house was already cordoned off as Bradley and the George walked up the street towards the Police Incident tape. Showing their respective identities which were added to a list; the uniformed Police Officer gave them each a pair of clear plastic shoe covers and black rubber gloves as they went up the short garden path.

Jonathan shuffled from foot to foot hunched over at the front entrance to the house looking completely bewildered as they approached him. He feigned a smile as Bradley grasped his left shoulder. Bradley could feel Jonathan tremble in the cold night air.

"I'm waiting for her; she's probably just gone to the village shops." blurted Jonathan; *now in denial*.

"We'll find her mate." responded Bradley; looking him firmly in the eye.

"Let's go into the kitchen and have a brew."

(Despite his mixed ancestry, Bradley had lived in the UK since he was three years of age and knew only too well that tea somehow had somehow evolved into the British panacea to most of life's dramas, ills and calamities.)

Now more than ever, Jonathan needed something to ground him; like it or not, Jonathan might well hold the key to Lucy's whereabouts.

Jonathan stood silently as they waited at the entrance to the kitchen for the *all clear* from Forensics to go in. The team had taken digital images and dusted surfaces. The kitchen revealed no signs of a struggle.

Bradley ushered his friend towards the kitchen table and made a large pot of English Breakfast Tea without being prompted. He rummaged through the kitchen cupboards for a pack of biscuits; to no avail.

George went into the snug and updated the M15 hot desk.

Bradley sat down and took in the scene around the kitchen whilst he waited for Jonathan to speak. The kitchen bore all the hallmarks of baking; of Lucy in home-maker mode.

"They think he may have taken her...after a struggle in the bedroom." He stared hard at the stone floor; taking in nothing.

"We don't know it was him." regretting the words; as soon as he uttered them; Bradley could have bitten his tongue with regret at his impetuous comment.

"Well WHO THE HELL ELSE would have wanted to kidnap Lucy; for FUCK SAKE Bradley?"

Dark thoughts crossed both their minds as Jonathan spoke; he was trembling and visibly trying to hold back tears.

"Let it go. It's just you and me mate. We'll find the Bastard; whatever it takes. Look at me Jon'."

Jonathan lifted his eyes to meet Bradley head on.

"He's not interested in Lucy. He wants 'Schultz. We know that from the 'phone messages which Dan received before we put him in a safe house."

"We'll give the Bastard what he wants and get Lucy back; whatever it takes."

Jonathan sipped his tea. The house was cold as forensics and specialist officers went about their work. The fire in the snug had long since gone out.

"You said the back door was open when you got back Jon': *had it been forced?"*

Jonathan didn't answer at first. "Yeah, I mean the door was open and one of her shoes was outside on the garden path; near the back gate."

"The police bagged it as soon as I'd identified it as Lucy's. I recognised it immediately: she'd bought them in Highgate Village barely a month ago."

Bradley put a hand on Jonathan's shoulder as he stood up and headed to the back door. The sturdy dead-lock and wooden frame had not been disturbed.

An expert job if that had been the mode of entry. There was no reason to assume otherwise. Similarly, It would almost certainly have been the exit route.

A uniformed Policeman stood at the back gate; which lead onto a small laneway: big enough for a car or van to park up without attracting much attention thought Bradley. Several of the other residents had cars parked up and the Police were already performing house to house enquires as the residents began arriving home from work.

Bradley returned to the kitchen.

There had to be at least two of them involved Bradley surmised: one to extract Lucy and one standing stag to ensure no nosey neighbours interfered. It was hard to envisage that Lucy would go quietly, so they had to have sedated her. The lost shoe was consistent with a rear exit strategy and a van would offer the security and privacy they needed.

The two of them sat huddled in conversation as Jonathan slowly recounted his actions earlier in the evening. Leaving the office by taxi only to return to an unusually cold house; the back door open and signs of Lucy's interrupted cooking. No sign of *Ginger the cat* and then when Jonathan went into their bedroom, the blood on the duvet. *That's when he had called Bradley*: first thought, first action.

"CHRIST!" shouted Jonathan as he suddenly sprang up; spilling his remaining tea as his discarded mug rolled onto the tiled floor and smashed into large fragments.

He ran into the hallway and stormed up the stairs, Bradley followed him somewhat bewildered by the sudden outburst.

Two masked forensics scientists dressed from head to toe in white overalls were carefully putting the duvet into a large clear forensic evidence bag when Jonathan ran headlong into the bedroom; narrowly missing *Dr Irma White-Law*, who looked visibly startled by Jonathan's sudden appearance.

In his enthusiasm, Jonathan almost tripped over as his leg caught the corner of the bed frame in his haste to get to Lucy's dressing table which stood in front of the window.

"WHERE IS IT?!!" yelled Jonathan as he began frantically pulling out drawers and discarding contents over the floor.

"*'Jon' what is it*?" called Bradley from the entrance to the bedroom; not wanting to further contaminate the crime scene and disrupt the vital work of the forensics team.

"*MR CLARKE*! Exclaimed Dr White-Law expressing her exasperation from behind her face-mask, in a stern voice.

"Please, you really *must allow us to do our job*."

After ransacking the drawers he seemed satisfied. With almost a hysterical tone in his voice Jonathan shouted:

"Lucy's new green broach it's not here; she MUST be wearing it."

"But what does that have to do with..." Bradley's question was cut short.

"I put a fucking *tracker* in it!!"

"We'd planned a skiing holiday in the Alps for the second week of March: *there's no way I wanted to lose her in the deep snow*!"

Chapter 24

20:25 Thursday 26th January

"Did I ever tell you, you're a fucking genius Jon'!" Bradley gave him a mock punch on his right shoulder.

Jonathan sat beside him silently in the back of the unmarked car; his face a picture of anguish. In between taking swigs from his bottle of sparkling water he began chewing the nails of his right fingers. A childhood habit which had long since extinguished itself until Lucy's abduction.

"Well I didn't foresee any of this when I asked for your help."

The car lurched as George accelerated briskly past a string of cars. He glanced in his rear-view mirror and chipped in to the conversation:

"The butterfly broach you bought Lucy is obviously sending a good signal Jonathan: the lead car on the M3 is keeping its distance, as instructed".

Always the master of understatement George was cool headed and a tough ally; having worked with Bradley on a number of surveillance, arrest and detainment operations at home and on foreign soil. He had worked for Special Forces in Australia for ten years before moving to British Security Services. His modest demeanour concealed his steely grit and determination to get the job done.

"We haven't deployed the chopper yet as we don't want to spook the driver. The van was reported stolen earlier today by a plumbing Company in Central London. It has a small insignia on the side so is unmistakable when combined with the registration. We're tracking progress using gantry cameras and they're two up in the front seat, so Lucy must be in the back of the van."

George exited the M40 joining the M25 London Orbital Motorway anticlockwise: heading Southbound towards Junction 12 for the M3 Motorway Exit. The sirens wailed and the busy evening traffic parted like the waves before the bow of a ship as the unmarked three car BMW cavalcade from the Security Services weaved through traffic in close formation.

The lead car was tracking detailed progress of the suspect vehicle which was heading down the M3 in heavy evening traffic and relaying back to Control.

The unmarked Police pursuit team were in already in place behind the lead car on the M3; awaiting final instructions to move in for a hard stop.

"He surely must be planning to hole up somewhere." said Bradley, above the grunt of the German made engine as George made short work of passing a large articulated lorry in the BMW M5.

Bradley checked his emails and texts. "We've had no further update from Russia yet."

"*As long as Lucy's okay; that's all I care about*." said Jonathan staring out of the window. As an afterthought he added: "*What about Dr Schultz*?"

"*Henry has just updated me by text*: Schultz' is in a car with a heavily armed tactical team standing by."

"*Like I said: whatever it takes Jon'*."

"How are you holding up mate?" asked Bradley, switching his attention back to Jonathan.

"I just need this to be over; I can't believe Lucy has got mixed up in all this crap."

"I hear you loud and clear but none of us could have predicted this."

"That means he's acting unpredictably then, *maybe irrationally*?"

"I didn't say that; he's a planner this creep. Sending me off to Leicester Square was obviously a decoy; he's smart and he knows that Lucy is his only bargaining chip. He won't hurt her."

George responded to a message in his earpiece as they joined the M3 Motorway heading Southbound.

"Roger that: *Alpha one*. Siren off. *Delta one out*."

"We are only three miles behind the target vehicle and closing fast." George smiled and added: "Not long now guys; the pursuit team are standing by. The motorway traffic is being slowed a few miles ahead of the target vehicle; it'll be easier to contain at low speed for a hard stop.

Tango One is ready to move in close; *Alpha One's* instructed us to turn off sirens in case there's a spotter anywhere along the route.

Alpha One sat in the control room monitoring progress. *Chief Inspector Liam Carter* was a steady-hand at the tiller, having worked in traffic division for the best part of twelve years. Standing next to him was *Henry Davidson* from Security Services [UK Head of Operations].

Tango Two and *Tango Three* moved into position with eyes on the target vehicle [*Xray One*] which was moving down the outside lane of the M3 motorway heading South. Having passed through road-works, the van was making steady progress in the evening rush hour. *Alpha one* was issuing instructions to the thee unmarked police vehicles some three miles ahead of them; Henry Davidson remained silent.

Chapter 25

Thursday 26th January 2017

21:15 Southbound carriageway of M3 Motorway, UK

Victor checked his rear-view mirror again, this time he was sure; they were being followed. The dark German saloon had now been on his tail for over five miles. There would be others. Time to make his move.

In the distance up ahead, he could see a broken down vehicle in the nearside emergency lane; hazard lights flashing.

Timing would be critical.

The outside overtaking lane was moving quickly and as a convoy of cars passed Victor seized his chance. From the inside lane he accelerated out in front of an articulated lorry in the middle lane, seconds before it was about to overtake him, and he braked hard: predictably with no where to go, the lorry raced up behind him sounded his horn then slammed on his brakes. Victor accelerated into the outside lane as *Rudolph* sat next to him, *grabbed the handrail*; sensing the unfolding drama.

In his left wing mirror he could see the rear end of the lorry start to jack-knife across the inside lane. But Victor had only just begun.

Accelerating again Victor cut recklessly back into the middle lane using the van as a battering ram and forcing a pick-up driver to veer left into the nearside lane. Following cars caught the rear end of the pick-up truck and began to concertina; five cars collided end to end as the pick-up turned over blocking the lane. Victor accelerated hard, struggling to steer the van as he swung left then right in front of an estate car on the middle lane of traffic. The driver reacted slowly and as the estate veered hard right into the central barrier causing the two lanes of traffic to snarl up as cars ploughed into the back and sides of the car. All three lanes were at a standstill behind him.

Victor checked his rear view mirror and a plume of smoke was visible cascading across the motorway as multiple flashing blue Police lights immediately lit up the eventide traffic mayhem.

Victor smiled arrogantly and let out a guttural laugh as Rudolph slapped him on the back and took a swig of whisky. Narrowly missing the broken down vehicle on the hard shoulder, he floored the accelerator and the van swerved taking out several cones as he struggled to stay planted on the wet slip road as he exited the Motorway. He drove hard left through the red traffic lights; narrowly missing an on-coming motorcyclist which swerved to avoid him, sending the rider sliding across the road to a hail of horns as motorists took evasive action and the motorcyclist lived to ride another day; as his leathers mercifully took the impact and allowed him to slide along the wet road.

Victor turned off the van's head lights and accelerated up the road and through a set of traffic lights before checking his satellite navigation and turning left into a near deserted residential road; illuminated only by intermittent dim street lights.

Driving slowly down past each house in turn he checked his rear view mirror and could see no signs that anyone had followed their vehicle. He pulled up outside a large extended house with no visible lights on inside. A four-by-four stood on the driveway. Perfect. He drove past the vehicle into the rear aspect of the front drive, close to the front of the house. *Rudolph* was out of the van in one bound and got to work on the four-by-four as it sat on the driveway.

Five minutes later, tailgate open and car engine idling, Victor transferred the bulky package into the rear compartment of the car and they drove slowly out of the drive. Victor heard sirens and could see an ambulance racing through the lights at the junction as he drove straight across the intersection; waiting for the satellite navigation on the aged Toyota to kick in.

He speed dialled as he drove; *"Hello"* said a voice at the end of the phone.

"We have the package; change of plan, we had company. Different transport arranged. We will head for the agreed location and await your orders."

"Good. When do you estimate?"

"I guess less than an hour."

"Don't fuck up." The phone went dead.

"Arrogant BASTARD!" croaked Rudolph; swigging more whiskey. Victor took the bottle and took a large swig for himself as he slowed for oncoming traffic.

Overhead they could hear a helicopter as the rain began to beat down on his windscreen. Victor switched the wipers upwards selecting fast mode and tried to look up as he drove. He checked his speed and slowed down from 45 m.p.h. to a sedate 35m.p.h., not wanting to attract any undue attention. The chopper was heading away from their direction of travel. Only the hypnotic sound of the wipers and the swish of rain, as it rhythmically cleared from the windscreen broke the silence.

Victor turned on the radio and tuned into the *Hampshire* travel update:

"M3 closed southbound by a multi-vehicle accident.....air ambulance expected on scene."

He smiled to himself, *"that should keep them busy for a while."*

Rudolph listened for any noise coming from the package in the rear of the car; nothing. The dose of intravenous hypnotic had done the job; *just as Alexei had instructed*. They didn't call Alexei *"The butcher"* without reason; he mused.

The results of his work brought admiration, even amongst their own Serbian community at home who knew little of the Russian, except by word of mouth reputation.

Chapter 26

22:30 Hampshire

None of this made sense unless she was a hostage. Lucy struggled in vain; unable to loosen the ties fastened around her wrists. Darkness prevailed around her taught body. She told herself this was a nightmare: willing herself to wake up.

Suddenly it all felt very real. The vehicle shuddered and she was thrown back and forth, winding her; making it harder for her to breath with the tape over her mouth. Lucy forced herself to breath calmly through her nose for she feared she might suffocate.

There was no doubt anymore in her mind: she was being driven over rough ground and her mobile prison was lurching left and right and she could feel the wheels spinning and slipping somewhere under her head.

A huge jolt left her fighting to breathe. A sudden stabbing pain in her head grew in intensity as warm fluid began trickling into her left eye. Deep guttural voices were raised in the front of the car, arguing in a tongue she did recognise. A thunderous noise grew louder from somewhere in the distance. Then she could hear it more clearly; the sound of a helicopter, coming closer; deafeningly loud. She yearned to cover her ears and wake up from this living nightmare.

In spite of the blindfold, she was aware of the light: moving closer yet coming and going as the vehicle continued to shudder and lurch haphazardly left; then right.

Lucy tried to calm her breathing again as her mouth started to fill with a metallic taste; *she was sure it was her blood.* She swallowed hard and tried to visualise Jonathan but that made her panic more, thinking she might never see him again. She focused her mind to visualise *Ginger* sat in front of the warm fire, in the snug. She pictured his long whiskers and patted the black and white fur on his head as he purred contentedly.

The vehicle lurched hard again and suddenly she heard an ear splitting bang as the vehicle collided with an unseen obstacle. Almost in slow motion she felt the car roll and her neck was twisted as her knees came crashing into her face; Lucy felt her chest compressed and she fought hard to take a last deep breath as her hands were forced upward by the impact; just far enough up to tear the corner of the tape away from her mouth. She gasped and struggled to breathe; her chest heaving. Her head was swimming wildly and darkness surrounded her once more.

Lucy's shoulders were hunched up around her head as she lay crumpled. Summoning her strength, she fought frantically to remove the rest of the tape from her mouth.

She froze as she heard a door opening ahead of her and shouting which grew louder. She knew they must be clambering out of the front seats as the vehicle was on its side.

An icy cold wind washed over her as she heard the hatchback door above her prised open. Lucy screamed and kicked hard as hands took her feet and arms.

A stern, calm, frigid voice commanded her from above:

"Don't struggle and you live."

"We must move you quickly." Victor growled in a tongue foreign to hear ears which were still ringing from the car's impact against a large boulder. A pungent familiar smell filled her nostrils.

Lucy was manhandled by two sets of hands from the car, then large muscular arms slung her over someone's shoulder as if she were a rag doll: shortly afterwards her hands were cut loose; flailing in the dark.

The blind fold remained over her eyes and Lucy shouted but her scream was inaudible over the sound of the explosion from the car as they stumbled away. She felt the sudden intense heat wave flash over her body and she imagined it was akin to a Tsunami in its ferocity as the pressure wave rolled over them. But the heat was short lived as they ran on into the frigid night.

Heavy footsteps followed her and she realised it was just the three of them as she'd surmised. The blindfold was slipping from her eyes and she could see flashes of woodland and suddenly it was back; the bright beacon of light; flashing across the undergrowth, blinding as it bounced off the corner of her eye. She screwed her eyes up tightly trying to protect her night vision just as Bradley had taught her when they went night fishing in Italy together: just the three of them.

The man following closely behind them suddenly tripped and she heard his voice, now angry, his tone harsh. "FUCK!" he cried out angrily as he hauled himself back up from the ground and began running to catch them up.

Lucy's head knocked against a tree and her heart was pounding and she feared she would pass out from the weariness she felt throughout her body; she could feel more blood trickling down her face now as she thrashed against her captor's back. Instinct told her to remain calm; whatever they'd given her explained her drowsiness and fatigue.

The overhead search-light was evidently trying to pinpoint them; as they began running through the dense woodland.

She tried clenching her fists to restore circulation, but they felt weak; she had pins and needles in both her hands and her fingers felt numb with the cold. Her right shoulder was painful and her legs felt listless. She could not tell how long she'd been unconscious but it was cold and dark and she was being held captive by two strong men. The Police were obviously searching overhead: it was the only plausible explanation.

But why her? They had no money to pay for a ransom….this must be some terrible mistake she consoled herself. Unless, could this somehow be related to Jonathan's work? So many questions flooded her brain.

She blocked her thoughts and concluded her best course of action was to do nothing; and wait. Bide her time and stay as calm as her body would allow. Her basic Biology from school days told her she was in *flight or fight mode*: adrenaline was coursing through her veins.

Rain began falling heavily around them, and Lucy began to shiver as the cold pierced her woollen jumper. The arm around her tightened and suddenly they were swiftly gaining ground, weaving through long grass like a threshing machine at harvest time.

Lucy's nose kept bumping against the waistline and belt worn by her abductor and she recognised he was wearing camouflage trousers. She'd laundered Bradley's for him on many an occasion when he'd come home for R&R with them.

She could smell the musty scent of damp clothing and hear the squelch of his boots in the muddy pools as they veered across the open farmland. She could hear cows in the distance and detect their distinct sweet faecal odour. The men ran on in silence and she concentrated on relaxing; biding her time.

A mobile phone started to ring and buzz simultaneously; it was in the trouser pocked of the man carrying her. He ignored it and pressed on; tightening his grip on her and fore warning: "*Hold on tight*"; as they descended a slippery bank. All at once she could hear the sound of a river; fast flowing. She held her breath expecting cold water but instead they had stopped and turning abruptly, and were evidently following the river along its bank.

Overhead, Lucy could hear thunder in the distance as the rain grew harder. The raindrops stung her eyes as she tried to lean her head up to look behind them. Her neck hurt and she willed herself to relax. They were running uphill again and she could hear the men starting to breathe more heavily as they began to slip on the muddy banks of the river.

Suddenly they started to fall backwards, it all felt surreal as her captor lurched in the darkness and unexpectedly she was jolted free of the hand around her thigh. She fell backwards in the darkness her head striking the cold mud and could hear the water gushing down-stream behind her. She scrambled free in the thick mud as the man toppled and she half-crawled, half dragged herself towards the sound of the water. She kicked back at hands trying to grab her legs and ran headlong into the water which rapidly engulfed her in a swirling sea with icy torrents of terrifying ferocity which stole her breath.

She kicked up and taking a deep breath she swam back underwater, using every ounce of strength she kicked with her feet and pushed her hands ahead of her, ensuring she didn't hit anything. The water was freezing and she gulped again before being dragged under by the unseen unyielding current. She swam hard and as fast as the current would allow her, gulping when she could.

This was her chance; she was determined to be free again.

Her right ankle felt wrenched and entwined in unseen undergrowth and she kicked out and was released again. She surfaced and took long gasps as the water lapped over her head. She couldn't hear anything except the sound of water, growing louder until it threatened to deafen her ears; the current was strong and she sensed danger; instinctively she veered right and kicked out but was dragged by the current now tumbling in deep water.

She reached out frantically with her outstretched fingers as she kicked again trying to force herself towards the bank, but the force of the water propelled her on and down underwater. Her lungs were bursting as she tried to hold the remnants of her breath. The deafening sound in her ears grew louder and she felt sure she was in mortal danger. Her heart was slowing and keeping beat like a tribal drum in her ears.

Something sharp stabbed her face and she let go the last of her breath and gulped in freezing cold water. Instinctively she circled her arms all around her and grasped something tethered to the river bank. She clung on for dear life, kicking and pulling herself with her arms, inch by inch along the branch as it pierced her skin, dragging herself towards the water's edge; gasping for air.

The cold air hit her face like an ice pick as she began to crawl out of the water's edge. She lay exhausted, coughing and panting for breath, barely able to move; all the time aware of the crashing sound of water up ahead and all around her.

A torrent of water was spraying around her head and a blinding light overhead stole her remaining vision as the giant hovering black bird whipped up leaves and bushes. She froze and covered her eyes with her arms. Her body shuddered and her legs buckled as she tried to stand. Everything grew dark as her head started to swim and lights flashed in front of her eyes. Then she was flying closer to the bird, closer to its open mouth; only to be consumed by the greedy predator as it growled and flew on to its nest.

Tortured demons prevailed in her head as she lost consciousness.

Chapter 27

23:35 Hampshire

"But have they found Lucy *alive*?"

Silence as George listened into the transmission.

"Alpha One: please repeat over. Delta One received: you have apprehended two suspects; both male? Over" clarified George.

"Roger that. Delta One out." said George; turning to Jonathan.

"They've picked up two guys from the four-by-four. Lucy's not with them and they're saying nothing." He looked concerned and sat quietly whilst Jonathan digested the latest update on his mobile.

"How could it all go so BLOODY wrong?" swore Jonathan, punching the side of the car with frustration. 'And how come *fucking blondie* is not *with them? Does he have her now?"*

"Unlikely mate, the Police think she may have escaped. Her tracker stopped working near the site they picked up the suspects; they were near a river, so she may have made a break for it. They are searching the area with spotlights; they'll find her. She's a bloody good swimmer. Remember how she put us both to shame on that holiday in Greece; made us look like bloody school-kids!"

George set off again as he received a new set of coordinates over his headpiece.

"Roger that. Delta One out."

"They've given us a location guys." George turned on the siren and hit the accelerator. *'Be there in thirty."*

The heavy rain pounded the windscreen and Jonathan could only think of how cold Lucy must be; alone and frightened. His heart pounded and he felt sickened to the core. He wanted to vomit, but he suppressed the urge and took a swig of water and closed his eyes. He picked up his small black case of medication and insulin; thought for a moment, then replaced it in the seat compartment without taking any of his regular meds.

George swore as someone pulled out in front of the car; forcing him to brake heavily and swerve left then right as he continued on down the narrow country road. He switched to full beam and listened into his earpiece as he received further directions.

Gravel flew up as George decelerated and executed a rapid "U-turn" before retracing the road to the T-junction and heading left. He accelerated rapidly again and overhead came the familiar sound of a helicopter flying low in the heavy rain.

Jonathan craned his neck down to look up into the sky and whispered a silent prayer.

Chapter 28

00:35: Friday 27th January 2017: Accident & Emergency Department

Royal Alderton Hospital, Hampshire

"Lucy, I'm Dr Redfield. You're perfectly safe now; I don't want you to worry about anything. My team will take good care of you. We are giving you some oxygen through your face mask and warming up your body slowly with a space blanket."

"The Army Helicopter which brought you into us took very good care of you. I realise it must have been very alarming all the same: the water you swam in was clearly ice cold."

"There's an infusion of glucose in your left arm which will help restore your circulation. You have a head injury and facial cuts; but they're not serious. We will need to carry out some further tests and keep you in hospital; but you should make a full recovery."

"Do you need a pain killer?" asked a nurse to her left.

Lucy shook her head slowly, trying to take in the scene around her; her head was throbbing in time with the heart monitor in the background. She looked back at the Doctor, and tried to speak; but the words didn't come out.

Dr Redfield sensed her request none the less.

"Your husband is on his way; he knows you're safe."

Lucy's eyes welled up and she could not see anything but swirling faces; she started to sob uncontrollably and she felt a warm hand grip her right hand and gently squeeze her over the space blanket she was wrapped in.

"Don't worry Lucy, I am here and will stay with you until your husband arrives. *My name is Amanda; I'm a staff nurse. Your husband is called Jonathan I believe?"*

Lucy nodded. It was the best she could do.

"Lucy we understand you've had quite an ordeal, but try to relax and sleep now until you feel stronger;" continued Amanda with a kind reassuring voice. "The doctor will give you something to help you relax now."

Very little made sense to her; whisked from the safety and security of her home to God knows where by two men. What had they done to her and why? She had so many questions but her head felt heavy and she could not focus her thoughts. Lucy started to drift away mentally; she tried to draw comfort from the cacophony of bleeps and buzzing monitors. The monsters came back into her dreams, wearing combats and leering down at her motionless, defenceless body as it lay next to a torrent of raging water.

Chapter 29

07:45 Friday 27th January 2017

Ward 5: Royal Alderton Hospital

Jonathan sat by her bedside, cradling her right hand. The small ball of cotton wool fastened with white tape on her left hand was the only evidence of the drip recently removed from Lucy's hand by Amanda. Lucy's fingernails were dirty and broken. Cuts and grazes on her hands and forearms were mirrored by bruises on her chin and face. Her scalp was largely hidden by bandaging. The skin around her mouth was red and grazed and her lips chapped.

She had lay sleeping peacefully for hours only to suddenly jerk and writhe as if tortured by some unseen enemy; amid screams and whimpers in equal measure.

'*God knows what she'd suffered*. Jonathan thought of home and Ginger, and wondered where he must be. He prayed against the odds, that Ginger too would be okay; Lucy loved him like the child she had never borne, he was quite simply part of the family.

Amanda popped her head around the door of the room.

"*Good morning Jonathan. How are you*? Can I get you a cup of tea before we hand-over?"

Jonathan smiled and nodded: "*Thank you, you're a star.*" His voice was weary but his tone appreciative.

Lucy moved and turned over onto her right side, wincing before slowly opening her eyes momentarily.

"*Good morning sleepy head....*" said Jonathan gently, moving closer to her as he spoke.

Lucy smiled and looked towards Jonathan; trying to focus on his face. She couldn't speak but simply grasped his hand and squeezed it tightly in her own.

"Rest Lucy, don't try to talk now." said Jonathan; as he gently touched her left cheek.

She closed her eyes again and slept again.

Dr John Redfield appeared at the door and walked quietly up to Jonathan.

"We will arrange a scan of Lucy's head this morning Mr Clarke; just to be sure there's no internal injury following Lucy's ordeal."

"We will be ready to examine Lucy and review her progress in a minute or two if that's okay with you?"

Jonathan gave a brief smile and nodded affirmatively.

An Armed Police Officer approached Bradley as walked through the automatic doors and approached Lucy's room. The Officer scrutinised Bradley's identity card before knocking twice on the door. After a few moments Jonathan came out and shook Bradley's hand; before they went slowly up the corridor in search of the visitors' coffee bar. As they left, a small huddle of doctors and nurses had assembled outside Lucy's room: morning ward rounds were already well underway.

Bradley sat down next to Jonathan armed with two coffees and four croissants, each plate accompanied by a small pot of raspberry jam.

"Tuck in mate." encouraged Bradley; cognoscente that Jonathan had barely eaten in the last twenty-four hours.

They ate silently watching a steady trickle of visitors and staff heading for their early morning refreshment. Bradley checked his watch: 8:15 a.m.

"Right that's better. *How is Lucy doing*?"

"She's still resting. The doctor gave her night sedation; she was distressed last night when we arrived."

"*She looks so...vulnerable*. God knows what she's been through. She'll have a scan later this morning, to rule out internal damage."

"*Well that's great mate*. They'll take real good care of her, don't worry. Lucy is fit and strong; more than a match for a few cuts and scrapes."

Jonathan looked deep in thought again.

"Well we know this much mate; she got away from those bastards and swam for her life – literally. *Thank the Lord* she got out of the water when she did, *she came damn close to that weir*. "

"*Blondie is nowhere to be found and the two bastards that held her are saying nothing.*"

"I've sent their mug-shots to Vladimir this morning; hopefully he can cast some light on their identities. Their mug-shots and prints have also gone to Interpol via the police."

"When they were lifted they were clean; no identities; PAYG mobiles. They sound ex-military."

"*Scumbags*." said Jonathan; looking weary: finally responding with a sigh.

"Why not get some rest Jon'; I can sit with Lucy if you like?"

"I want my face to be the first thing she sees when she's wide awake Bradley. She opened her eyes just before you arrived and promptly went back to sleep."

"Best thing for her; *rest and recuperation*!" Bradley replied, giving Jonathan a playful punch.

"Followed by a bloody stiff Gin and Tonic, as soon as she's back home Jon'!"

"That makes *three* of us." Jonathan replied with a chuckle.

"That's the spirit mate!" smiled Bradley, just as Jonathan reciprocated with a firm punch.

Bradley got a refill of their coffee cups and they sat quietly; Jonathan's eyelids starting to close between sips of coffee.

"Bloody hell, I needed that. Just like old times 'eh Bradley; shit coffee and no sleep."

Jonathan jumped as a fire alarm above his head began ringing with a fury all of its own.

"Shit, now what?" groaned Jonathan. *"Of all the bloody times..."*

"Yep: probably a test." They waited but the klaxon continued to ring.

"Okay let's go Jon'." Bradley barked with a sudden sense of urgency as he jumped up. He was already heading for the door and Jonathan caught up with him as he headed for the stair case.

"So do you think there's real fire Bradley?"

"I hope that's all it is." came the cryptic reply.

They waited impatiently at the ward entrance for the nurse to buzz them onto the ward.

Amanda waved and let them through the security doors, calling back to them:

"The fire-brigade is on the way; the panel shows a problem in an adjacent supplies building. *We should be fine, so don't worry.*"

They headed along the corridor past the nurses' station and turned left towards Lucy's room. The armed policeman was no longer stood outside her room. Looking perplexed, Jonathan barged through the door; his jaw dropped. Lucy's bed was empty. He checked her en-suite toilet: empty.

Bradley was ahead of him; searching for Amanda. Jonathan found Dr Redfield on his rounds.

"*We're booking a scan now Mr Clarke*, one of my juniors is on the case; so Lucy should still be in her bed....." His voice trailed off as Jonathan dashed back up the corridor in search of Bradley.

Bradley was quizzing Amanda outside one of the four bedded bays; worry graven into his facial features. He caught Jonathan's eye and headed back up the ward.

"*Okay let's do a sweep of the ward; where the hell is Lucy's guard*?"

Two minutes later Amanda rushed up to Bradley on the ward.

"The door to the ward toilet is unlocked but the door is wedged closed." said Amanda. "One of the patient's may have collapsed inside."

"LUCY?!!" shrieked Jonathan; knocking loudly on the door.

Bradley stepped forward and heaved the door open as Amanda pushed the emergency buzzer to summon medical help.

The Policeman lay face down on the floor; barely conscious. His firearm was nowhere to be seen.

Chapter 30

11:05 Ward 5

The SMS on Bradley's phone read:

"I have her. My only interest is Schultz. This time: NO mistakes."

Bradley read the text: He called the mobile. No response.

"That bastard Blondie." he heard himself say out loud. He handed the phone to Jonathan who looked pale and miserable as he sat in the Hospital corridor; outside what had been Lucy's room just a few hours earlier.

Bradley marched down the corridor in search of the Hospital Manager and found him in Amanda's office.

"We need to examine the hospital CCTV cameras *now*."

Bradley stood squarely in front of the *Alastair Long*, who stood impassively in his grey pin striped suit and responded haughtily:

"There are procedures to be followed."

Bradley turned around briefly to watch Amanda as she set off down the corridor, ready to lock Lucy's room to preserve vital evidence.

Bradley lowered his voice and took a further step towards Alastair Long: clearly invading his personal space.

"I made this request over an hour ago. This is highly likely to be an abduction of a vulnerable adult. If you want to keep your job and good looks; I suggest you make it happen *now*."

"There are serious consequences for threatening hospital staff; we have a zero tolerance to..."

Bradley could feel his blood starting to boil and the pulses in his neck grow stronger. He clenched his fists and forced his knuckles down into his trouser pockets in shear frustration.

"Let me stop you right there buddy. If you don't cut through your red tape right now, *I will make it my mission in life...*"

Bradley felt a hand on his right shoulder; Jonathan stood behind him.

"*They've found Lucy's wheelchair Bradley.*" He exclaimed breathlessly.

Chapter 31

11:20 Short Stay Car Park

"He discarded the wheelchair 'once he'd put Lucy in the back of the transit; the guys in Forensics are working on it now. We have a partial index on the van's number plate. The rear bumper was already damaged. We've got cars on each of the main arterial routes in and out of the area. An armed response team is on standby and a mobile team has Dr Schultz."

Having updated them on the getaway vehicle, George exited the car park drove steadily to the hospital exit.

Outside the hospital George parked up in a lay-by and they waited in silence. Jonathan held his head in his hands and dug into nails into an imaginary scab on his scalp. His whole body ached with the agony of loosing Lucy. Bradley looked long and hard at him; he appeared as though all the zest for life had been sucked out of him.

How could they have lost his beloved Lucy for a second time?

Bradley stood in the drizzling rain using his mobile phone; trying to piece together next steps with Henry Davidson. The Policeman who had been guarding Lucy had almost certainly received a large blow to the back of his head. He was already undergoing surgery to remove a life threatening intracranial haematoma: a large clot pressing on his brain.

The CCTV camera on the ward had been inactivated at the time of Lucy's abduction.

Bradley checked his watch then headed swiftly in and out of a local convenience store where he stocked up with water, iced coffee cans and a variety of snacks and chocolate bars.

Bradley climbed back into the front seat; alongside George. A text pinged on his phone. *Map coordinates from Blondie.* Bradley forwarded the text to Henry Davidson who was in the control room: having now taken command of the operation.

George listened as instructions were relayed through his earpiece; he punched the details into the sat nav.

"*Roger that Delta One out.*" Right let's nail this bastard, once and for all." He hit the accelerator as the rain started to fall more heavily; part-clearing, part-smearing the pigeon excrement which had accumulated on the windscreen.

Jonathan lay across the back seat; Bradley's overcoat spread over him. His dreams had now transformed into nightmares. He tossed and turned as the car sped through the heavy traffic with the blue beacon flashing, George was taking no prisoners as he made swift progress.

Chapter 32

16:40 Dorset

George slowed to a snail's pace as the road suddenly narrowed to form a single track, barely wide enough for a car to snake through. The road was bounded by tall hedges and overhanging willowy trees which interlaced in parts, creating a virtual canopy. The light was fading fast and George adjusted his lights to full beam. The teaming rain created a drum roll on the roof of the car and Jonathan sat up with a jump, yawning and stretching; trying to relieve the knot in the nape of his neck.

They emerged onto a gravel drive and immediately ahead of them a large unlit dark red brick Georgian house slowly emerged from the thick veil of darkness which shrouded the property as the light from the car's headlights swept over the property.

George slowed their approach to walking pace as they surveyed the scene. In front of the main entrance to the house, a transit was visible, parked up, the rear doors open wide; a damaged rear bumper visible as they draw nearer. The license plate tallied with the CCTV from the hospital short stay parking bay.

George stopped three car lengths behind the transit and looked for any signs of activity: nothing. A dense copse of woodland formed the backdrop to the property and there were no visible outbuildings.

George edged forwards and slowly implemented a wide U-turn; passing initially in front of the house, giving Bradley eyes on the front entrance; before they completed the one-eighty degree turn and parked up on the far side of the van, shielding them from direct vision and giving them cover; just in case they needed a quick exit from the drive. George parked close enough to prevent the driver from easily accessing the cab to the transit.

They sat in silence for a moment as Bradley text an update to Henry, whilst George spoke into his mouthpiece; checking his automatic weapon as he did so. In the rear of the car, Jonathan looked agitated and began to chew his bottom lip nervously. Bradley wondered about the state of Jonathan's blood sugar; he'd barely eaten or slept and the stress must have been playing havoc with his diabetes.

(So much for enhanced control of his blood sugar by the addition of twice daily insulin shots; which his GP had insisted would optimise his long term health.)

(Jonathan had refused to use his injectable insulin while Lucy was absent. Opting instead for his simple daily oral dose of metformin. He was fully aware that he was unlikely to experience a very low blood sugar which many diabetics feared more than anything; [a *"hypo=hypoglycaemia", which might lead to unconsciousness in the absence of a well planned calorie intake*]: whilst taking his single oral tablet once a day.)

George relayed instructions from Henry: they were to wait for back up.

Bradley handed Jonathan a selection of chocolate bars and he chose a Kit-Kat and munched swiftly through the four chocolate fingers before drinking a few mouthfuls of sparkling Welsh water from one of the collection Bradley had left in the rear footwell.

George declined food or water and they sat quietly listening as Jonathan selected a Mars Bar which went the way of the Kit-Kat: munched down with water. He saved the remaining bars for Lucy's benefit: he was sure she'd be ravenous by the time they rescued her.

"For once the bloody weather is on our side. Right I will go in through the front entrance George and once I am inside, you find a rear entry point; it should be dark enough for you to get around without drawing too much attention. Once inside I will play for time; we don't want any dramas before back up arrives. You concentrate on locating Lucy; we'll secure her release together."

"Jonathan, you stay put, ready for a quick extraction; *God willing.*"

They sat where they were, windows down; listening for any signs that their arrival had stirred up any activity outside the house. After five long minutes, they had heard only the sound of raindrops falling on the car roof. George closed the windows.

Jonathan broke the tension with the question on everyone's mind: "*Where the fuck is everyone*? That rain is like bloody water torture."

"All this waiting around doesn't feel right." said George.

"Fuck this" said Bradley and sent a text to Blondie; "We're outside."

"Come in ALONE;" came the brisk text response.

"Yeah and fuck you too Blondie. Okay, remember I'm going in alone Jon' *with George as back up: no heroics from you.*

If Lucy see's you she'll freak out and he'll manipulate the situation. Stay in the car mate and wait for back up."

George got out of the car and spoke to Bradley out of earshot of Jonathan, then he crouched down between the front wing of the car and rear of the van as Bradley headed for the house. Jonathan sat back with only grizzly visions for company.

Darkness fully engulfed the house as Bradley walked briskly across the loose gravel on the drive to the front door and rang the large white button marked: *Bell*.

He waited; there was no movement in either of the bay windows on either side of the front door. He glanced up; the first floor windows were all undisturbed; curtains closed. Minutes later he heard a bolt pulled back and then silence. He waited, anticipating instructions; he would do nothing to endanger Lucy but needed to get on top of the situation quickly and without alarming her captors.

A clear voice shouted "COME IN." The voice was certainly not a Russian accent; *not* Blondie. That figures, there are at least two of them hosting this charade.

Bradley gripped the large wet wooden door knob on the ageing dark wood front door; it slipped in his hand as he turned it. The heavy door opened with a loud creak to reveal a cavernous dark void: the entrance hall. He walked in and closed the door behind him. Silence filled the house. The air smelled musty, evoking memories of family holidays in France when he was a teenager; long relaxing holidays filled with home cooking, leisurely hikes and open-air swimming. Times that had long since passed.

He had little time to develop his night vision before a voice commanded:

"Lie down on the floor with your hands behind your head. Spread your legs and don't move."

Bradley knelt and then lay face down on the cold tiled floor; he felt grit stippling his face and dust penetrating his nose. Either the owners were not house-proud or the house had been closed for a while.

Bradley kept looking left, away from the front door; in the direction of the rear of the house. Heavy footsteps walked up behind him; the sound of rubber boots on the tiled flooring.

"Are you armed Mr Jones?" asked a calm authoritative voice from behind his head: an Eastern European accent.

"No." Even as he replied Bradley felt a heavy boot land on his back and a trained hand patting him down.

"Where is Dr Schultz?" The heavy weight on his lumbar spine was swiftly replaced by a boot wedged painfully between his shoulder blades.

"He'll be here; with the cavalry."

"Where's Lucy?"

"Safe. She will be unharmed if you cooperate."

"And you'll be fucking dead if you harm a hair...."

"Don't waste your breath; our only interest is *'Schultz.'*"

"Is Lucy here?" pressed Bradley playing for time to enable George to get oriented and find Lucy.

"All in good time Mr Jones: she is your *friend's* wife, or so I understand." came the reply, in a mocking tone. "Maybe you have a *particular* interest in the sexy lady."

Bradley stayed silent; though he wanted to ram his fist down the bastard's throat. This guy was a wind up merchant and no mistake.

Two can play at that game.

"You seem to know a lot about me and my friends. What are you some kind of stalker?

No response.

"So have we met before Boris?"

"Maybe you think only the British have Intelligence sources Mr Jones?" the mocking continued; playing into Bradley's hands.

"I'm impressed; are you ex-FSB?"

"Does my accent *sound* Russian to you, Mr Jones?" he spat out the words with heavy sarcasm as he spoke; stamping his heavy boot on Bradley's back. "Now keep still or I will put a bullet in your head and you will never *hug* your *friend's wife again.*"

Bradley knew this dickhead's game; he was trying to provoke him; any excuse to doll out a good kicking. He was not about to give him an opportunity if he could help it: but he had to play for time.

"Don't you have anyone you care about Boris?" Bradley responded; in mocking retaliation.

"Surely somebody misses you when you don't come home at night?"

The heavy boot stomped twice on his back, winding him. Bradley lay gasping for breath all the time adjusting to the darkness. As he bent his chin to his chest, trying to appear more distressed than he felt, he could now clearly see a passage leading off to the rear of the property and there was a stairwell behind them just out of his peripheral vision.

"Oh dear, I hope I didn't hurt you Mr Jones?"

"Too much time in fancy hotels, chasing *pussy*?

"Maybe Boris, but at least I don't need to pay for mine!"

Boris understood that insult alright.

The stomping began again, four good heavy blows; but Bradley was ready for them, he braced himself. He knew the more time he distracted Boris, the more time George had to deliver a surprise welcome. Bradley started to cough, spitting blood from his split lip as he did so; writhing around a bit for good measure; surprised he was not yet hand cuffed. Our guys could teach this wannabe a thing or two.

Bradley felt something cold in the nape of his neck; a gun muzzle. Boris was astride him, his knees either side of his torso, digging in under his armpits and pinning him down as a hand grabbed his hair and yanked his head back, pushing the barrel deep under the base of his skull:

"Now if you want to play your little games, then say hello to my best friend which will blow your F-U-C-K-I-N-G head clean off!"

He heard the trigger cocked and hoped for his sake the bloody safety catch was still on.

The sudden searing pain in his scalp came without warning as Boris pistol whipped him ferociously. Bradley's head began to swim. He could smell Boris' putrid breath as he came down close to his left ear.

"What's the matter arsehole, cat got your tongue Mr Bradley Jones? *NOT..SO...CLEVER...NOW...*" the pistol whipping kept time with the words as he spat them out into Bradley's ear; like a human metronome. Stars filled the darkness before his eyes, his vision swirling as Bradley tried to focus again.

"Okay Boris, I get the message..."

Suddenly something moved swiftly in his peripheral vision. Bradley began coughing again and turned his head around to the right, towards the front door, doing his best to distract Boris.

Drawing in a couple of noisy deep breaths: "So what's the plan Boris; how do we do this?"

"We wait until your cowboy friends arrive."

"I am going to cuff you; if you move again I WILL KILL YOU ."

Cold steel clamped around his right wrist and cut into his flesh as it locked. His left arm was yanked up to meet his wrist and as he relaxed his shoulders Bradley felt Boris unexpectedly violently jerking backwards. George evidently had Boris in a choke hold. As his hands flailed, Bradley heard the gun slide across the tiles in the darkness; towards the door way.

Bradley twisted his body trying to loosen Boris' grip around his ribs and he grabbed out for Boris' flailing hands. The left hand smacked him hard on the back of the head and Bradley went down hard against the tiled floor; warm blood filling his mouth. George had his right arm secured around Boris' neck and was heaving backwards trying to choke Boris' bull-like neck. The vice-like grip loosened momentarily around Bradley, so he twisted around and bucked forward crashing his forehead into Boris' nose as hard as he could. He felt warm blood spatter over his face as skin sheared and bones crunched. Boris was spitting and bucking like a horse; his arms forced up to grab George.

Bradley twisted to the right and forced his left knee towards Boris' crotch as hard as he could; then he lay on his right side and kicked repeatedly into the thug's groin. Boris was now writhing and George was dragging him backwards and digging his left hand into his enemy's eyes, panting with the exertion. Boris reciprocated by digging into George's face with his right hand.

Bradley clambered to his feet, slipping on a pool of his own blood and started raining blows down into Boris' face, concentrating on his fractured nose and right eye as George continued to gouge his left.

Bradley stomped firmly into Boris' groin with all his might; he grabbed his short hair and kicked hard into his chest repeatedly.

George finally twisted the brute's neck with a fearsome crunch and as Boris' body began to flail limply, Bradley leapt over towards the door and scoured the floor for the pistol. He felt, as much as he heard, the slump of Boris' body on the floor. Bradley secured the gun and checked the safety catch was still applied, before releasing the cocked trigger.

They heaved and rolled Boris' huge body towards the far wall in the hallway; then checked the pockets. Nothing: no mobile or identification.

Momentarily exhausted, they sat against the wall, panting heavily and drawing breath as they were actively listening for any sound. An eerie silence ruled in the cold, damp darkness.

Where was their back-up? Bradley's heart was pounding and he checked everything was secure in his pockets before retrieving the pistol from his waist band.

The handcuffs hanging freely from his right wrist would have to wait until they got into the car for removal.

George stood and gestured behind him as Bradley motioned forward and headed towards the room ahead of him. He checked the room was empty and emerged just as George began moving slowly upstairs. The short staircase was covered in old dark threadbare carpet which silenced George's footsteps as he cautiously ascended the staircase, whilst Bradley waited at the bottom of the stairs, listening intently; safety catch off and trigger cocked.

Chapter 33

17:45

"So where the FUCK is Lucy Bradley?"

A sense of panic was beginning to grip Jonathan as he looked at the blood oozing from Bradley's lacerated head, face and lip.

Jonathan felt sick and he sat motionless in the back seat of the car; gripping the upholstery.

"And where are the rest of the team?"

George's face revealed the same preoccupation as he exchanged glances with Bradley; whilst Jonathan vented his frustration.

"Jon', she's alive and Blondie has her hidden somewhere."

"Our friend Boris was a diversion to make sure we were out of the picture; I'm sure of it. The rest of the house was empty but George recovered a mobile phone from one of the bedrooms. The text message exchanges from earlier in the evening are the only messages in the memory. No dialled calls, only one incoming mobile number: *it has to be Blondie's*. So he must be holed up somewhere else with Lucy; giving instructions."

Bradley wondered what on earth was taking so long with the exchange of Lucy for Schultz? What was Henry holding back from them?

Jonathan began to retch and got out of the car, steadying him-self against the transit as he did so. He stood, looking helpless before gulping a lung- full of the cold night air.

George retrieved the First Aid kit from the boot and dressed Bradley's wounds. He used a small pocket torch which he held in his mouth as he applied adhesive strips to seal the lacerations made by the pistol whipping Boris had metered out; they were deep but with the edges opposed the blood loss was minimal.

He took out his Leatherman from the pocket of his denims and removed the Soviet manufactured handcuffs from Bradley's right wrist.

Bradley updated Henry, pacing up and down outside the car as he did so; he listened intently as Henry issued instructions within the control room during their conversation. *M15 were now firmly in control.* They were tracing the location from the last known use of the unknown mobile cell used to call Boris. Henry agreed that was likely to be the new number which Blondie was using. It was simply a case of triangulation from the last known signal coordinates.

"We locate the mobile, we find Babichev." Henry stated dryly.

But why had the back-up not arrived Bradley wanted to know? What piece of the jig-saw was Henry holding back? And what about Dr Schultz, where the hell was he being held?

"Sit fast Bradley and await further instructions." Then the line went dead.

"BASTARD!" shouted Bradley climbing back into the car. "He's keeping us in the dark. He wanted us out of the way; quite happy for us to be the fall guys dealing with bloody two-ton Boris!"

"The bigger they are, the harder they fall!" chanted George, lightening the mood.

"Judging from his body language in the dark, he looked like a bear on heat as you needled him with your one-liners."

"And boy did you take that mammoth down with a crash!" chimed in Bradley.

"Sorry I missed all the fun." responded Jonathan managing a weak smile as he reclined across both back seats; realising he needed some carbohydrates to keep his blood sugar topped up. He ate the second Kit Kat and drank more water.

The tension broken, they relaxed back in the darkness; each with his own thoughts.

George and was listening to his ear-piece: impatiently awaiting further instructions. He tapped his fingertips on the dash board.

"*Roger that. Delta one out.*" responded George and started the ignition. He keyed coordinates into the satellite navigation and set off long before the device located regional satellites. Gravel went flying as the tyres squealed under the firm command of his right foot.

Chapter 34

18:30 Somerset: location undisclosed

The plastic ties dug painfully into her aching taut wrists. Lucy squirmed around as she tried to manoeuvre her bottom to sit more comfortably on the steel chair. She hated her wrists bound behind her; her shoulders ached with every movement, no matter how slight. The tape over her mouth was making her chapped lips sore and as she swallowed saliva it felt as though someone had sandpapered her dry throat; she longed for a sip of cool water.

Sleep was denied her: an unrelenting bell clanged inside her head.

A pungent oily smell infiltrated Lucy's nostrils; an odour she couldn't place. In the background she could hear a buzz of activity, voices blurring into obscurity; overshadowed by the sound of a chaotic symphony of metallic clangs and crashes: distant yet familiar sounds. Her thoughts continued to whirl uncontrollably like an abandoned carousel.

She craned her head to one side and concentrated hard, trying to focus. The voices were not English; Asian may be?

The room was stark; a square room with dirty grey walls, illuminated by a small green shade, brass framed desk lamp on the bare floor boards in the far corner of the room.

I pity the poor student who had to study in here, thought Lucy. She wandered back in time to her days studying English Literature. She tried hard to recount the detail of her favourite Thomas Hardy novel; trying to raise her spirits and distract her from the constant burning pain in her shoulders and pounding in her head.

Everything of late was a bad dream and she told herself over and over: just like all bad dreams it would could come to an end and she would wake up from this nightmare.

From somewhere outside the room, heavy footsteps drew closer and the door opened. A head looked around the door at her; she stared back, not moving, not even daring to breathe. The door closed abruptly. Lucy caught her breath and made an effort to breathe slowly and calmly through her nose. Her body began shivering again, this time, uncontrollably.

The hospital gown she had been dressed in was covered in a large white woollen jumper which smelled of moth balls. She was wearing grey tracksuit bottoms which were made for someone twice her size and weight. They felt damp. She needed the bathroom but wouldn't be asking anytime soon. Had that creep dressed her? Had he touched her body? She felt sick at the thought and blocked out the sordid visions which invaded her thoughts.

Footsteps, louder and faster; the door opened and this time he came in. The seal on the bottle of water was opened; she clearly heard the crinkling of the cellophane. She looked ahead and didn't meet his eyes. Lucy focused on the lamp and its soothing warm light.

"Drink only; scream and you will sleep for a very long time." The accent was Russian; the words delivered in a slow deliberate way. The message was chillingly cold, like the chair under her buttocks.

The tape was suddenly ripped from her mouth, rearing memories of a bikini line waxing Lucy had undergone just before her honeymoon. Never again she had told Jonathan; he laughed until he rolled off the bed. She smiled inwardly; distancing herself from the monster stood over her and her desperate desire to urinate.

Lucy drank the water slowly; it felt like fire burning her throat. The hand that held the bottle was steady. A sweet smell wafted into her nostrils as she drank, *Indian cooking: there's a kitchen nearby*!

A kitchen meant people: and hope.

Her cracked lips felt painful as she used them to grip the bottle.

"Thank you." she whispered; without looking at him; her voice was croaky and alien to her ears. He let the bottle fall onto the floor.

She could feel his eyes watching her. He tore a piece of duct tape from a roll and replaced the covering on her mouth. He picked up the empty bottle and headed for the door; then stopped and looked round at her.

Piercingly blue eyes met hers. He smirked briefly, turned off the light and left Lucy in darkness.

Lucy closed her eyes and shivered uncontrollably for a second time; part fear, part relief.

She needed to rest, despite her pain. *"Okay, you can do this,"* she told herself: *"You're Lucy, you're strong. People love you and will find you."*

Cold engulfed her once more. She dilated her nostrils and took in the smell of Indian cooking; trying hard to visualise the ingredients they would be using to create a masala: the Indian mixed spice sauce which formed the basis for so many Indian dishes. She pictured one of her cooking idols: skilfully blended spices as she spoke directly to camera in her kitchen.

Lucy began thinking about Jonathan; he would be sick with worry. She thought maybe she'd seen him momentarily earlier that day, at the hospital; by her side. *Or was that just a dream*? She couldn't be sure.

Why did she feel so muddled? Was it the medication - something the hospital had given her, or maybe this monster? She could feel her tears welling. She gulped and sucked in more air through her nose, breathing deeply. *What did he want with her*? The carousel started to whirl again; she stepped aboard and let her mind float away; too weary and weak to resist.

(She lay curled up on the sofa with Jonathan, in front of a crackling log fire; the flames, the heat, so comforting. The winter sun was streaming through the porthole cottage window enhancing the warm glow on their faces. She nestled into his shoulder and he touched her cheek tenderly, brushing her forehead with his lips; caressing her hair. Her hand wandered down onto his thigh then moved slowly upwards. He moaned and moved closer; his tongue glancing down her neckline. She rubbed the bulge in his jeans and he grew under her palm. Lucy lowered her body as his hand moved down her lower back, caressing her body....)

A sudden loud noise startled her; the door slammed open. A sickening hollow pain started to radiate across Lucy's stomach. Swirling dusty sickly air passed by her nostrils; she froze.

The large figure stood for a moment looking at her in the dark room; silhouetted against the bare light coming in from the hallway, as the door slowly closed. He moved across to the far corner of the room, bent down and turned on the angle-poise lamp: before turning and moving slowly towards Lucy.

He transfixed his eyes on her face. Lucy willed herself not to return his gaze; her heart was pounding relentlessly. She willed her body to move and escape his dark intentions. It was then she saw his dark gloves.

Slowly he circled her like a beast ready to devour its prey. He stopped behind her and rested his hands on her trembling shoulders; flaunting his superiority. She shivered uncontrollably and urinated involuntarily. Lucy could smell coffee on his rancid breath as he moved closer to her left ear, groaning; she retched and acid filled her mouth. His breathing was slow and laboured as she closed her eyes; sensing what was about to happen.

She could smell his leather clad fingers and she tensed her body as hands stroked her taught neck; ice cold shivers racked her body. His breathing grew faster and harsh and suddenly with his hands under her chin, he wrenched her head back. Lucy coughed and pulled forwards instinctively. She forced her shoulders forwards and wrenched her tethered hands upwards and backwards trying to injure his crotch.

She gagged and felt herself choking on her own saliva and fighting to draw air as her nose congested. Vice-like fingers slowly but steadily squeezed her throat as his groaning became more intense. She struggled but couldn't breathe, drowning in her saliva. Pain overwhelmed her body. The lights blurred and swirled and her vision dimmed as her body crumpled and she was pulled backwards into a deep long dark tunnel.

A blinding flash was followed by a deafening symphony, overwhelming her senses. The room was full of dark unearthly figures, captured rapturously in slow motion; lights flashing in unison. Powerful forces lifted her weight-less, worthless body up as she floated effortlessly upward and soared like a bird; free from the demon's hands. Her eyelids dropped and in one last act of defiance she prayed that that Lucifer would spare her this final ordeal.

Chapter 35

02:30 Saturday 28th January 2017

Straps prevented her from moving; Lucy no longer had the will to resist her confinement. She was ready to accept her final destiny: heaven or hell.

Lucy found herself staring up at a swirling cauldron of fluorescent lights, dancing across the ceiling as the vehicle hurtled on its timeless journey.

The pain in her head felt like a hand crushing a discarded beer can. Her body started to float away.

"Stay with me Lucy. You're safe now. Try to relax as much as you can. We are taking you to hospital. Your husband will be waiting for you."

The paramedic smiled down at her, like her very own Guardian Angel.

Hayley adjusted the oxygen mask on Lucy's face and checked the five percent dextrose infusion in her right arm. She tended the space blanket to ensure it was wrapped snugly around Lucy's cold, battered body.

Hayley re-checked the oxygen saturation monitor, and smiled with satisfaction as the monitor displayed ninety-nine percent. She turned off the oxygen stream but left the mask on for good measure.

Lucy's electrocardiogram monitor displayed a normal heart rhythm, with a heart rate of eighty-eight beats per minute. No surprise that her heart rate is high, thought Hayley; with everything this lady had evidently endured. Blood continued to seep through the bandage applied to her head; her laceration would require re-stitching at the hospital.

Hayley knew that Lucy had been a kidnap victim but little else about the circumstances of her captivity. The Police at the scene had told her only that Lucy had been rescued by Special Forces [the British SAS].

Too exhausted to speak, Lucy closed her eyes and drifted away to the soothing rhythm of the racing ambulance rocking her to sleep; sirens whining in the distance. She dreamed of cold, gut churning waters engulfing her, of drowning, and of floating up and soaring up and away towards innumerable heavenly bright lights. Hayley gently lifted Lucy's eyelids in turn and shone a light into her eyes.

"I'm sorry to disturb you again Lucy, I just need to check your pupil reactions; in light of your head injury; nothing to worry about. I'm sorry about this uncomfortable collar; hopefully the doctors will take it off at the hospital, once they have checked the x-rays of your neck."

As she'd applied the neck support, Hayley had seen the early bruising around Lucy's neck; consistent with someone having tried to strangle her. Thus far, there was no sign of Lucy's airway having been compromised. No sign of any breathing difficulties; her oxygen saturations remained steady.

The beeps and clangs clashed with Lucy's raw nerves and she flinched when the driver encountered speed bumps or veered out of the way of oncoming traffic as the ambulance pressed on quickly through the heavy traffic lanes.

She looked up at Hayley's face smiling down at her, her warm hazelnut eyes; but she could still see his cold vacant blue eyes: the windows to hell. She screwed her eyes up tight and tried to block out the images which came flooding into her mind. Lucy started to breathe quickly, fighting for oxygen and she felt the belt tighter around her chest.

"Okay Lucy, you're so brave; not long to go now. Try to relax and take deep breaths." She squeezed Lucy's right hand through the space blanket.

"E.T.A FIVE MINUTES" b*oomed a loud unknown male voice from the front of the ambulance. Lucy felt her throat tightening and her heart pounding; this time she couldn't relax. Panic filled every morsel of her body.*

Chapter 36

07:30 Monday 30th January 2017

"Will there be any *lasting damage* doctor?"

Jonathan looked exhausted; his four day stubble and tangled hair only served to highlight his unkempt appearance. Dark rings encircled his bloodshot eyes. He rubbed a weary hand through his hair as he spoke and absent-mindedly scratched his nose.

"Lucy's injuries are not serious. None the less, we'll continue to monitor your wife for the next few days. Physically she should recover quickly; psychologically, *well it's more difficult to say. Time will tell Mr Clarke.* "

"We will arrange comprehensive counselling of course; *for you both.*"

Dr Phillips looked over his black rimmed glasses at Jonathan; his pained look of concern was obvious to Jonathan despite his personal exhaustion.

They both realised there was a metaphorical *"elephant in the room."*

Jonathan rubbed his eyes and took a long deep breath before meeting Dr Phillip's gaze.

"Is there any sign that Lucy has been....." he tailed off, looking down at the immaculately white tiled floor and mentally searched for the words he didn't know how to phrase or utter; he crossed his arms and uncrossed them again, releasing a deep sigh; then chewed the broken nail on his right forefinger.

"Injured elsewhere?"

"If you mean did we find any signs of *sexual assault;* I am pleased to say the answer is a definitive no."

Jonathan did not meet Dr Phillip's eyes and simply continued to look at the floor; concentrating hard on a single cracked tile; chewing the inside of his upper lip in preference to his fingernail.

Steven Phillips placed his right hand on Jonathan's left shoulder and spoke quietly, but firmly.

"Lucy may find it *very hard* to talk to you about the details of what's happened to her. My advice is to be patient and most importantly, *just listen*, more than ever; let Lucy talk whenever she needs to open up to you. Lucy is obviously very strong physically and from what we know of her ordeal, she has coped amazingly well; you *both* have. "

"Take some time out from work Mr Clarke, and don't try to make everything *normal*; nothing will seem normal to Lucy for a while. That may be true for a *very* long time. Just be yourself and let her see you're there for her; no matter what."

"What do you mean, *no matter what* Doc'?"

Jonathan was searching Steven Phillip's eyes for answers. Listening carefully to his tone of voice as much as what he said.

"I'm sure you're aware of Post Traumatic Stress Disorder?"

"Lucy may display quite rapid mood swings: anger or feelings of extreme anxiety alternating with dark days: *she may talk of her shame and guilt: though not in so many words, or of suicide or even wishing she was already dead…. "*

Jonathan's bottom lip began to quiver and he felt an eerie cold course through his body as he encountered the words, *suicide and dead….*

"The counselling will help, but it may be a slow process. Be prepared and be open with your close family and close friends."

"Yes – I see what you're getting at now." Jonathan looked Steven Phillips in the eyes again and smiled briefly.

"You can be sure Lucy will get whatever she needs. Thank you for *everything you've done for us; for Lucy.*"

Steven Phillips nodded appreciatively; smiled and left.

Jonathan slumped down onto the fading brown leather sofa which sighed under his weight. He closed his weary eyes and slept.

Chapter 37

11:30 15th June 2017

Highgate Village, North London

Jonathan felt the colour drain from his face; his stomach churned and he felt physically repulsed by the increasingly sordid truths about Alexei Babichev: *the monster who'd masterminded the abduction of Lucy and been the source of so much heartache and pain for them both.*

Jonathan knew he must endure Bradley's full de-brief to have any hope of achieving the psychological closure he craved.

He took several long slow deep breaths; just as his Counsellor had advised in times of stress.

"Let me try and get my head around this Bradley:" he spoke slowly and deliberately despite his thoughts racing at lightening speed. He was trying to confront words which he could not bear to hear; yet alone begin to comprehend.

"What you're saying is that Alexei Babichev wanted to kill Lucy?"

"He intended to kill her after he had her kidnapped form this house; from our own bedroom: she was not simply a bargaining chip to get hold of Christophe Schultz?"

Jonathan could feel anger and resentment beginning to rise and resurface again through every fibre of his being: emotions he had worked so hard to displace from his heart and soul.

He was determined to externalise such feelings and then sweep them clean away from the emotional corridors of his mind. That way, maybe he could sleep soundly again and leave Lucy alone for more than a few hours without fearing her disappearance from his life forever.

He knew that anger and resentment would only grow stronger and calcify like a hard rock and weigh him down on the road to recovery from the ordeal which had been so close to robbing him of the one person who mattered most in his life: the woman who was his life and would always complete his heart.

Lucy truly was his soul mate.

He could barely imagine his life without her tenderness and devotion.

Jonathan sat back on his chair and looked mortified as he stared disbelievingly across the table; trying to take in what he was hearing. His jaw sagged open and he took several long deep breaths; disbelief etched across his furrowed brow. He ran his fingers through his hair. Tears began to well up and he brushed them away absentmindedly.

Bradley nodded slowly, watching him intently; letting his words sink in. He knew it was a crushing blow to receive: but he owed a debt of honesty to his closest friend.

Bradley was acutely aware that this pivotal piece of the jigsaw had the potential to change both their lives, *forever*.

Jonathan remained silent; then continued:

"Lucy must never know Bradley: PROMISE ME." he raised his eyes beseechingly to Bradley.

"She's only just stopped having regular nightmares, this would take her right back to......'God knows where."

Bradley nodded affirmatively: he maintained eye contact with Jonathan, his promise was given without words, because words would have been superfluous. Their friendship was welded with a bond no mortal could destroy: the rescue of Lucy had been a defining moment for them both.

Jonathan was shaking his head; trying to solve the riddle.

"But he could have killed Lucy in cold blood at any time; yet he kidnapped her and put her through all that *SHIT*; even after she escaped the first time. So why go to all that trouble; why wait and prolong her agony: *our agony?* "

"I just can't comprehend what was going through his head!"

He raised his hands and looked up to the heavens for inspiration.

None was forthcoming.

Jonathan swallowed hard and felt his eyes welling up again. He felt physically sick; covering his mouth with his right hand he closed his eyes and took deep breaths as the reality flooded his mind.

All at once the flashbacks resurfaced - the hospital, fire alarms, Lucy's disappearance and car pursuits played haphazardly through his mind while he looked on in horror, drawn further and further into this web of dark forces..unable to resist.

Jonathan sat concentrating and clenched his fists and teeth and the muscles of his body....then visibly relaxed as he re-played his memorised personal mental relaxation scenario and followed his Benediction.

"All this time, we've assumed she was the innocent bystander; a means to an end for that Bastard to get to 'Schultz."

"That was easier to accept somehow, through our counselling. Lucy was just an innocent pawn in a sick game of chess, with 'Schultz as the prize..."

"I don't get it. He wanted Schultz incarcerated; banged up in prison for life: *but he wanted* Lucy *DEAD*?"

He hung his head and sighed, shaking his head; thinking out loud.

"There has to be a link between them; there has to be...."

"What am I missing?"

Bradley waited patiently as Jonathan spoke. He knew how bright Jonathan was; intellect was his strong card; he was often the first in the team to make a connection when sifting evidence; even on "shifting sands" he could see a pattern emerge, when others just saw tangled webs and unfathomable complexity.

Jonathan sat, gathering his thoughts; rubbing his chin. He brushed away fresh tears from his eyes, then looked directly at Bradley. There was an element of desperation in his eyes.

"You'll need to spell this one out to me mate. What the hell is it all about?"

"Let me refill your coffee."

Bradley took his time and walked across the kitchen to fetch the coffee flask, all the time organising his own thoughts as he slowly and deliberately delivered the facts:

(Common starting ground thought Bradley before he spoke.)

"Schultz' was born in Stuttgart."

Jonathan nodded affirmatively.

"He lived there with his mother *Helga* and his father *Anton*; his dad was a dentist."

"The family inherited their house from Schultz' grandfather *Wolfgang*. He was a prison guard during World War Two. Most of his detainees were Russian prisoners of war."

Wolfgang Schultz probably oversaw the incarceration and demise of *Andrei* Babichev."

"Alexei Babichev's *grandfather*?" interjected Jonathan.

Bradley nodded sagely.

"By the time Alexei kidnapped Lucy from the hospital; *he had already abducted and tortured Christophe Schultz.*"

Another bombshell exploded inside Jonathan's psyche.

"You mean..." his face looks ashen and voice spelled incredulity......his voice was faltering.

Bradley continued slowly.

"Whilst we dealt with *Boris* at the deserted farmhouse, a team of Special Forces raided a disused ware-house where 'Schultz had been held, tortured and was found critically ill: *close to death."*

"He required months of intensive treatment and given the media coverage of his trial and acquittal; the news of his rescue and recovery were kept out of the media. He's now making a slow but steady recovery in an Army facility near Porton Down Chemical and Biological Defence Establishment. The chemicals they gave Christophe were caustic to his skin and highly noxious to his nervous system; to say nothing of the insignia carved across his face."

"The medical report makes for painful reading…." Bradley stopped and cleared his throat.

"In addition to the chemically induced skin burns Christophe sustained after his abduction, Babichev engraved Christophe's face with a Swastika: he indelibly tattooed his face but ironically didn't imbue it with a *right tilt*; so it looks more like a hideous attempt at a depiction of divinity or spiritualism, to give it the original Eurasian interpretation."

Jonathan listened quietly with his head bowed.

"Whatever his intention, he failed to kill Christophe and is now being held at a maximum security institution. It's unlikely Christophe will need to give evidence against him as his fingerprints are literally all over the crime scene and the injuries speak for themselves, never mind the horrors he inflicted upon Lucy."

"*Henry meanwhile held all the cards*: he didn't reveal details of Christophe's abduction to me until a face-to-face meeting last week at 'Viktoria [Secret Service Headquarters]."

"*Thank God that Christophe's alive*." Jonathan breathed a sigh of relief. He liked Christophe and the realisation of what he must of endured made the pill taste even more bitter. But they had to be grateful for his merciful survival.

Jonathan sat quietly; sipping his coffee.

"*Christophe Schultz was abducted early in the morning on Wednesday 25th January....whilst driving to work.*"

He paused while Jonathan took on board that by the time Lucy was abducted on Thursday 26th January 2017: Christophe Schultz was already under Alexei Babichev' control.

"So....there was never a question of a trade of Lucy for 'Schultz: Henry didn't have 'Schultz: Babichev had already...*abducted him*?

Bradley nodded slowly.

"Christ that guy is a real *bastard and no mistake...I've a good mind to...*"

"*Let it go mate.*" Counselled Bradley. "*I felt the same when he told me..*"

"But look at it this way: if we'd known we had no bargaining chip..we'd have felt a whole lot worse.....disempowered completely."

They sat in silence and Bradley sipped his coffee; preparing himself to serve the next volley of revelations.

"But what's *any of this* got to do with Lucy?"

"*I believe Lucy was adopted when she was barely a year old*?" Bradley responded.

"Absolutely, she never hid that from me or our friends."

"But Lucy had no way of knowing that her paternal grandfather worked in an SS death-camp."

Jonathan swallowed hard and looked up to the roof as he took long slow breaths.

Bradley could clearly see the Carotid arteries in Jonathan' neck pulsating in time with his heart beat.

"*Is this going where... I think it's going?*" Jonathan looked pale and spoke slowly and deliberately. "*Is this some kind of revenge.....for.....?*" Jonathan fell silent.

"Precisely; at least, according to information gathered by Interpol and the War Crimes Unit in Geneva."

"There's no easy way to tell you this bit mate." Now it was Bradley's turn to take a deep breath. He lowered his voice, his hand wandered over his breast bone as he spoke.

"Lucy's grandfather died before he could be charged with war crimes."

"Eye witness testimony suggests it is highly likely that he was in charge of a group of soldiers who murdered prisoners; *in many cases by strangulation after committing unspeakable acts.....*"

He looked down at the kitchen floor for a moment: "mostly female prisoners – in many cases after they'd been – sexually assaulted or abused by the guards."

The two men sat looking at each other; unspoken words and indescribable acts of War: bridged the silence.

Jonathan's body started to rock involuntarily as he thought of his own distant family who'd been killed during the Holocaust. He cried silently and Bradley stood up and walked across to the kitchen window with his own horror stories flooding before his eyes.

He walked across the kitchen and filled two glasses of cold water from the fridge dispenser and put them down on the table, one in front of Jonathan.

Jonathan stood up and raised his glass as Bradley spoke softly:

"Lest we forget."

The tears welled up and trickled down Jonathan's face as his lips moved to a silent Benediction.

Bradley looked away for a moment, faces ran like a movie real through his brain. He held back tears and swallowed hard. Moments later he raised his glass for a second time:

"Here's to absent friends and tortured souls: may they finally Rest In Peace."

Chapter 38

10:30 30th July 1917

The large newly painted Royal Blue heavy wooden front door slowly creaked open and shopping bags replete with fresh farm eggs, wholemeal flour, live yeast, along with fresh lemons and organic butter; were placed carefully onto the dark orange quarry tiled floor.

"You two look very conspiratorial!" declared Lucy chirpily as she came bounding into the kitchen, carrying her purchases in two brown paper bags cradled in her arms akin to identical twins.

"We're just planning your Birthday party."

Jonathan gave her a big *"welcome home smile"* as he responded, despite carrying a rather guilty look on his face which Lucy had instantly seen through.

She placed the shopping bags next to the fridge then turned and replied playfully...

"Now I know you're lying: that's a long way off." Her voice was scornful as she began wrinkling up her nose; with a wink to Bradley:

"He always forgets!" She mocked playfully placing her right palm under her chin theatrically and rolling her eyes skyward with a frown.

"Well just to prove you wrong....." Jonathan looked veritably delighted with his successfully completed secret shopping mission as he delved into his denim jacket pocket and produced a small square hinged white box edged in silver, which he placed in the centre of the kitchen table: just out of Lucy's reach."

"Happy Un-Birthday!"

Lucy squealed with unexpected delight and leaning across the table, snatched the box, as her face lite up like the early morning sunrise and her pale cheeks blossomed pink in front of their eyes; delight written instantaneously across her slim face.

Jonathan's heart sang as he watched her reaction: exactly what he'd hoped for after months of counselling and heart searching following the chain of events of the previous six months.

Today maybe, just maybe, they could start to put all that behind them and turn around their precious lives together.

She delicately pinned the White Gold broach onto her short woollen green jacket and rushed to the hallway to admire it in the full length mirror. It seemed to her that the wings of the Dove almost came to life in front of her gleaming eyes.

(The Dove became a World renowned symbol for Peace after its use in April 1949 when it was used by Picasso as the central theme to the illustrative Poster for the "Exposition De La Paix [World Peace Congress in Paris]).

After the revelations surrounding the ancestry of Lucy and Dr Christophe Schultz, Jonathan for his part had resolved to ensure that Lucy would be exposed to as much of the World's truth, Peace and kindness; as he could engage.

Much of his work historically, had by necessity been in the shadows whilst working with MI5, and In resolving his own personal conflicts, Jonathan planned to travel with Lucy; to see more, do more and experience more of the World: recognising that life is indeed both fragile and best lived in the sunshine, rather than the dark corridors of Counter-Terrorism and combating Organised Crime on line.

The Green Emerald encrusted eyes cast into the Dove twinkled in the glorious morning sunlight as Lucy headed back into the kitchen to show the two boys in her life how happy she was with her gift.

"Have you bugged....?" Bradley asked quietly directly into Jonathan's right ear....

Jonathan raised his right hand to respond, interrupting Bradley mid-sentence:

"*The answer to your question is a big fat NO!*"

"You boys!" beamed Lucy, skipping around the kitchen like a teenage schoolgirl:

"*Always sharing your little secrets!*"

"*If only you knew......!*" blurted out Jonathan; before they too regressed to their teenage years, burst into laughter and shadow boxed around the kitchen table and out into the garden via the newly constructed UPVC back door, fitted with privacy shatter-resistant reinforced glass and state of the art deadlocks.

"*Nothing changes, Thank The Lord!*" exclaimed Lucy, blissfully unaware of the transformation in security their two-up, two-down had undergone.

Watching "the boys" playfully pummel each other, she laughed until tears rolled down her slender pink cheeks.

Ginger wandered up to her and began rubbing his bushy black and white tail up against her legs, vying for her personal attention as usual.

She scooped him up into her arms and hugged him close; feeling the strength of his purr as she kissed the soft fur on his head.

"Just wait until *daddy finds out our news*!

She lay her right hand gently over her lower abdomen where the miracle of life was just beginning to take shape: marking a new dawn in their married lives.

Chapter 39

Dark Deceit

One year previously…..

Saturday 13th August 2016

Chicago, USA

His private mobile pinged and vibrated as the SMS message landed; just as he glanced at his Rolex watch.

Seated imperially at the head of table, he surveyed the expressions and body language of each of his twelve guests one by one, as they were served by the duo of wine waiters; immaculately dressed in black suits with contrasting crisp white shirts. Each was impeccably groomed reflecting the quality of the dining experience he'd paid handsomely for: courtesy of his Corporate Charge Card.

He removed his mobile from his right inside tuxedo pocket and used the fingerprint and facial recognition simultaneously. The SMS was the one he'd been expecting……

"It's done. A.B confirmed.

"Any resistance?"

"nope. putty in my hands!"

"Unexpected issues?"

"nope. he listened to my advice. didn't pitch up. took a cab home…"

"…..he paid for his one night stand..with me and her……."

"….A.B. will deposit glove for good measure."

A look of concern crept across his face..wondering about her true feelings….he knew she'd spent the night with him - just the one time - she'd kept the condom not knowing if she'd ever need to use it against him…..

"R. U. OK T?"

"yeah, horny as hell: can't wait to f*** your brains out."

"Mmmm….sounds good…..what you wearing?"

"black G string and ur fav long black socks…."

A pic landed in his Dropbox.

"Mmmmmmmmmm……I'm hard already."

"call me later G…..more to cum….."

No one took any notice as *George Latimer* laughed out loud as he read her SMS: his guests were all deep in conversation and enjoying the best steaks Chicago had to offer: eased down with a spectacular Merlot from a Gold-Medal winning Californian Vineyard.

"Can't wait T."

She puckered her red lipstick coated lips and poked out the tip of her tongue suggestively before sending him a selfie with one of the straps on her low cut bra worn tantalisingly off the shoulder…

"see u later big boy….."

"…hurry home daddy….I'm hot for U xxx. Luv T.

He lounged back on his wooden chair and visualised her lean hips in the figure hugging grey dress she'd worn just twenty-four hours ago: he hadn't take his eyes off her curves when they'd met momentarily in the corridor just before he'd addressed the Board.

He loved seeing her parade around in Versace which he'd gifted her: the look in her eyes captivated his very soul and he imagined her cupping his ample testicles as she stared longingly into his eyes.

He closed his eyes momentarily....her fragrant body covered in his favourite lemon scent riding on his engorged member......

He drank a large mouthful of sparkling water and sighed.

Finally, he text his right hand man.

"T has taken care of business."

"Anglo-Russian cooperation at its best."

"Watching brief only. Expect C.S. soon unexpectedly detained..." Regards G."

He smiled disingenuously as he re-read the SMS before hitting send.

Clive McGregor read the SMS and smirked as he lay next to his outdoor pool: confident that he had seen the last of his least favourite Medical Director.

The End

Sequel to this novel: **Available on-line 2021…..**

"The Visionary"

A fast-paced Politically charged thriller set in a Brave New World witnessing the Post Apocalyptic fall-out of a World-Wide Collapse of the Economy: where the future of Nations lies in the hands of a select few….

"The Visionary"

Chapter One

Seven Heads of State

06:47 November 4th 2025

Merthyr Tydfil Town Centre, Wales, United Kingdom

A myriad of mobile digital cameras flashed in unison and captured thousands of pixellated images as Prime Minister **Gwen Thomas** exited the jet black Range Rover positioned in the centre of the three car cavalcade. She stepped decisively onto the wet pavement which glistened in the reflection of two intersecting artificial arcs of light created by a pair of portable lamps.

The (supposedly) unscripted photo opportunity was set in the small Welsh town of Merthyr Tydfil: just twenty-three miles due North of the P.M.'s Birth Place in Cardiff, South Wales.

For the town's folk, it was nothing short of a homecoming: they regarded Gwen Thomas as their very own *"First Lady."*

Well-wishers had gathered to line the route since long before dawn on a wet and otherwise damp and dreary November morning, hoping for the merest glimpse of the Prime Minister. The Ministerial drive-by had been intentionally leaked to the BBC twenty-four hours before her scheduled arrival in Wales.

Police Road blocks had been in place for two hours prior to the arrival of the Prime Ministerial' entourage of Security and Administrative Staff. The High Street was only accessible in two directions both of which were rendered free of traffic as the Police advance party of outriders halted all traffic and closed tributaries to the Town Centre. Diversion signs re-routed all but Emergency Services vehicles.

Local Army sniffer dogs and their handlers from the Battalion of the Welsh Guards had checked for explosives and improvised electronic devices whilst local Government employees and specialised Police Officers had cleared the road side of all refuse and inspected the drains beneath all manhole covers before leaving highly visible yellow security seals in place.

The owners, landlords and lessees of all shops, houses and apartments lining the town High Street had been vetted by a plain clothed security inspectorate a week before the details of the planned route had been released to the BBC. That very same inspectorate mingled with local residents, shop owners and farmers; all of whom had come to pay their respects, rather than air their differences; which had been so common with by-gone Administrations.

During her four years in the Highest Office of the Land, *The First Lady of Wales* had delivered on her promises: an unparalleled historical achievement in Politics.

Few were privy to the PM's plan to stop and give a brief speech to the local electorate. Final plans were confirmed at 5 a.m. that morning as the P.M. flew into RAF Brize Norton in Oxfordshire, U.K. and was picked up by her security entourage, ready for the 110 mile drive; with an E.T.A. of 6.45 a.m.

Fresh from recent face-to-face meetings with the **Seven Heads of State Authority [S.H.S.A.]** in Geneva, Switzerland; Gwen Thomas felt buoyed by the recent election results which had been the first opportunity for the entire United Kingdom Electorate to vote by personal computer; *empowered by her Government: engaging her initiative that every household should have internet connectivity and a new or recycled computer laptop: at Government expense.*

Her Party's land-slide victory giving her a second term in Office had been unprecedented in British Politics with so many Ministers having defected from their traditional Parties in a quest for a brighter, cleaner, healthier Britain where jobs were more important than Corporate Profits and Land more valuable than new transportation links and *accommodation for all*: trumped multiple Property ownership.

The Prime Minister's **Press Secretary *Ivan Roberts*** and her **Personal Assistant *Myra Small*** proudly unravelled the Party "Go To Slogan" as she prepared to make her short improvised statement.

"All hands to the pump" was one of the PM's favourite mantras; of which she had many. The Green coloured cotton material sourced from the Mills in Lancashire was emblazoned with the Party slogan:

"**Do it Once, Do it Right, Vote Conservation Party**"

With the Party banner unfurled, gently flapping in the early morning breeze, and a microphone set up on a portable plinth on the pavement outside a local Greengrocers, the PM spoke to her impromptu audience.

"Ladies and Gentlemen I am delighted to announce that following successful negotiations during the weekend, the **Seven Heads of State Authority** has asked me to continue my work as Chairperson and in this capacity I am honoured to announce a package of fiscal measures which will further empower individuals within our Great Nations to elect the Leaders they see fit to Govern."

"Do it Once, Do it Right, Vote Conservation Party!"

Her green eyes were positively gleaming as a flurry of flash photography followed her every word and her exultant gesture as she raised her left hand and punched the air as she enunciated the words: *"Conservation Party!"*

A muted cheer rang out along the street as Welsh Flags were raised in honour of *one of their own*. The First Welsh female Prime Minister to grace the corridors of Whitehall and call Number 10 Downing Street: *Home.*

"Our policies aimed at improving the Quality of Life for all, and not just the privileged few, have resulted in more Welsh Jobs, a return to farming and a regeneration of the British Steel industry; powered by British workers paid in Pounds Sterling and not Euros!"

More cheers and energised flag waving as the PM talked of Welsh jobs.

"Those Countries who predicted our isolation from World Trade have found themselves sliding into an economic abyss as the European Utopia they envisaged had crumbled under the weight of fiscal mis-management and lavish expenditure."

"For generations to come, our families and our children will benefit from home grown produce: not foreign imports laced with illegal insecticides."

The BBC TV Camera panned out and captured a full view of *"Roberts' Family Green Grocers" the backdrop for the Prime Minister's Announcement.*

Two hundred and fifty metres up the High Street in a top floor apartment above **Iris' Florist Shop**, she lay flat on the long chest of drawers with the stock of the Russian machined ordnance embedded firmly in place, wedged snuggly in her left shoulder; abutting her Police stab vest.

She slowly altered the horizontal adjustment control of the reticle on the telescopic sight ensuring that her target remained in the epicentre of the cross hairs.

She blinked and re-focused her eyes momentarily as she slowed her breathing and gently exhaled milliseconds before she gently squeezed the trigger……

Printed in Great Britain
by Amazon